# A Devil and Her Love Song

### Story & Art by
## Miyoshi Tomori

## Volume 9

# A Devil and Her Love Song

## Volume 9
### CONTENTS

The devil
makes me
LOVELY!!!

## STORY THUS FAR

As Maria enters her second year of high school, she meets a first-year boy named Shintaro Kurosu. Shintaro immediately begins trying to get close to her and initiating as much physical contact as he can. He quickly finds himself at odds with Shin, who worries that being touched so much will trigger Maria's memories of her painful past.

When the group takes a weekend trip to Shin's family's beach house, Shintaro is included. During the visit, Maria and Shin share a wonderful moment when he accompanies her on piano while she sings "Ave Maria." Seeing this makes Shintaro jealous—jealous enough to make a move on Maria!

# prise!
## You may be reading
## the wrong way!

*It's true: In keeping with the original Japanese comic
format, this book reads from right to left—so action,
sound effects, and word balloons are completely
reversed. This preserves the orientation of the original
artwork—plus, it's fun! Check out
the diagram shown here to get
the hang of things, and then
turn to the other side of the
book to get started!*

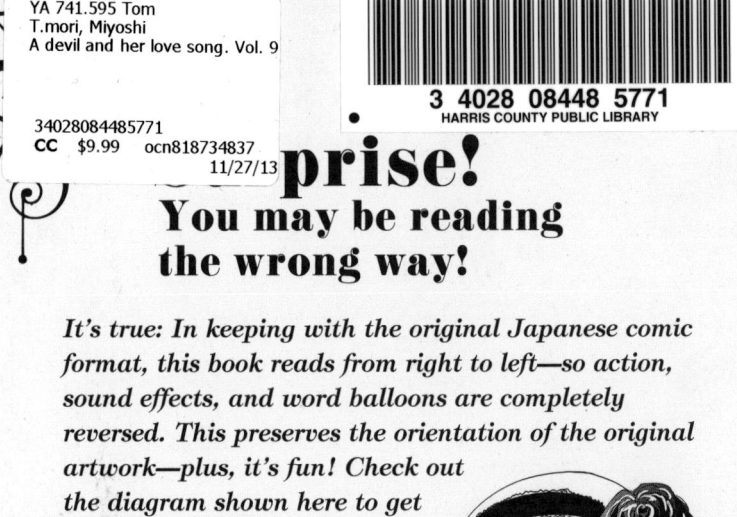

# A DEVIL AND HER LOVE SONG
## Volume 9
### Shojo Beat Edition

STORY AND ART BY
## MIYOSHI TOMORI

English Adaptation/Ysabet MacFarlane
Translation/JN Productions
Touch-up Art & Lettering/Monalisa de Asis
Design/Courtney Utt
Editor/Amy Yu

AKUMA TO LOVE SONG © 2006 by Miyoshi Tomori
All rights reserved. First published in Japan in 2006
by SHUEISHA Inc., Tokyo.
English translation rights arranged
by SHUEISHA Inc.

Printed in the U.S.A.

Published by VIZ Media, LLC
P.O. Box 77010
San Francisco, CA 94107

10 9 8 7 6 5 4 3 2 1
First printing, June 2013

www.viz.com   www.shojobeat.com

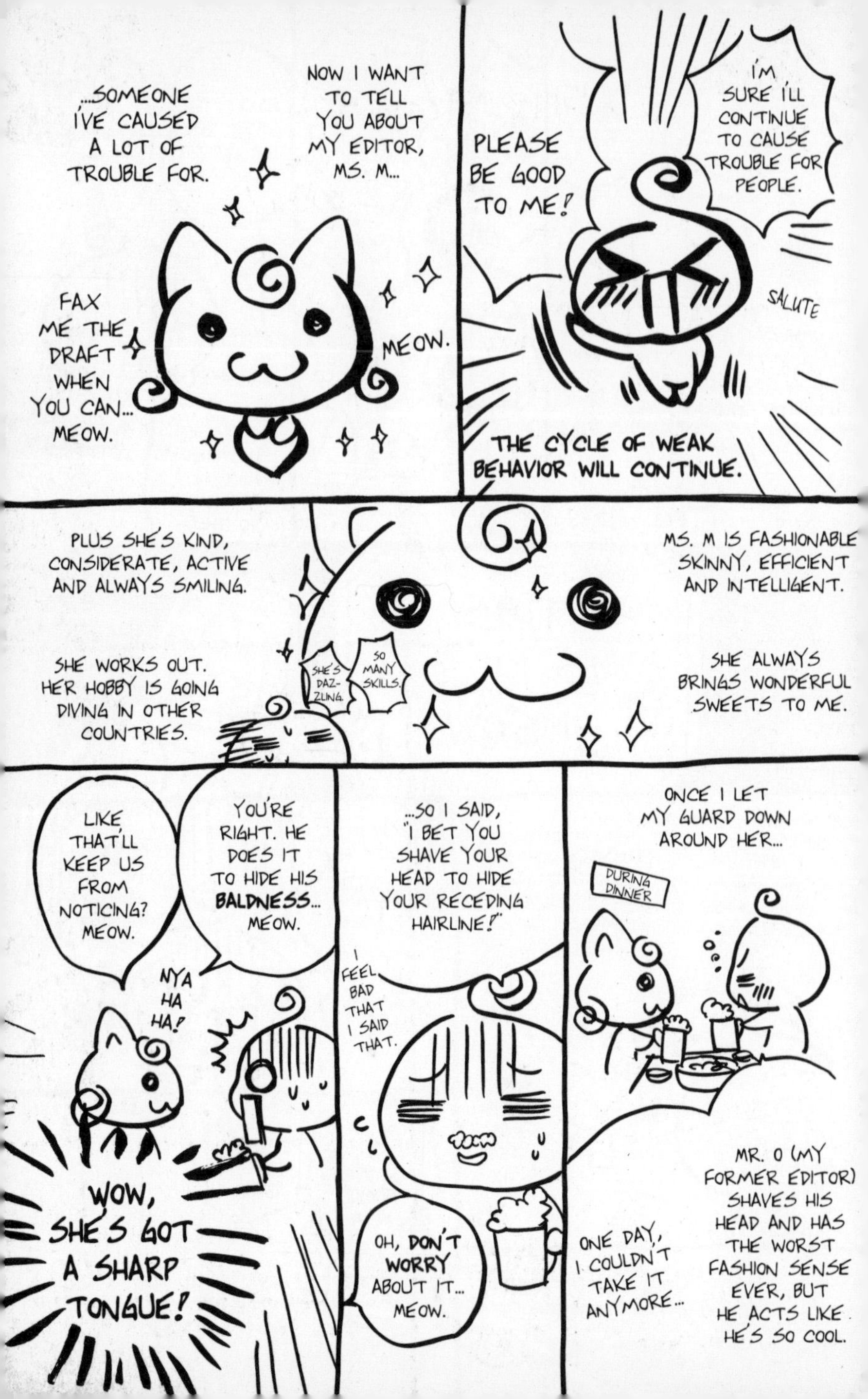
I'M SURE I'LL CONTINUE TO CAUSE TROUBLE FOR PEOPLE.
PLEASE BE GOOD TO ME!
SALUTE
THE CYCLE OF WEAK BEHAVIOR WILL CONTINUE.
NOW I WANT TO TELL YOU ABOUT MY EDITOR, MS. M...
...SOMEONE I'VE CAUSED A LOT OF TROUBLE FOR.
MEOW.
FAX ME THE DRAFT WHEN YOU CAN... MEOW.
MS. M IS FASHIONABLE SKINNY, EFFICIENT AND INTELLIGENT.
SHE ALWAYS BRINGS WONDERFUL SWEETS TO ME.
SO MANY SKILLS.
SHE'S DAZ-ZLING.
PLUS SHE'S KIND, CONSIDERATE, ACTIVE AND ALWAYS SMILING.
SHE WORKS OUT. HER HOBBY IS GOING DIVING IN OTHER COUNTRIES.
ONCE I LET MY GUARD DOWN AROUND HER...
DURING DINNER
MR. O (MY FORMER EDITOR) SHAVES HIS HEAD AND HAS THE WORST FASHION SENSE EVER, BUT HE ACTS LIKE HE'S SO COOL.
ONE DAY, I COULDN'T TAKE IT ANYMORE...
...SO I SAID, "I BET YOU SHAVE YOUR HEAD TO HIDE YOUR RECEDING HAIRLINE!"
I FEEL BAD THAT I SAID THAT.
OH, DON'T WORRY ABOUT IT... MEOW.
YOU'RE RIGHT. HE DOES IT TO HIDE HIS BALDNESS... MEOW.
LIKE THAT'LL KEEP US FROM NOTICING? MEOW.
NYA HA HA!
WOW, SHE'S GOT A SHARP TONGUE!

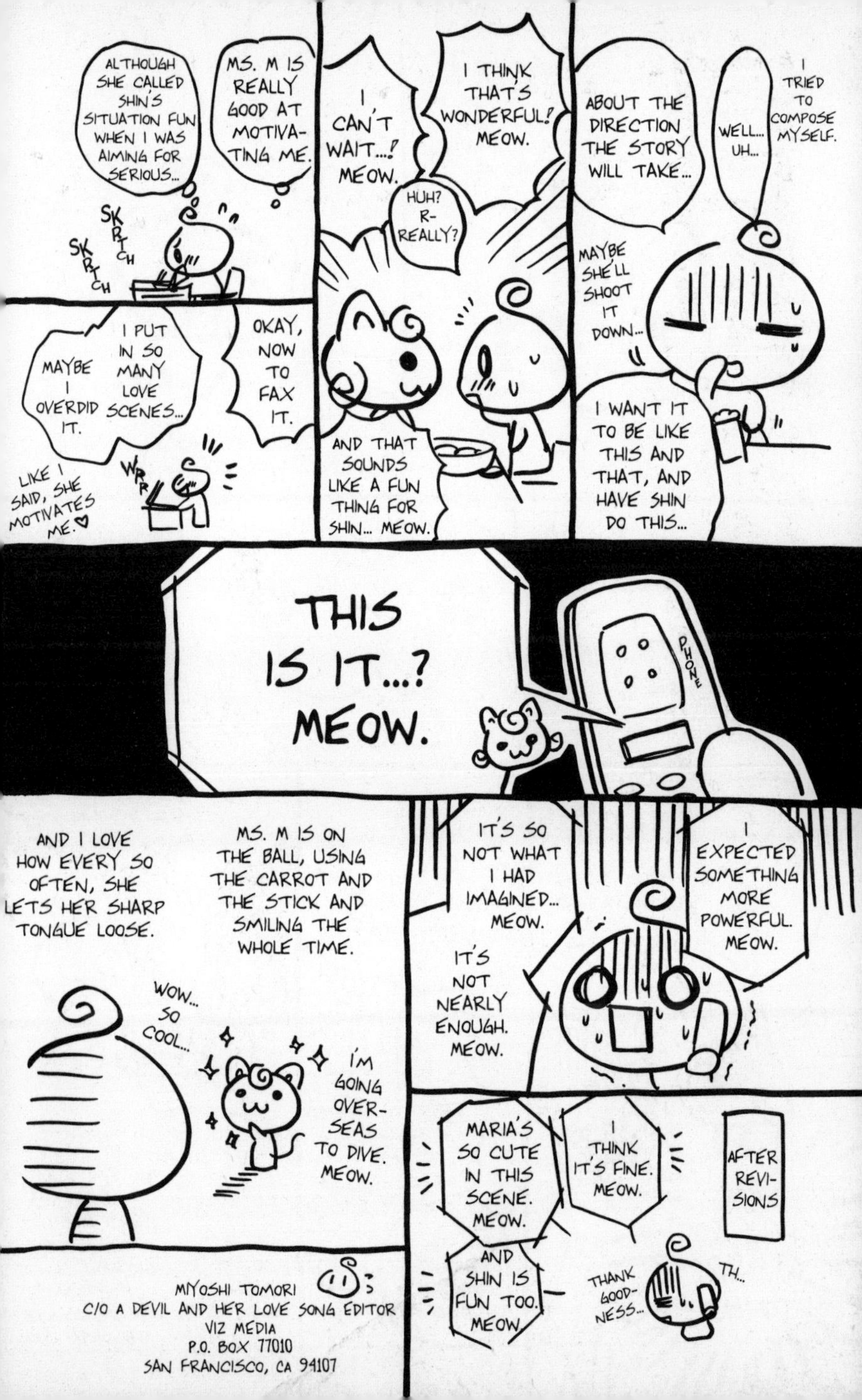
I TRIED TO COMPOSE MYSELF.
WELL... UH...
ABOUT THE DIRECTION THE STORY WILL TAKE...
MAYBE SHE'LL SHOOT IT DOWN...
I WANT IT TO BE LIKE THIS AND THAT, AND HAVE SHIN DO THIS...
I THINK THAT'S WONDERFUL! MEOW.
I CAN'T WAIT...! MEOW.
HUH? R-REALLY?
AND THAT SOUNDS LIKE A FUN THING FOR SHIN... MEOW.
MS. M IS REALLY GOOD AT MOTIVATING ME.
ALTHOUGH SHE CALLED SHIN'S SITUATION FUN WHEN I WAS AIMING FOR SERIOUS...
SKRTCH SKRTCH
OKAY, NOW TO FAX IT.
I PUT IN SO MANY LOVE SCENES...
MAYBE I OVERDID IT.
WRR
LIKE I SAID, SHE MOTIVATES ME.♡
THIS IS IT...? MEOW.
PHONE
I EXPECTED SOMETHING MORE POWERFUL. MEOW.
IT'S SO NOT WHAT I HAD IMAGINED... MEOW.
IT'S NOT NEARLY ENOUGH. MEOW.
AFTER REVISIONS
I THINK IT'S FINE. MEOW.
MARIA'S SO CUTE IN THIS SCENE. MEOW.
AND SHIN IS FUN TOO. MEOW.
TH...
THANK GOODNESS...
AND I LOVE HOW EVERY SO OFTEN, SHE LETS HER SHARP TONGUE LOOSE.
MS. M IS ON THE BALL, USING THE CARROT AND THE STICK AND SMILING THE WHOLE TIME.
I'M GOING OVERSEAS TO DIVE. MEOW.
WOW... SO COOL...
MIYOSHI TOMORI
C/O A DEVIL AND HER LOVE SONG EDITOR
VIZ MEDIA
P.O. BOX 77010
SAN FRANCISCO, CA 94107

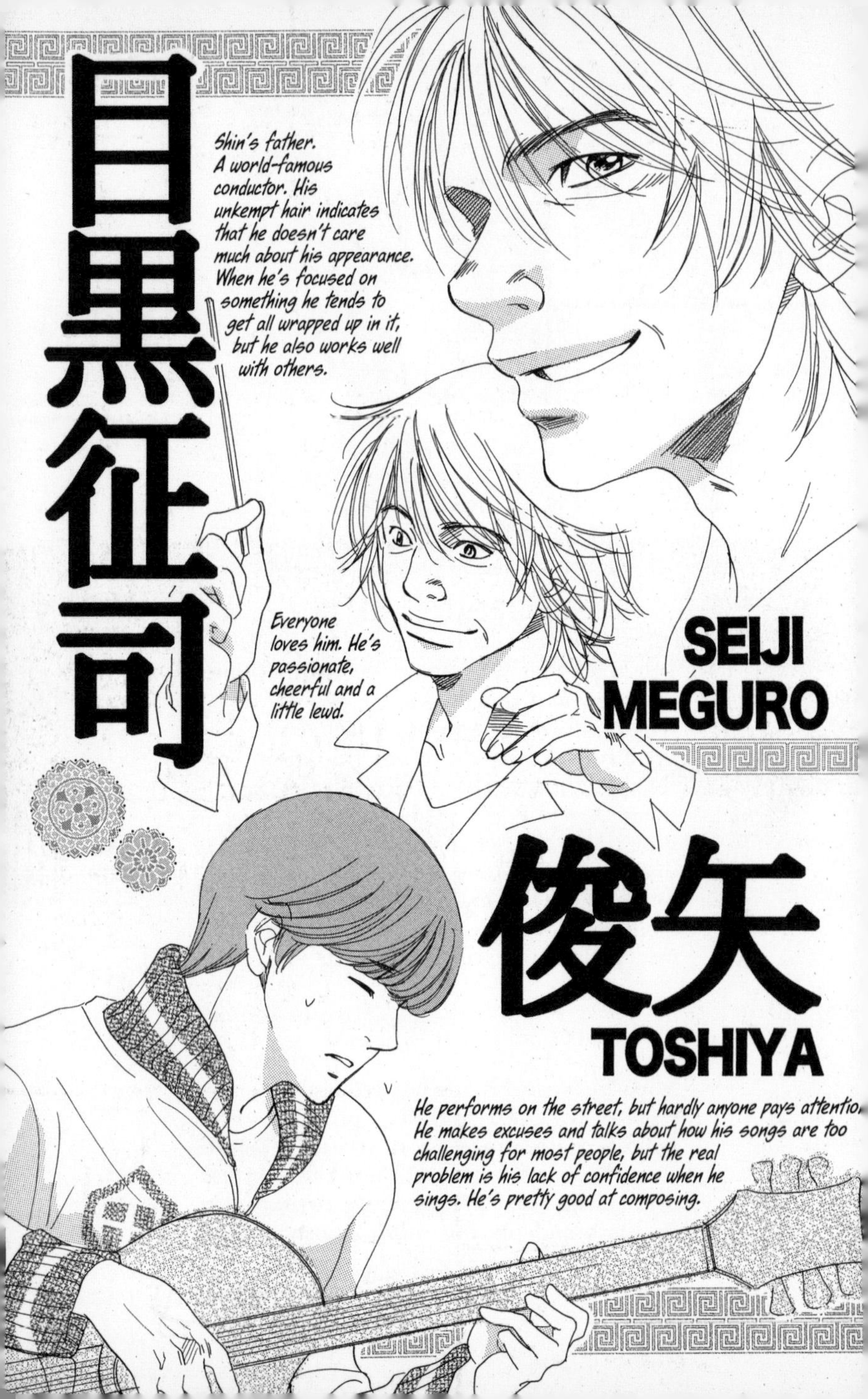
目黒征司
SEIJI MEGURO
Shin's father. A world-famous conductor. His unkempt hair indicates that he doesn't care much about his appearance. When he's focused on something he tends to get all wrapped up in it, but he also works well with others.
Everyone loves him. He's passionate, cheerful and a little lewd.
俊矢
TOSHIYA
He performs on the street, but hardly anyone pays attentio
He makes excuses and talks about how his songs are too challenging for most people, but the real problem is his lack of confidence when he sings. He's pretty good at composing.

I thought that 3D movies were something you view at a special science expo or a ten-minute show you pay 1,000 yen at the amusement park to see. But lately, many 3D movies have been released in theaters, and it has made me reflect on how times have changed. Then one day, I discovered that they sell 3D television sets for the home! What I had dreamt of as a child has now become reality!! Maybe one day, comics will become 3D too…?

-Miyoshi Tomori

Miyoshi Tomori made her debut as a manga creator in 2001, and her previous titles include *Hatsukare* (First Boyfriend), *Tongari Root* (Square Root), and *Brass Love!!* In her spare time she likes listening to music in the bath and playing musical instruments.

# CHARACTERS

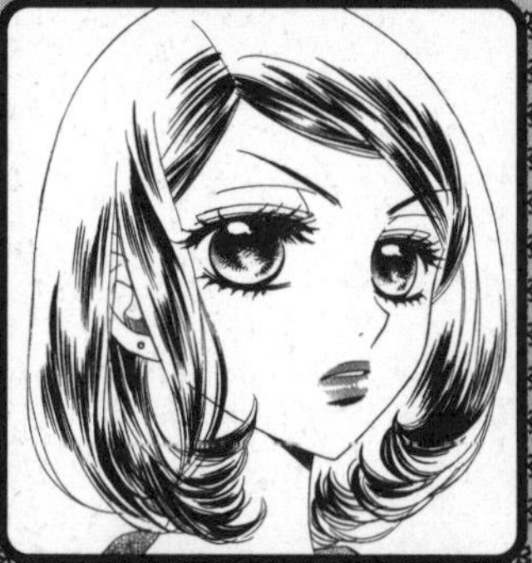

**Maria Kawai**

Maria transferred to Totsuka High after being expelled from St. Katria, a private girls' school. At first, her keen instincts and frank opinions isolated her from her new classmates, but they eventually began to appreciate her honesty. She is in love with Shin.

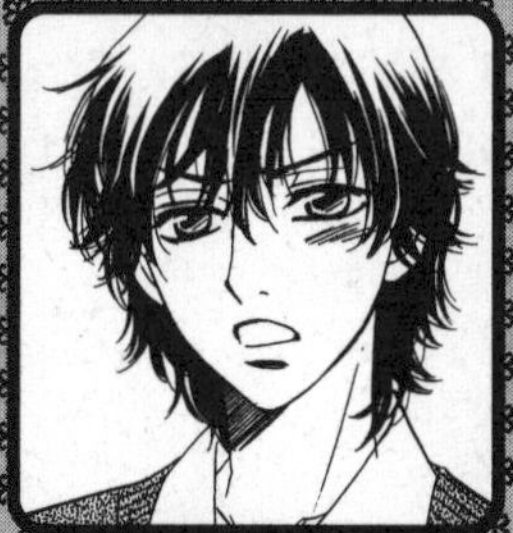

**Shin Meguro**

Shin is a man of few words and comes across as curt, but the truth is he cares deeply about his friends and gets embarrassed easily. His father is a famous orchestra conductor.

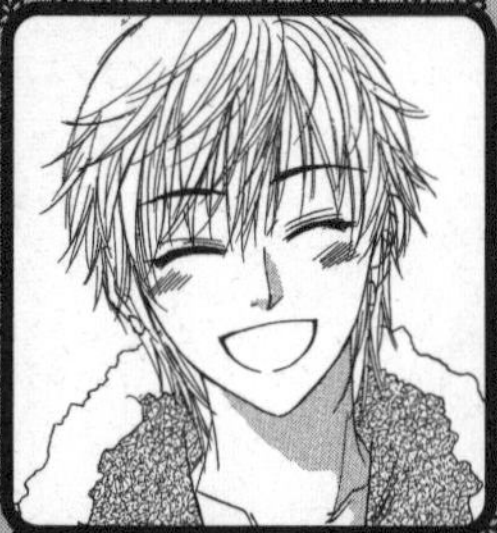

**Yusuke Kanda**

Yusuke is cheerful and kind to everyone, which makes him a class favorite. He's also very considerate, and he understands Maria very well.

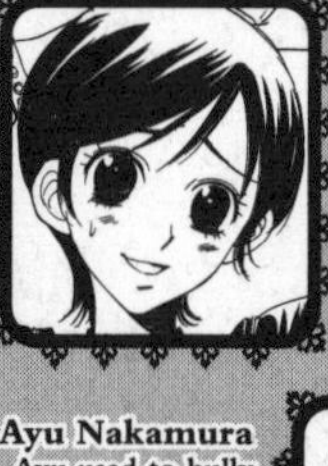

**Tomoyo Kohsaka**

Tomoyo used to be picked on by her classmates. Becoming friends with Maria has had a huge impact on her.

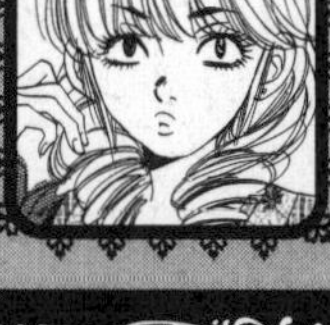

**Ayu Nakamura**

Ayu used to bully Maria, but now she counts Maria as a friend. She's in love with Yusuke.

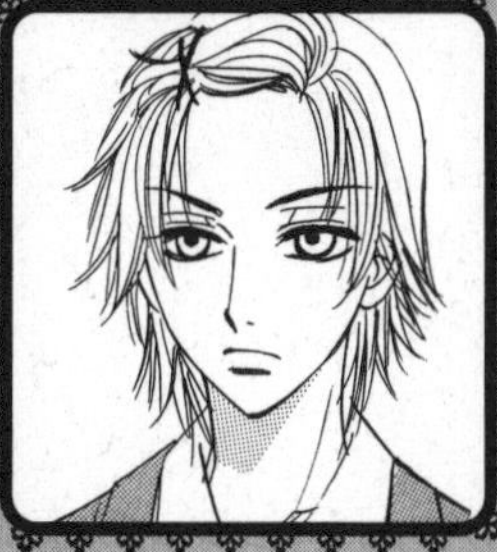

**Shintaro Kurosu**

A first-year boy who doesn't hesitate to say what's on his mind. He's in love with Maria. His nickname is... Eros?!

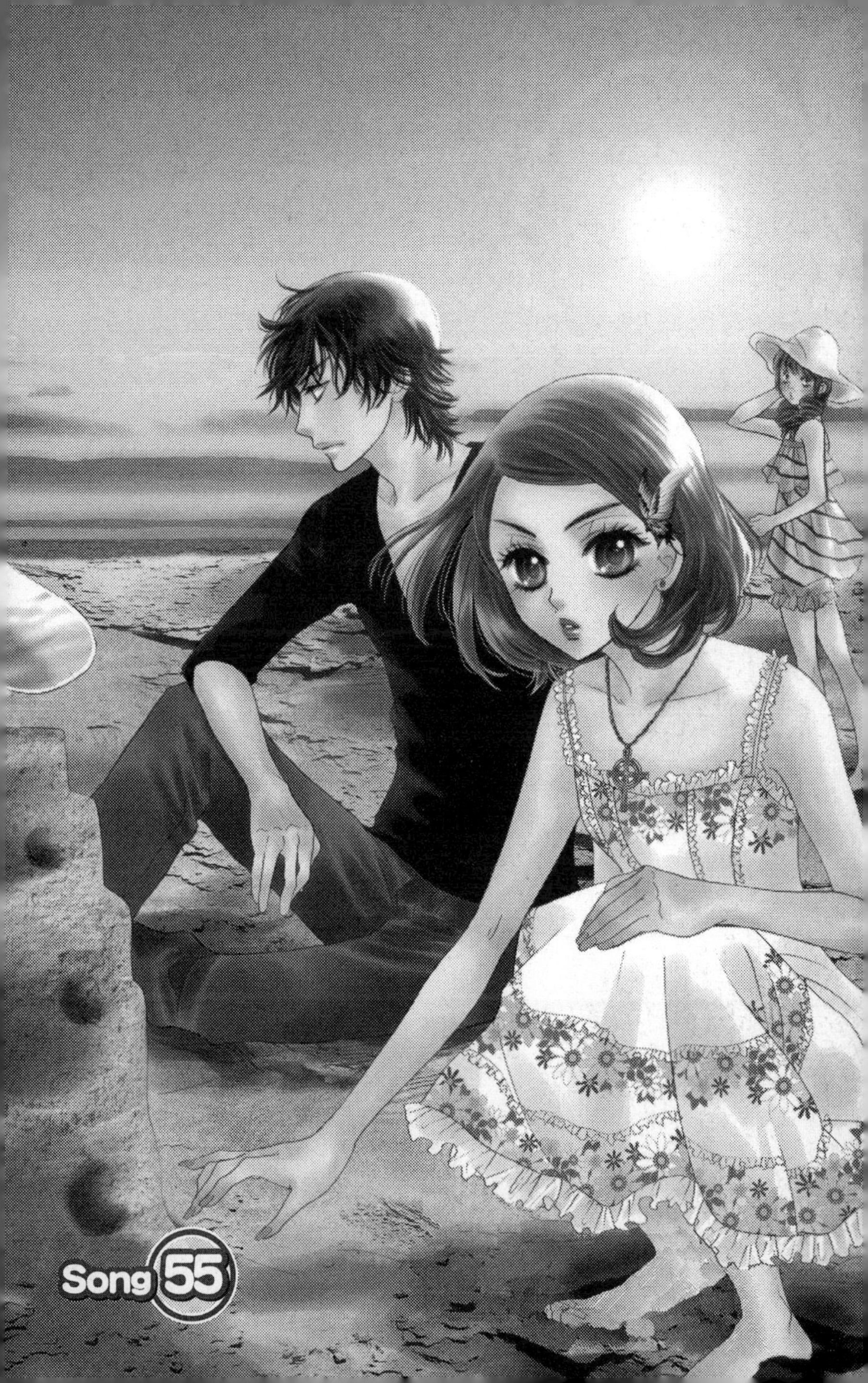
Song 55

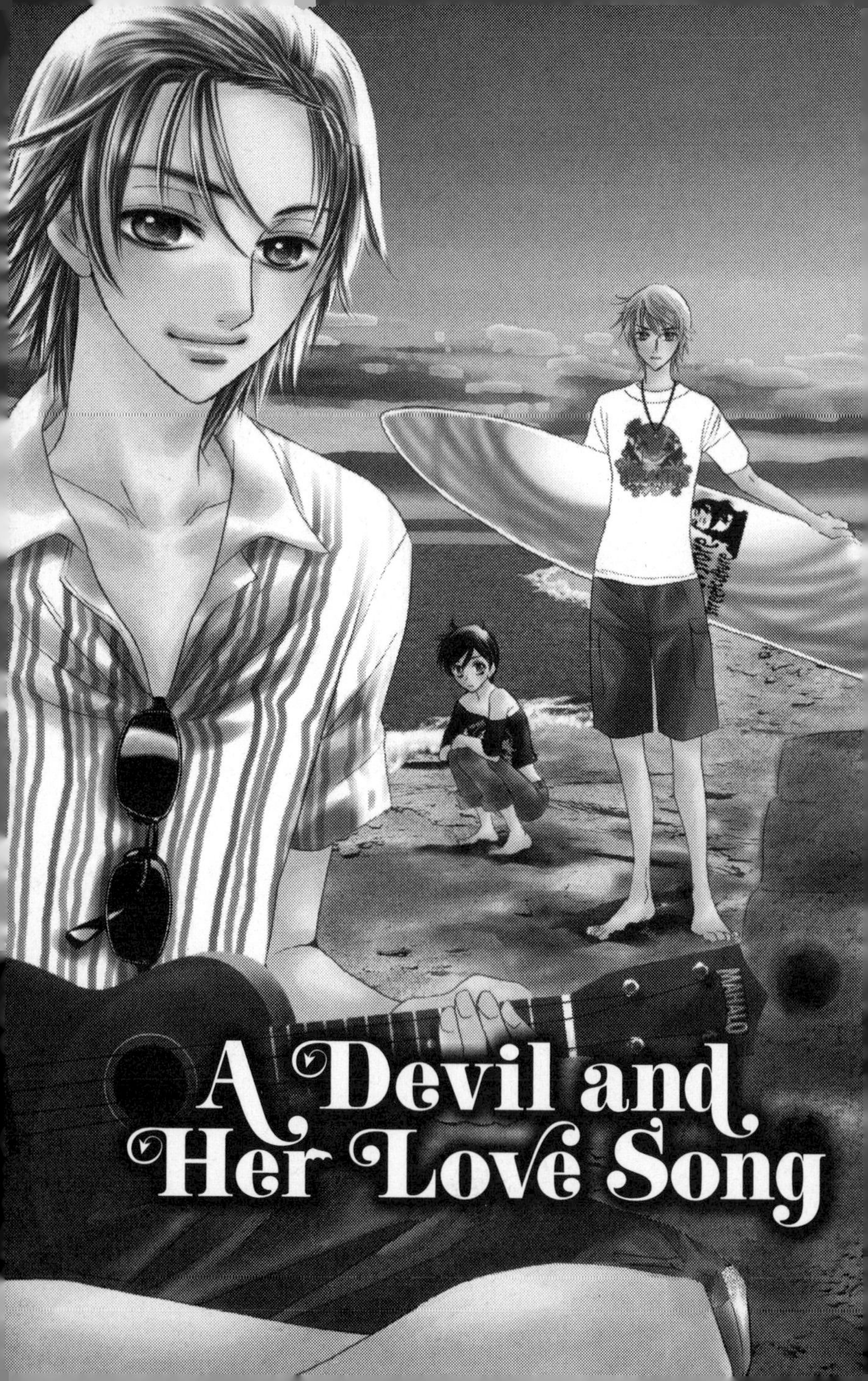
A Devil and Her Love Song

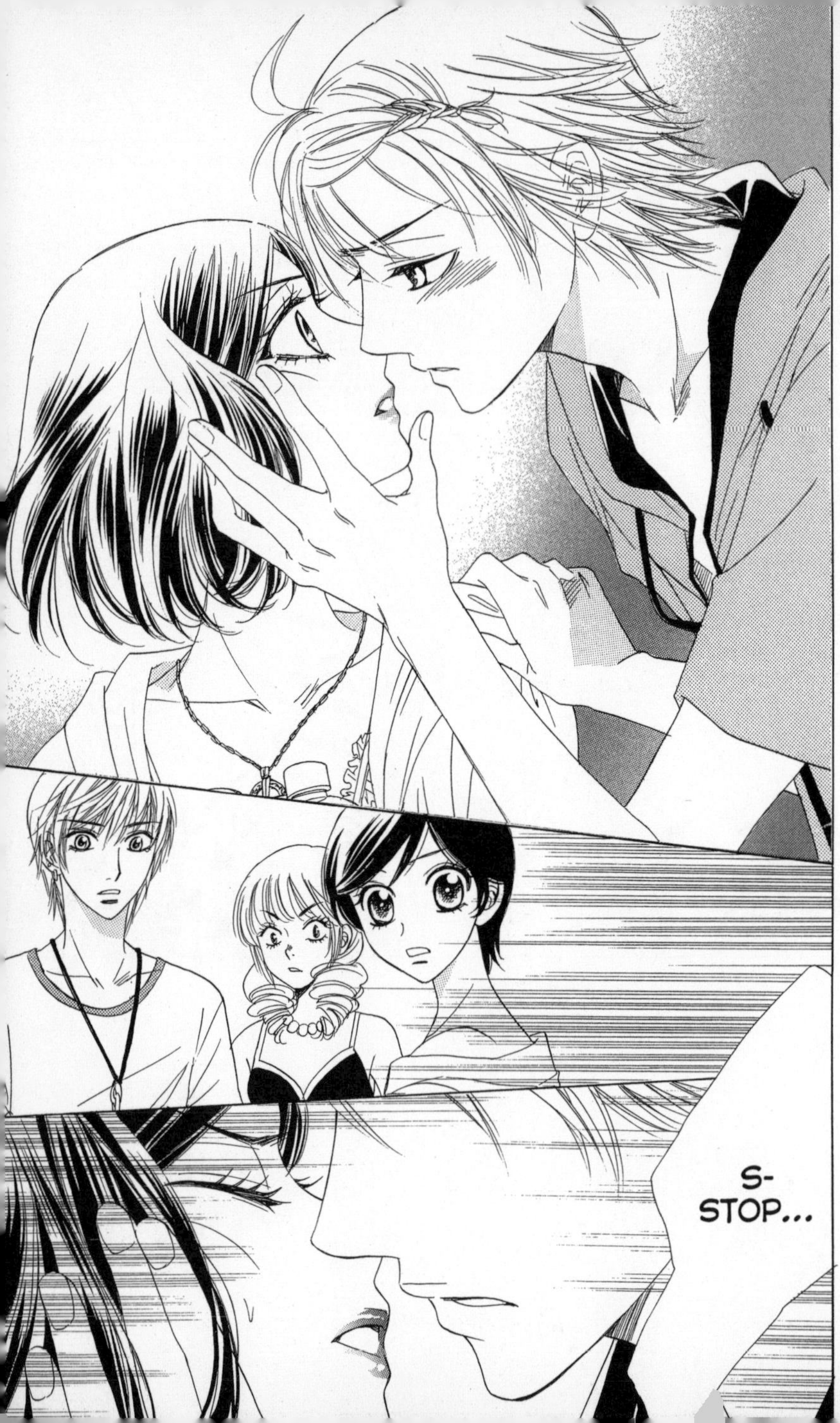
S-
STOP...

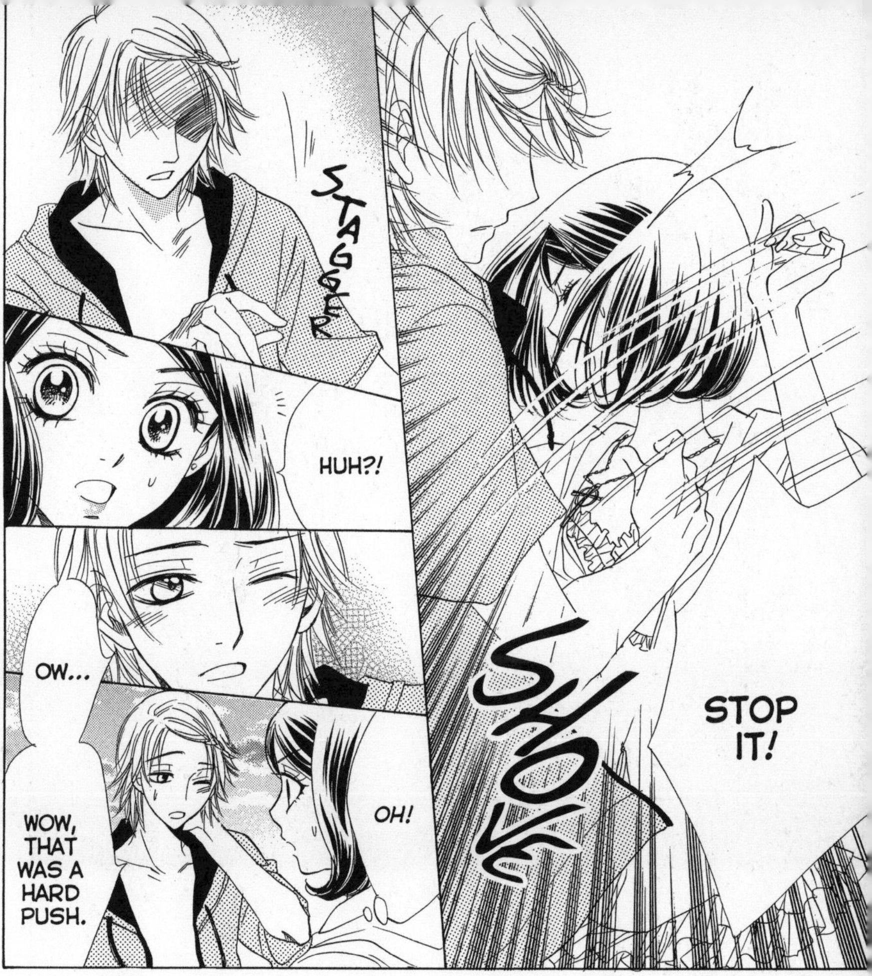
STOP IT!
SHOVE
STAGGER
HUH?!
OW...
OH!
WOW, THAT WAS A HARD PUSH.

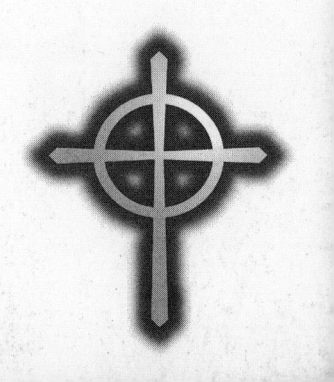

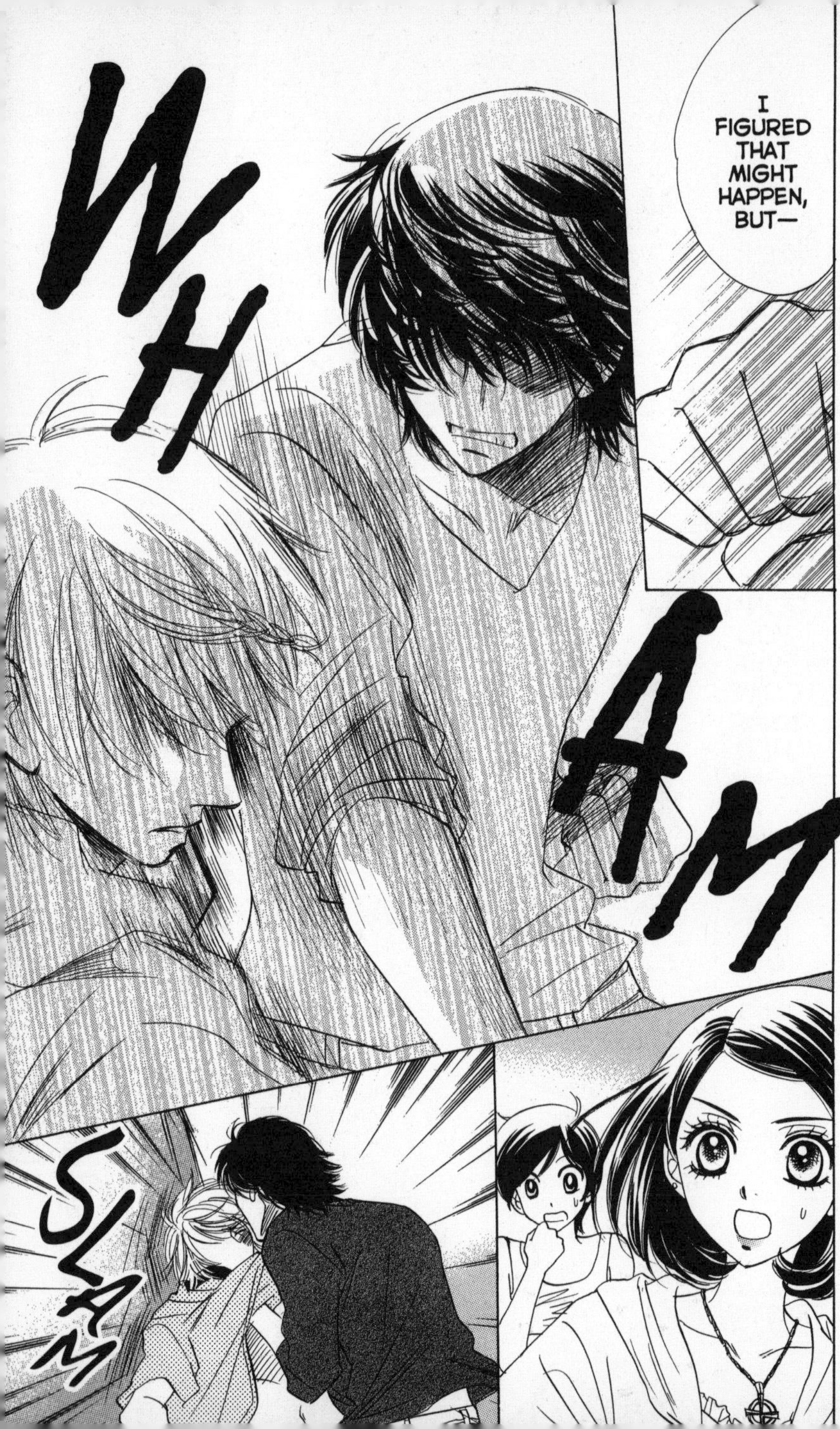
I FIGURED THAT MIGHT HAPPEN, BUT—
WHAM
SLAM

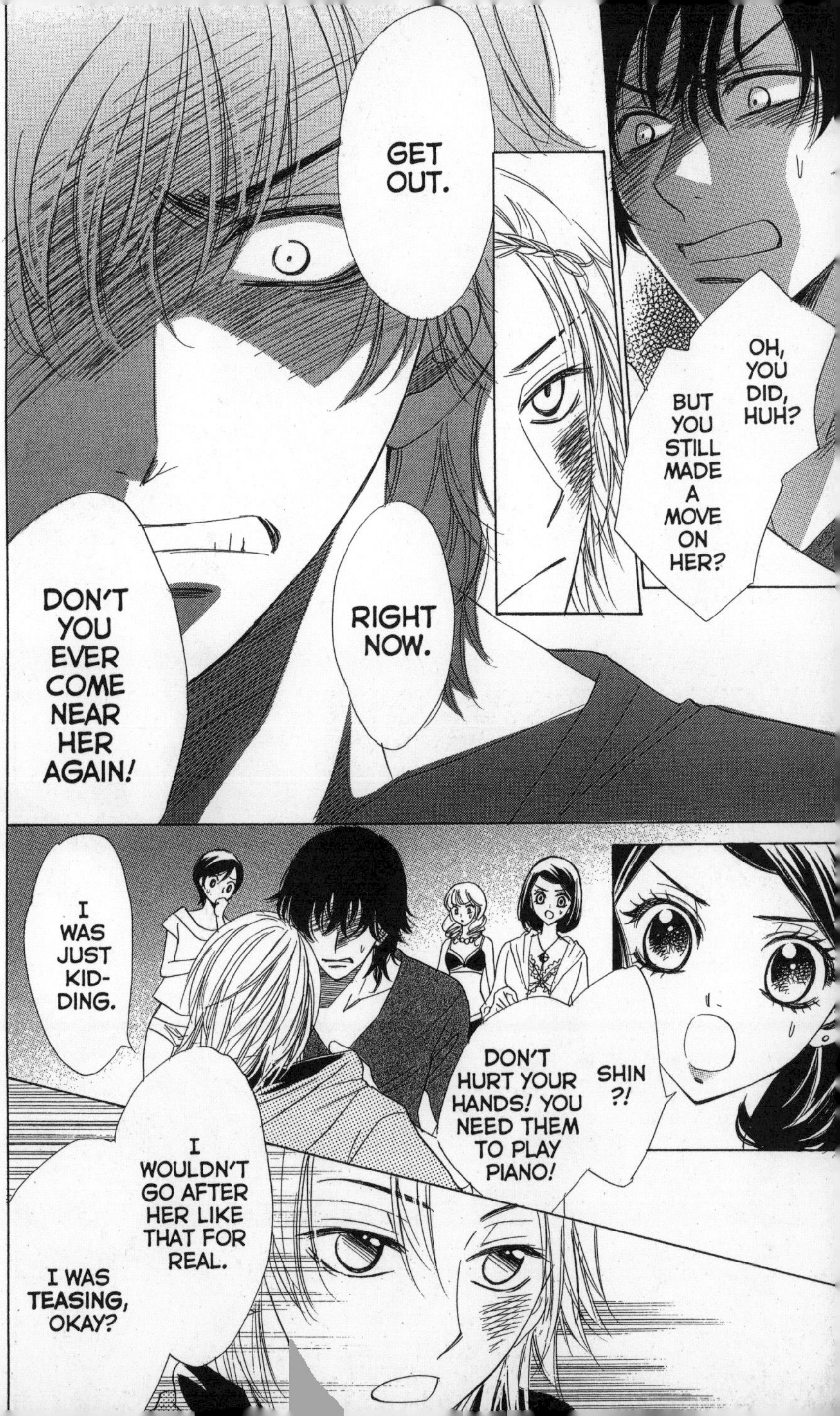
OH, YOU DID, HUH?
BUT YOU STILL MADE A MOVE ON HER?
GET OUT.
RIGHT NOW.
DON'T YOU EVER COME NEAR HER AGAIN!
SHIN ?!
DON'T HURT YOUR HANDS! YOU NEED THEM TO PLAY PIANO!
I WAS JUST KID-DING.
I WOULDN'T GO AFTER HER LIKE THAT FOR REAL.
I WAS TEASING, OKAY?

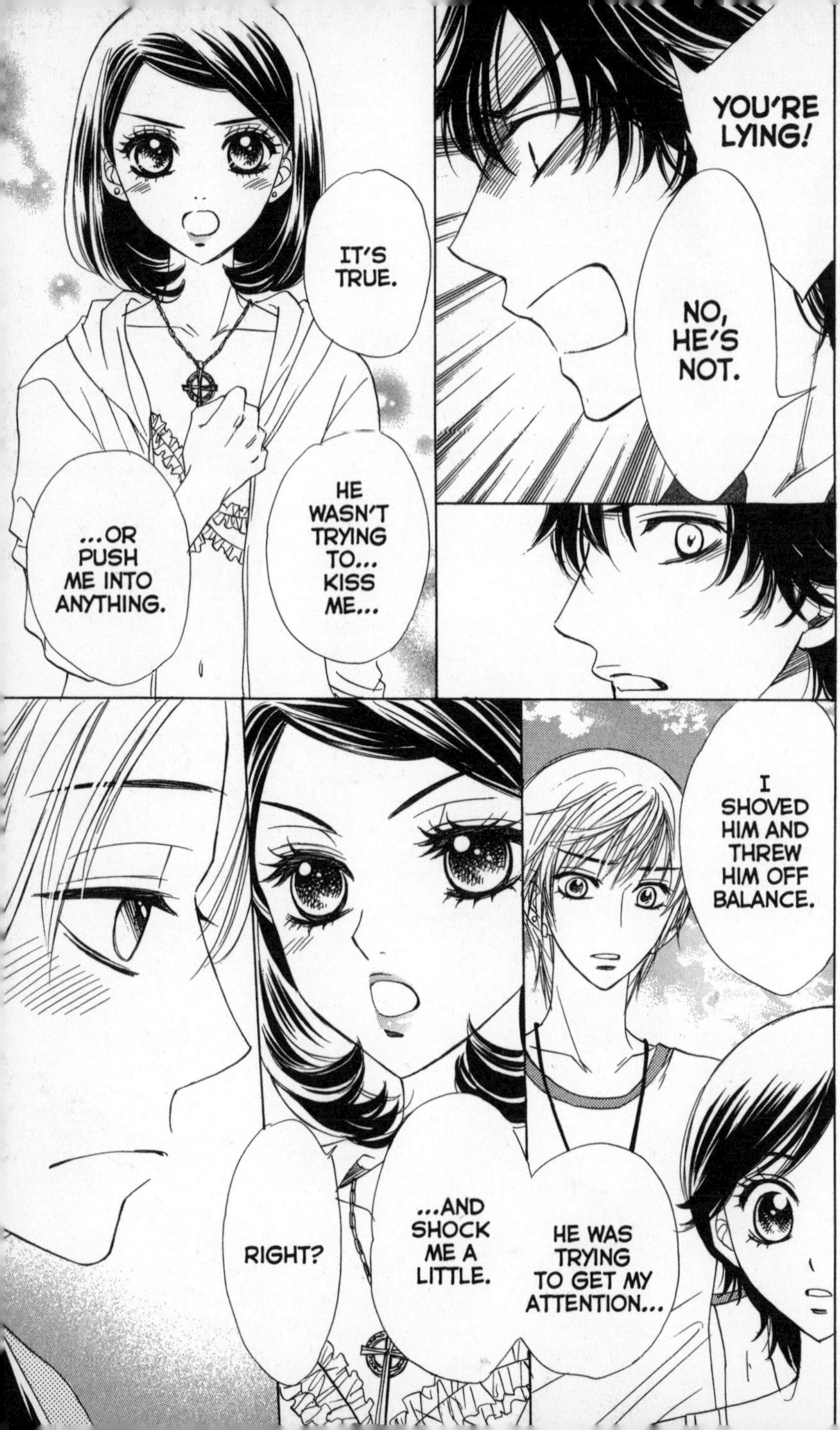
YOU'RE LYING!
NO, HE'S NOT.
IT'S TRUE.
HE WASN'T TRYING TO... KISS ME...
...OR PUSH ME INTO ANYTHING.
I SHOVED HIM AND THREW HIM OFF BALANCE.
HE WAS TRYING TO GET MY ATTENTION...
...AND SHOCK ME A LITTLE.
RIGHT?

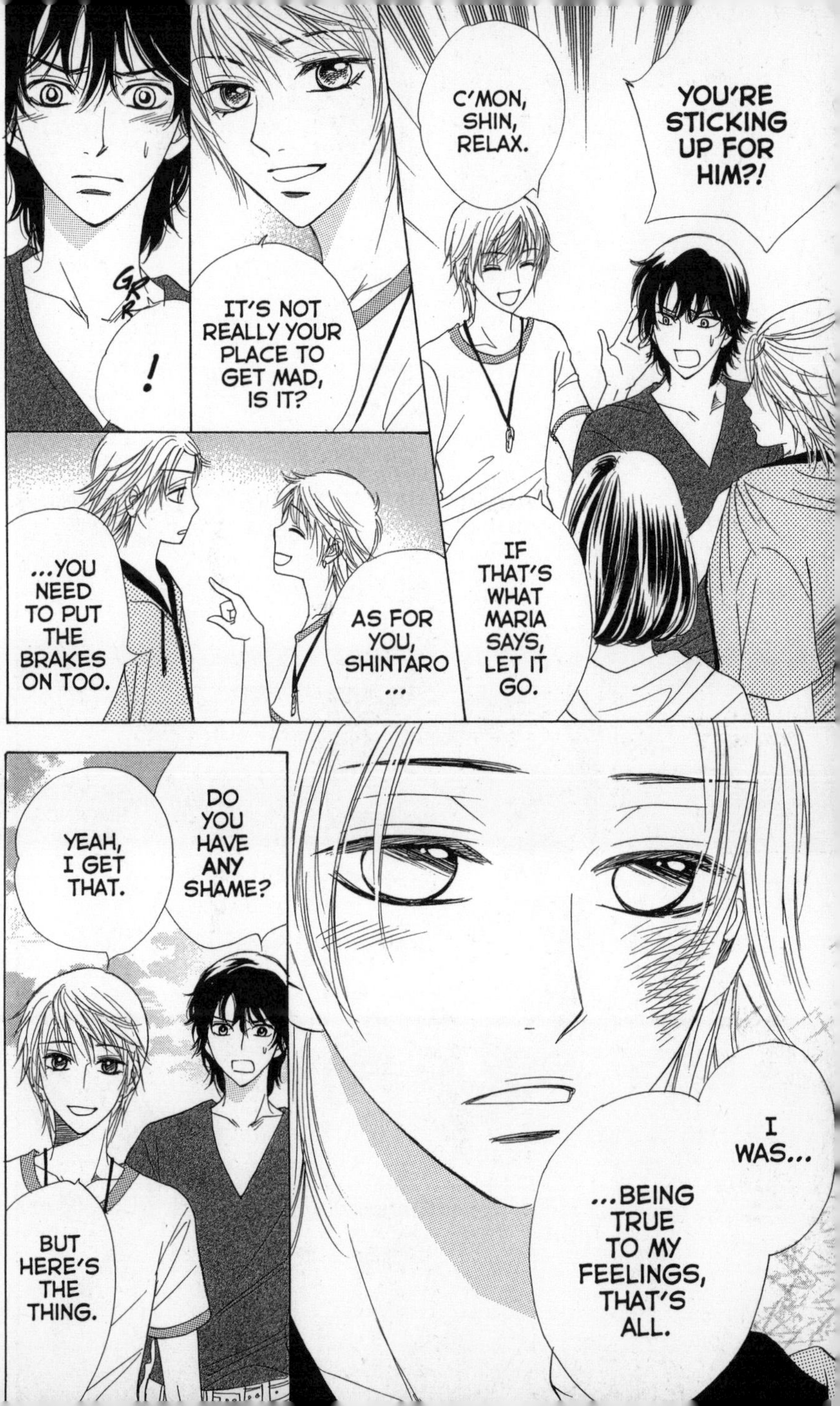
YOU'RE STICKING UP FOR HIM?!
C'MON, SHIN, RELAX.
IT'S NOT REALLY YOUR PLACE TO GET MAD, IS IT?
GRR
!
IF THAT'S WHAT MARIA SAYS, LET IT GO.
AS FOR YOU, SHINTARO...
...YOU NEED TO PUT THE BRAKES ON TOO.
I WAS...
...BEING TRUE TO MY FEELINGS, THAT'S ALL.
DO YOU HAVE ANY SHAME?
YEAH, I GET THAT.
BUT HERE'S THE THING.

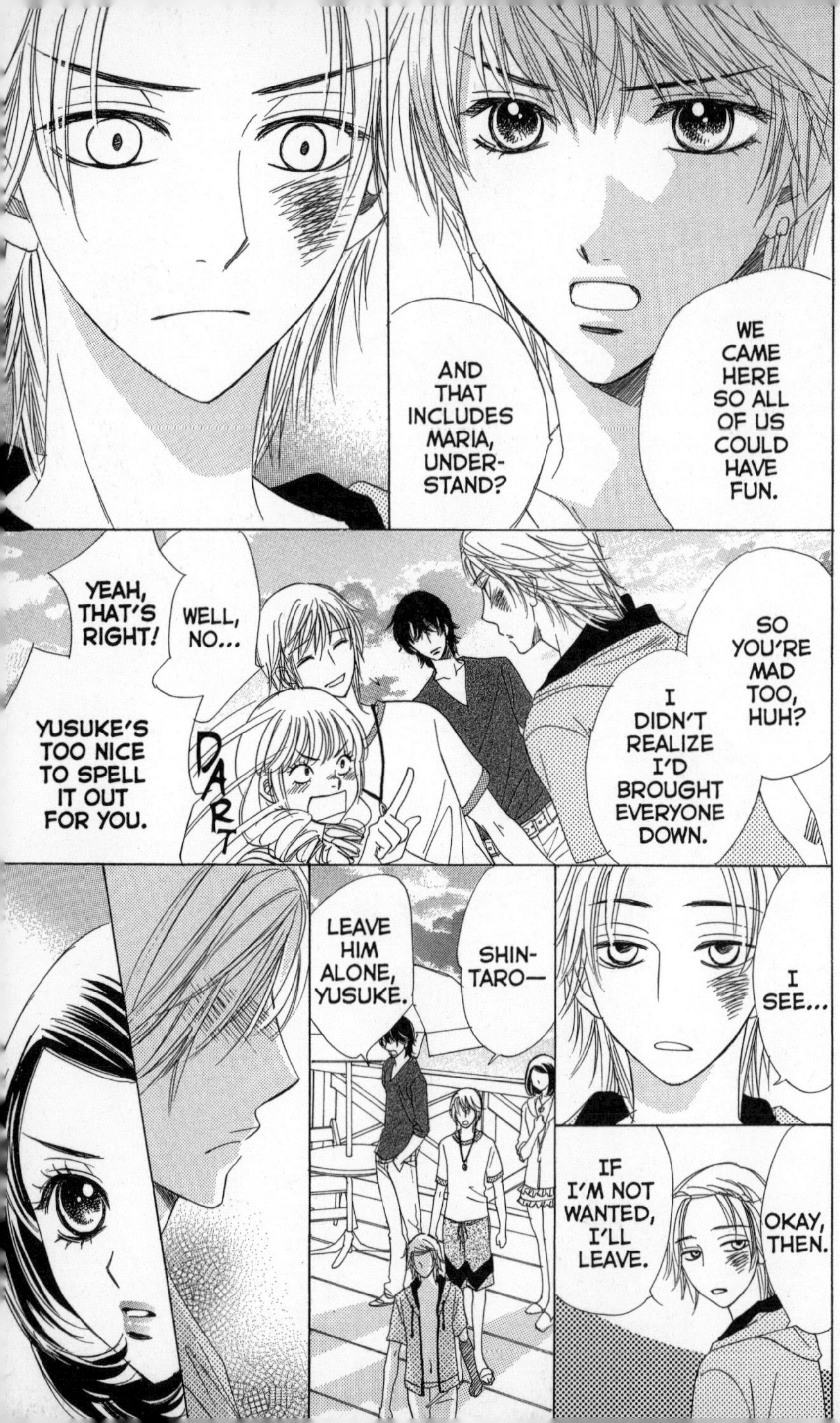
WE CAME HERE SO ALL OF US COULD HAVE FUN.
AND THAT INCLUDES MARIA, UNDER-STAND?
SO YOU'RE MAD TOO, HUH?
I DIDN'T REALIZE I'D BROUGHT EVERYONE DOWN.
WELL, NO...
YEAH, THAT'S RIGHT!
DART
YUSUKE'S TOO NICE TO SPELL IT OUT FOR YOU.
I SEE...
IF I'M NOT WANTED, I'LL LEAVE.
OKAY, THEN.
SHIN-TARO—
LEAVE HIM ALONE, YUSUKE.

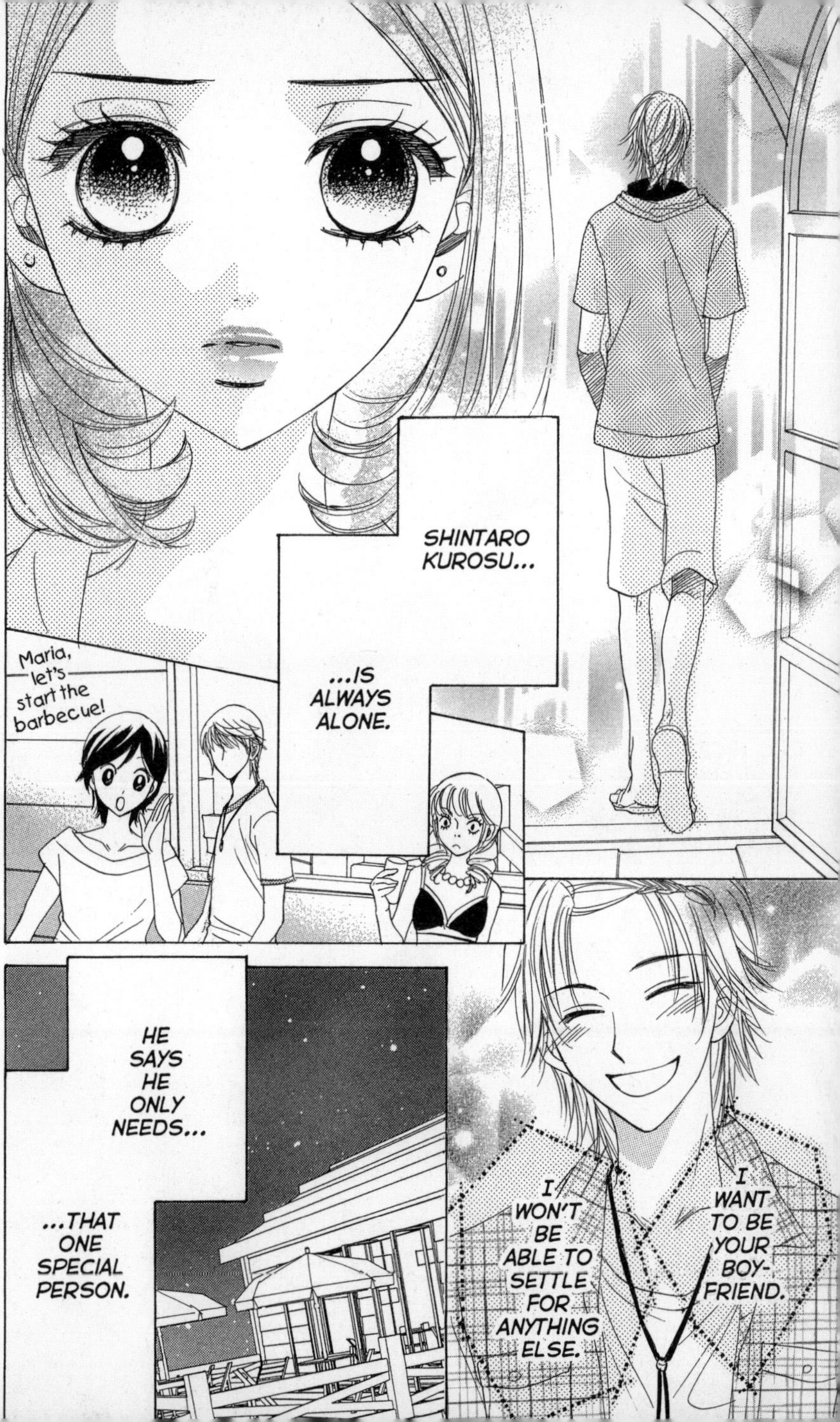
SHINTARO KUROSU...
...IS ALWAYS ALONE.
Maria, let's start the barbecue!
I WANT TO BE YOUR BOY-FRIEND.
I WON'T BE ABLE TO SETTLE FOR ANYTHING ELSE.
HE SAYS HE ONLY NEEDS...
...THAT ONE SPECIAL PERSON.

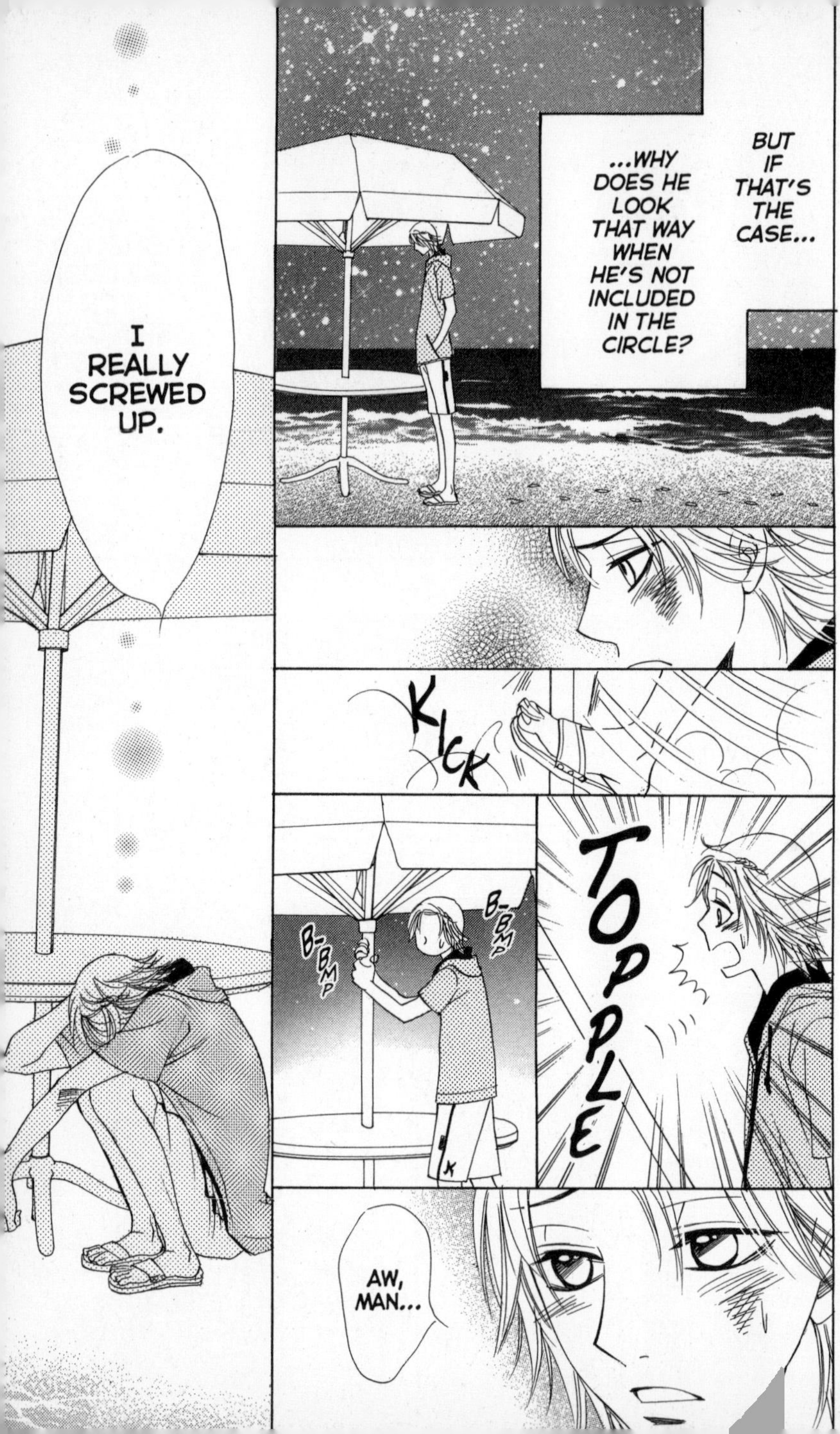
BUT IF THAT'S THE CASE...
...WHY DOES HE LOOK THAT WAY WHEN HE'S NOT INCLUDED IN THE CIRCLE?
KICK
TOPPLE
B-BMP
B-BMP
AW, MAN...
I REALLY SCREWED UP.

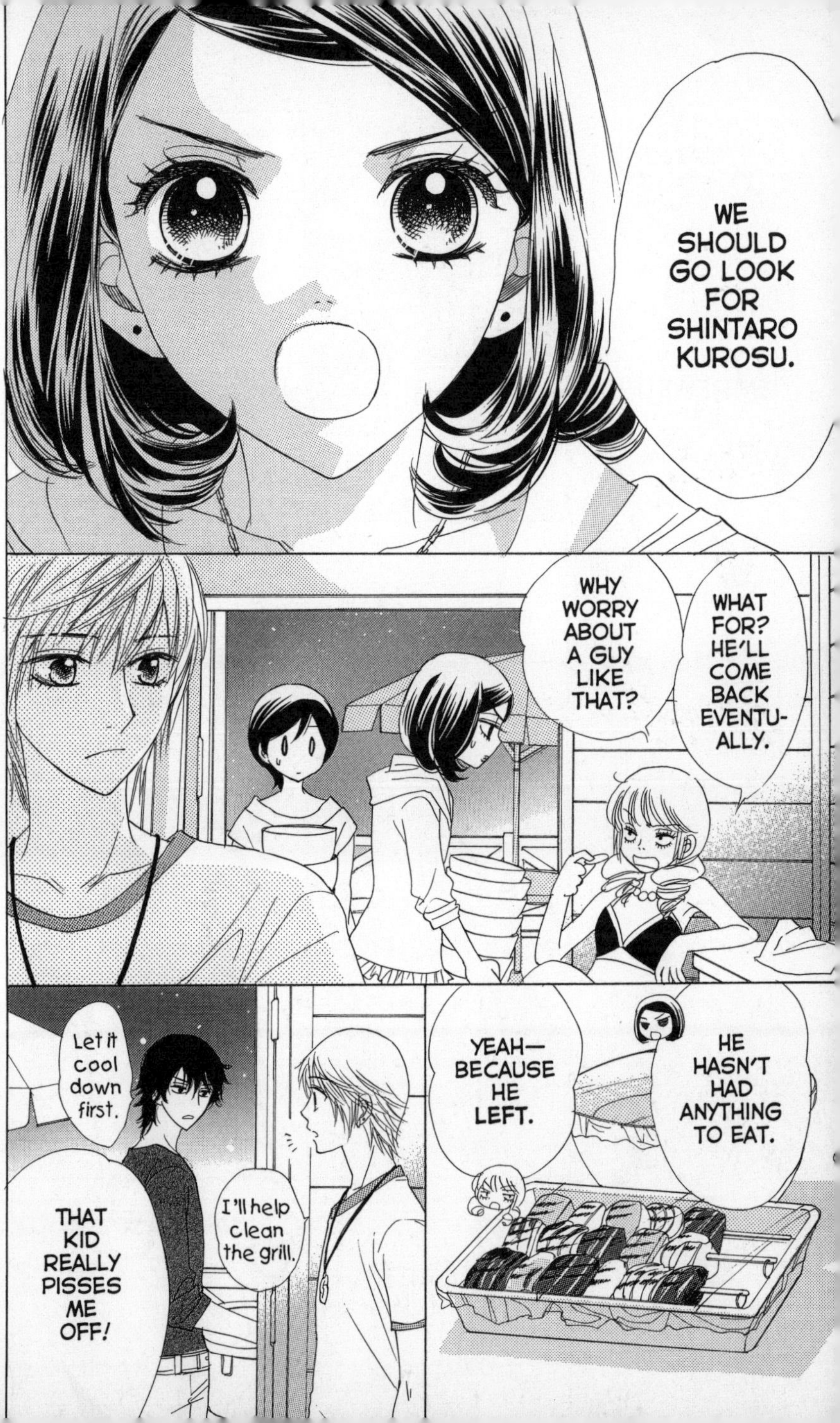
WE SHOULD GO LOOK FOR SHINTARO KUROSU.
WHAT FOR? HE'LL COME BACK EVENTU-ALLY.
WHY WORRY ABOUT A GUY LIKE THAT?
HE HASN'T HAD ANYTHING TO EAT.
YEAH— BECAUSE HE LEFT.
I'll help clean the grill.
Let it cool down first.
THAT KID REALLY PISSES ME OFF!

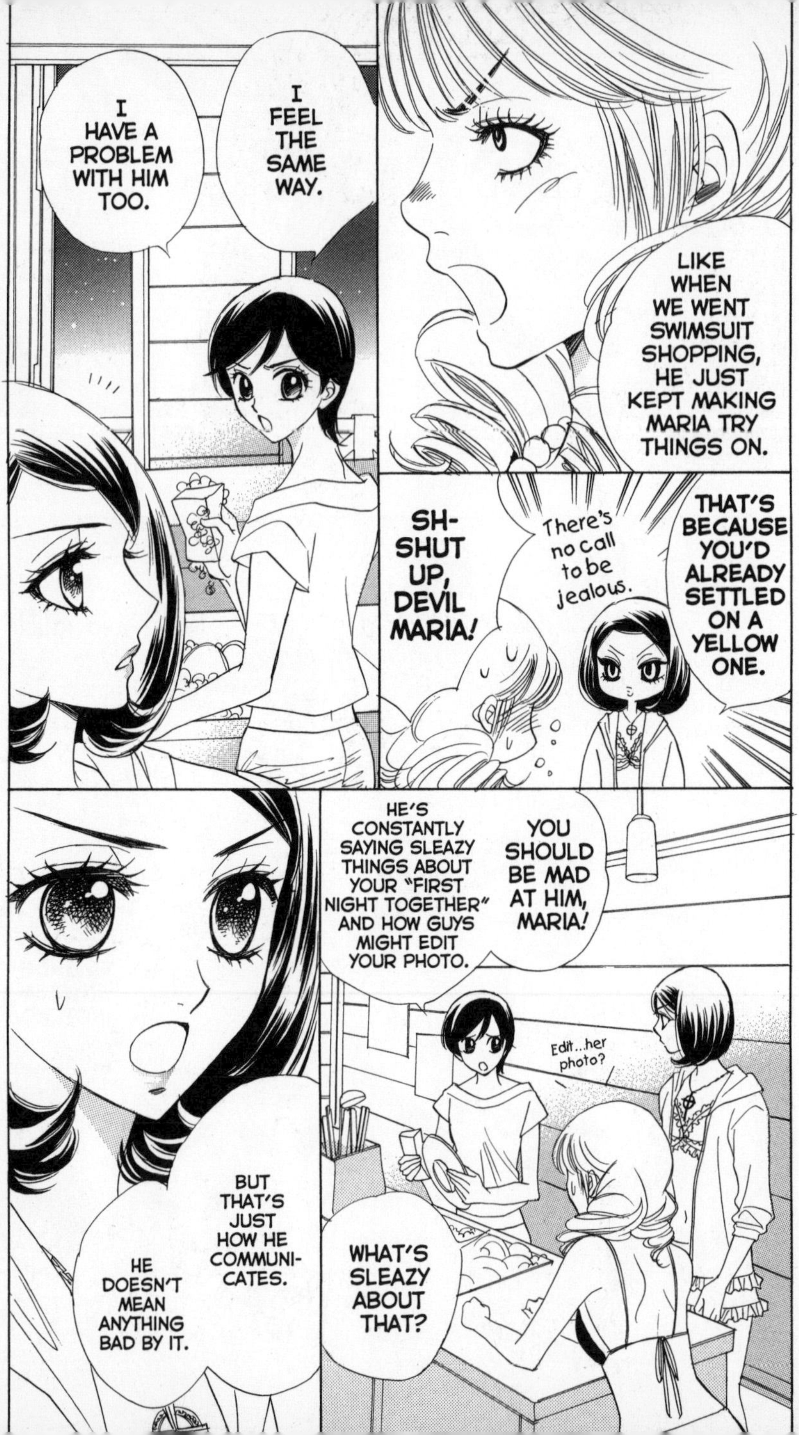
LIKE WHEN WE WENT SWIMSUIT SHOPPING, HE JUST KEPT MAKING MARIA TRY THINGS ON.
I FEEL THE SAME WAY.
I HAVE A PROBLEM WITH HIM TOO.
THAT'S BECAUSE YOU'D ALREADY SETTLED ON A YELLOW ONE.
There's no call to be jealous.
SH-SHUT UP, DEVIL MARIA!
YOU SHOULD BE MAD AT HIM, MARIA!
HE'S CONSTANTLY SAYING SLEAZY THINGS ABOUT YOUR "FIRST NIGHT TOGETHER" AND HOW GUYS MIGHT EDIT YOUR PHOTO.
Edit...her photo?
WHAT'S SLEAZY ABOUT THAT?
BUT THAT'S JUST HOW HE COMMUNICATES.
HE DOESN'T MEAN ANYTHING BAD BY IT.

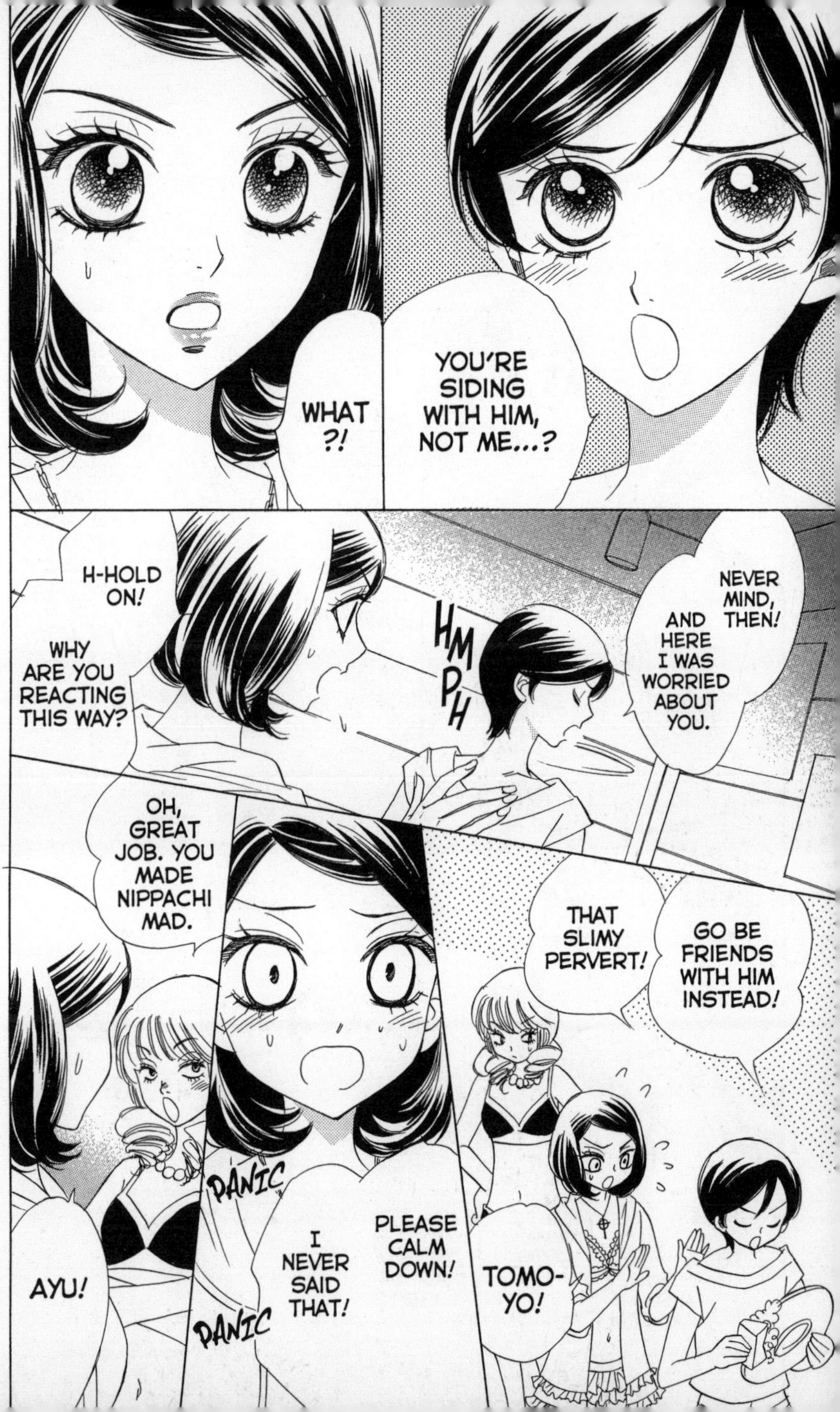
YOU'RE SIDING WITH HIM, NOT ME...?
WHAT ?!
NEVER MIND, THEN!
AND HERE I WAS WORRIED ABOUT YOU.
HMPH
H-HOLD ON!
WHY ARE YOU REACTING THIS WAY?
GO BE FRIENDS WITH HIM INSTEAD!
THAT SLIMY PERVERT!
TOMO-YO!
PLEASE CALM DOWN!
I NEVER SAID THAT!
PANIC
PANIC
OH, GREAT JOB. YOU MADE NIPPACHI MAD.
AYU!

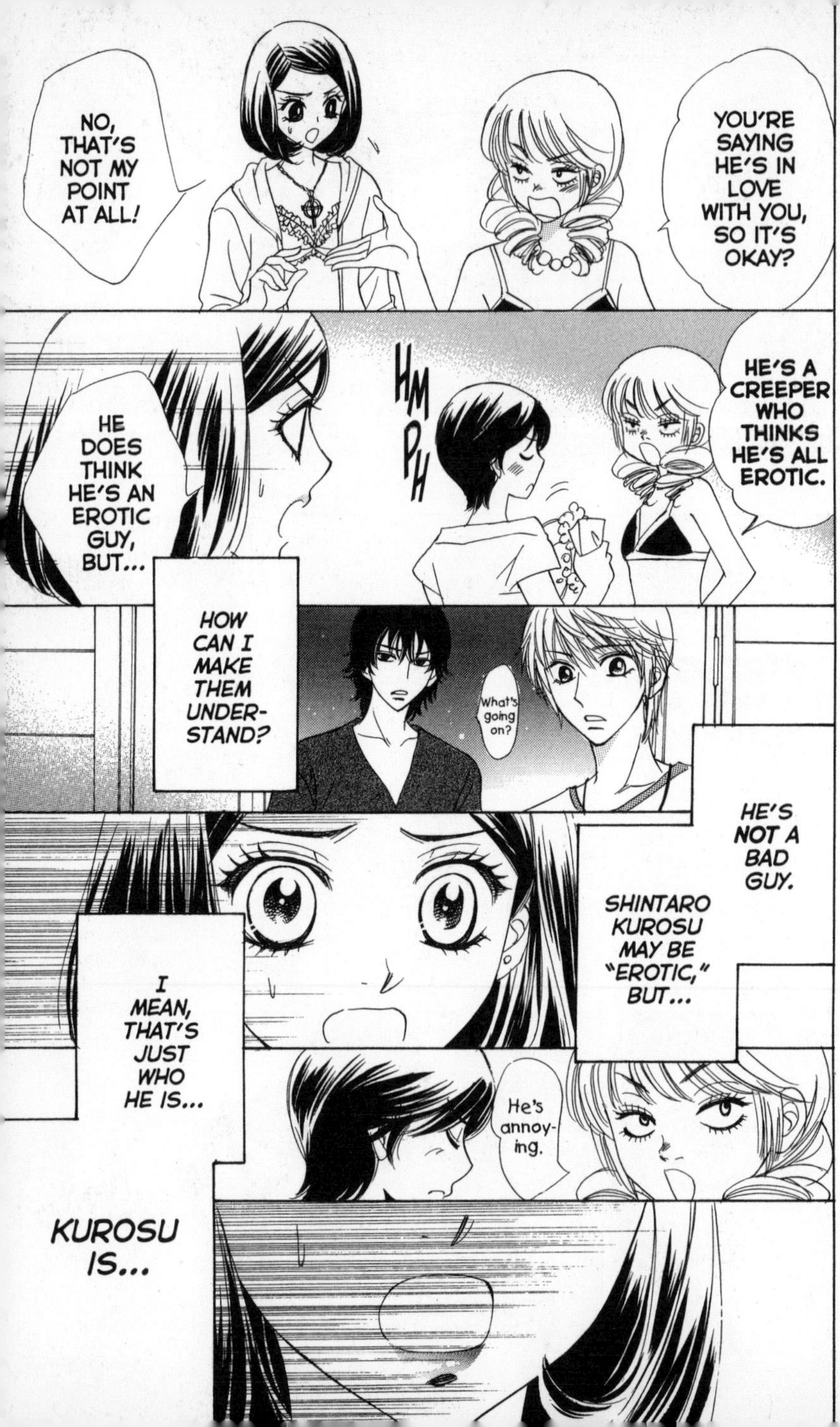
YOU'RE SAYING HE'S IN LOVE WITH YOU, SO IT'S OKAY?
NO, THAT'S NOT MY POINT AT ALL!
HE'S A CREEPER WHO THINKS HE'S ALL EROTIC.
HMPH
HE DOES THINK HE'S AN EROTIC GUY, BUT...
What's going on?
HOW CAN I MAKE THEM UNDERSTAND?
HE'S NOT A BAD GUY.
SHINTARO KUROSU MAY BE "EROTIC," BUT...
I MEAN, THAT'S JUST WHO HE IS...
He's annoy-ing.
KUROSU IS...

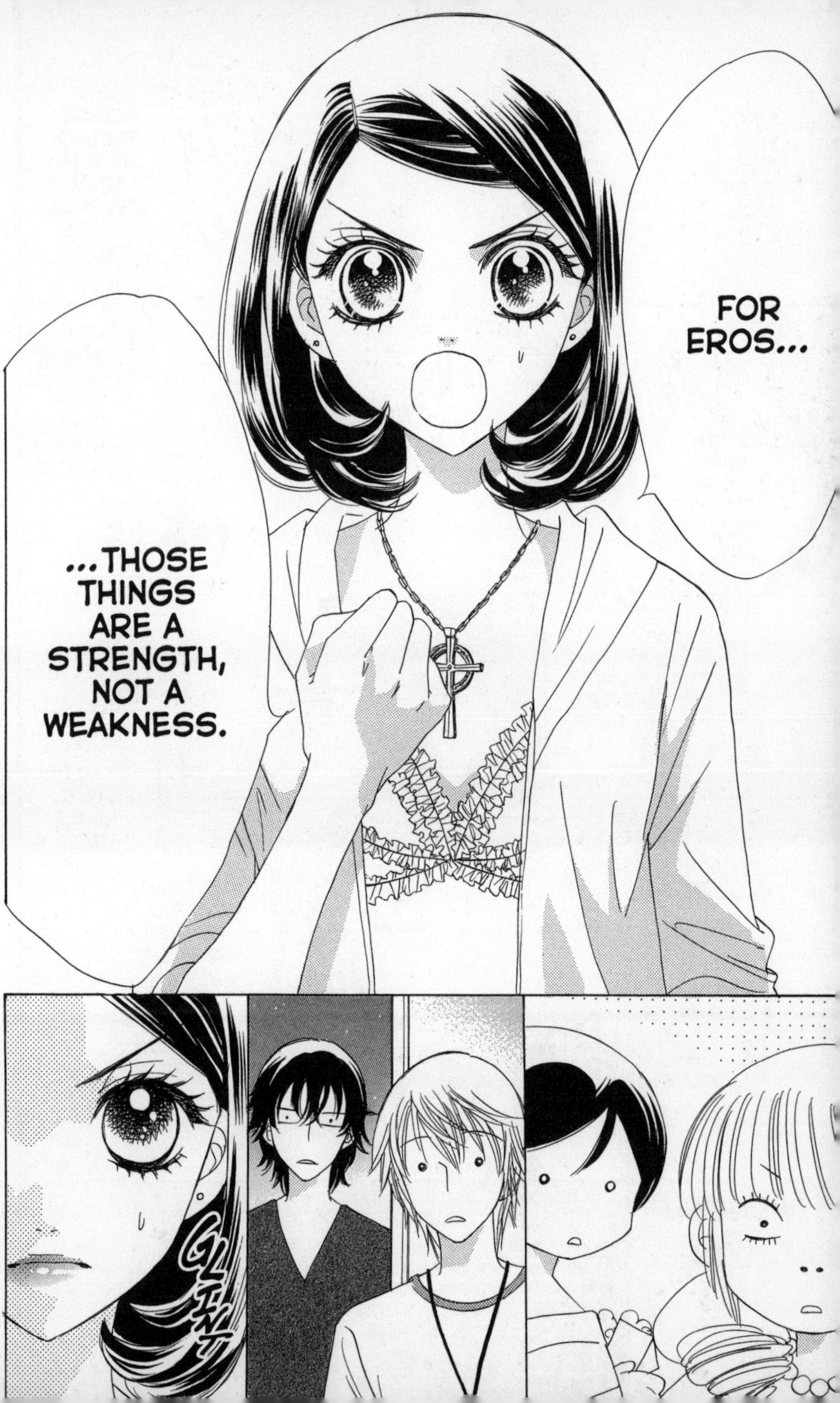
FOR EROS...
...THOSE THINGS ARE A STRENGTH, NOT A WEAKNESS.
GLINT

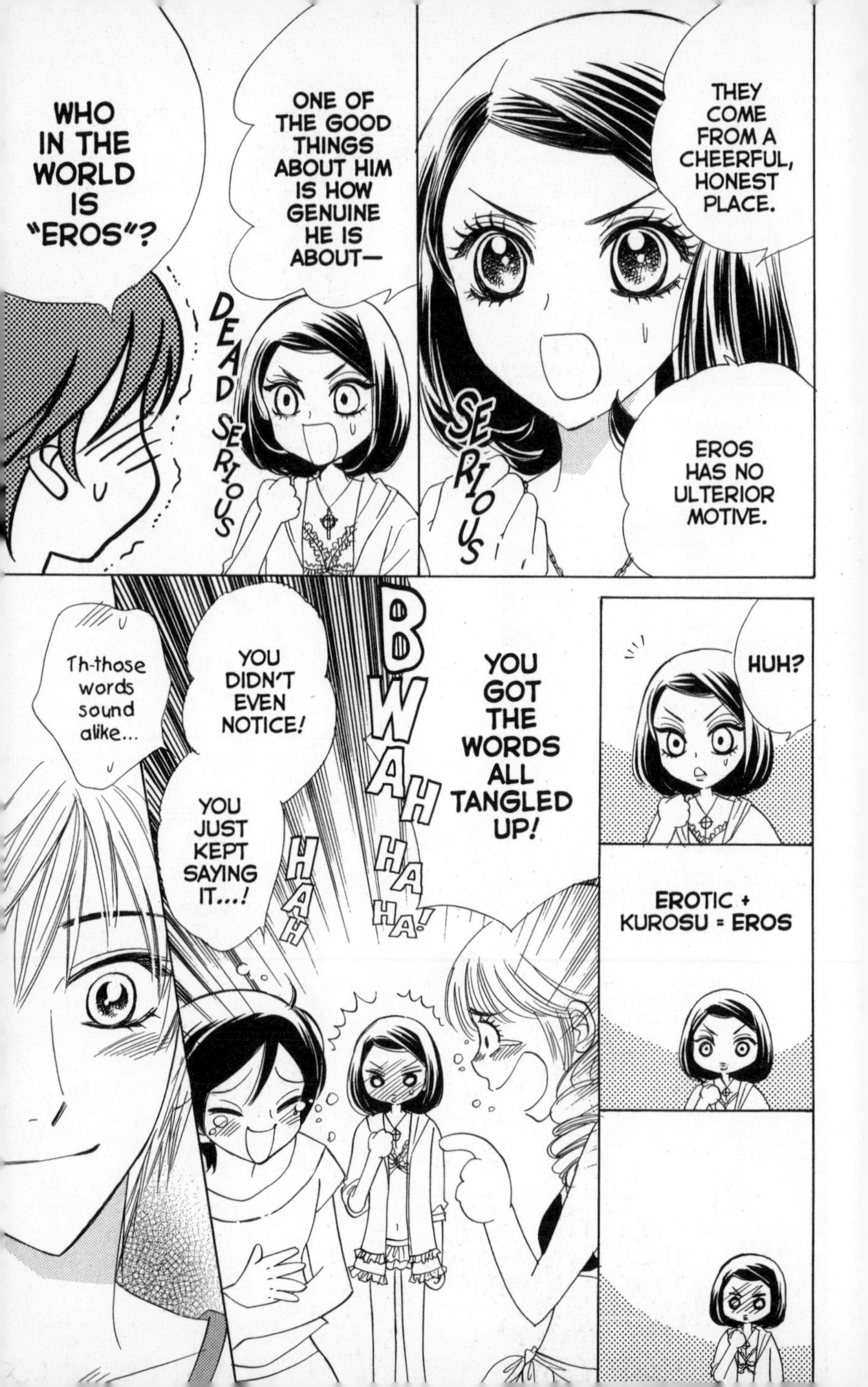
THEY COME FROM A CHEERFUL, HONEST PLACE.
SERIOUS
EROS HAS NO ULTERIOR MOTIVE.
ONE OF THE GOOD THINGS ABOUT HIM IS HOW GENUINE HE IS ABOUT—
DEAD SERIOUS
WHO IN THE WORLD IS "EROS"?
HUH?
EROTIC + KUROSU = EROS
BWAH HA HA HA!
YOU GOT THE WORDS ALL TANGLED UP!
HAHAH
YOU DIDN'T EVEN NOTICE!
YOU JUST KEPT SAYING IT...!
Th-those words sound alike...

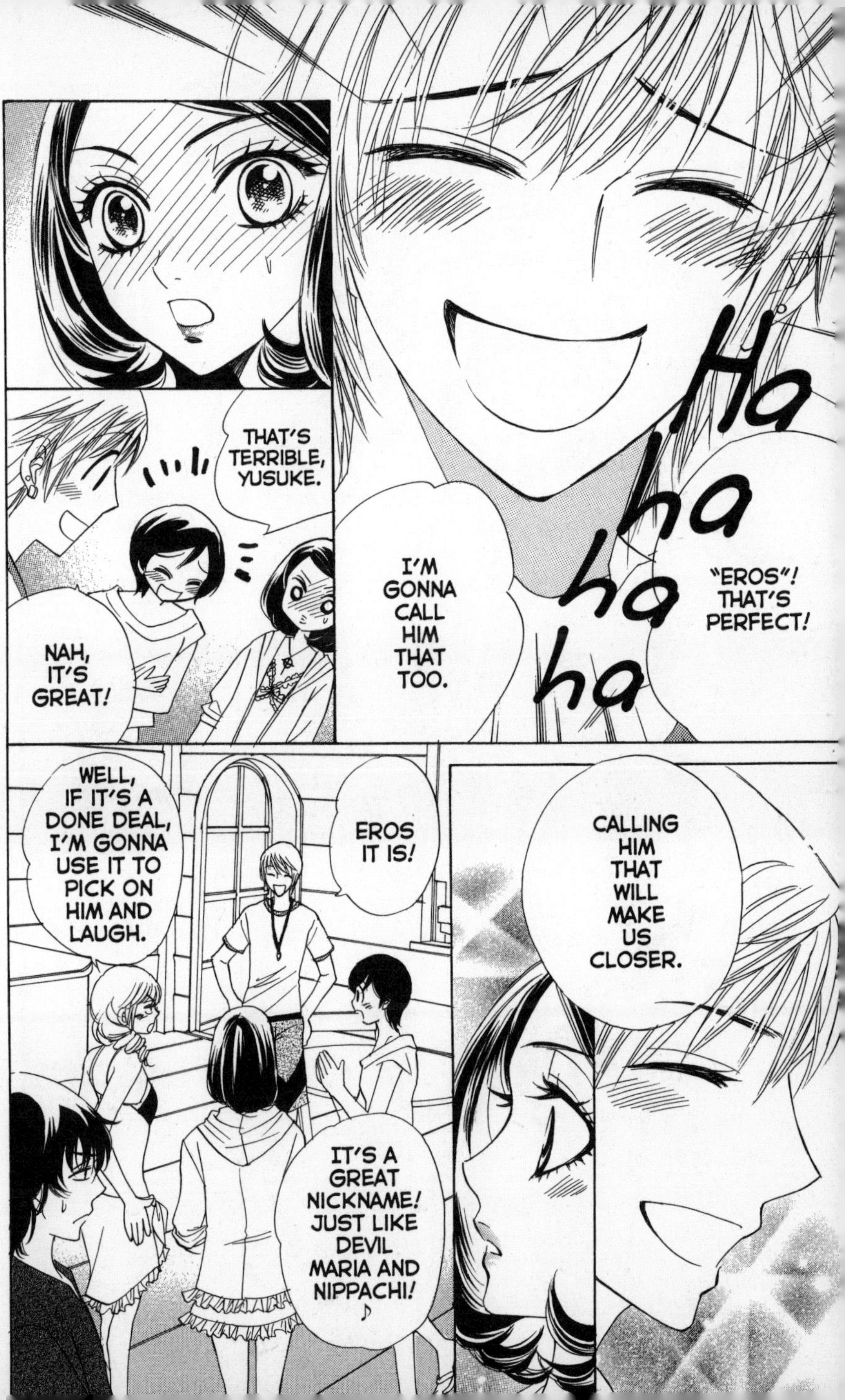
Ha ha ha ha
"EROS"! THAT'S PERFECT!
I'M GONNA CALL HIM THAT TOO.
THAT'S TERRIBLE, YUSUKE.
NAH, IT'S GREAT!
CALLING HIM THAT WILL MAKE US CLOSER.
EROS IT IS!
WELL, IF IT'S A DONE DEAL, I'M GONNA USE IT TO PICK ON HIM AND LAUGH.
IT'S A GREAT NICKNAME! JUST LIKE DEVIL MARIA AND NIPPACHI! ♪

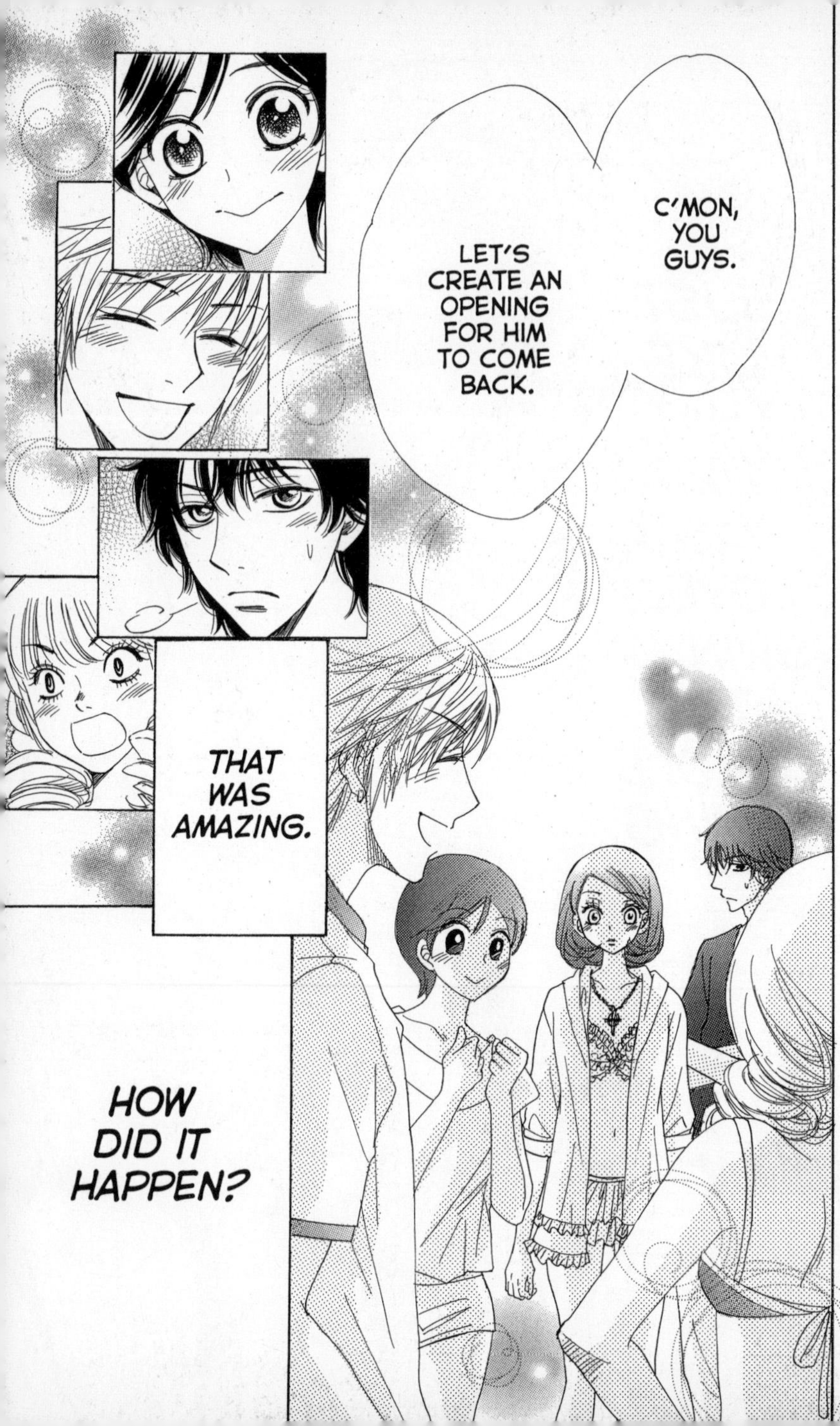
C'MON, YOU GUYS.
LET'S CREATE AN OPENING FOR HIM TO COME BACK.
THAT WAS AMAZING.
HOW DID IT HAPPEN?

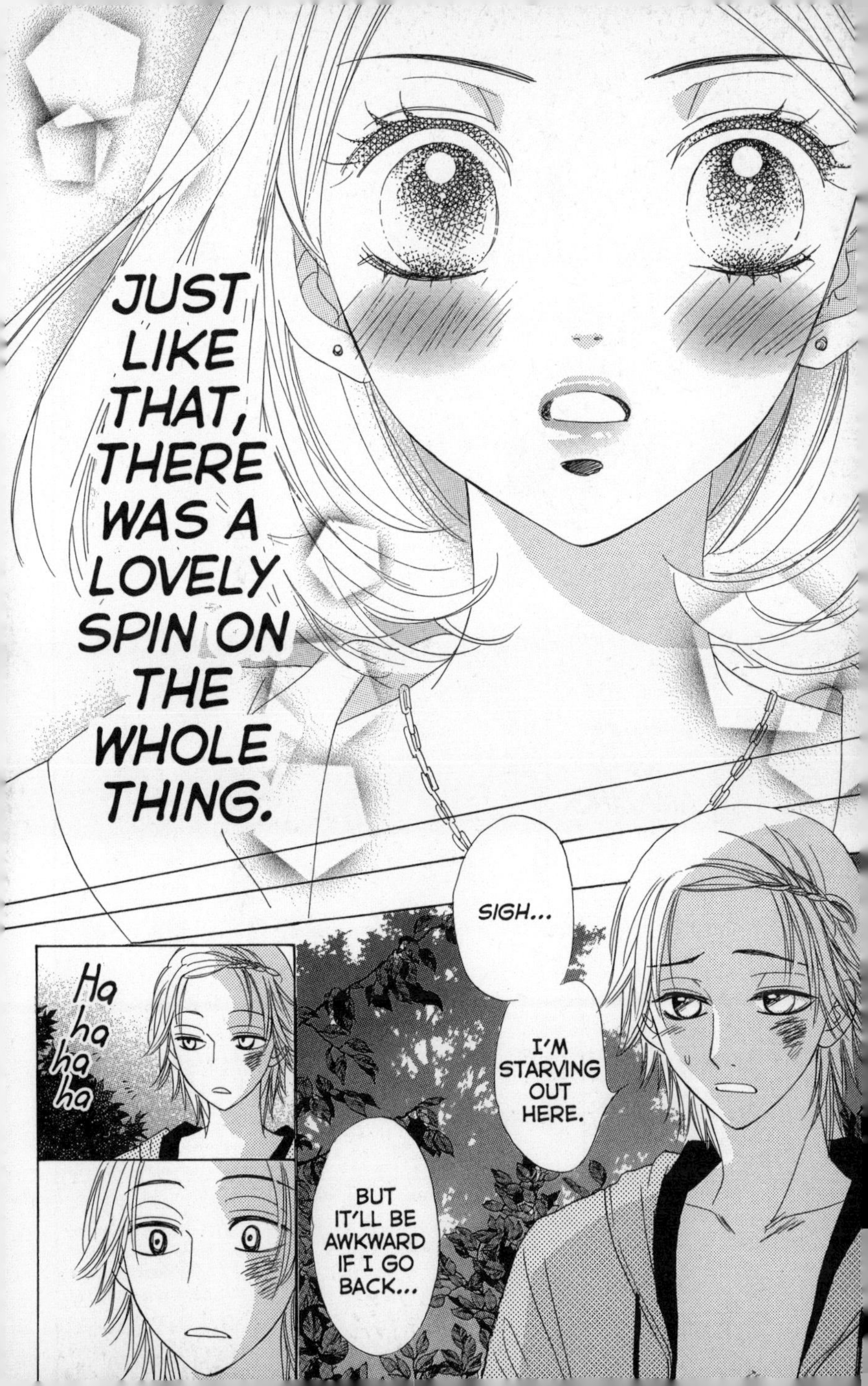
JUST LIKE THAT, THERE WAS A LOVELY SPIN ON THE WHOLE THING.
SIGH...
I'M STARVING OUT HERE.
BUT IT'LL BE AWKWARD IF I GO BACK...
Ha ha ha ha

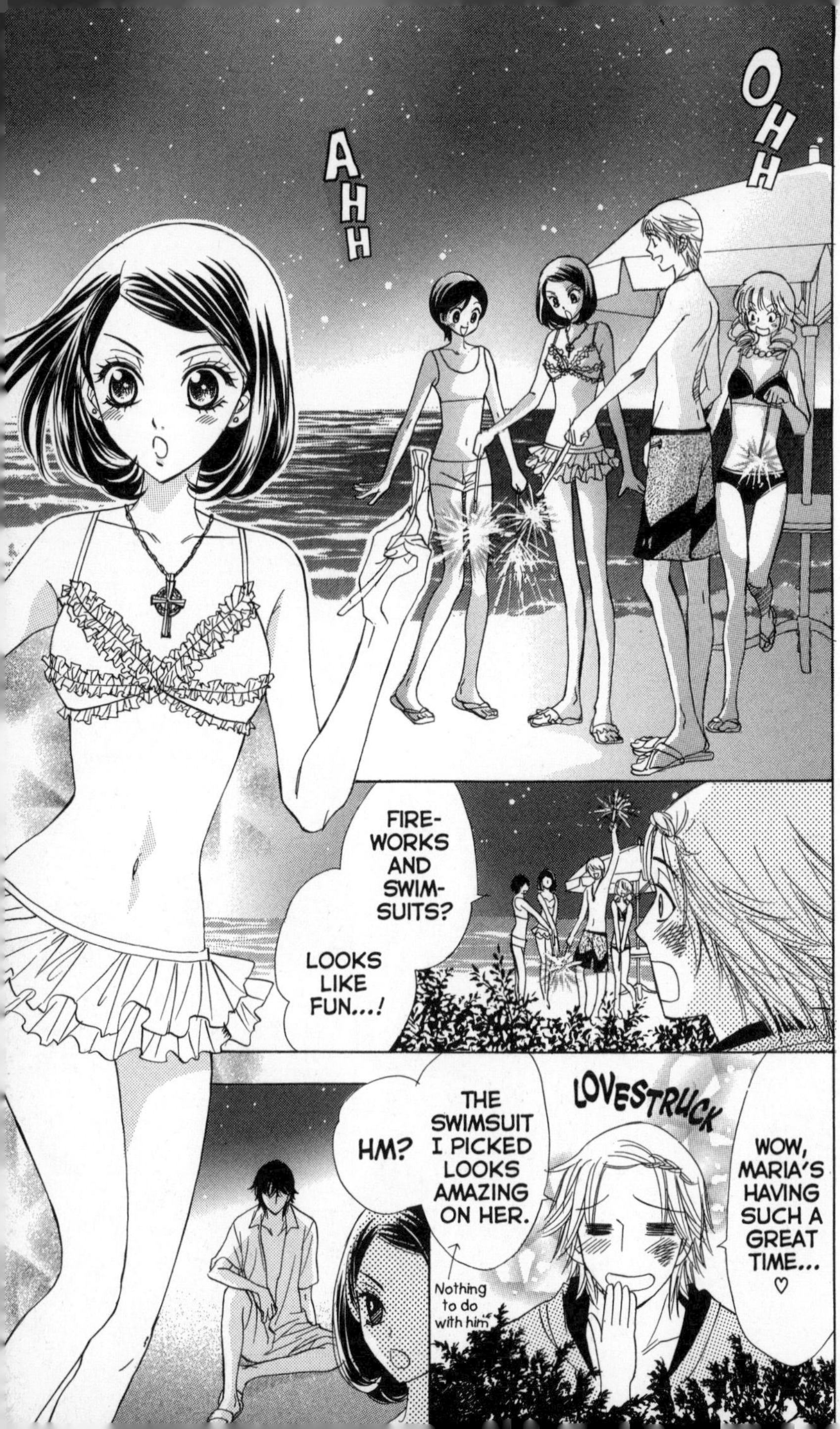
OHHH
AHH
FIRE-WORKS AND SWIM-SUITS?
LOOKS LIKE FUN...!
WOW, MARIA'S HAVING SUCH A GREAT TIME... ♡
LOVESTRUCK
THE SWIMSUIT I PICKED LOOKS AMAZING ON HER.
Nothing to do with him
HM?

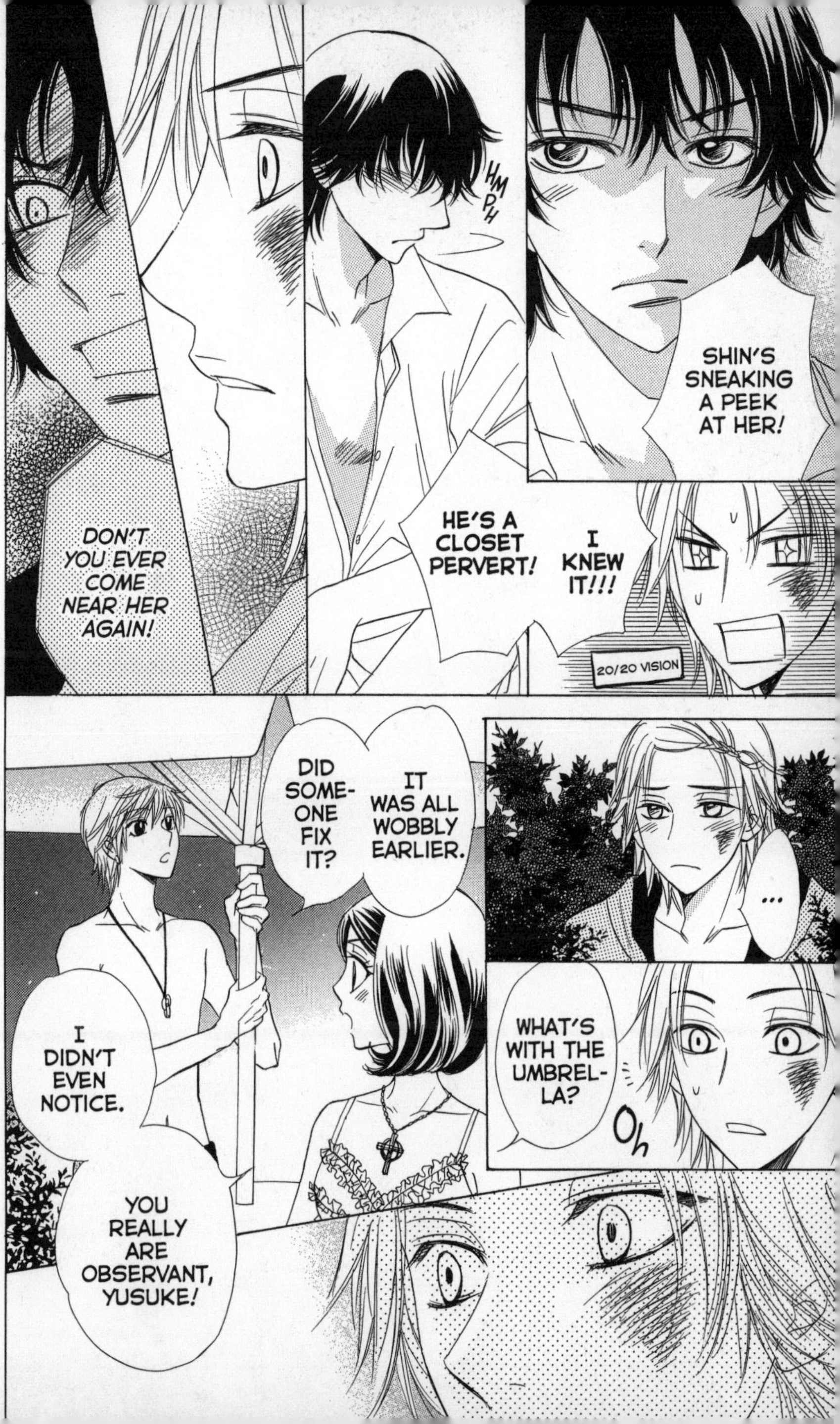
SHIN'S SNEAKING A PEEK AT HER!
HE'S A CLOSET PERVERT!
I KNEW IT!!!
20/20 VISION
HMPH
DON'T YOU EVER COME NEAR HER AGAIN!
...
WHAT'S WITH THE UMBREL-LA?
Oh
DID SOME-ONE FIX IT?
IT WAS ALL WOBBLY EARLIER.
I DIDN'T EVEN NOTICE.
YOU REALLY ARE OBSERVANT, YUSUKE!

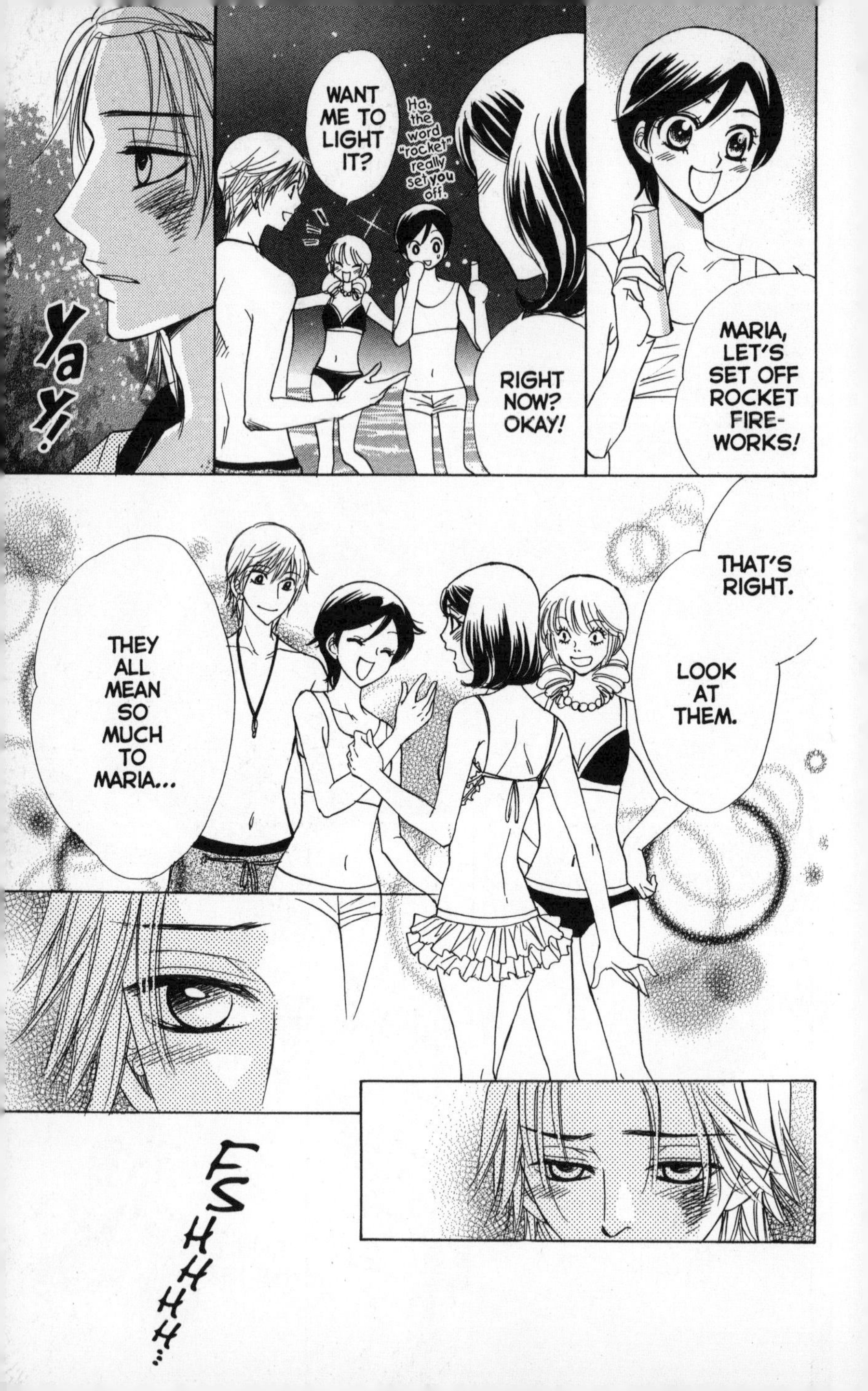
MARIA, LET'S SET OFF ROCKET FIRE-WORKS!
RIGHT NOW? OKAY!
WANT ME TO LIGHT IT?
Ha, the word "rocket" really set you off.
YAY!
THAT'S RIGHT.
LOOK AT THEM.
THEY ALL MEAN SO MUCH TO MARIA...
FSHHHH...

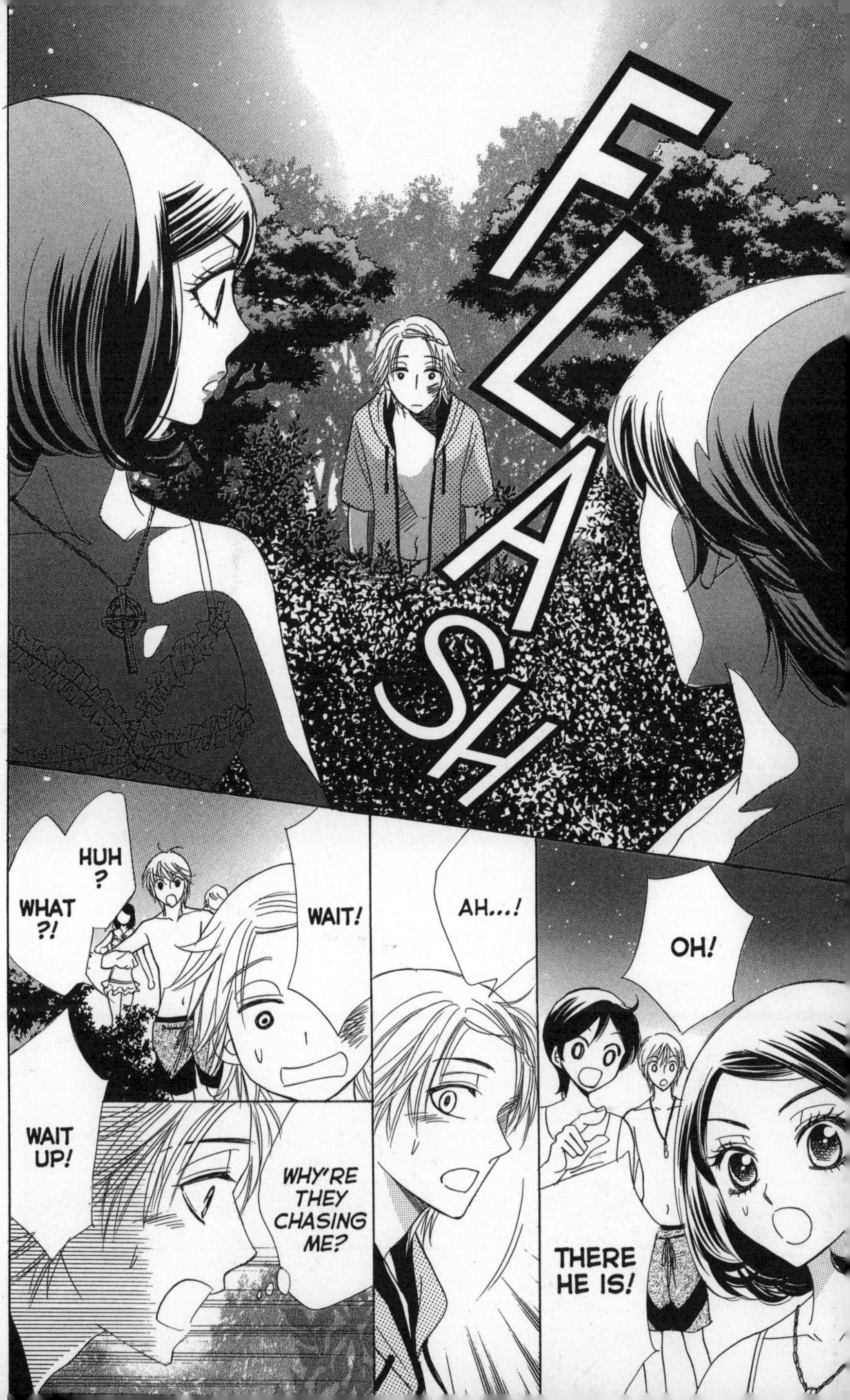
FLASH
OH!
THERE HE IS!
AH...!
WAIT!
HUH ?
WHAT ?!
WHY'RE THEY CHASING ME?
WAIT UP!

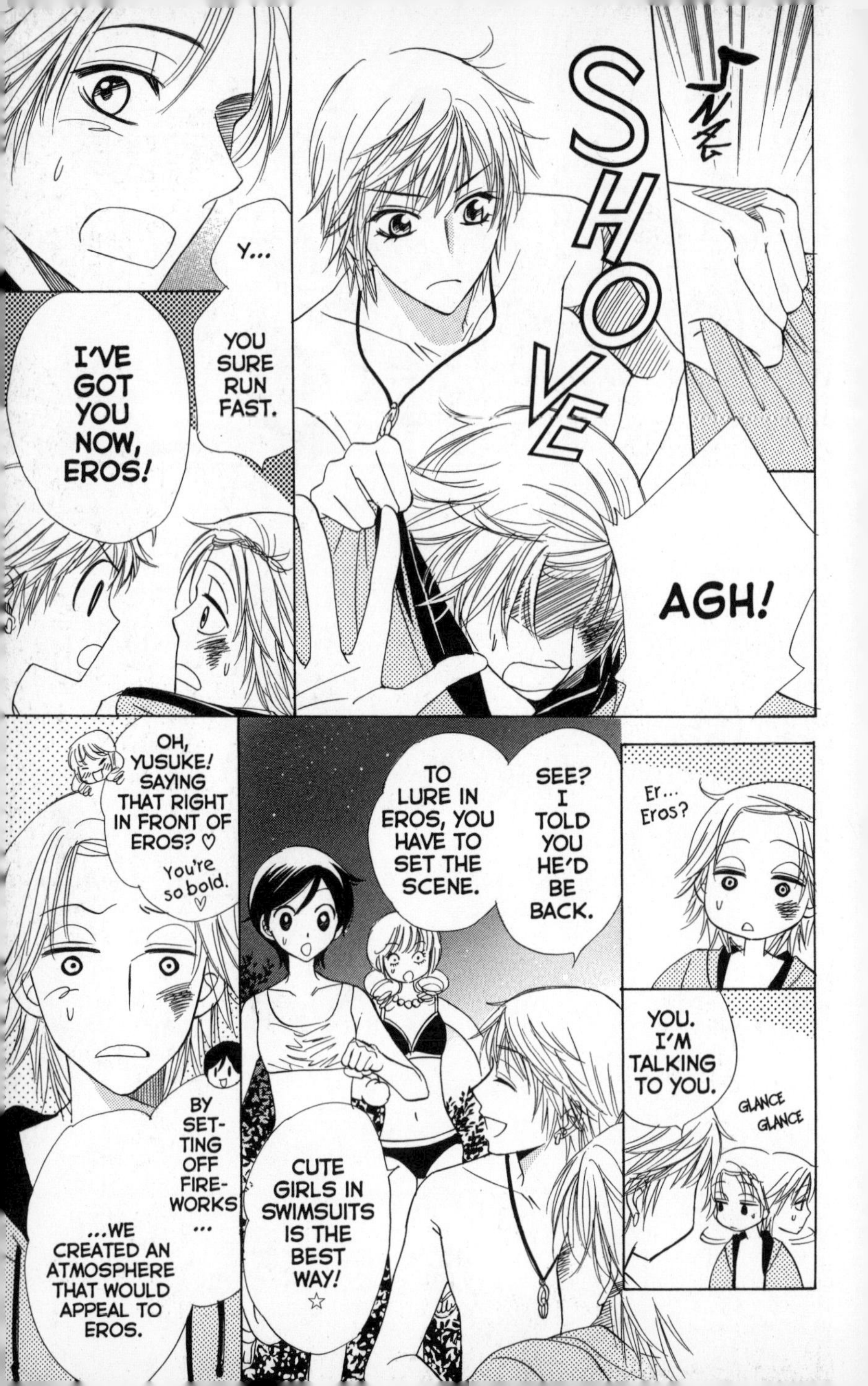
SHOVE
ZNG
AGH!
Y...
YOU SURE RUN FAST.
I'VE GOT YOU NOW, EROS!
Er... Eros?
YOU. I'M TALKING TO YOU.
GLANCE GLANCE
SEE? I TOLD YOU HE'D BE BACK.
TO LURE IN EROS, YOU HAVE TO SET THE SCENE.
CUTE GIRLS IN SWIMSUITS IS THE BEST WAY! ☆
OH, YUSUKE! SAYING THAT RIGHT IN FRONT OF EROS? ♡
You're so bold. ♡
BY SETTING OFF FIREWORKS...
...WE CREATED AN ATMOSPHERE THAT WOULD APPEAL TO EROS.

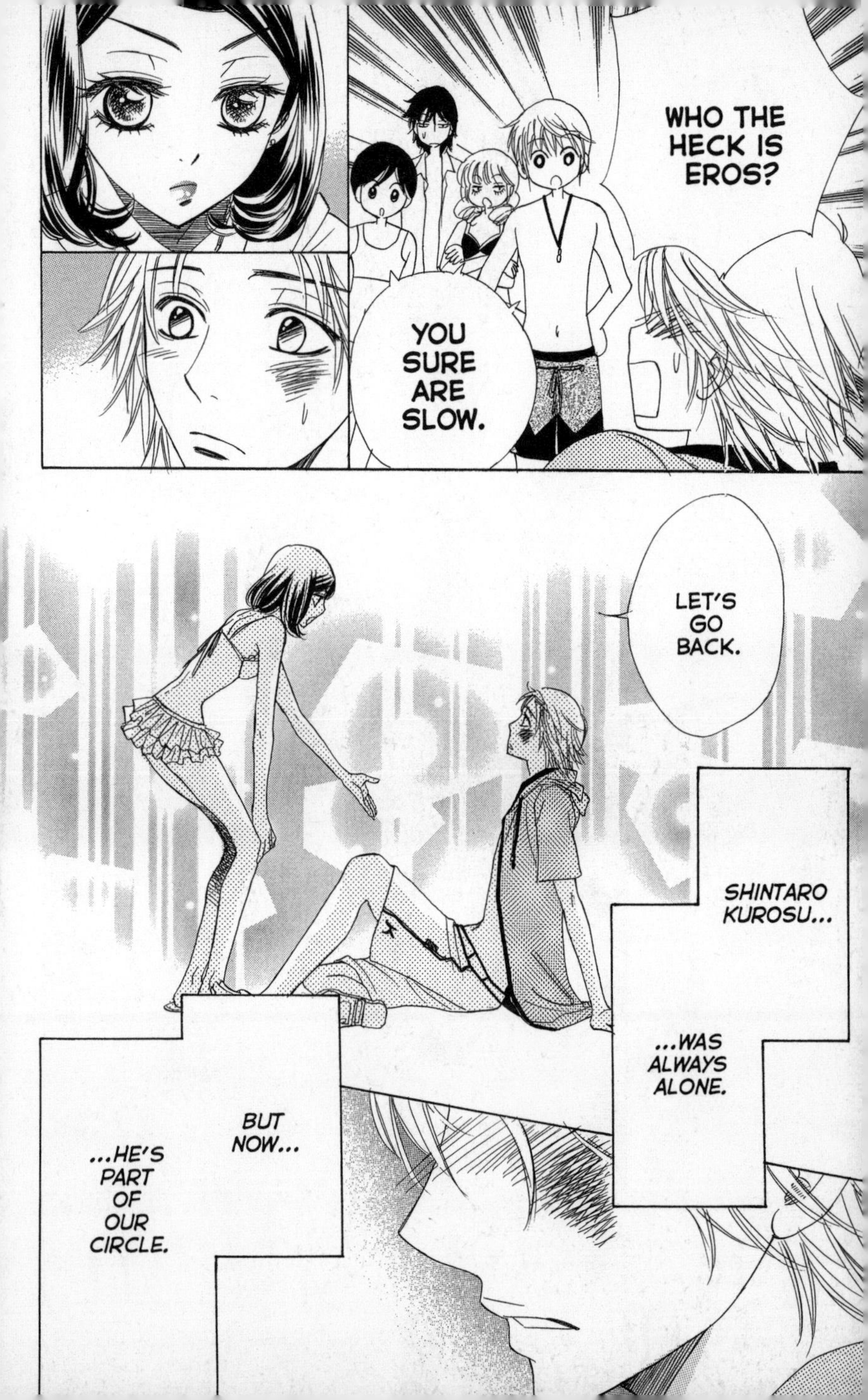
WHO THE HECK IS EROS?
YOU SURE ARE SLOW.
LET'S GO BACK.
SHINTARO KUROSU...
...WAS ALWAYS ALONE.
BUT NOW...
...HE'S PART OF OUR CIRCLE.

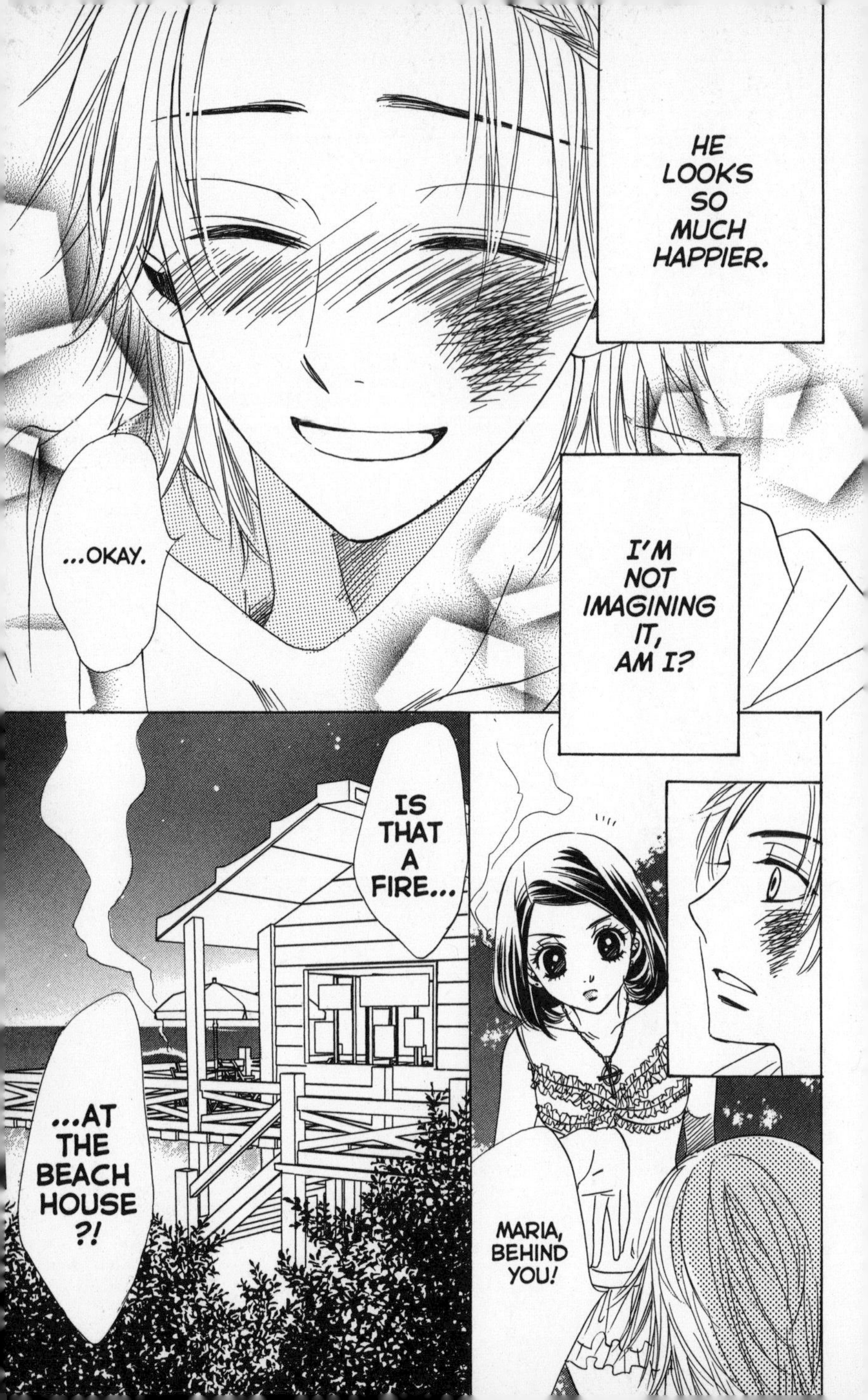
HE LOOKS SO MUCH HAPPIER.
I'M NOT IMAGINING IT, AM I?
...OKAY.
MARIA, BEHIND YOU!
IS THAT A FIRE...
...AT THE BEACH HOUSE ?!

A Devil and
Her Love Song

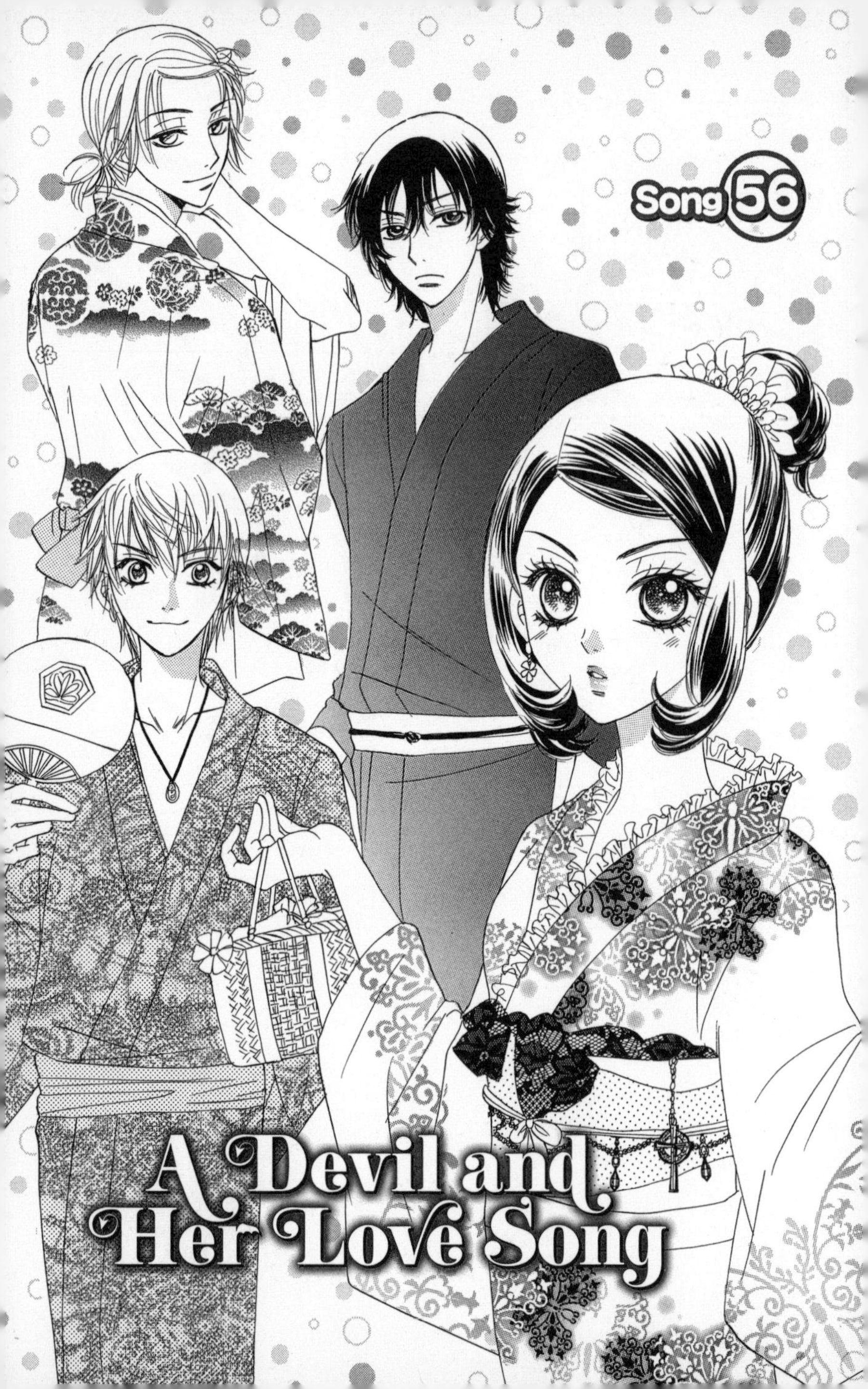
Song 56
A Devil and Her Love Song

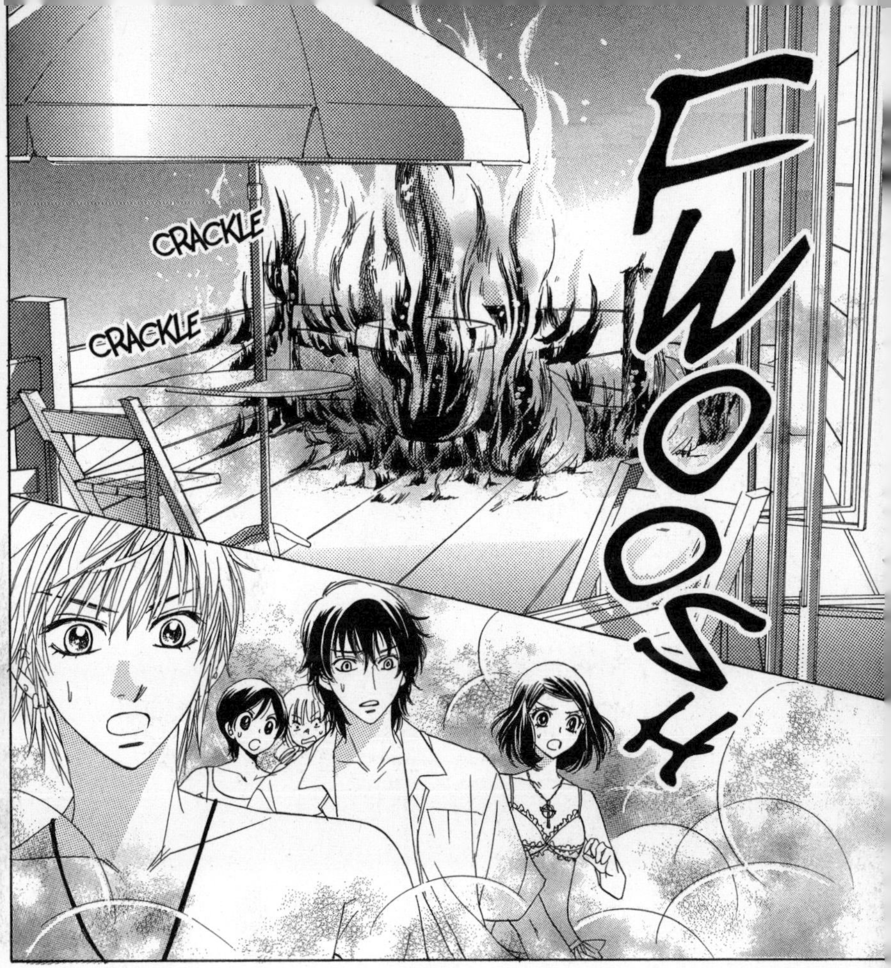
FWOOSH
CRACKLE
CRACKLE

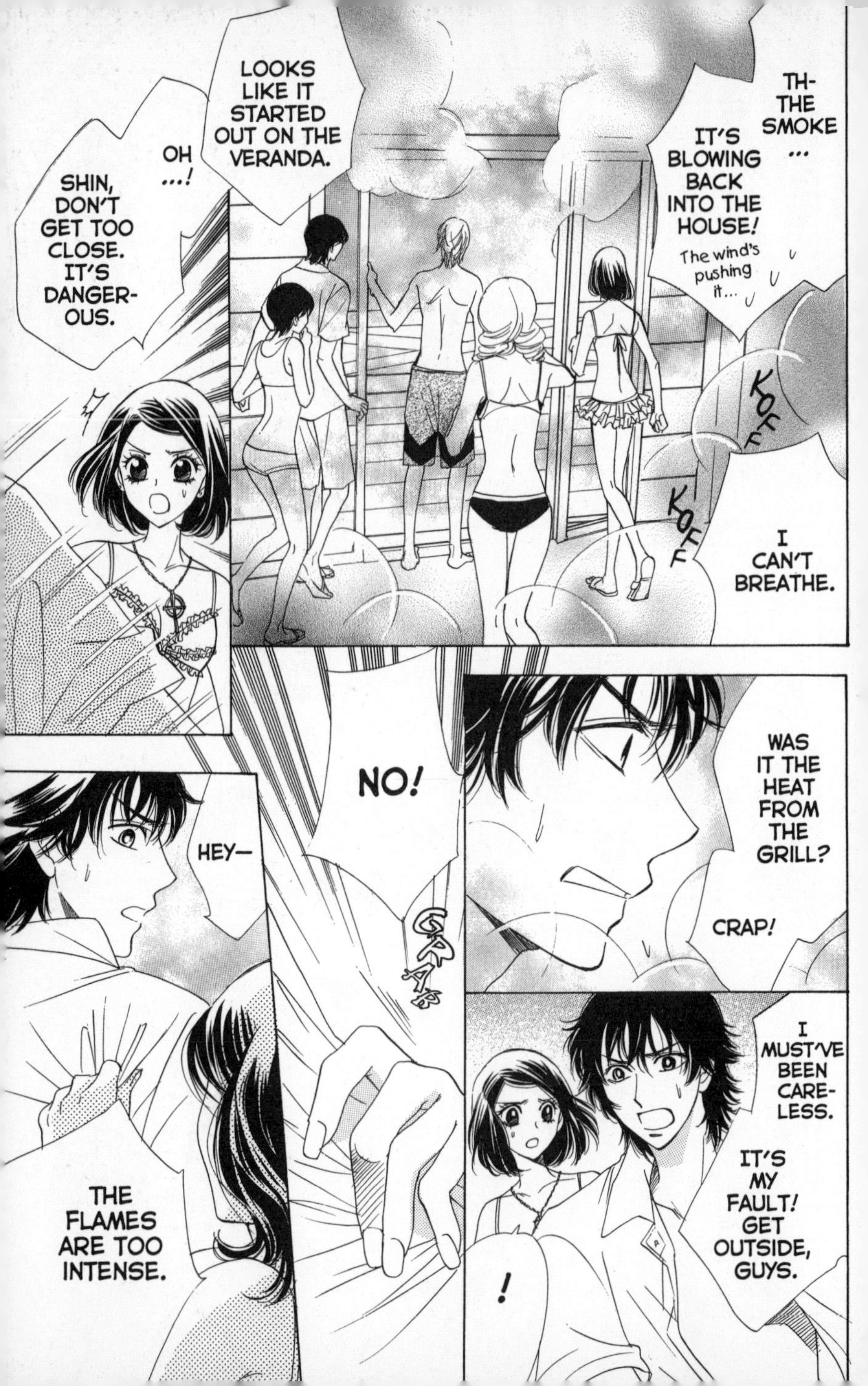
TH- THE SMOKE ...
IT'S BLOWING BACK INTO THE HOUSE!
The wind's pushing it...
LOOKS LIKE IT STARTED OUT ON THE VERANDA.
KOFF
KOFF
I CAN'T BREATHE.
OH ...!
SHIN, DON'T GET TOO CLOSE. IT'S DANGER-OUS.
WAS IT THE HEAT FROM THE GRILL?
CRAP!
NO!
HEY—
GRAB
I MUST'VE BEEN CARE-LESS.
IT'S MY FAULT! GET OUTSIDE, GUYS.
!
THE FLAMES ARE TOO INTENSE.

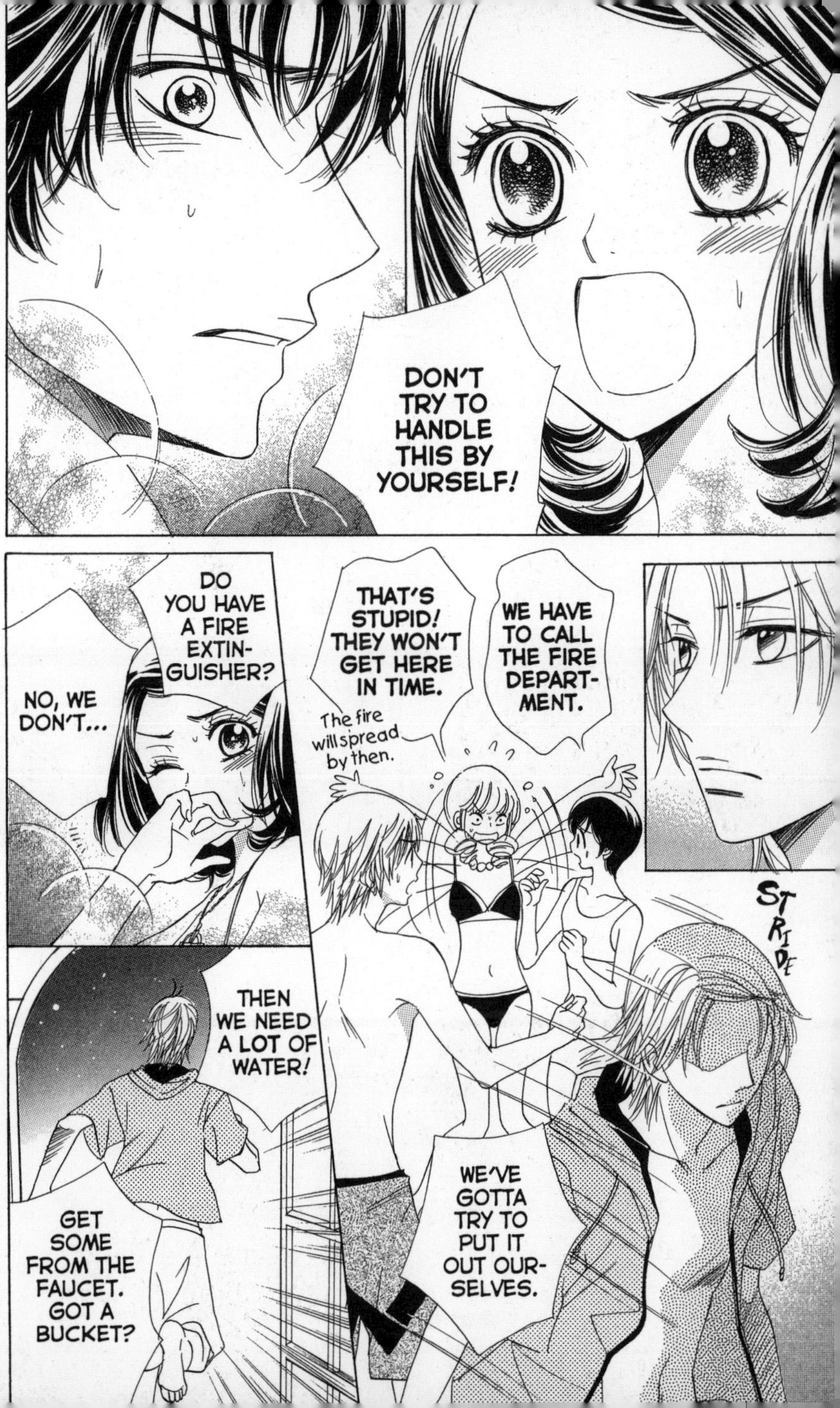
DON'T TRY TO HANDLE THIS BY YOURSELF!
WE HAVE TO CALL THE FIRE DEPARTMENT.
THAT'S STUPID! THEY WON'T GET HERE IN TIME.
The fire will spread by then.
DO YOU HAVE A FIRE EXTINGUISHER?
NO, WE DON'T...
STRIDE
WE'VE GOTTA TRY TO PUT IT OUT OURSELVES.
THEN WE NEED A LOT OF WATER!
GET SOME FROM THE FAUCET. GOT A BUCKET?

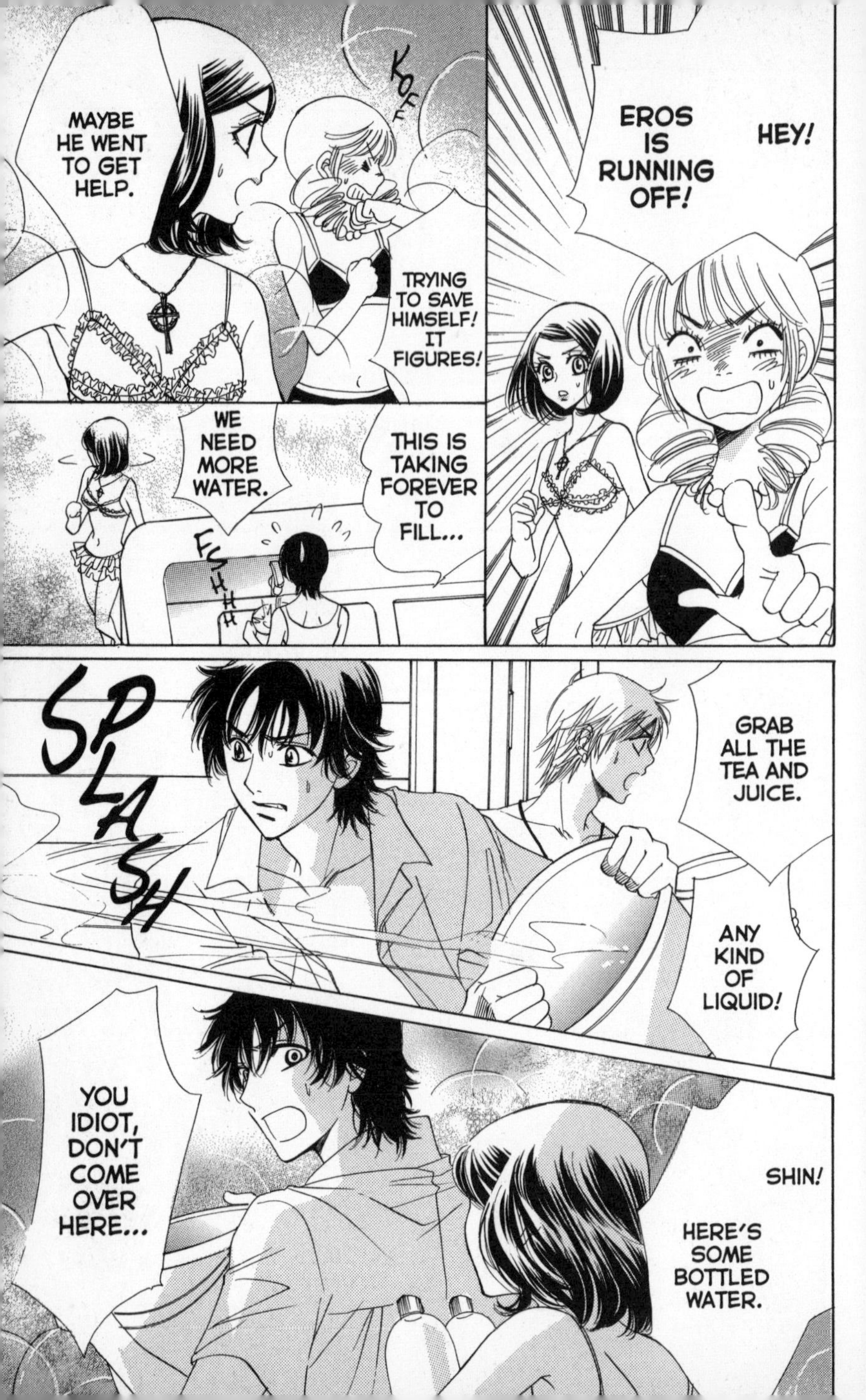
HEY!
EROS IS RUNNING OFF!
TRYING TO SAVE HIMSELF! IT FIGURES!
KOFF
MAYBE HE WENT TO GET HELP.
THIS IS TAKING FOREVER TO FILL...
FSHHH
WE NEED MORE WATER.
GRAB ALL THE TEA AND JUICE.
ANY KIND OF LIQUID!
SPLASH
SHIN!
HERE'S SOME BOTTLED WATER.
YOU IDIOT, DON'T COME OVER HERE...

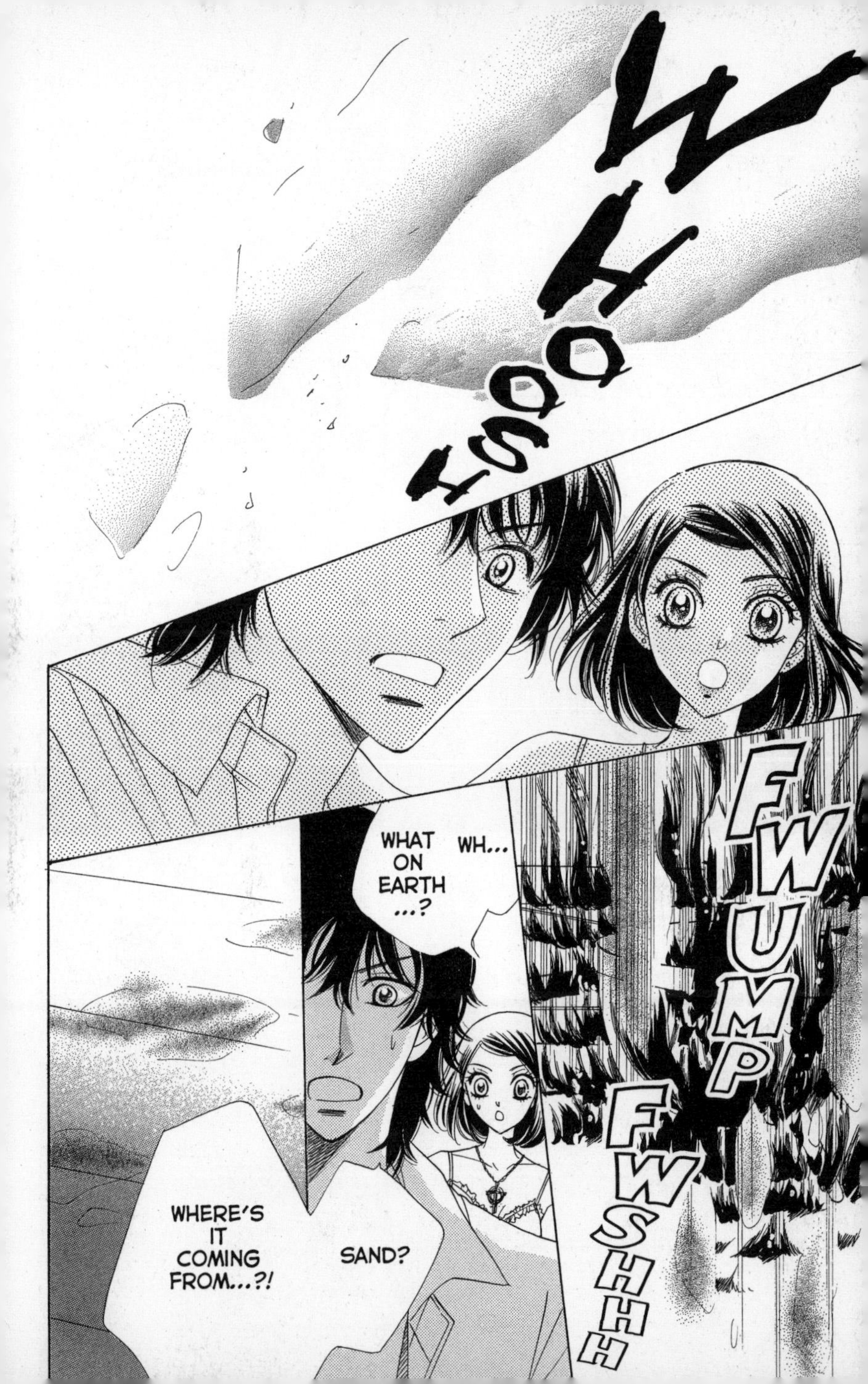
WHOOSH
FWUMP
FWSHHH
WH...
WHAT ON EARTH ...?
SAND?
WHERE'S IT COMING FROM...?!

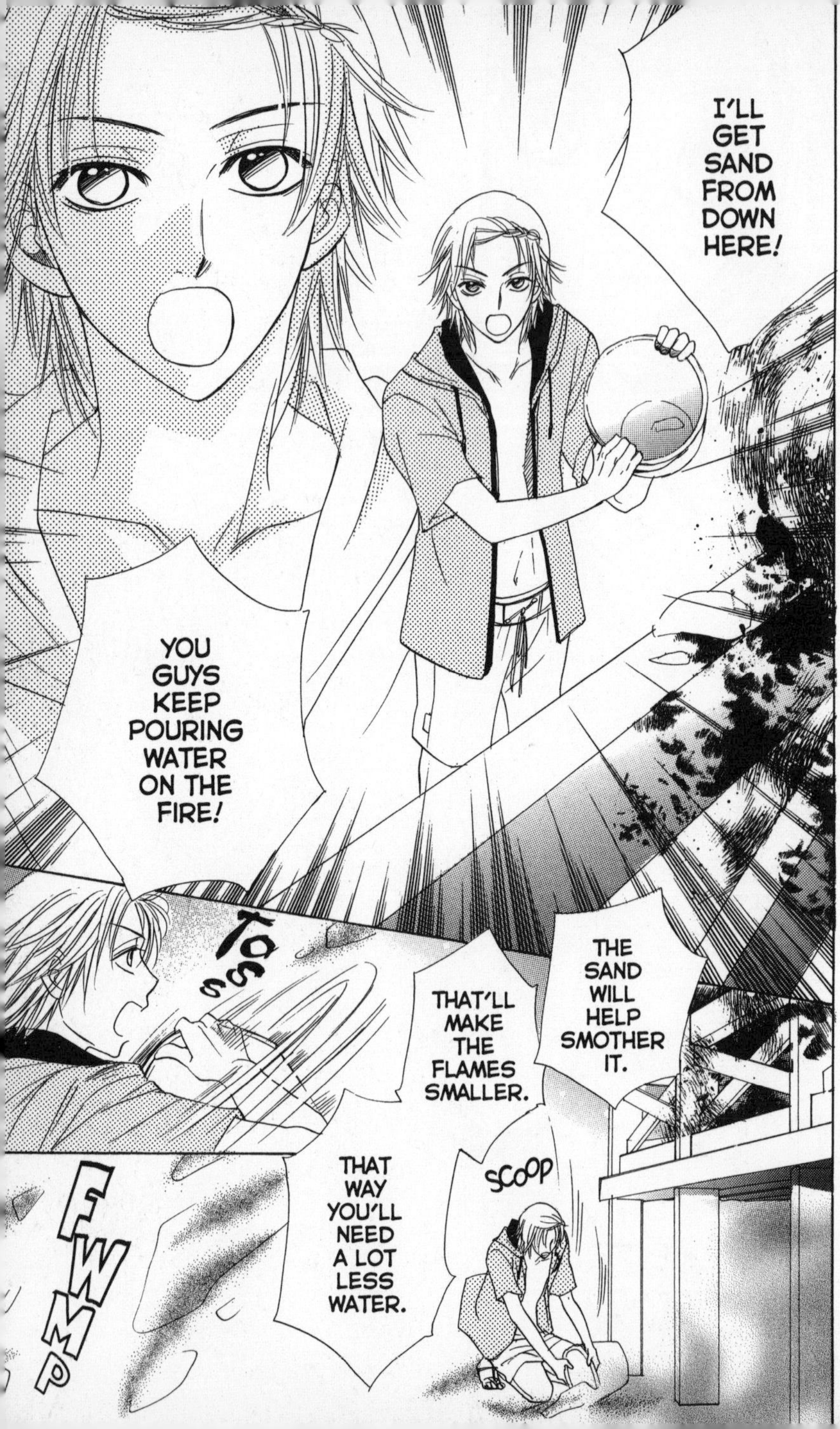
I'LL GET SAND FROM DOWN HERE!
YOU GUYS KEEP POURING WATER ON THE FIRE!
THE SAND WILL HELP SMOTHER IT.
THAT'LL MAKE THE FLAMES SMALLER.
TOSS
SCOOP
THAT WAY YOU'LL NEED A LOT LESS WATER.
FWWMP

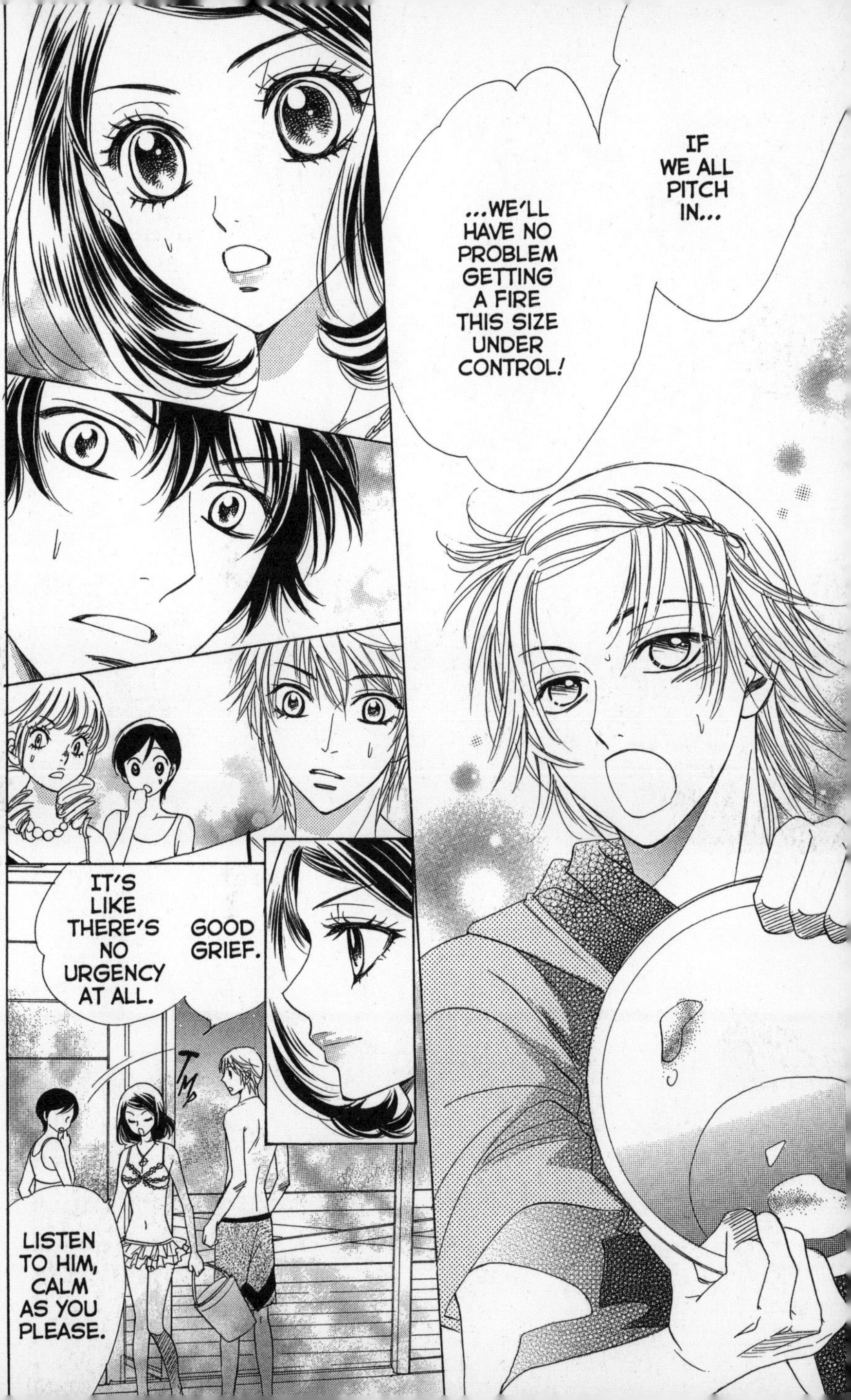
IF WE ALL PITCH IN...
...WE'LL HAVE NO PROBLEM GETTING A FIRE THIS SIZE UNDER CONTROL!
GOOD GRIEF.
IT'S LIKE THERE'S NO URGENCY AT ALL.
LISTEN TO HIM, CALM AS YOU PLEASE.

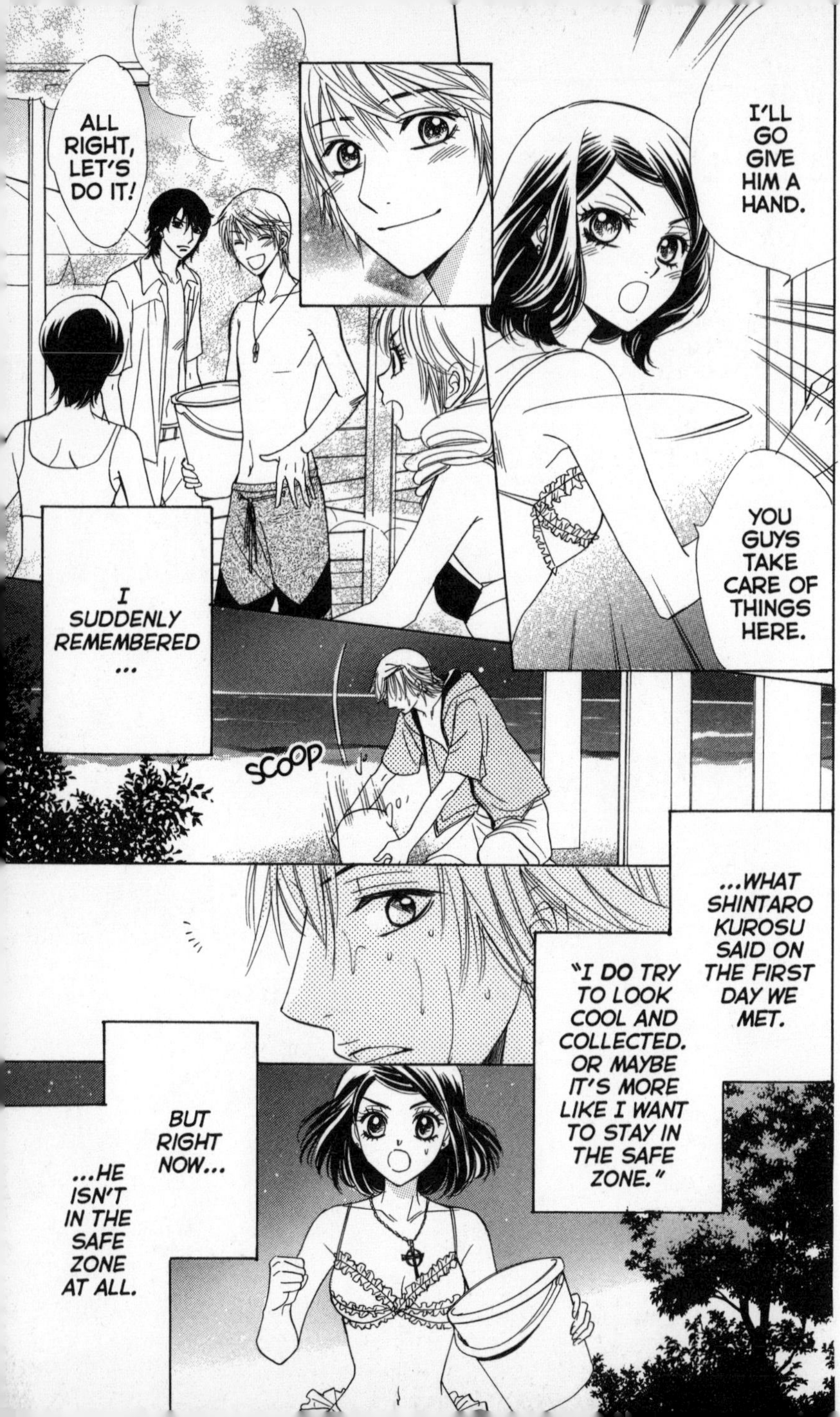
I'LL GO GIVE HIM A HAND.
YOU GUYS TAKE CARE OF THINGS HERE.
ALL RIGHT, LET'S DO IT!
I SUDDENLY REMEMBERED ...
SCOOP
...WHAT SHINTARO KUROSU SAID ON THE FIRST DAY WE MET.
"I DO TRY TO LOOK COOL AND COLLECTED. OR MAYBE IT'S MORE LIKE I WANT TO STAY IN THE SAFE ZONE."
BUT RIGHT NOW...
...HE ISN'T IN THE SAFE ZONE AT ALL.

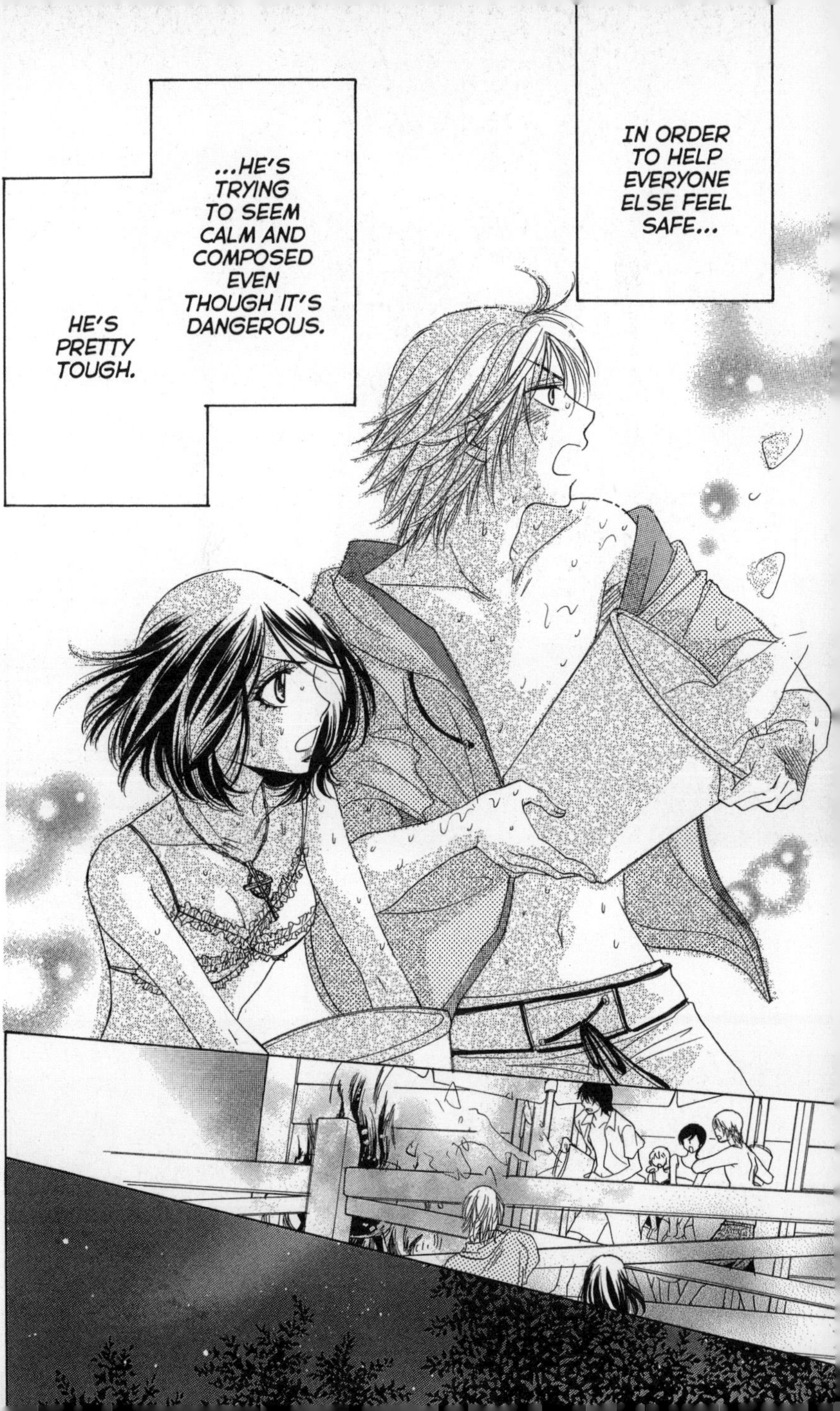
IN ORDER TO HELP EVERYONE ELSE FEEL SAFE...
...HE'S TRYING TO SEEM CALM AND COMPOSED EVEN THOUGH IT'S DANGEROUS.
HE'S PRETTY TOUGH.

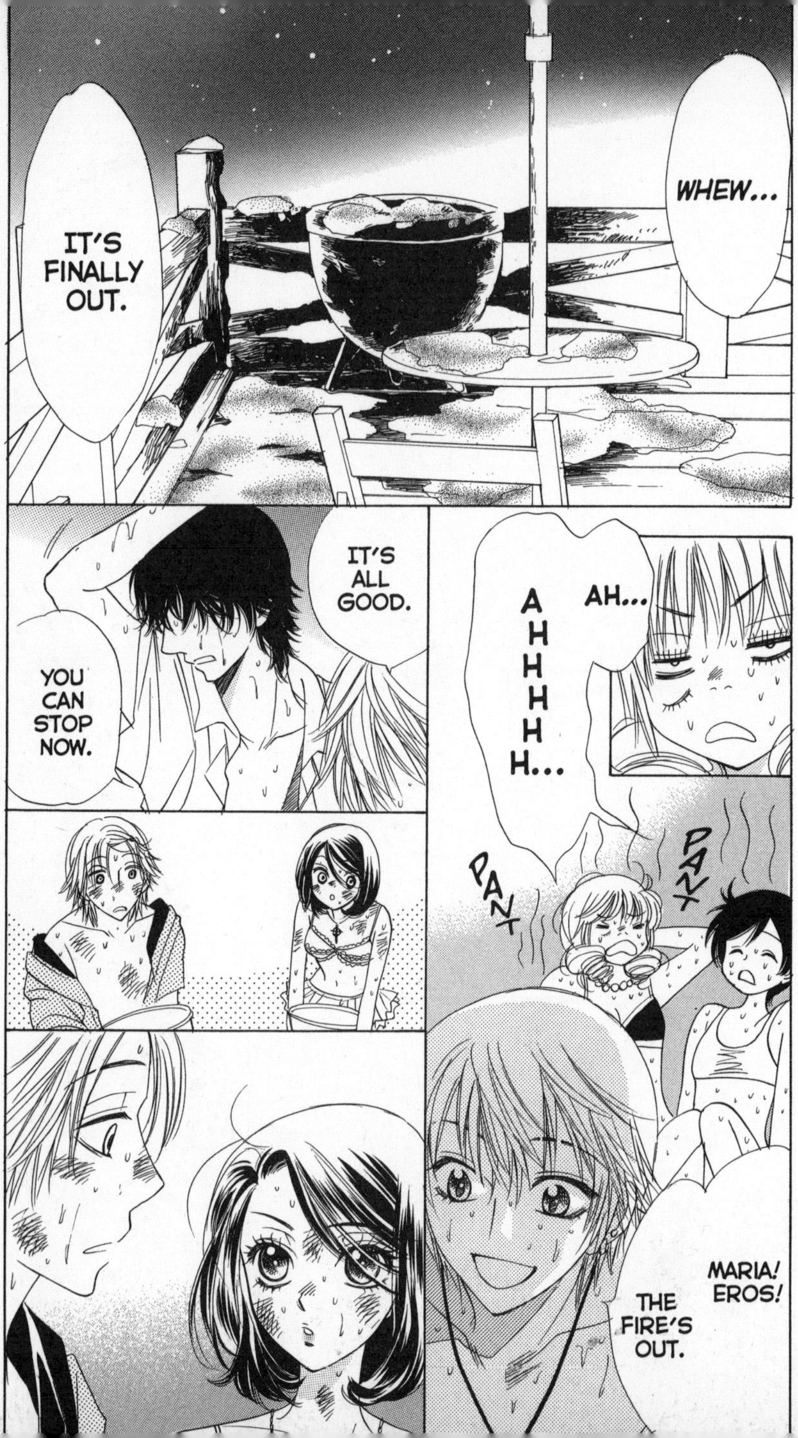
WHEW...
IT'S FINALLY OUT.
AH...
AHHHHH...
PANT
PANT
MARIA! EROS!
THE FIRE'S OUT.
IT'S ALL GOOD.
YOU CAN STOP NOW.

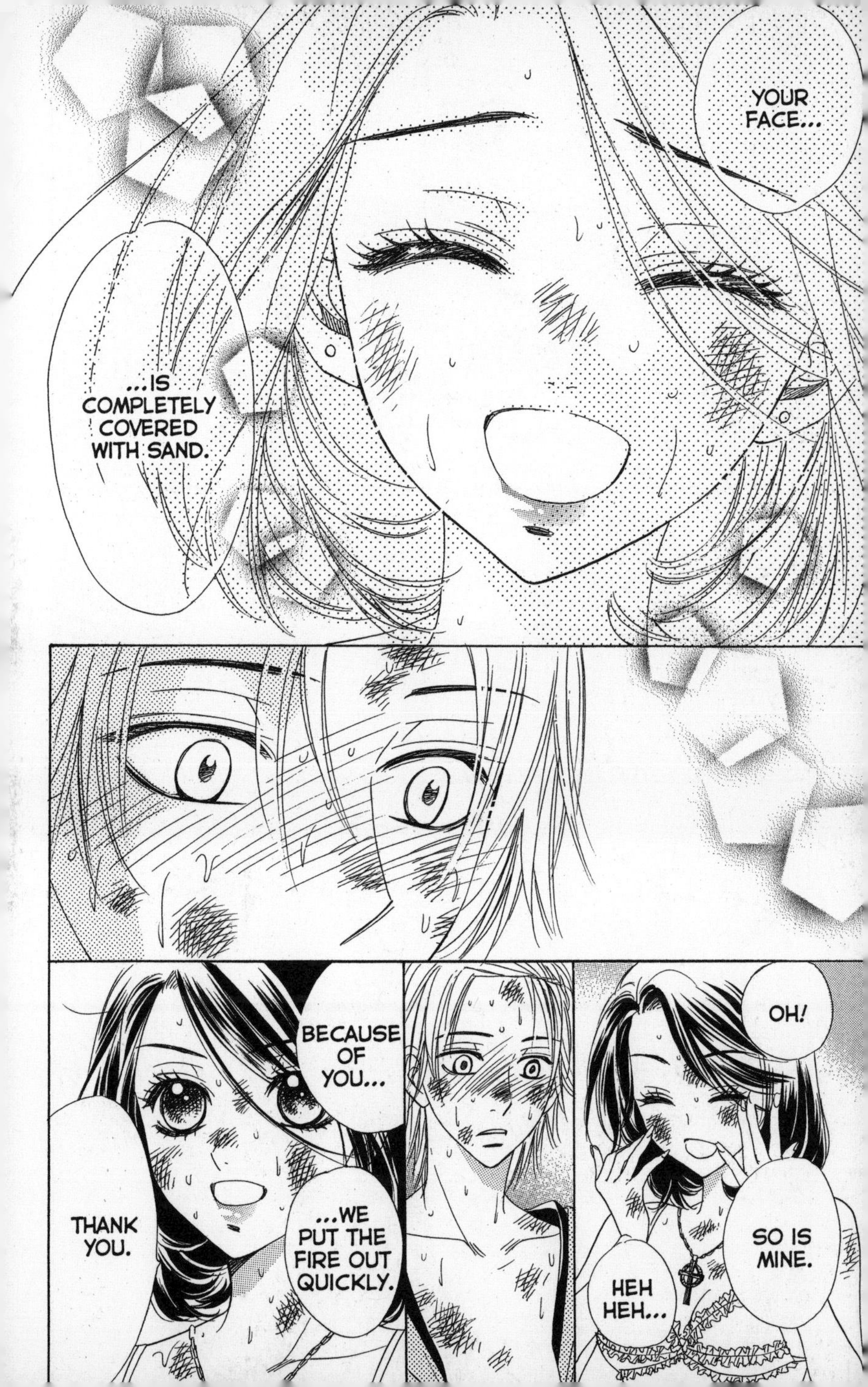
YOUR FACE...
...IS COMPLETELY COVERED WITH SAND.
OH!
SO IS MINE.
HEH HEH...
BECAUSE OF YOU...
...WE PUT THE FIRE OUT QUICKLY.
THANK YOU.

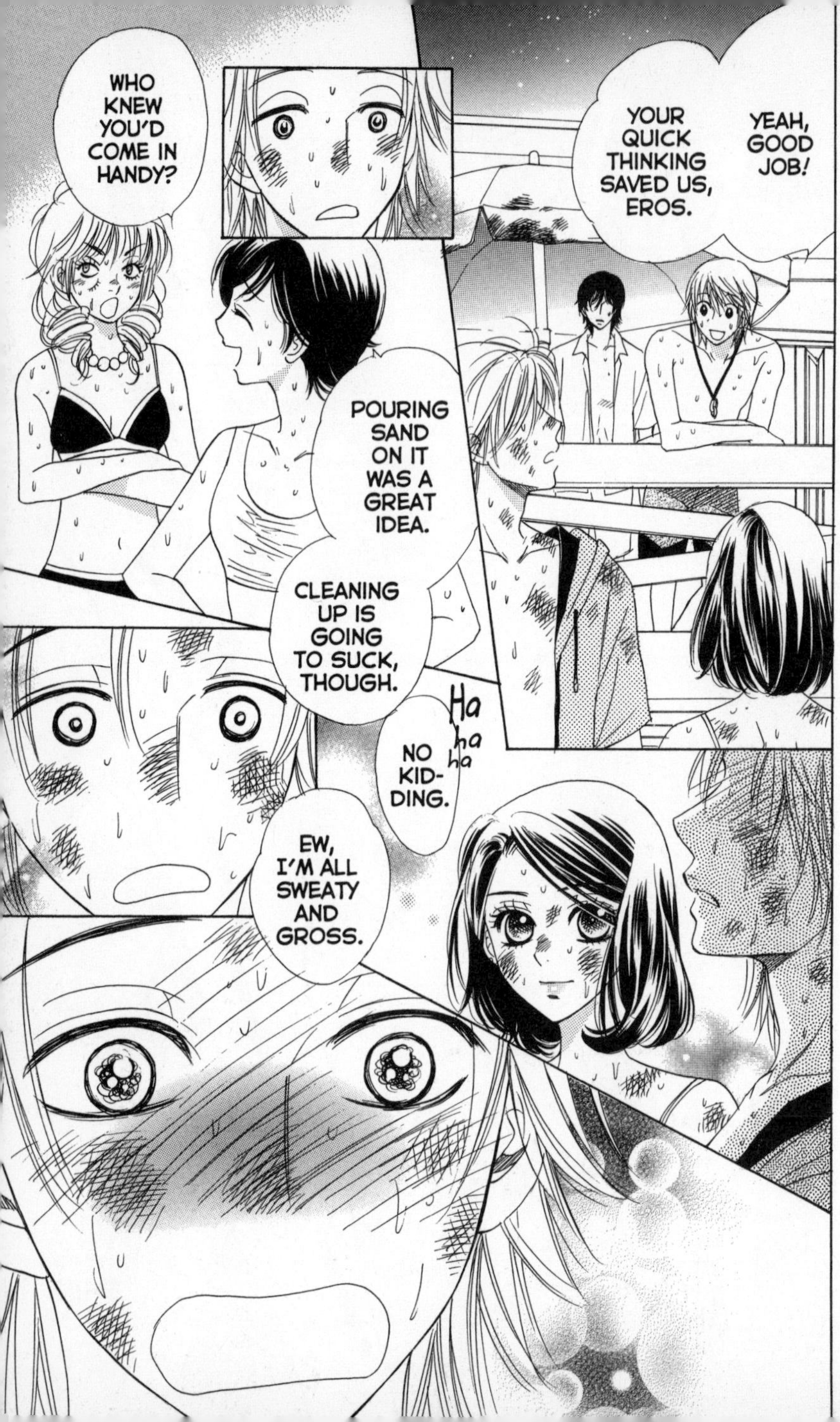
YEAH, GOOD JOB!
YOUR QUICK THINKING SAVED US, EROS.
WHO KNEW YOU'D COME IN HANDY?
POURING SAND ON IT WAS A GREAT IDEA.
CLEANING UP IS GOING TO SUCK, THOUGH.
Ha ha ha
NO KID-DING.
EW, I'M ALL SWEATY AND GROSS.

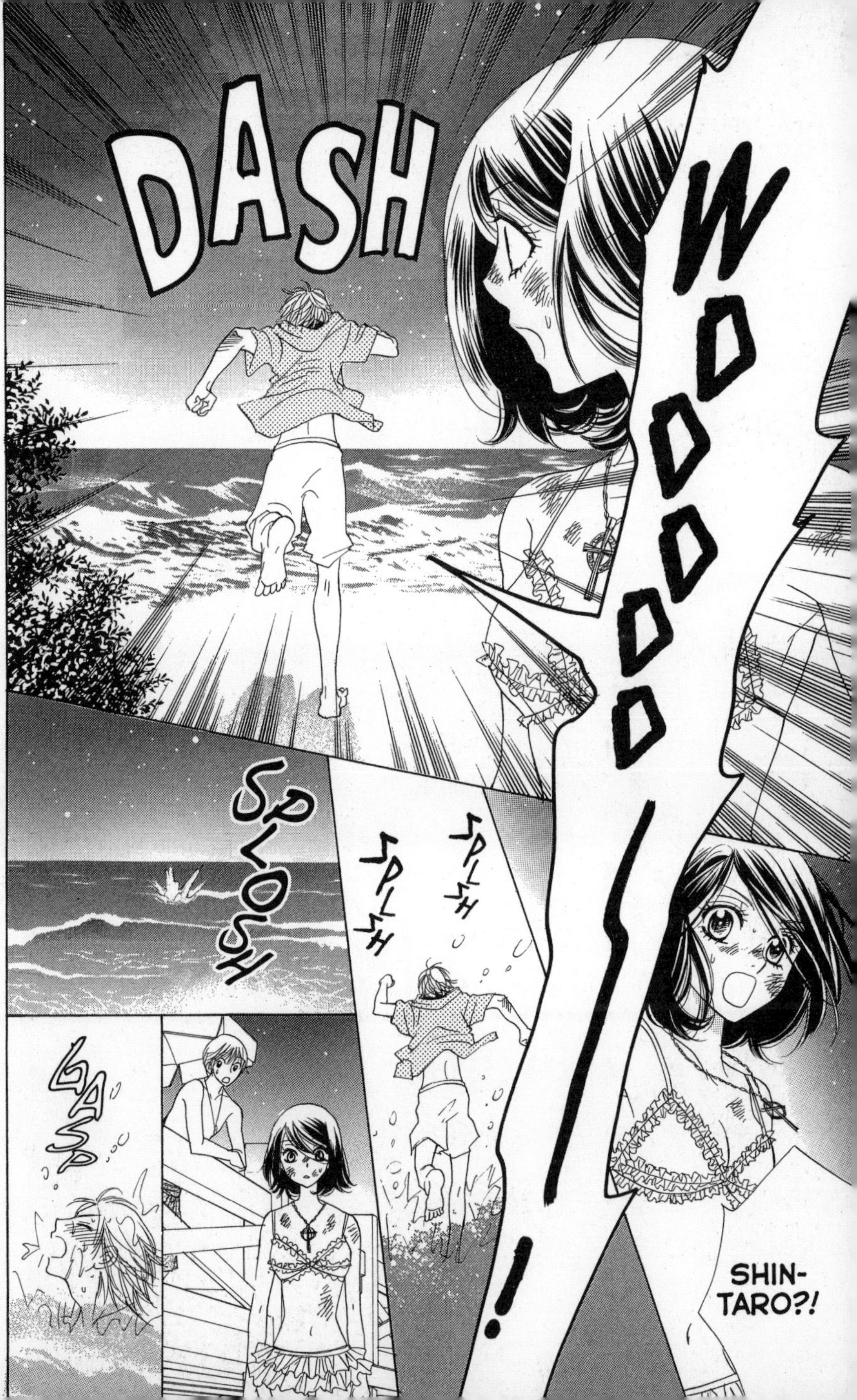
WOOOOOO—!
SHIN-
TARO?!
DASH
SPLSH
SPLSH
SPLOSH
GASP

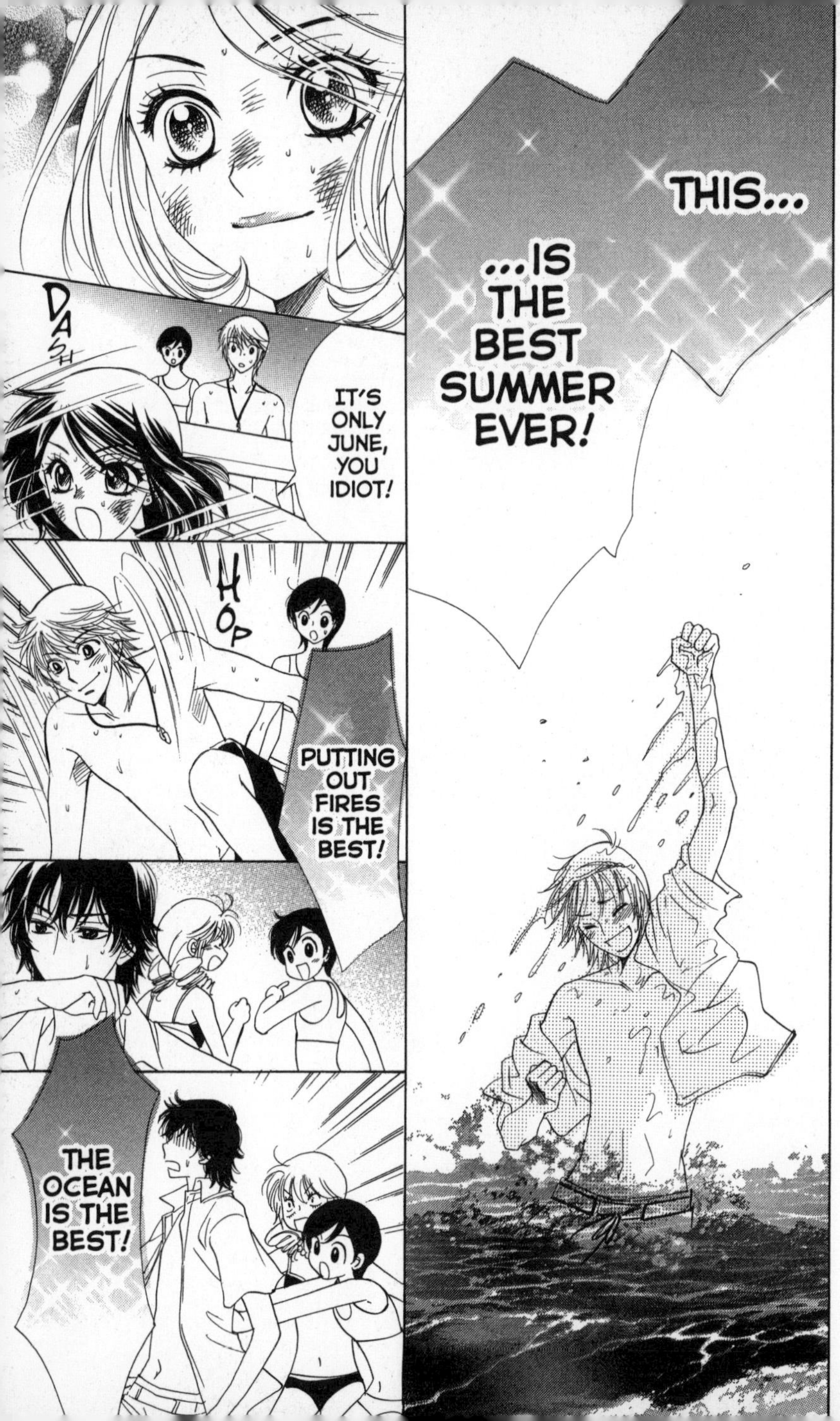
THIS...
...IS THE BEST SUMMER EVER!
DASH
IT'S ONLY JUNE, YOU IDIOT!
HOP
PUTTING OUT FIRES IS THE BEST!
THE OCEAN IS THE BEST!

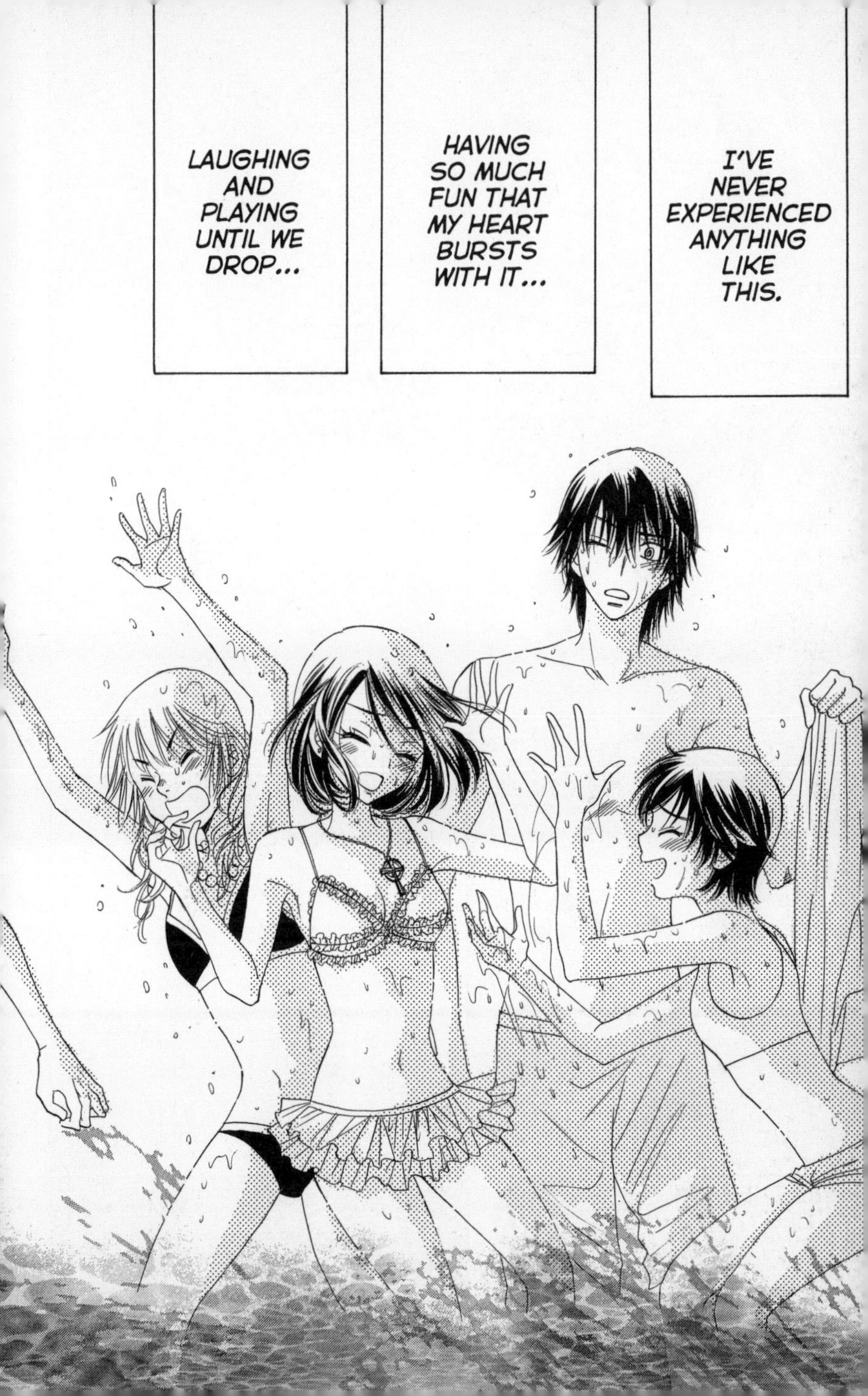
I'VE NEVER EXPERIENCED ANYTHING LIKE THIS.
HAVING SO MUCH FUN THAT MY HEART BURSTS WITH IT...
LAUGHING AND PLAYING UNTIL WE DROP...

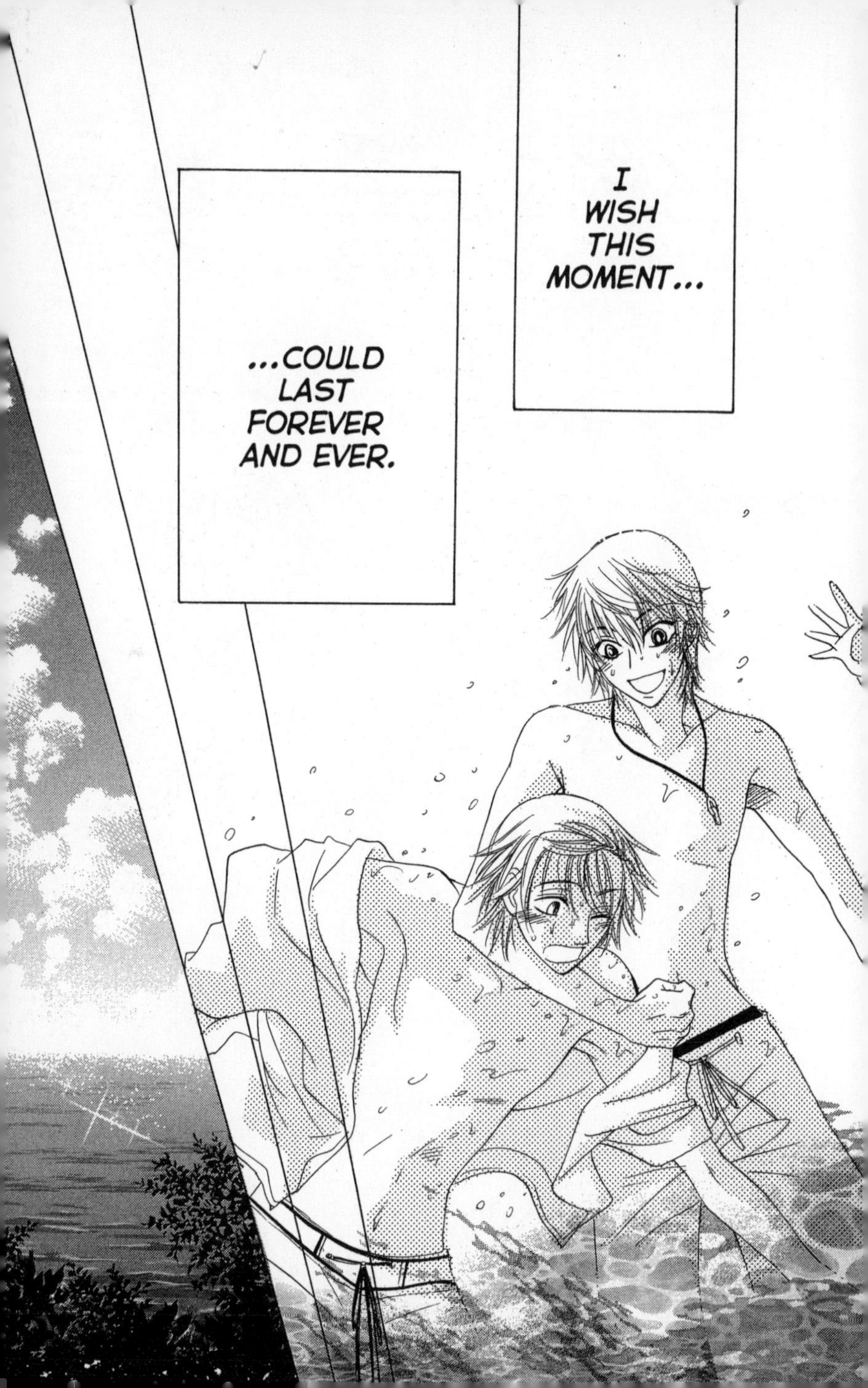
I WISH THIS MOMENT...
...COULD LAST FOREVER AND EVER.

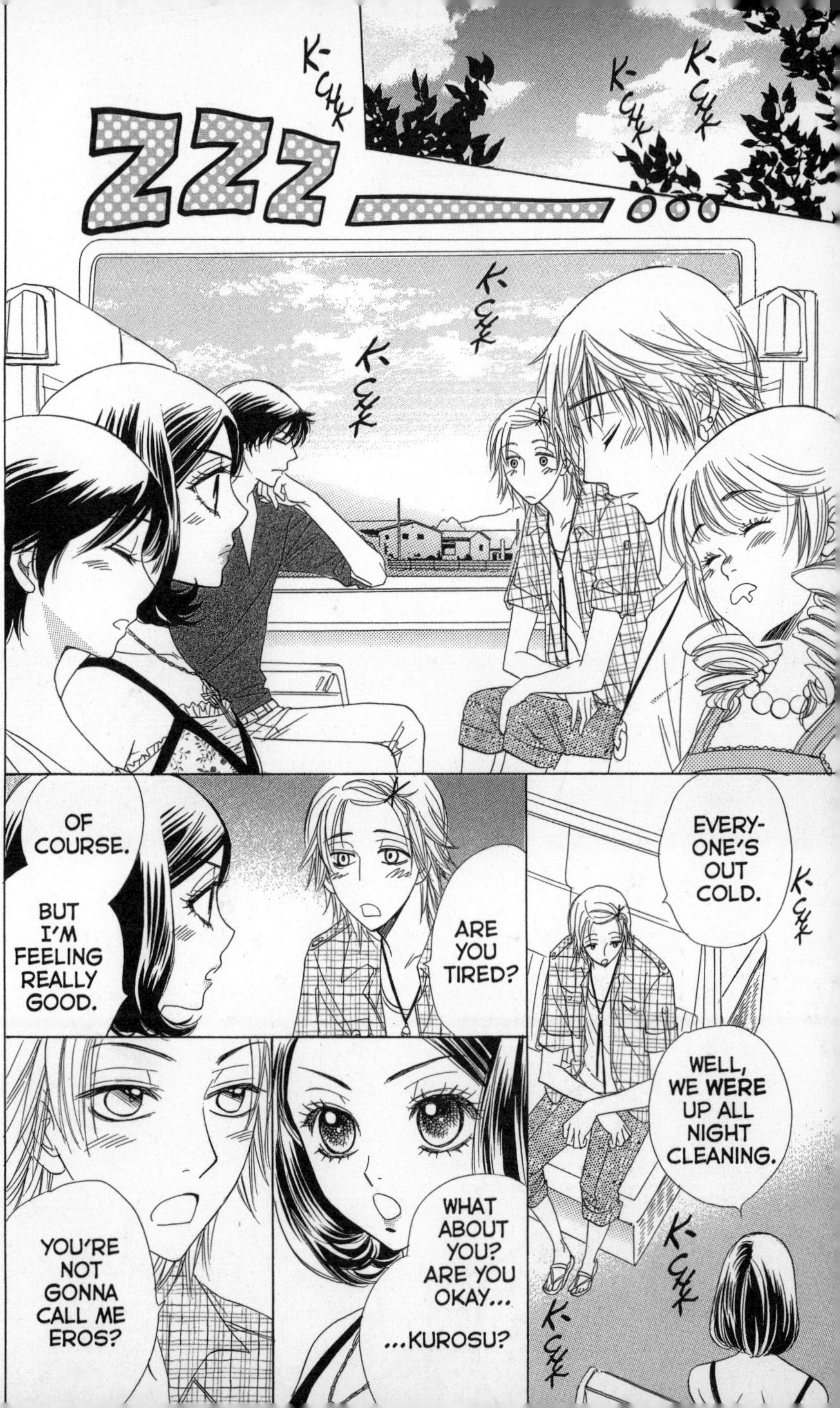
K-CHK
K-CHK
K-CHK
ZZZ...ooo
K-CHK
K-CHK
EVERY-ONE'S OUT COLD.
K-CHK
WELL, WE WERE UP ALL NIGHT CLEANING.
K-CHK
K-CHK
ARE YOU TIRED?
OF COURSE.
BUT I'M FEELING REALLY GOOD.
WHAT ABOUT YOU? ARE YOU OKAY...
...KUROSU?
YOU'RE NOT GONNA CALL ME EROS?

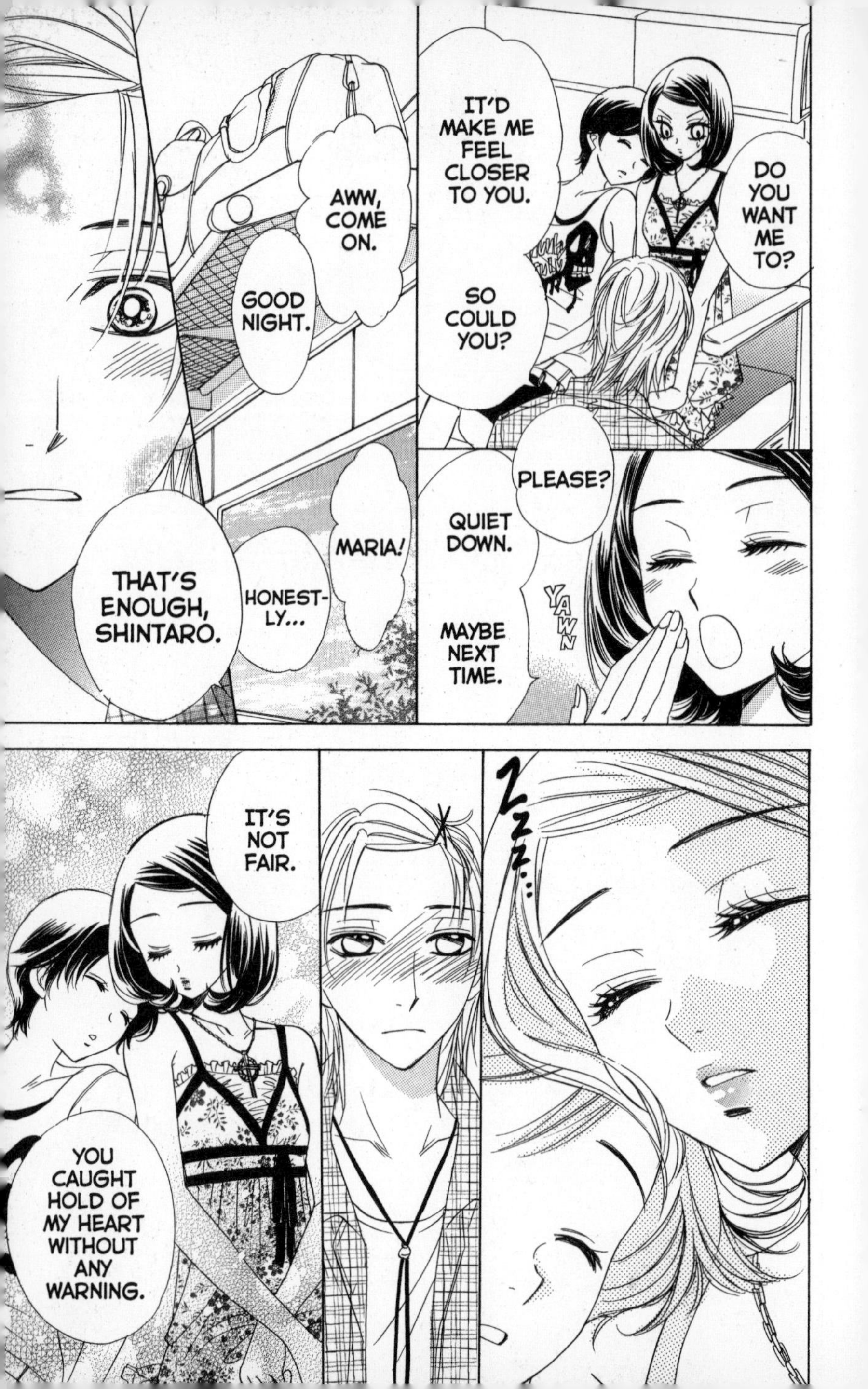
DO YOU WANT ME TO?
IT'D MAKE ME FEEL CLOSER TO YOU.
SO COULD YOU?
AWW, COME ON.
GOOD NIGHT.
PLEASE?
QUIET DOWN.
YAWN
MAYBE NEXT TIME.
MARIA!
HONEST-LY...
THAT'S ENOUGH, SHINTARO.
ZZZ...
IT'S NOT FAIR.
YOU CAUGHT HOLD OF MY HEART WITHOUT ANY WARNING.

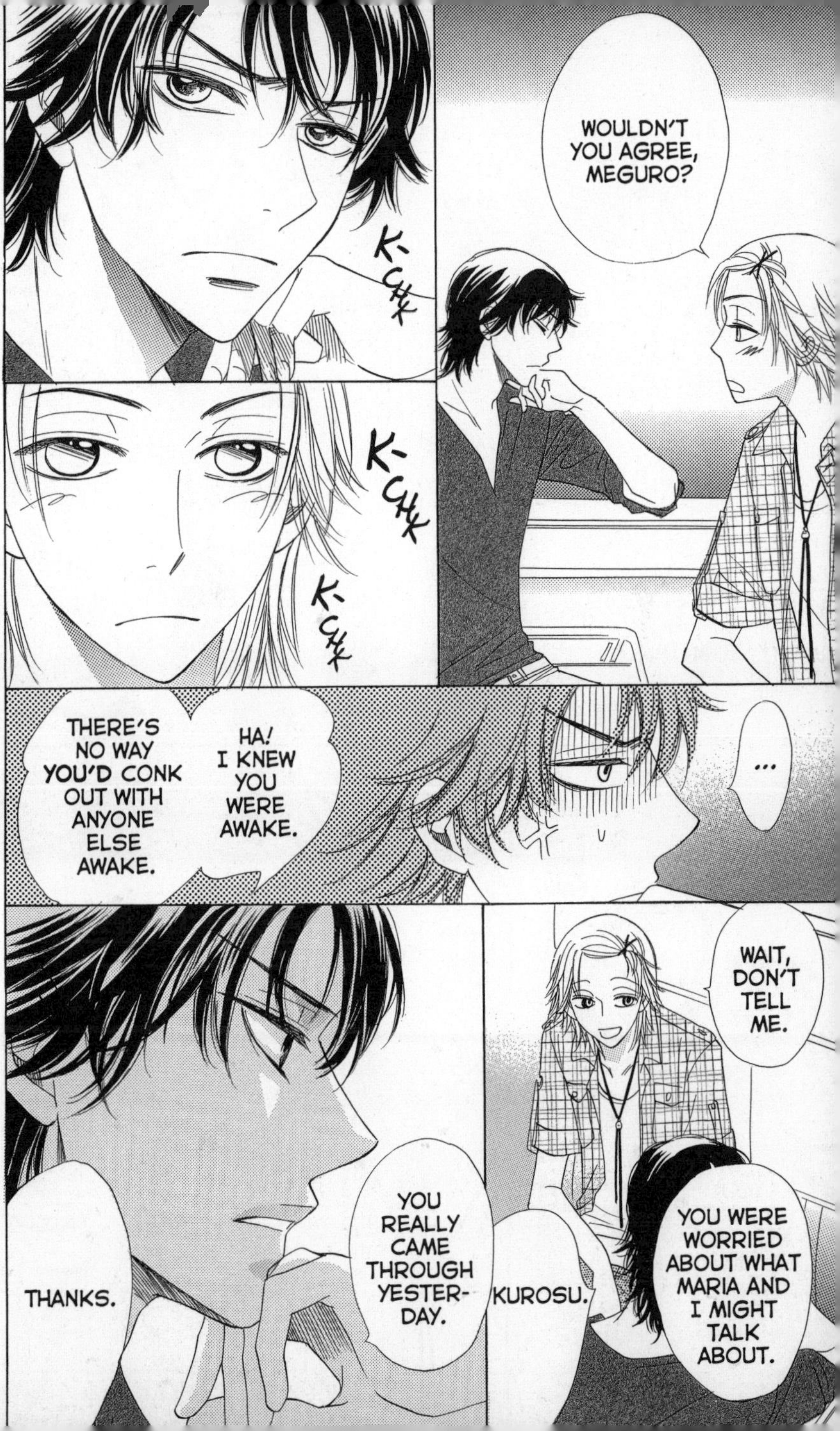
WOULDN'T YOU AGREE, MEGURO?
K-CHK
K-CHK
K-CHK
...
HA! I KNEW YOU WERE AWAKE.
THERE'S NO WAY YOU'D CONK OUT WITH ANYONE ELSE AWAKE.
WAIT, DON'T TELL ME.
YOU WERE WORRIED ABOUT WHAT MARIA AND I MIGHT TALK ABOUT.
KUROSU.
YOU REALLY CAME THROUGH YESTER-DAY.
THANKS.

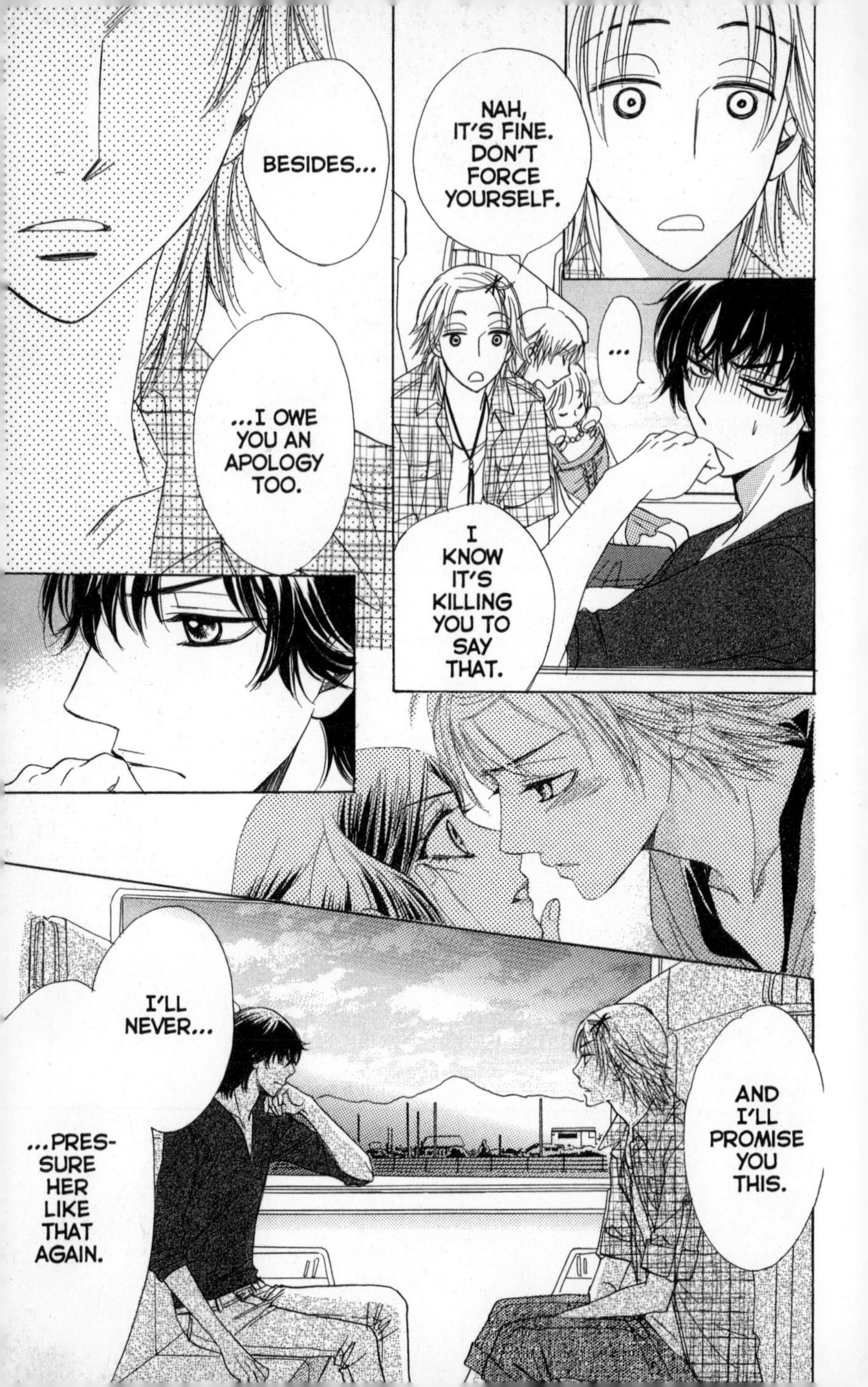
NAH, IT'S FINE. DON'T FORCE YOURSELF.
...
I KNOW IT'S KILLING YOU TO SAY THAT.
BESIDES...
...I OWE YOU AN APOLOGY TOO.
AND I'LL PROMISE YOU THIS.
I'LL NEVER...
...PRESSURE HER LIKE THAT AGAIN.

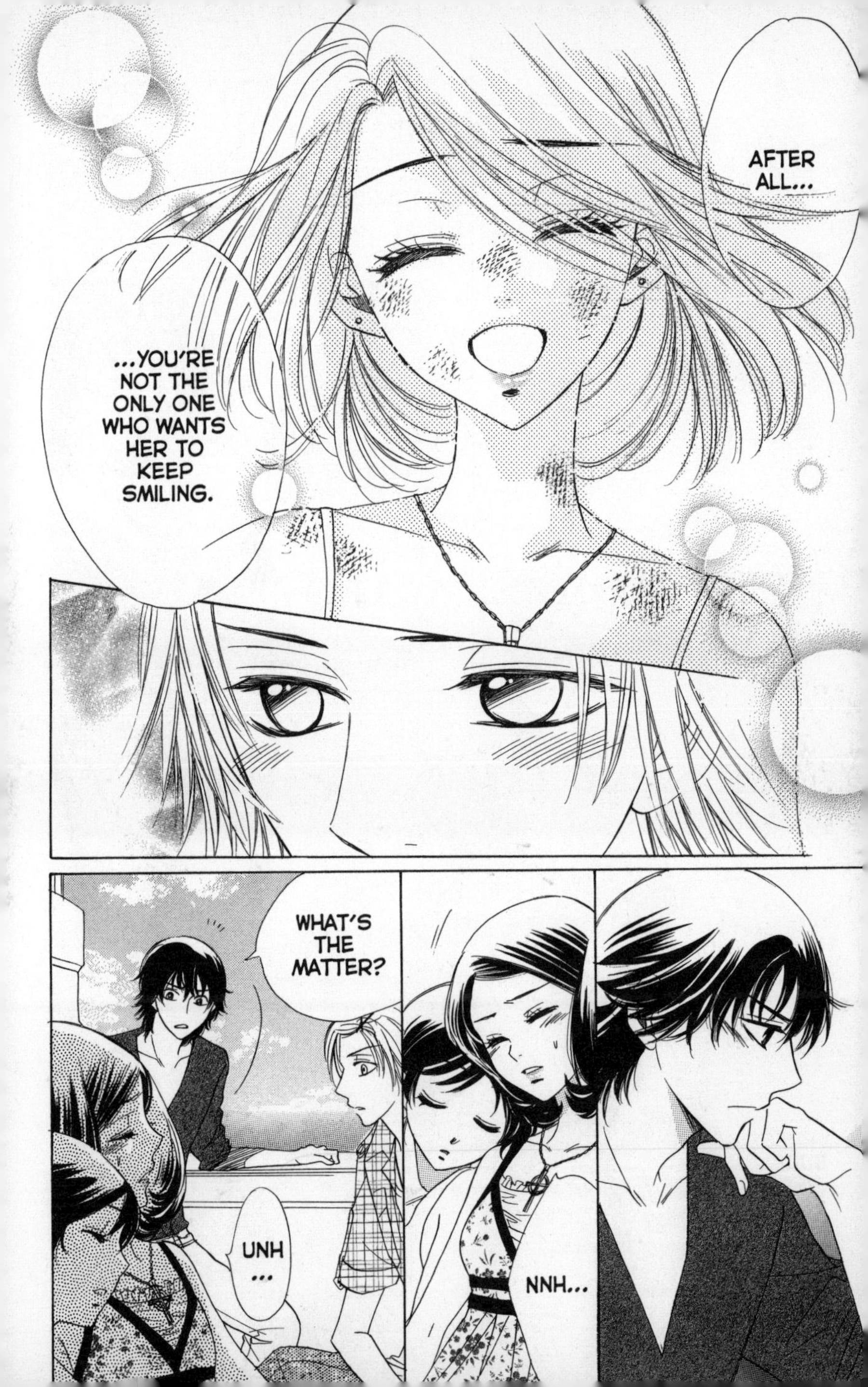
AFTER ALL...
...YOU'RE NOT THE ONLY ONE WHO WANTS HER TO KEEP SMILING.
NNH...
WHAT'S THE MATTER?
UNH ...

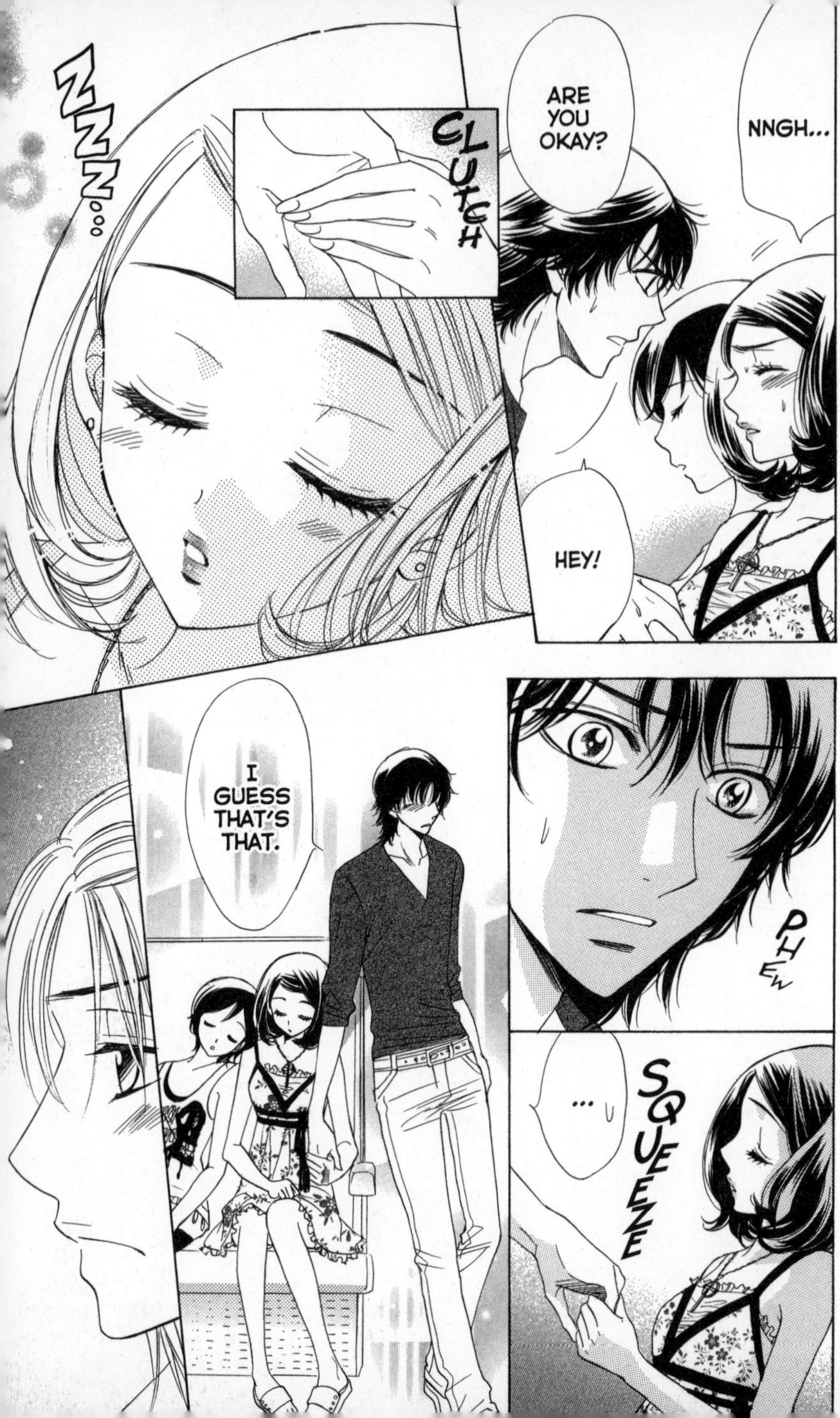
NNGH...
ARE YOU OKAY?
HEY!
CLUTCH
ZZZ...
PHEW
SQUEEZE
... !
I GUESS THAT'S THAT.

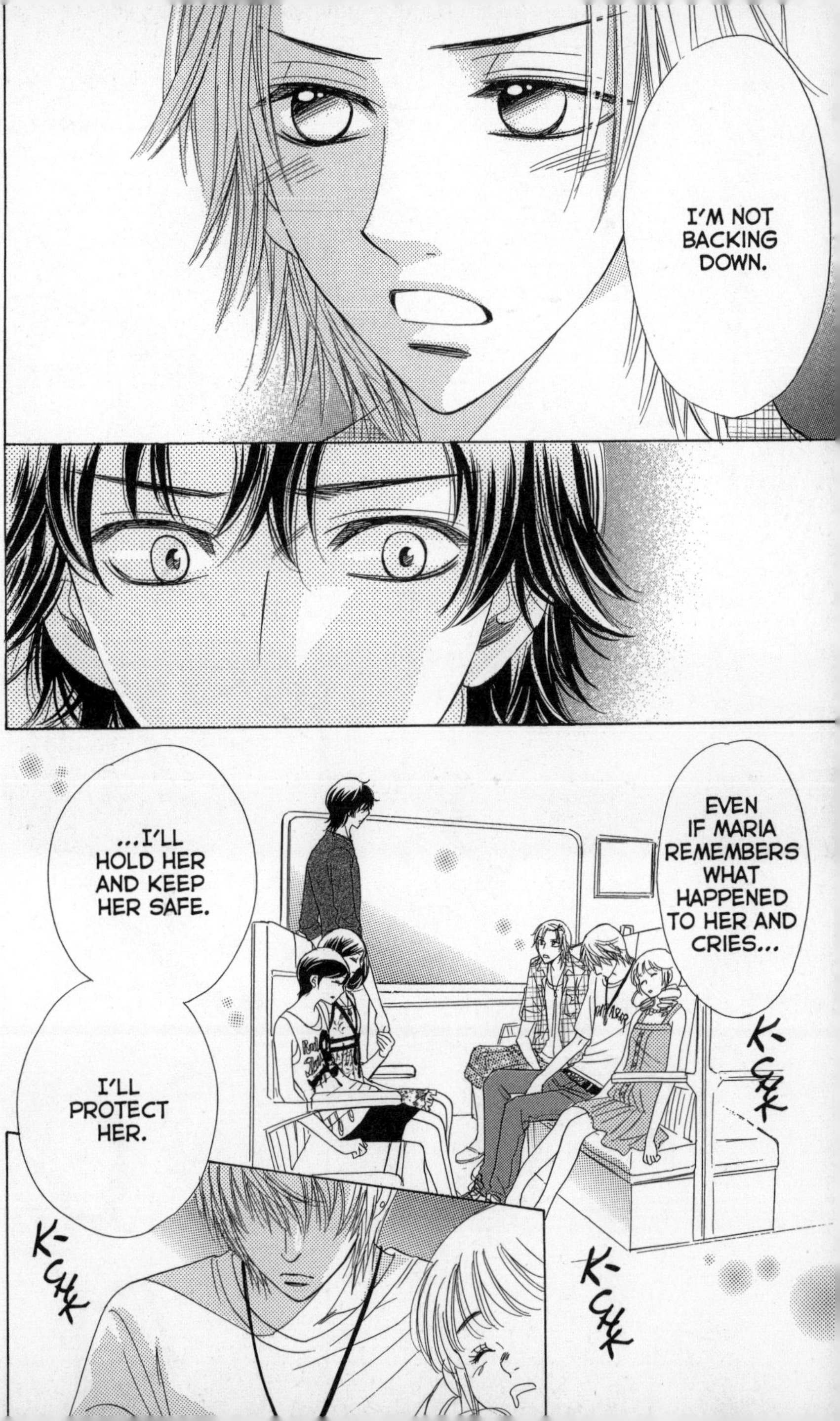
I'M NOT BACKING DOWN.
EVEN IF MARIA REMEMBERS WHAT HAPPENED TO HER AND CRIES...
K-CHK
...I'LL HOLD HER AND KEEP HER SAFE.
I'LL PROTECT HER.
K-CHK
K-CHK

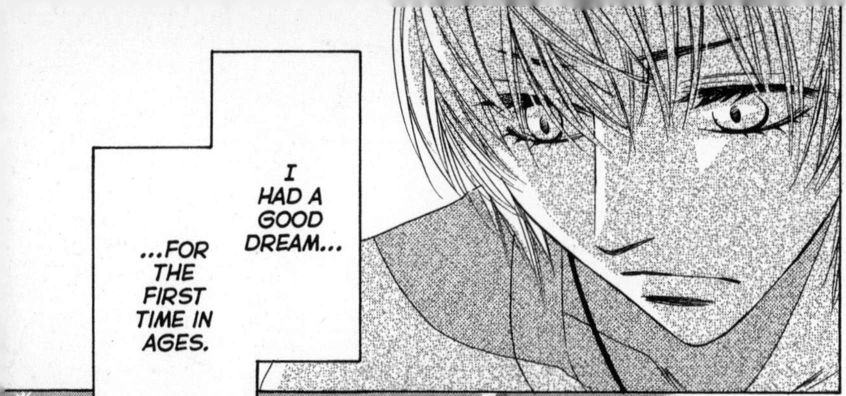
I HAD A GOOD DREAM...
...FOR THE FIRST TIME IN AGES.
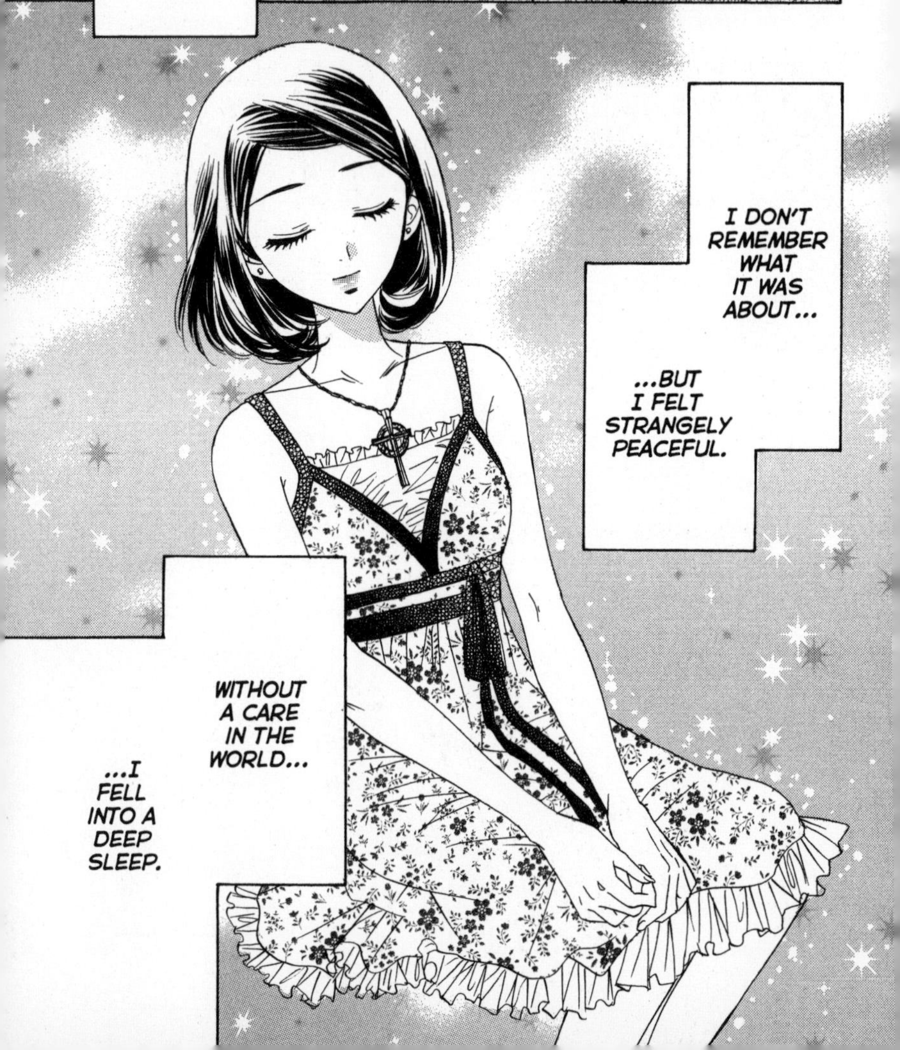
I DON'T REMEMBER WHAT IT WAS ABOUT...
...BUT I FELT STRANGELY PEACEFUL.
WITHOUT A CARE IN THE WORLD...
...I FELL INTO A DEEP SLEEP.

# A Devil and Her Love Song

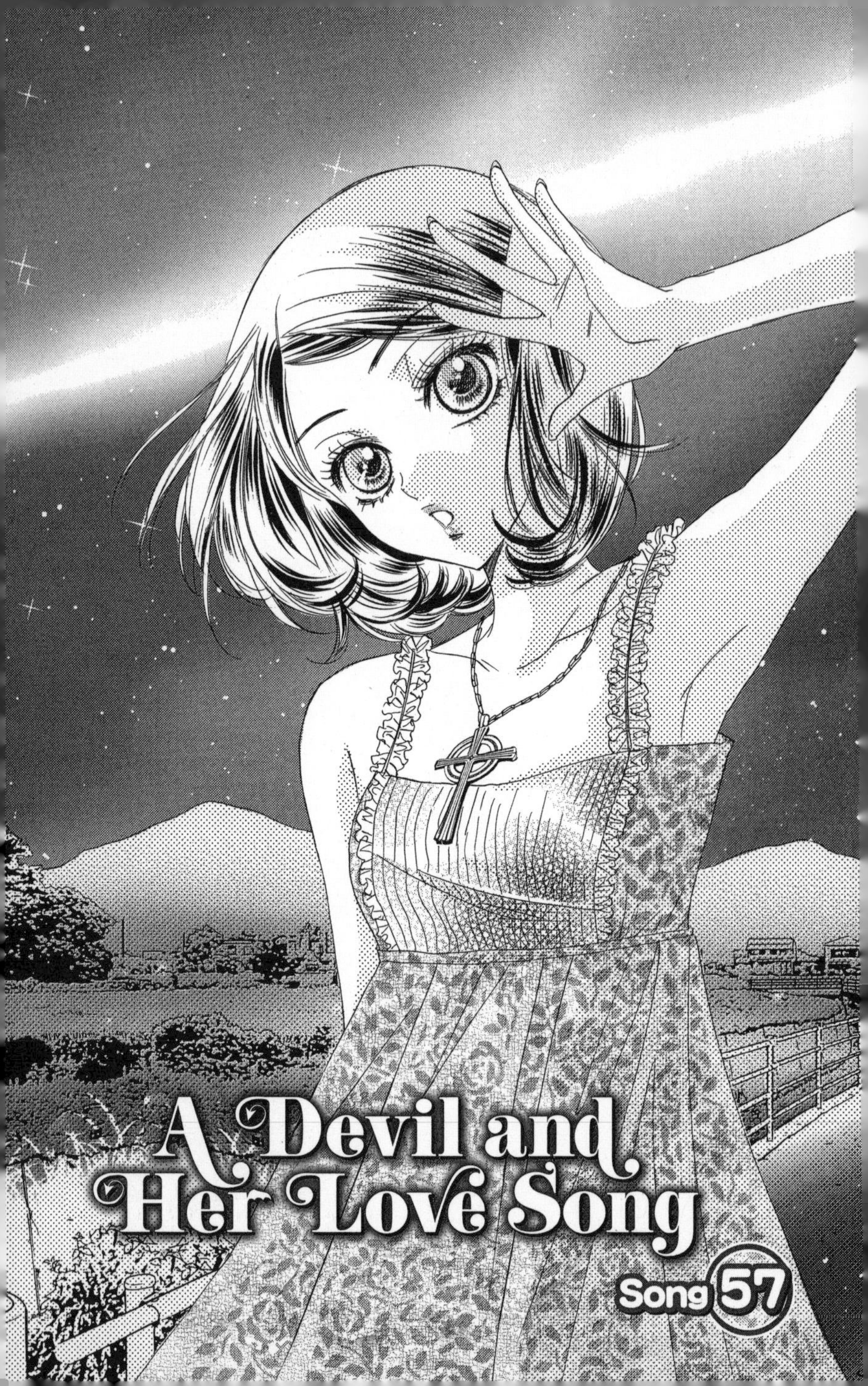
A Devil and Her Love Song
Song 57

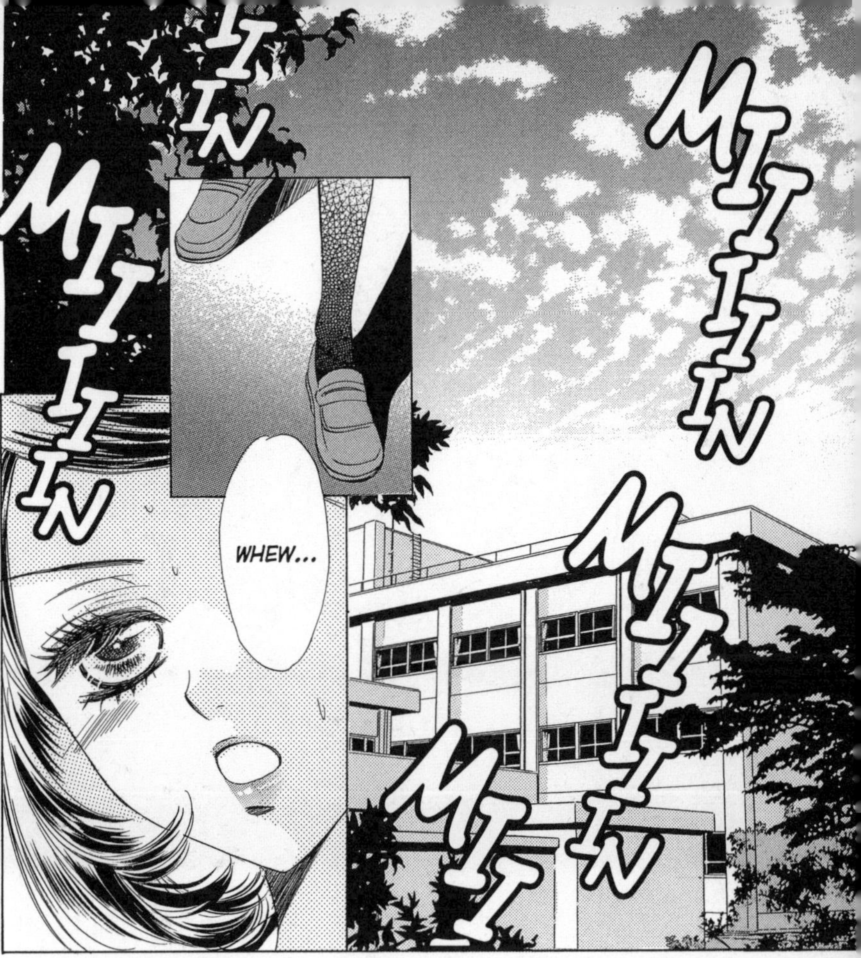
MIIIIN
MIIIIIN
MII
IIIN
MIIIIN
WHEW...

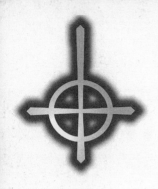

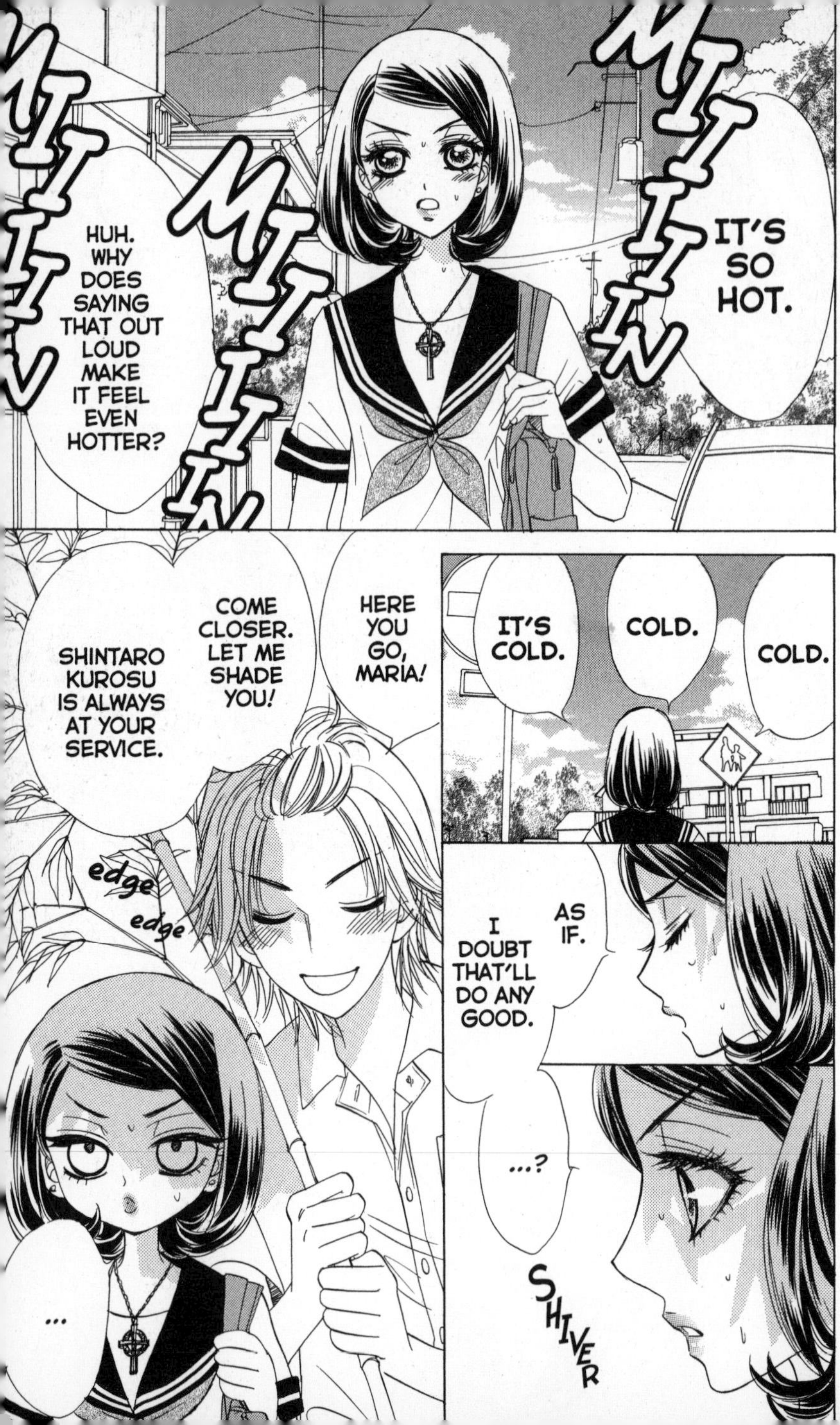
MIIIN
IT'S SO HOT.
MIIIN
HUH. WHY DOES SAYING THAT OUT LOUD MAKE IT FEEL EVEN HOTTER?
MIIIN
COLD.
COLD.
IT'S COLD.
AS IF.
I DOUBT THAT'LL DO ANY GOOD.
...?
SHIVER
HERE YOU GO, MARIA!
COME CLOSER. LET ME SHADE YOU!
SHINTARO KUROSU IS ALWAYS AT YOUR SERVICE.
edge edge
...

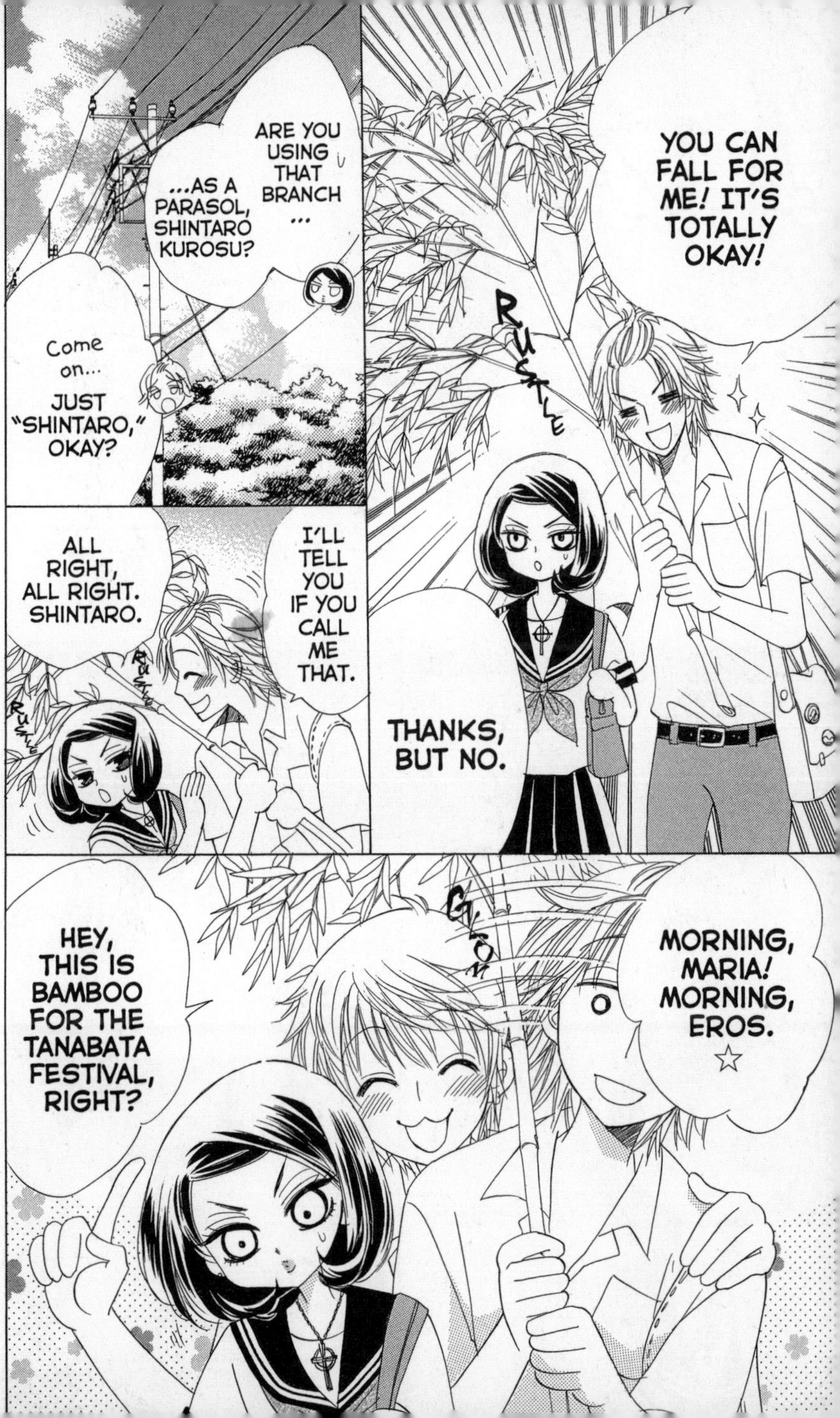
YOU CAN FALL FOR ME! IT'S TOTALLY OKAY!
RUSTLE
THANKS, BUT NO.
ARE YOU USING THAT BRANCH ...
...AS A PARASOL, SHINTARO KUROSU?
Come on...
JUST "SHINTARO," OKAY?
I'LL TELL YOU IF YOU CALL ME THAT.
ALL RIGHT, ALL RIGHT. SHINTARO.
RUSTLE
RUSTLE
MORNING, MARIA! MORNING, EROS. ☆
GLOM
HEY, THIS IS BAMBOO FOR THE TANABATA FESTIVAL, RIGHT?

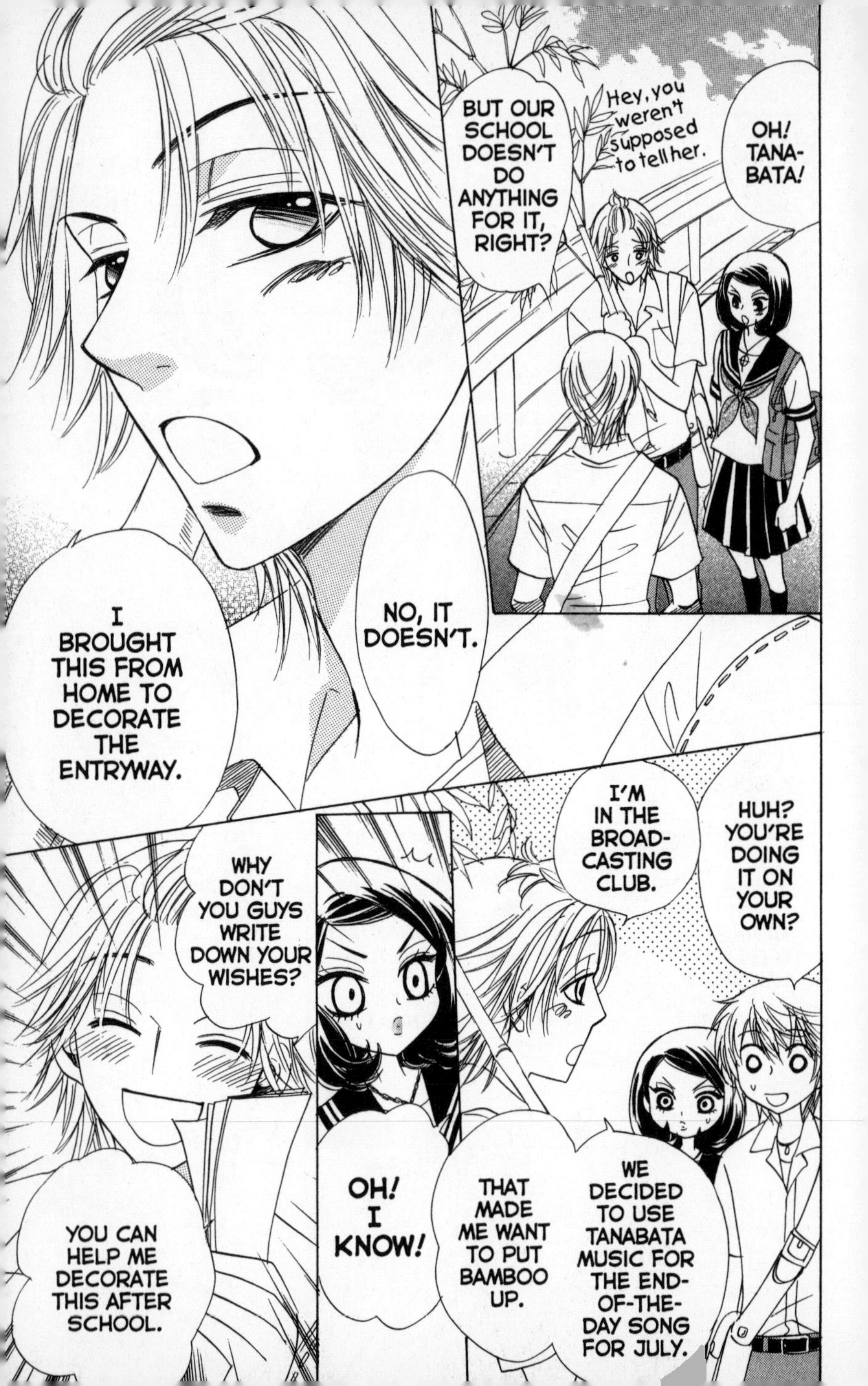
OH! TANABATA!
Hey, you weren't supposed to tell her.
BUT OUR SCHOOL DOESN'T DO ANYTHING FOR IT, RIGHT?
NO, IT DOESN'T.
I BROUGHT THIS FROM HOME TO DECORATE THE ENTRYWAY.
HUH? YOU'RE DOING IT ON YOUR OWN?
I'M IN THE BROADCASTING CLUB.
WE DECIDED TO USE TANABATA MUSIC FOR THE END-OF-THE-DAY SONG FOR JULY.
THAT MADE ME WANT TO PUT BAMBOO UP.
OH! I KNOW!
WHY DON'T YOU GUYS WRITE DOWN YOUR WISHES?
YOU CAN HELP ME DECORATE THIS AFTER SCHOOL.

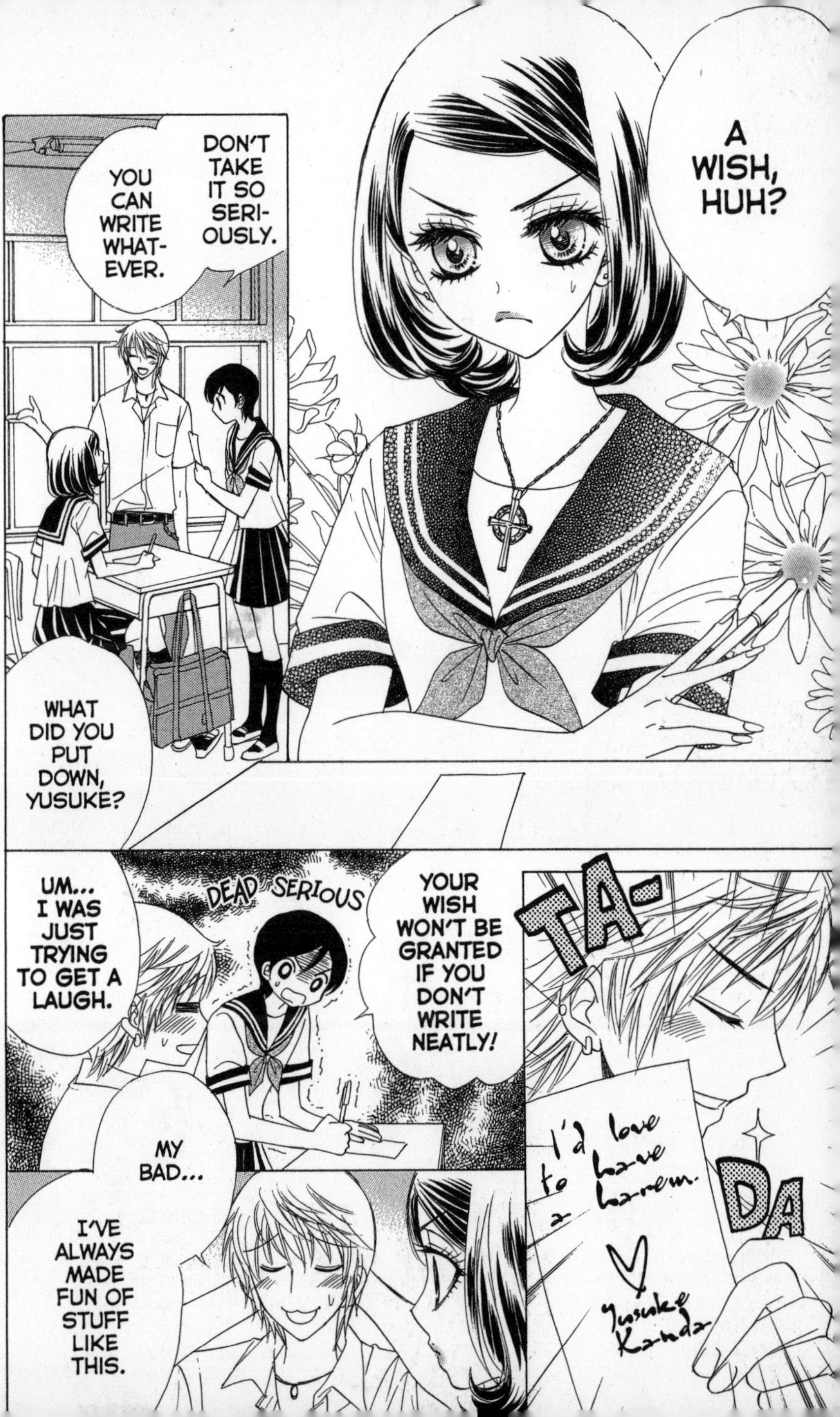
A WISH, HUH?
DON'T TAKE IT SO SERI-OUSLY.
YOU CAN WRITE WHAT-EVER.
WHAT DID YOU PUT DOWN, YUSUKE?
TA-
DA
I'd love to have a harem. ♥ Yusuke Kanda
YOUR WISH WON'T BE GRANTED IF YOU DON'T WRITE NEATLY!
DEAD SERIOUS
UM... I WAS JUST TRYING TO GET A LAUGH.
MY BAD...
I'VE ALWAYS MADE FUN OF STUFF LIKE THIS.

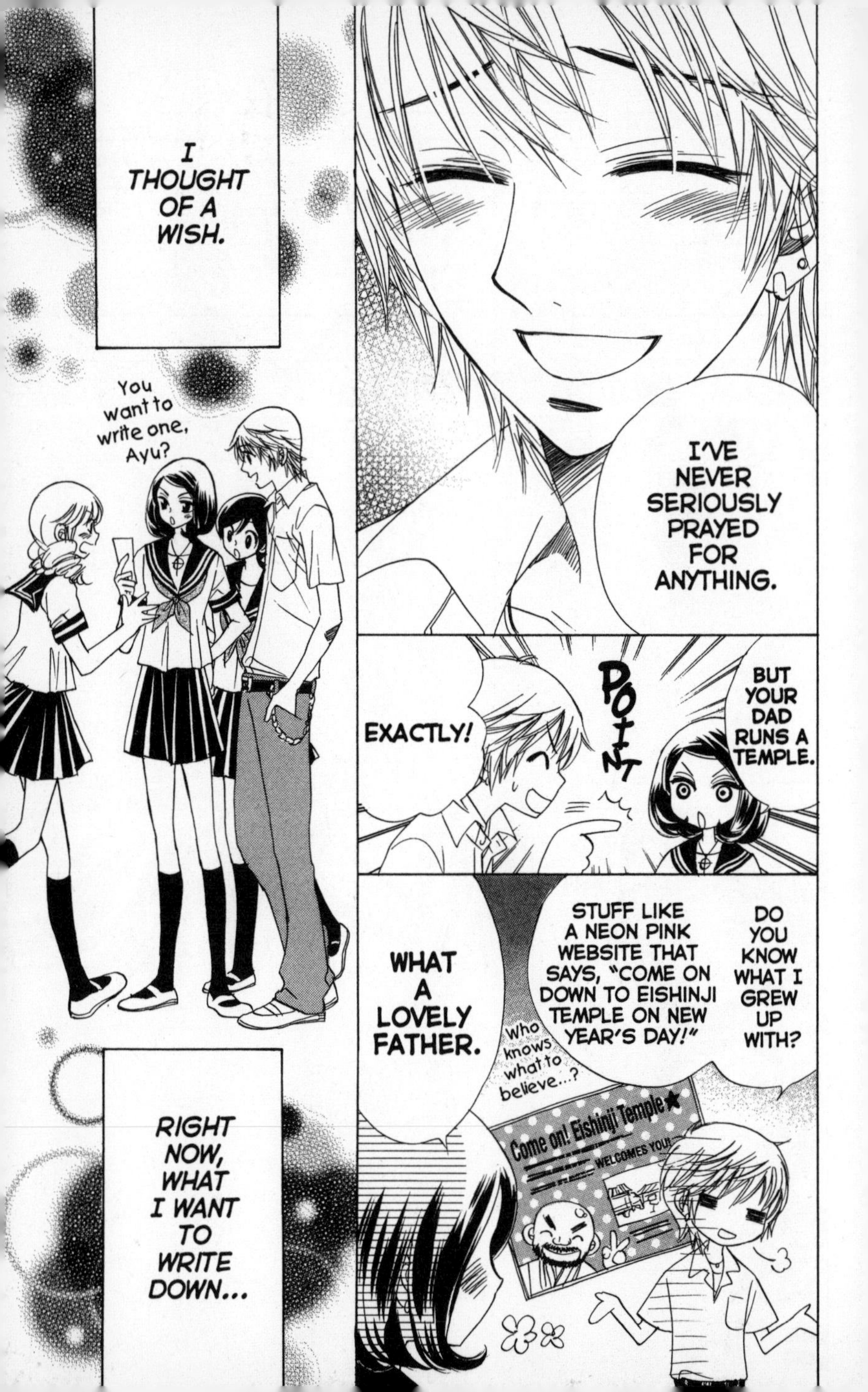
I'VE NEVER SERIOUSLY PRAYED FOR ANYTHING.
BUT YOUR DAD RUNS A TEMPLE.
POINT
EXACTLY!
DO YOU KNOW WHAT I GREW UP WITH?
STUFF LIKE A NEON PINK WEBSITE THAT SAYS, "COME ON DOWN TO EISHINJI TEMPLE ON NEW YEAR'S DAY!"
Come on! Eishinji Temple★
WELCOMES YOU!
WHAT A LOVELY FATHER.
Who knows what to believe...?
I THOUGHT OF A WISH.
You want to write one, Ayu?
RIGHT NOW, WHAT I WANT TO WRITE DOWN...

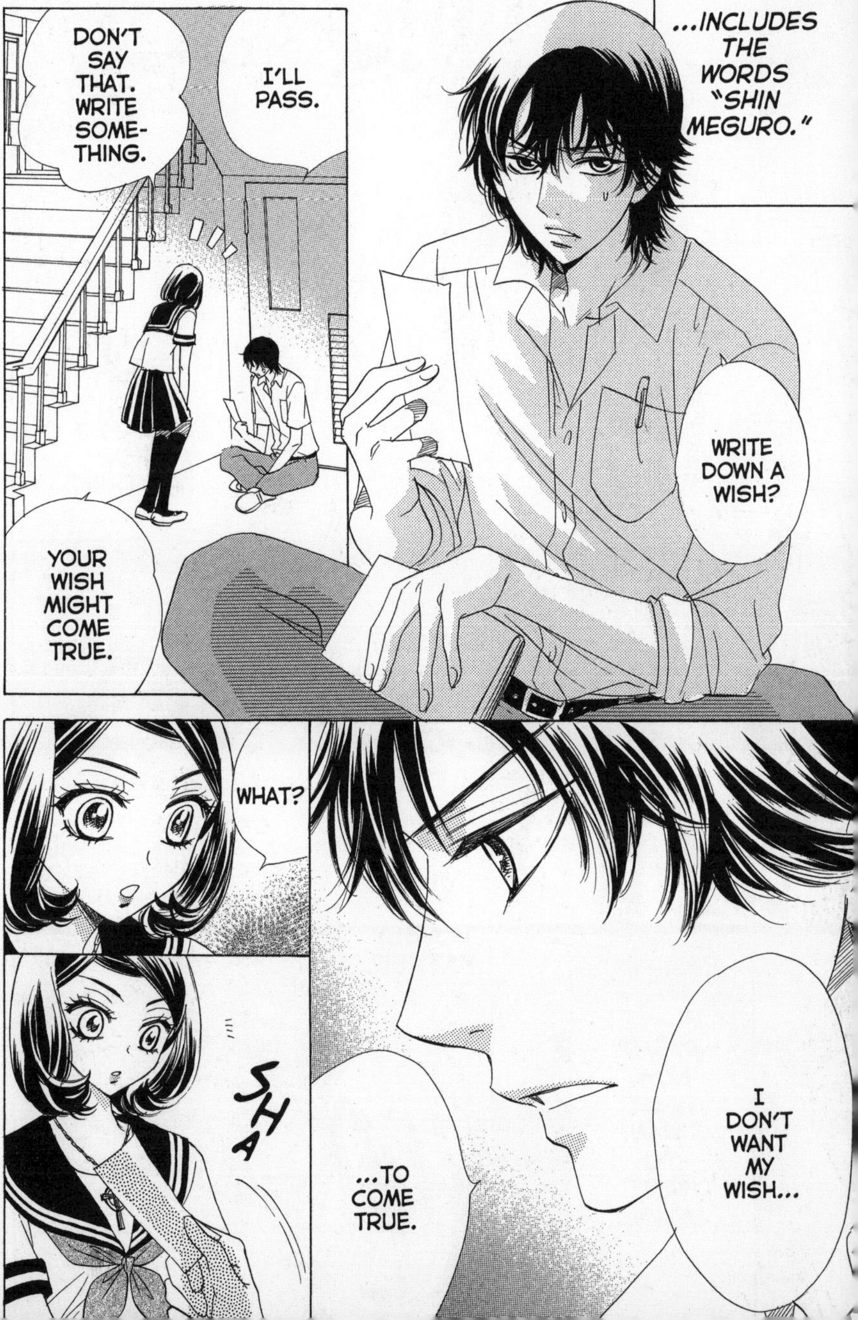
...INCLUDES THE WORDS "SHIN MEGURO."
WRITE DOWN A WISH?
I'LL PASS.
DON'T SAY THAT. WRITE SOME-THING.
YOUR WISH MIGHT COME TRUE.
I DON'T WANT MY WISH...
...TO COME TRUE.
WHAT?
SHA

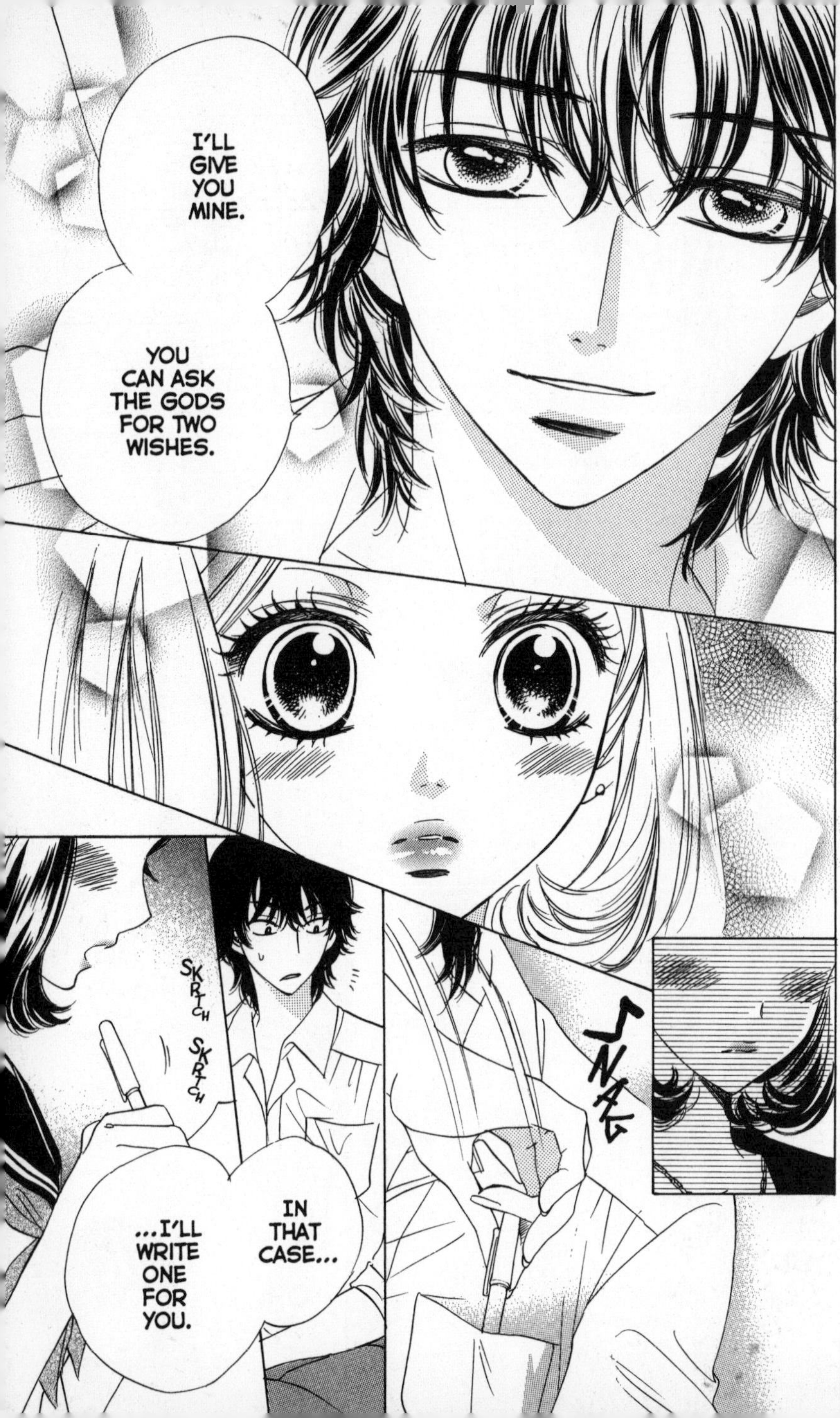
I'LL GIVE YOU MINE.
YOU CAN ASK THE GODS FOR TWO WISHES.
SNAG
IN THAT CASE...
...I'LL WRITE ONE FOR YOU.
SKRTCH SKRTCH

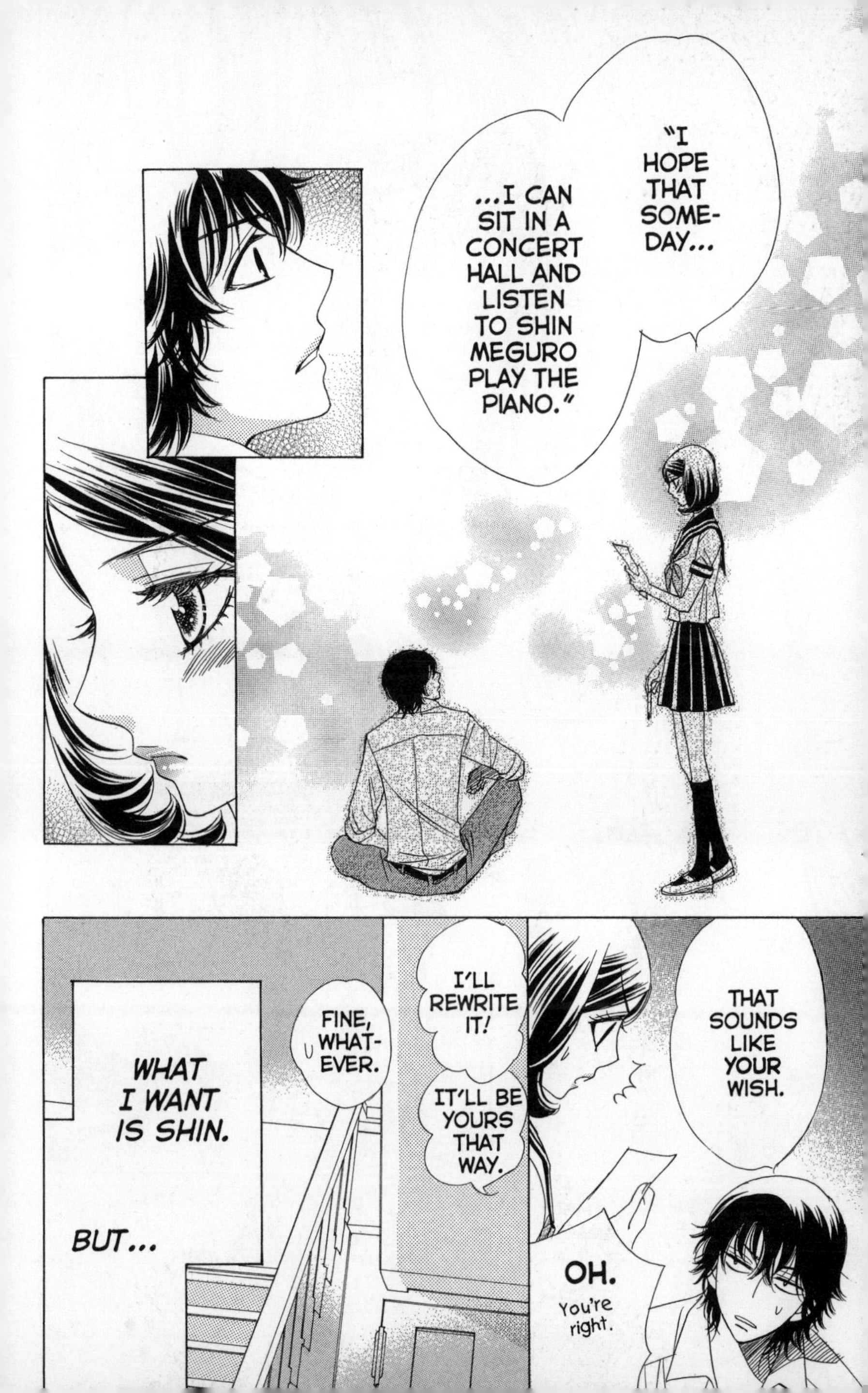
"I HOPE THAT SOME-DAY...
...I CAN SIT IN A CONCERT HALL AND LISTEN TO SHIN MEGURO PLAY THE PIANO."
THAT SOUNDS LIKE YOUR WISH.
OH.
You're right.
I'LL REWRITE IT!
IT'LL BE YOURS THAT WAY.
FINE, WHAT-EVER.
WHAT I WANT IS SHIN.
BUT...

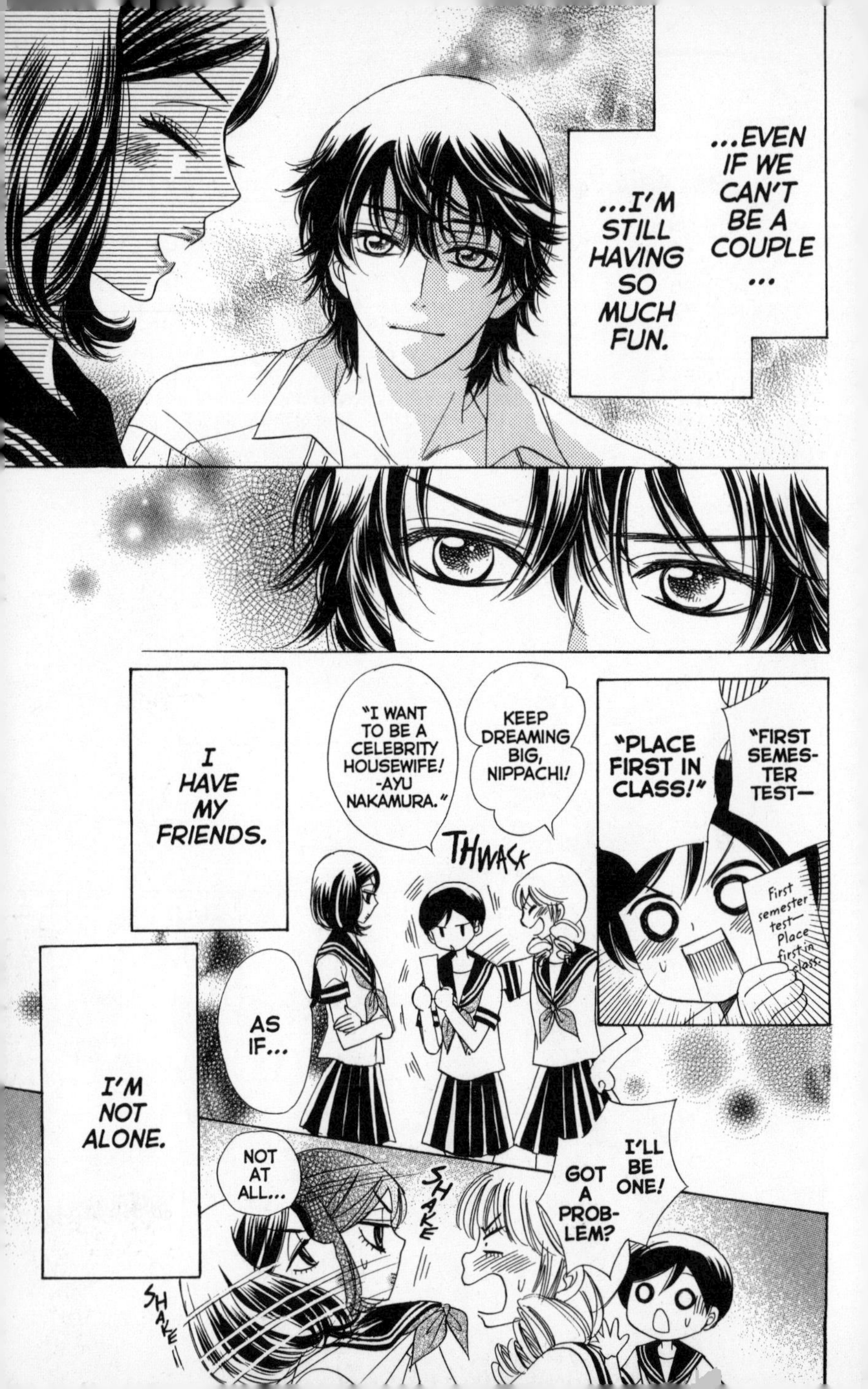
...EVEN IF WE CAN'T BE A COUPLE...
...I'M STILL HAVING SO MUCH FUN.
"FIRST SEMESTER TEST—
"PLACE FIRST IN CLASS!"
First semester test—Place first in class.
I HAVE MY FRIENDS.
KEEP DREAMING BIG, NIPPACHI!
"I WANT TO BE A CELEBRITY HOUSEWIFE! -AYU NAKAMURA."
THWACK
AS IF...
I'M NOT ALONE.
I'LL BE ONE!
GOT A PROBLEM?
SHAKE
NOT AT ALL...
SHAKE

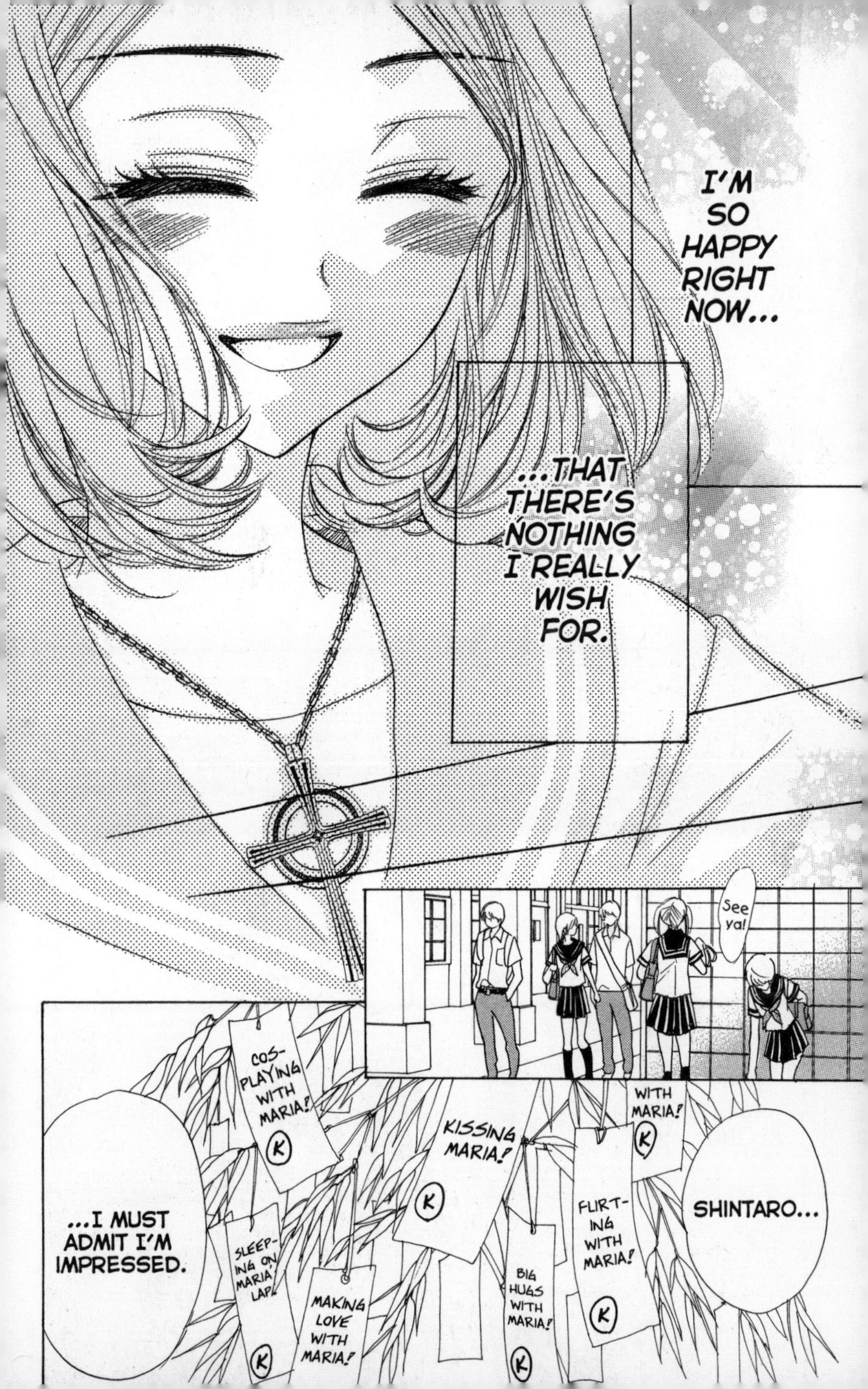
I'M SO HAPPY RIGHT NOW...
...THAT THERE'S NOTHING I REALLY WISH FOR.
See ya!
SHINTARO...
WITH MARIA!
FLIRT-ING WITH MARIA!
KISSING MARIA!
BIG HUGS WITH MARIA!
COS-PLAYING WITH MARIA!
MAKING LOVE WITH MARIA!
SLEEP-ING ON MARIA'S LAP!
...I MUST ADMIT I'M IMPRESSED.

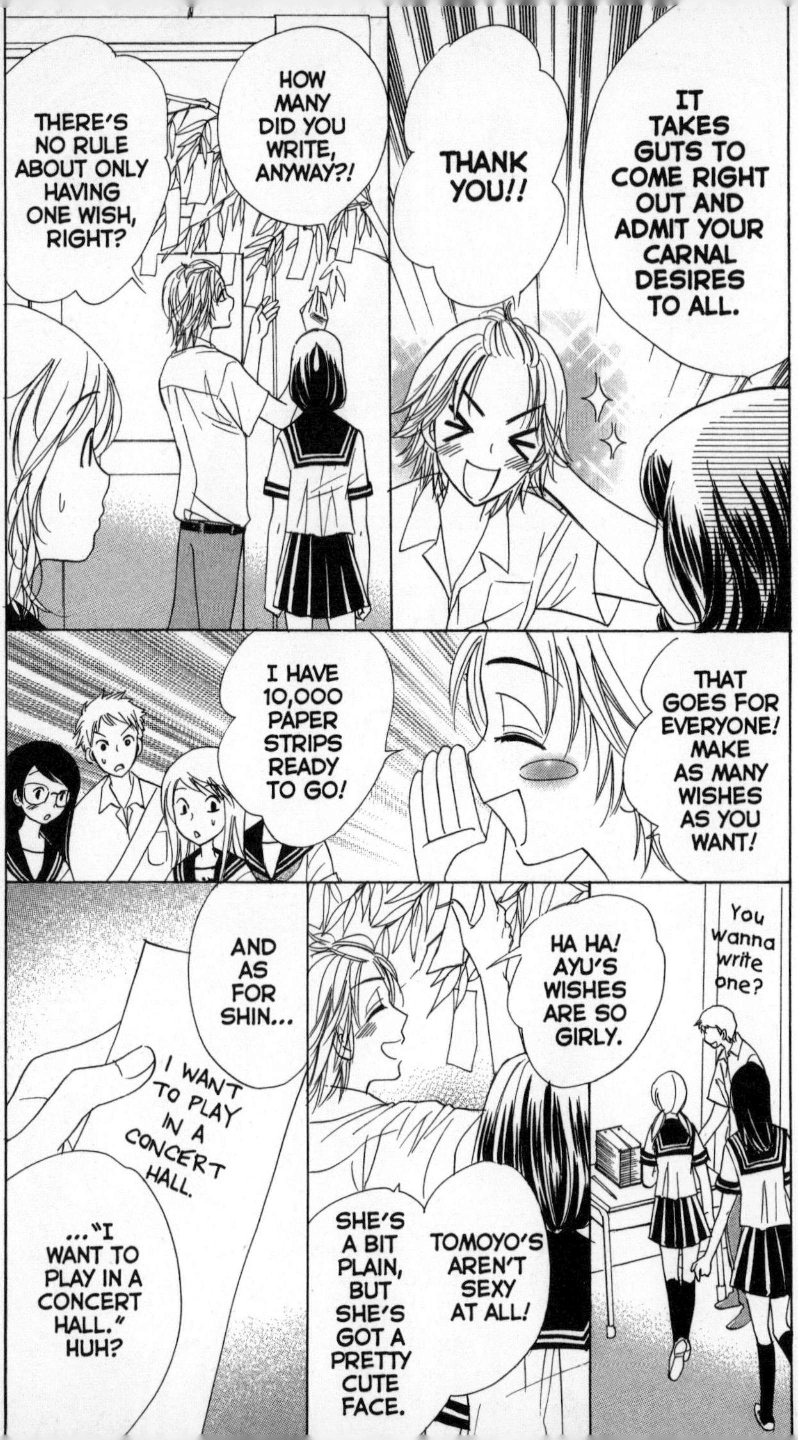
IT TAKES GUTS TO COME RIGHT OUT AND ADMIT YOUR CARNAL DESIRES TO ALL.
THANK YOU!!
HOW MANY DID YOU WRITE, ANYWAY?!
THERE'S NO RULE ABOUT ONLY HAVING ONE WISH, RIGHT?
THAT GOES FOR EVERYONE! MAKE AS MANY WISHES AS YOU WANT!
I HAVE 10,000 PAPER STRIPS READY TO GO!
You wanna write one?
HA HA! AYU'S WISHES ARE SO GIRLY.
TOMOYO'S AREN'T SEXY AT ALL!
SHE'S A BIT PLAIN, BUT SHE'S GOT A PRETTY CUTE FACE.
AND AS FOR SHIN...
I WANT TO PLAY IN A CONCERT HALL.
..."I WANT TO PLAY IN A CONCERT HALL." HUH?

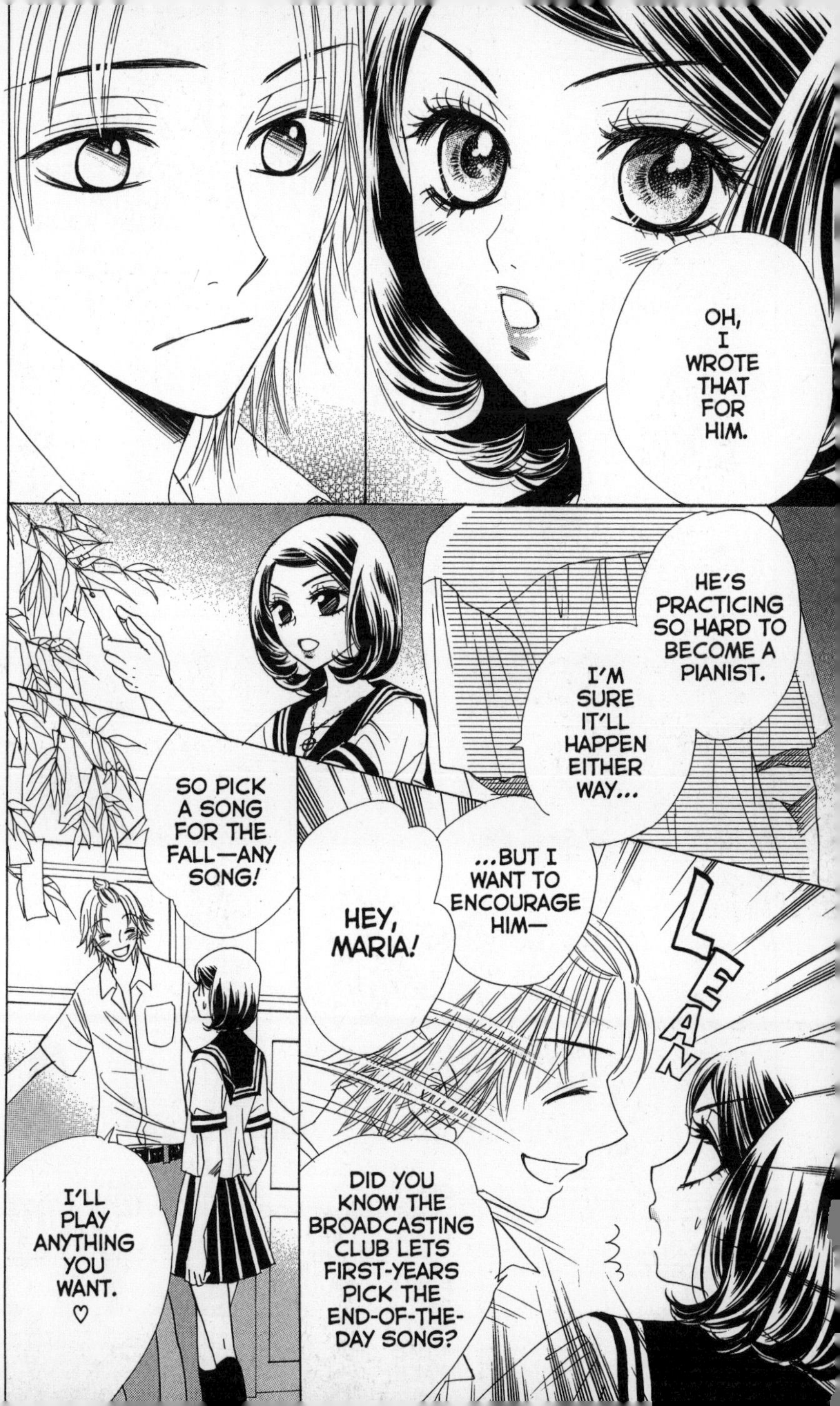
OH, I WROTE THAT FOR HIM.
HE'S PRACTICING SO HARD TO BECOME A PIANIST.
I'M SURE IT'LL HAPPEN EITHER WAY...
...BUT I WANT TO ENCOURAGE HIM—
HEY, MARIA!
SO PICK A SONG FOR THE FALL—ANY SONG!
LEAN
DID YOU KNOW THE BROADCASTING CLUB LETS FIRST-YEARS PICK THE END-OF-THE-DAY SONG?
I'LL PLAY ANYTHING YOU WANT. ♡

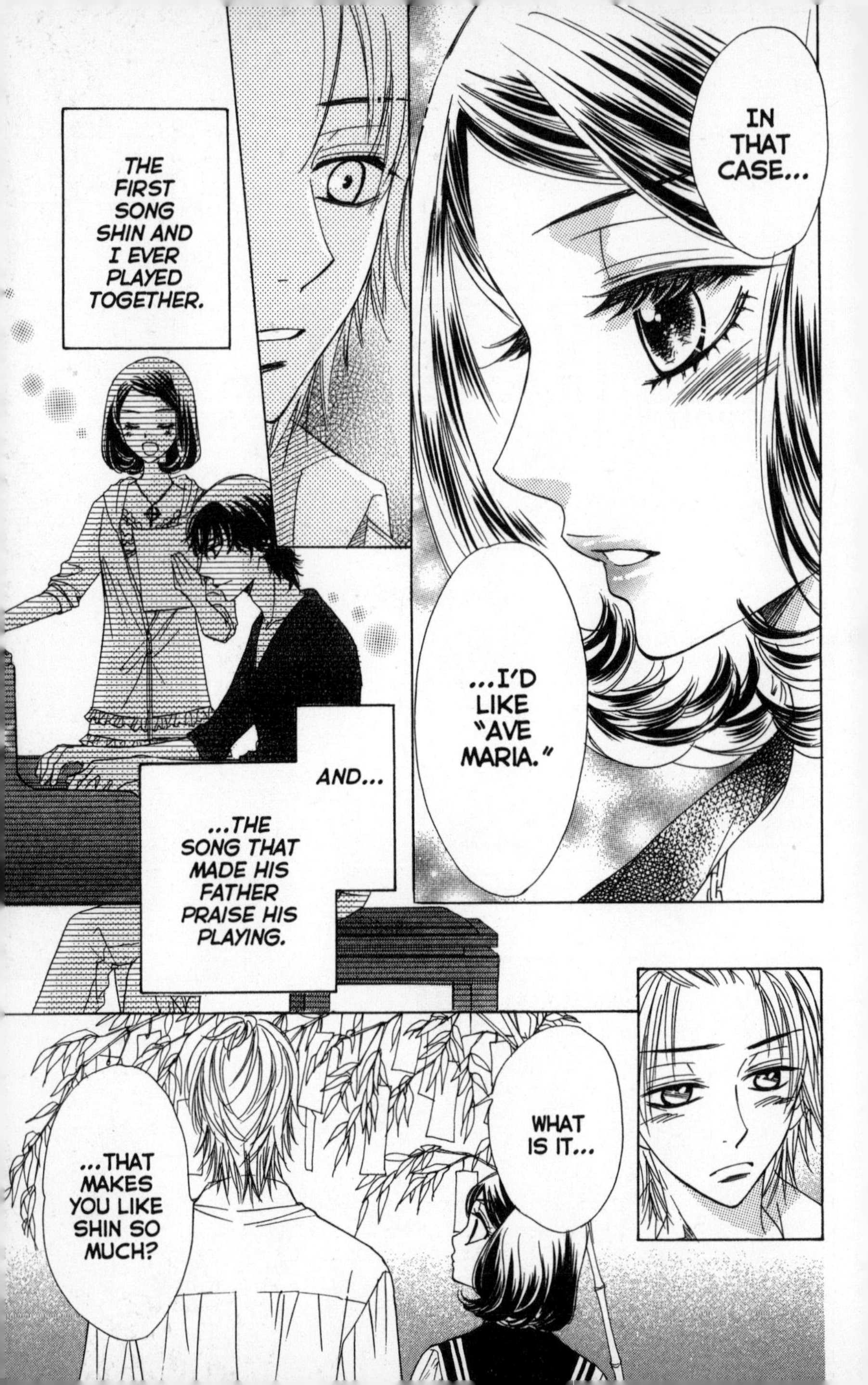
IN THAT CASE...
...I'D LIKE "AVE MARIA."
THE FIRST SONG SHIN AND I EVER PLAYED TOGETHER.
AND...
...THE SONG THAT MADE HIS FATHER PRAISE HIS PLAYING.
WHAT IS IT...
...THAT MAKES YOU LIKE SHIN SO MUCH?

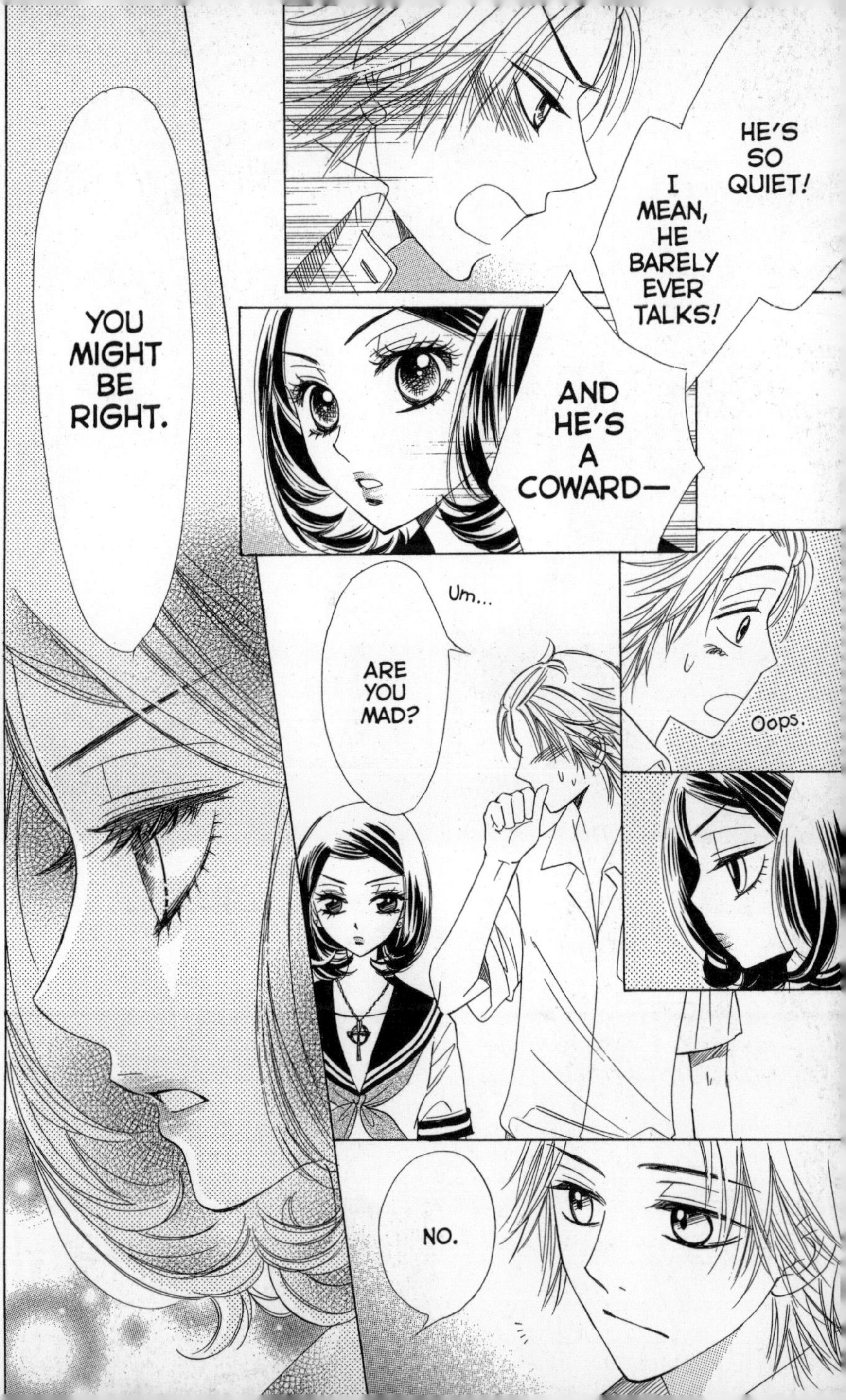
HE'S SO QUIET!
I MEAN, HE BARELY EVER TALKS!
AND HE'S A COWARD—
Oops.
Um...
ARE YOU MAD?
NO.
YOU MIGHT BE RIGHT.

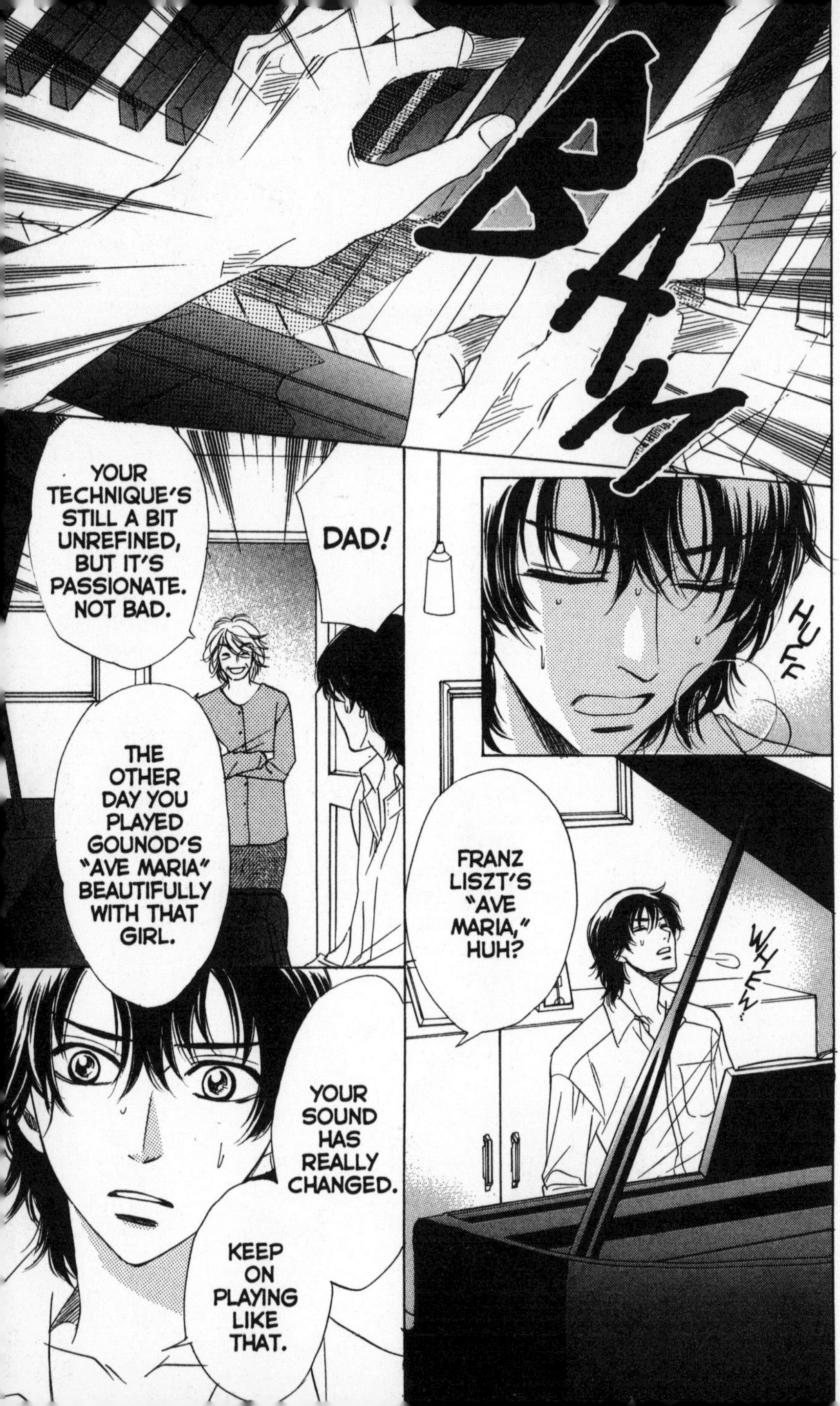
BAM
HUFF
WHEW...
FRANZ LISZT'S "AVE MARIA," HUH?
DAD!
YOUR TECHNIQUE'S STILL A BIT UNREFINED, BUT IT'S PASSIONATE. NOT BAD.
THE OTHER DAY YOU PLAYED GOUNOD'S "AVE MARIA" BEAUTIFULLY WITH THAT GIRL.
YOUR SOUND HAS REALLY CHANGED.
KEEP ON PLAYING LIKE THAT.

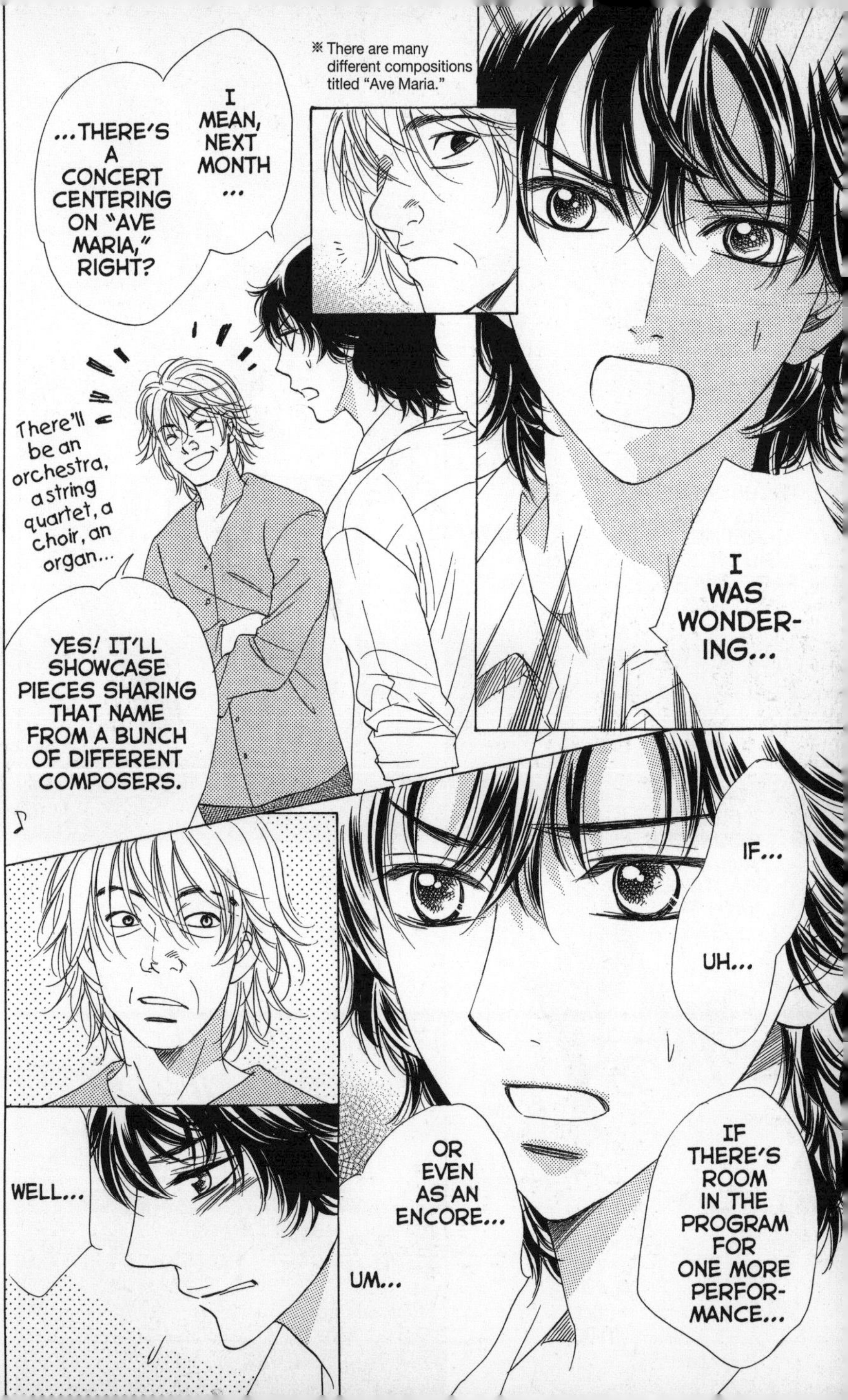
I WAS WONDERING...
I MEAN, NEXT MONTH...
...THERE'S A CONCERT CENTERING ON "AVE MARIA," RIGHT?
※ There are many different compositions titled "Ave Maria."
There'll be an orchestra, a string quartet, a choir, an organ...
YES! IT'LL SHOWCASE PIECES SHARING THAT NAME FROM A BUNCH OF DIFFERENT COMPOSERS.
IF...
UH...
IF THERE'S ROOM IN THE PROGRAM FOR ONE MORE PERFORMANCE...
OR EVEN AS AN ENCORE...
UM...
WELL...

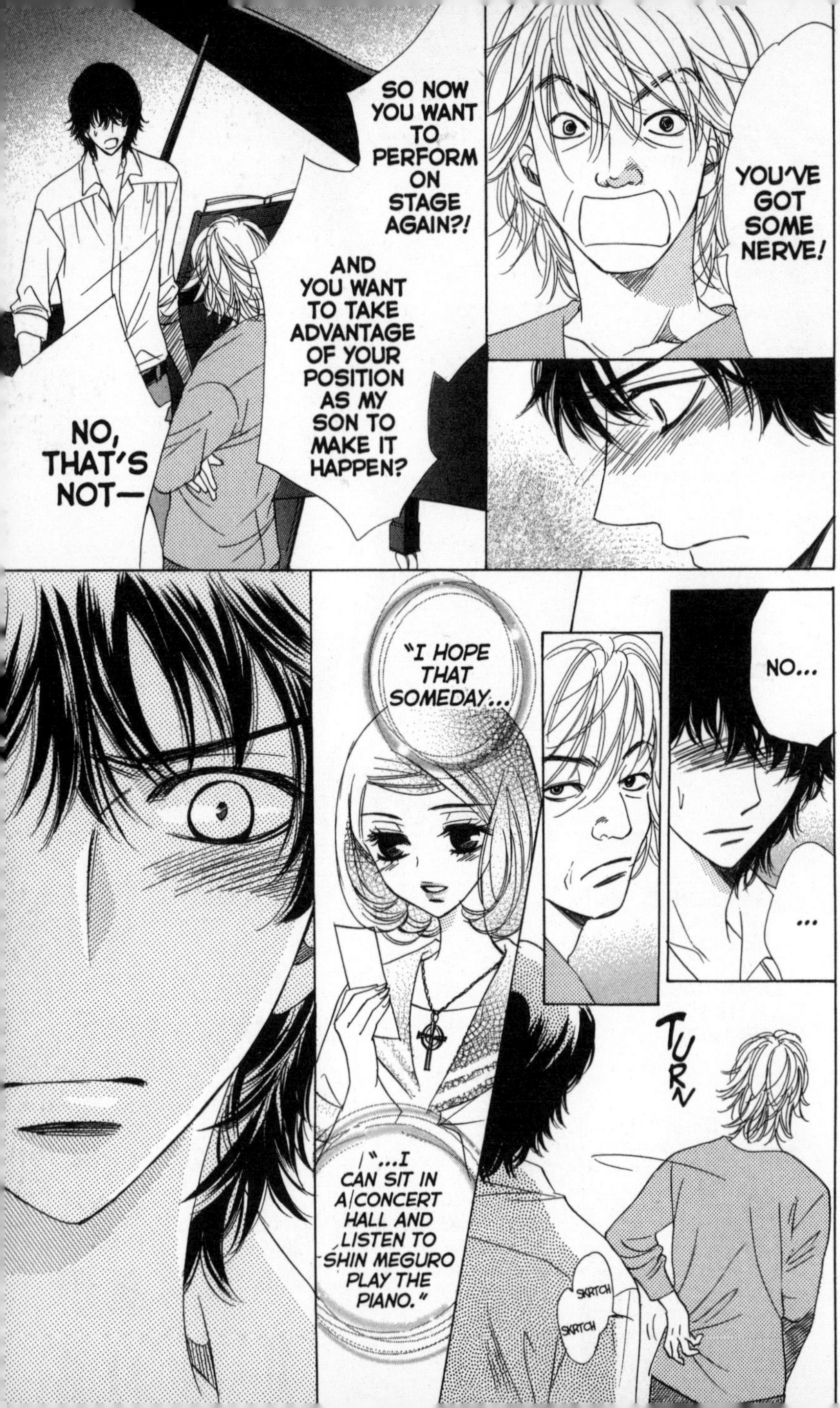
YOU'VE GOT SOME NERVE!
SO NOW YOU WANT TO PERFORM ON STAGE AGAIN?!
AND YOU WANT TO TAKE ADVANTAGE OF YOUR POSITION AS MY SON TO MAKE IT HAPPEN?
NO, THAT'S NOT—
NO...
...
TURN
SKRTCH
SKRTCH
"I HOPE THAT SOMEDAY...
"...I CAN SIT IN A CONCERT HALL AND LISTEN TO SHIN MEGURO PLAY THE PIANO."

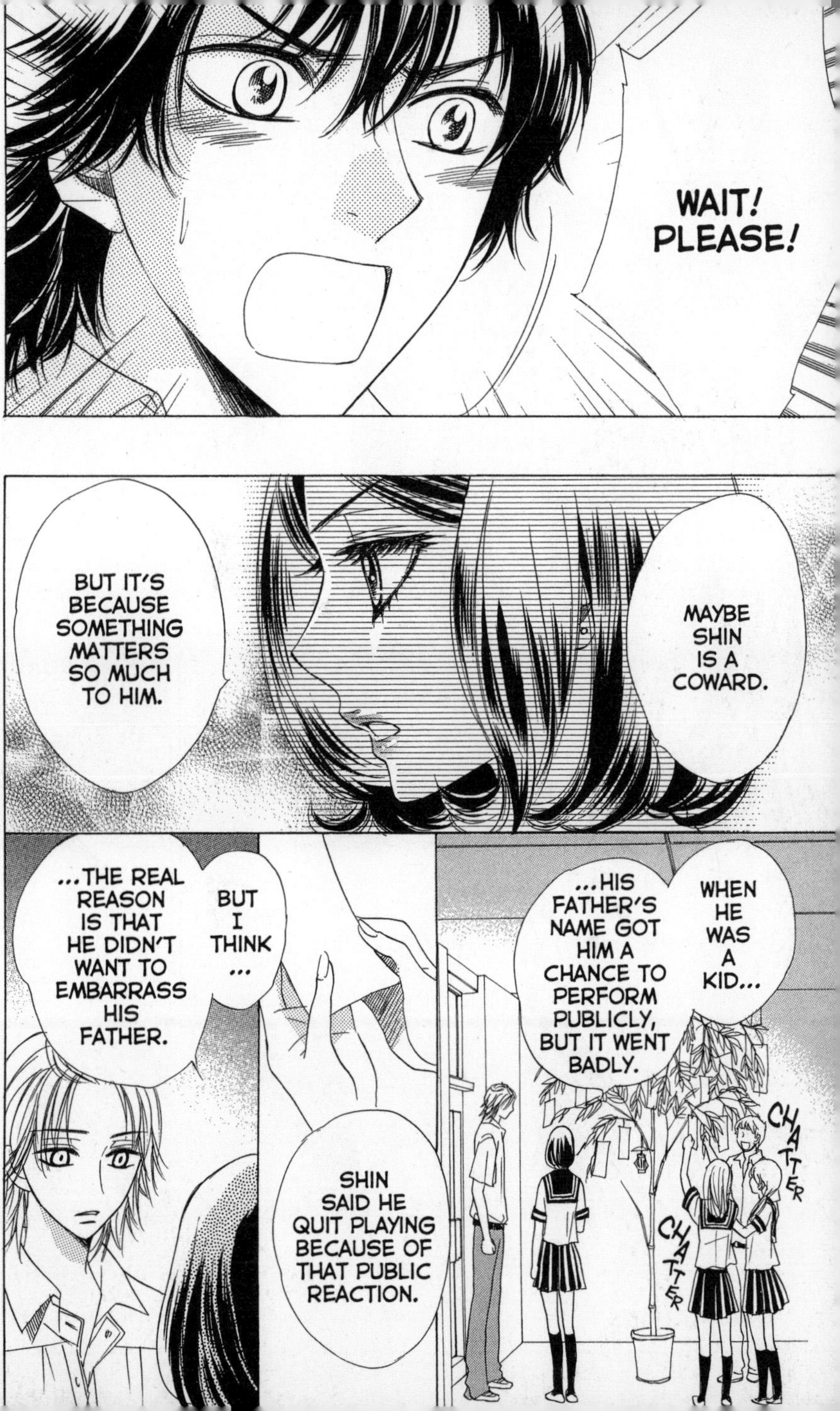
WAIT! PLEASE!
MAYBE SHIN IS A COWARD.
BUT IT'S BECAUSE SOMETHING MATTERS SO MUCH TO HIM.
WHEN HE WAS A KID...
...HIS FATHER'S NAME GOT HIM A CHANCE TO PERFORM PUBLICLY, BUT IT WENT BADLY.
CHATTER
CHATTER
SHIN SAID HE QUIT PLAYING BECAUSE OF THAT PUBLIC REACTION.
BUT I THINK ...
...THE REAL REASON IS THAT HE DIDN'T WANT TO EMBARRASS HIS FATHER.

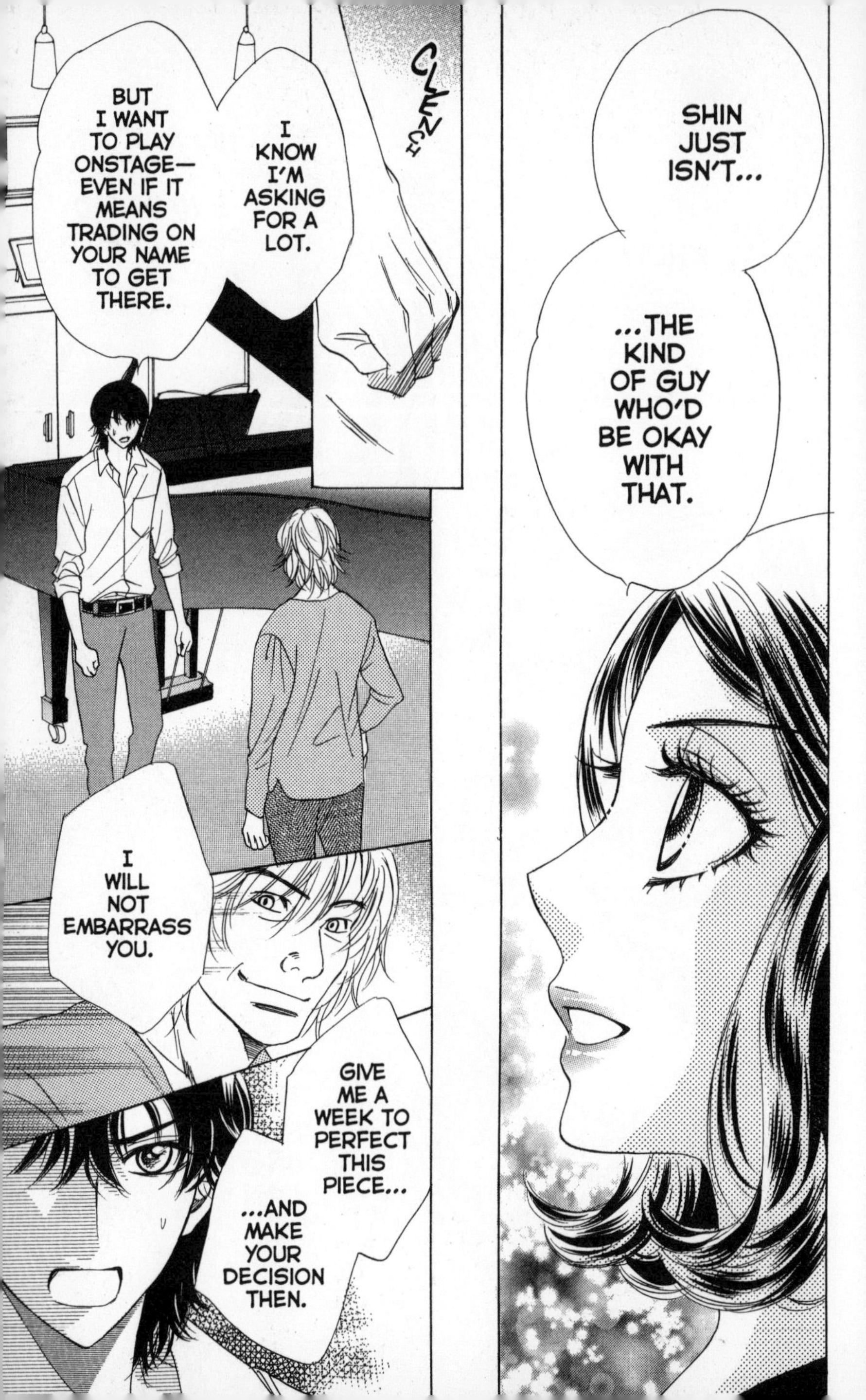
SHIN JUST ISN'T...
...THE KIND OF GUY WHO'D BE OKAY WITH THAT.
CLENCH
I KNOW I'M ASKING FOR A LOT.
BUT I WANT TO PLAY ONSTAGE—EVEN IF IT MEANS TRADING ON YOUR NAME TO GET THERE.
I WILL NOT EMBARRASS YOU.
GIVE ME A WEEK TO PERFECT THIS PIECE...
...AND MAKE YOUR DECISION THEN.

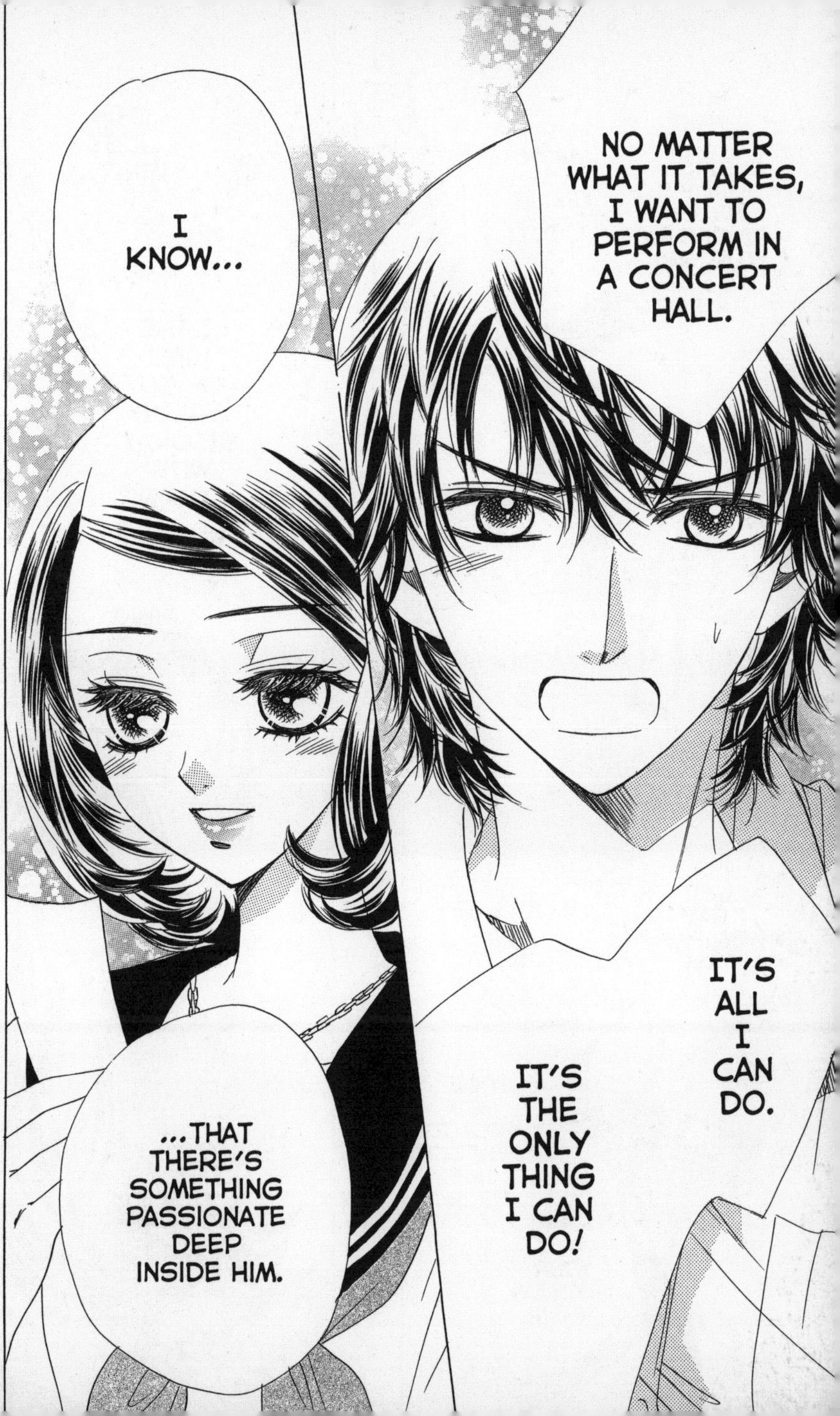
NO MATTER WHAT IT TAKES, I WANT TO PERFORM IN A CONCERT HALL.
I KNOW...
IT'S ALL I CAN DO.
IT'S THE ONLY THING I CAN DO!
...THAT THERE'S SOMETHING PASSIONATE DEEP INSIDE HIM.

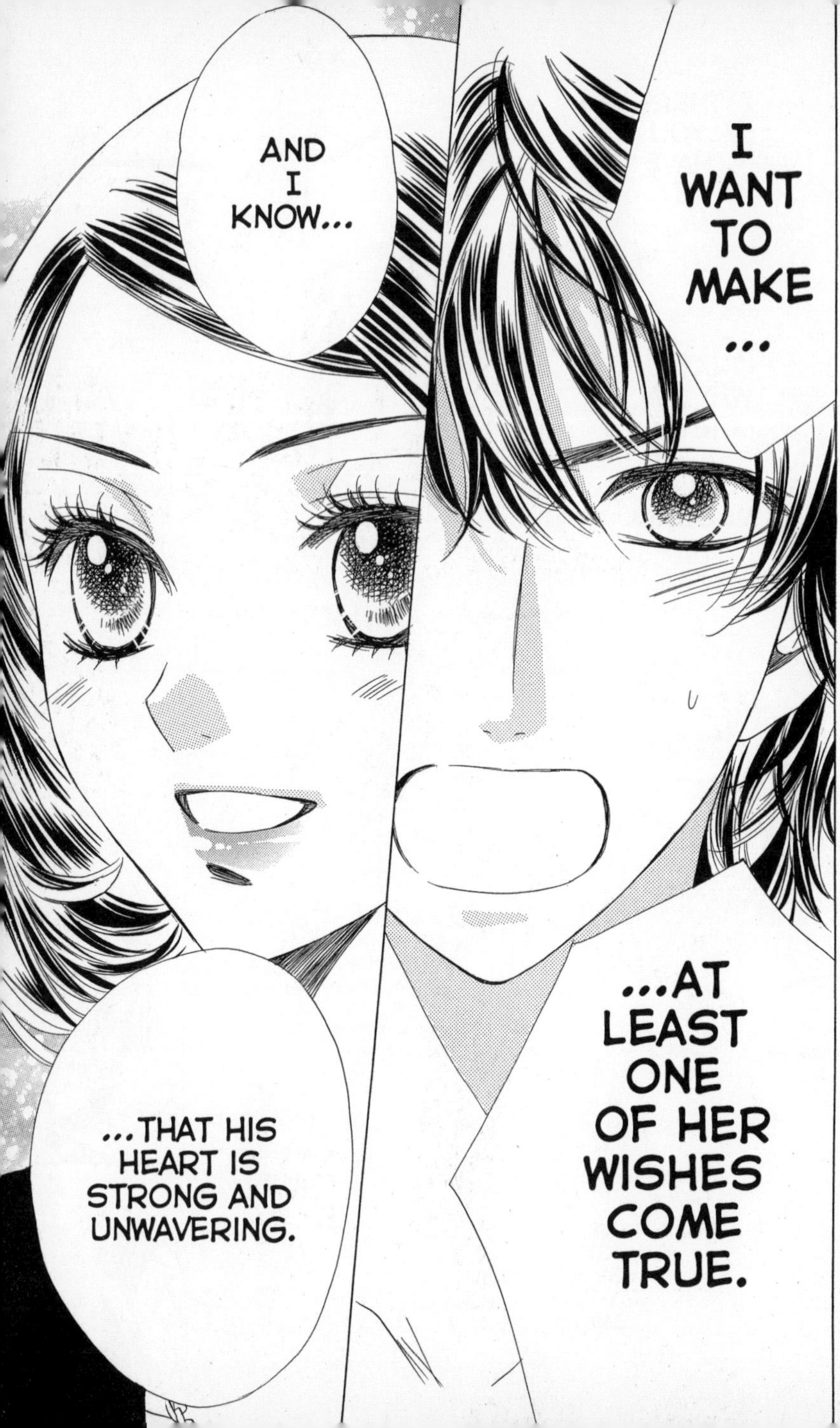
I WANT TO MAKE ...
...AT LEAST ONE OF HER WISHES COME TRUE.
AND I KNOW...
...THAT HIS HEART IS STRONG AND UNWAVERING.

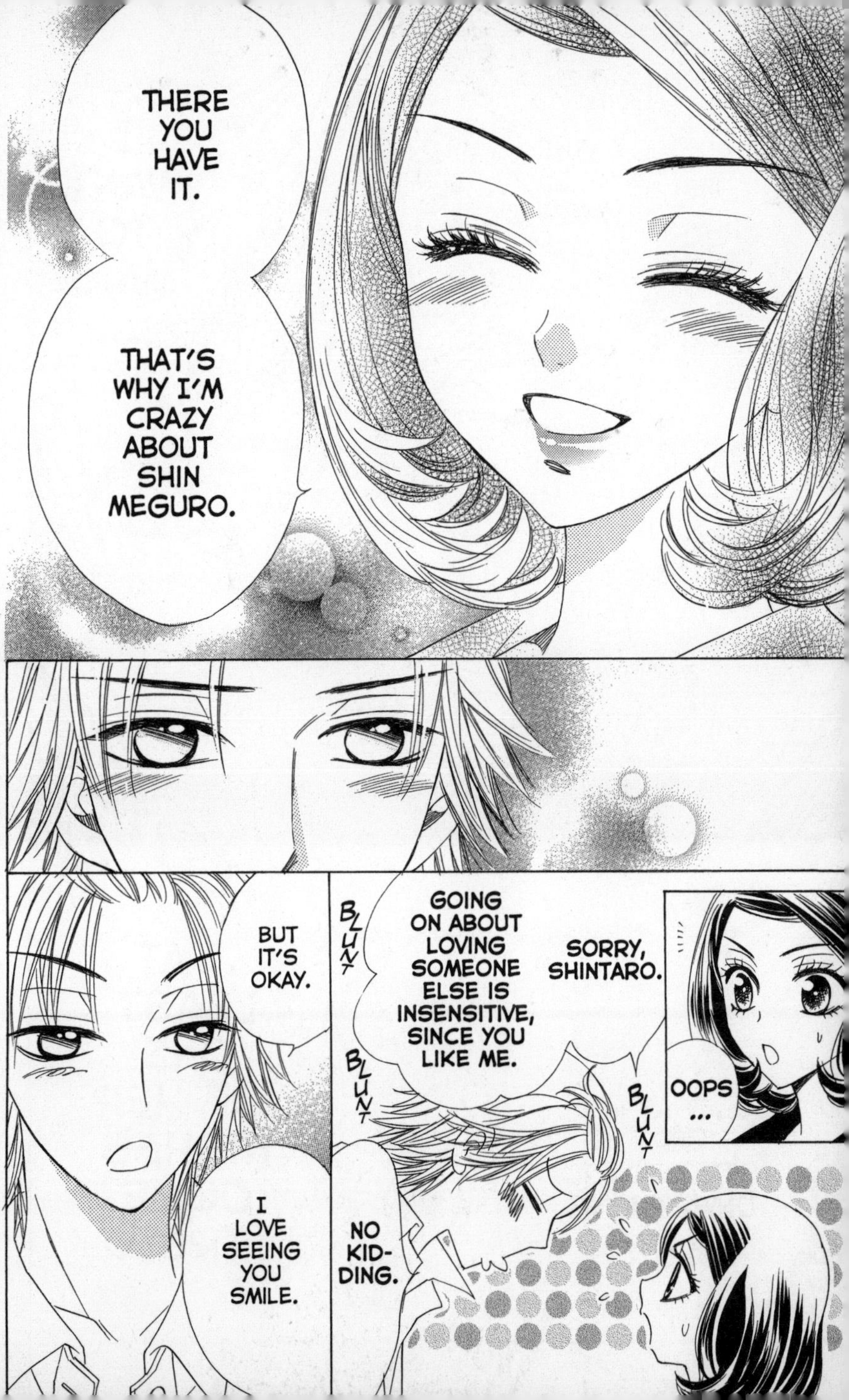
THERE YOU HAVE IT.
THAT'S WHY I'M CRAZY ABOUT SHIN MEGURO.
OOPS...
SORRY, SHINTARO.
GOING ON ABOUT LOVING SOMEONE ELSE IS INSENSITIVE, SINCE YOU LIKE ME.
BLUNT
BLUNT
BLUNT
NO KIDDING.
BUT IT'S OKAY.
I LOVE SEEING YOU SMILE.

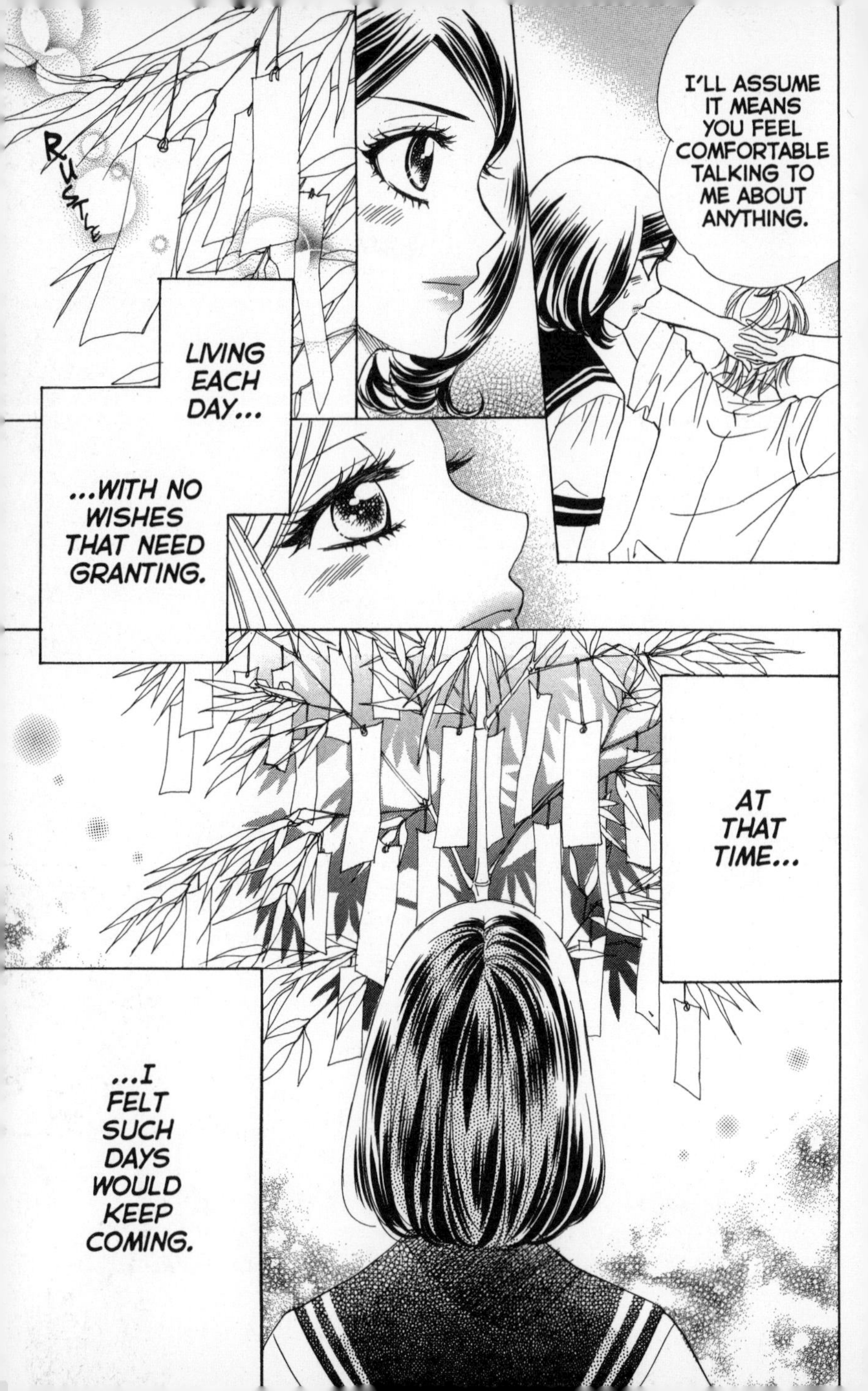
I'LL ASSUME IT MEANS YOU FEEL COMFORTABLE TALKING TO ME ABOUT ANYTHING.
RUSTLE
LIVING EACH DAY...
...WITH NO WISHES THAT NEED GRANTING.
AT THAT TIME...
...I FELT SUCH DAYS WOULD KEEP COMING.

A Devil and Her Love Song

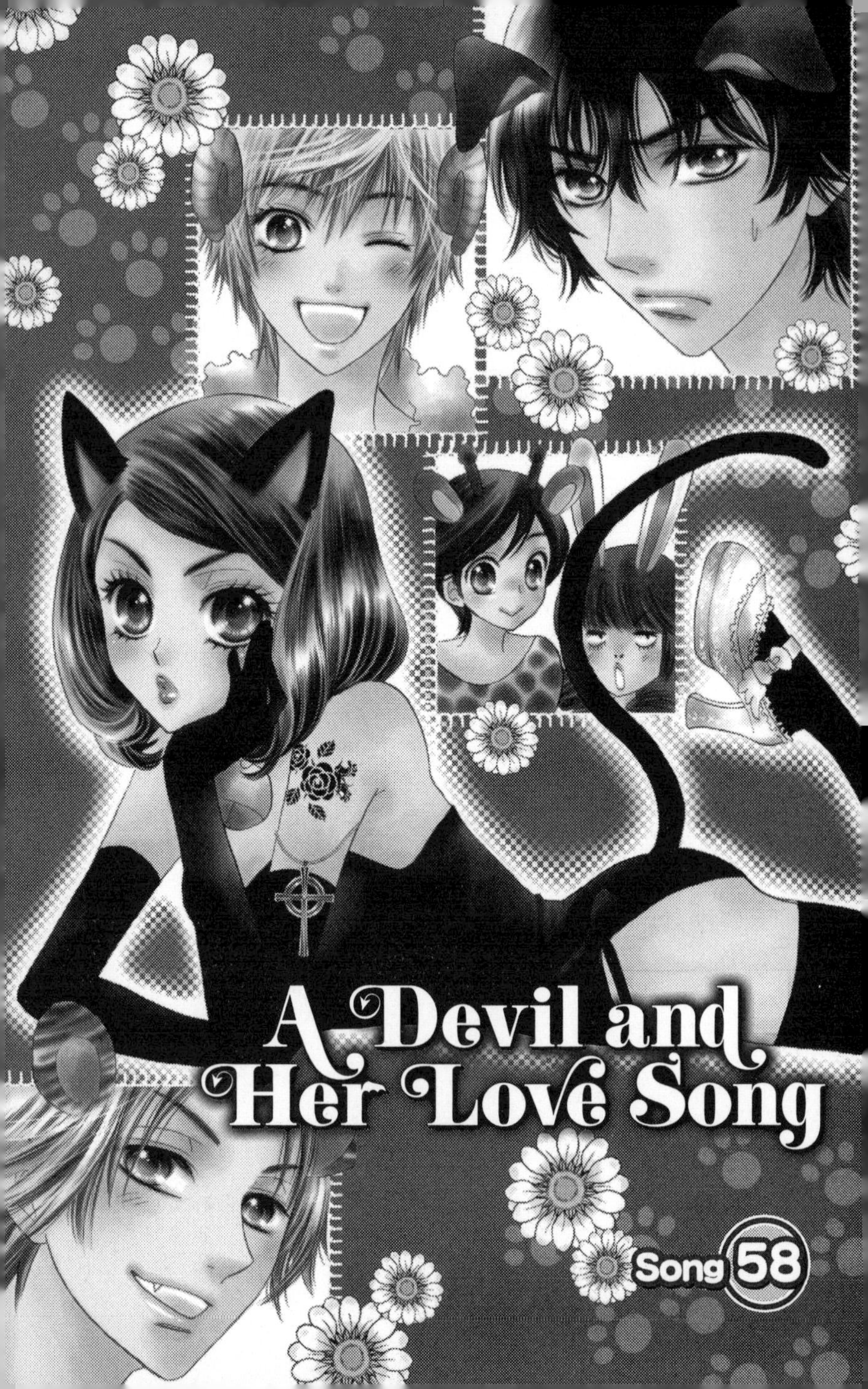
A Devil and Her Love Song
Song 58

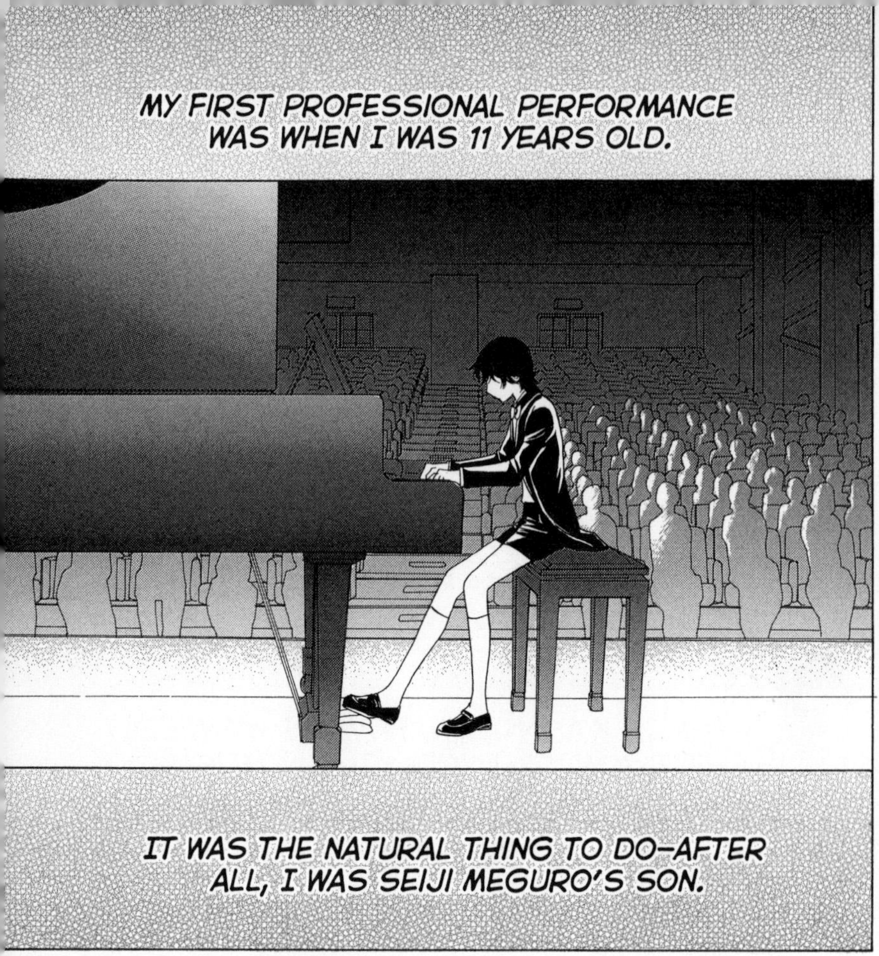
MY FIRST PROFESSIONAL PERFORMANCE WAS WHEN I WAS 11 YEARS OLD.
IT WAS THE NATURAL THING TO DO—AFTER ALL, I WAS SEIJI MEGURO'S SON.

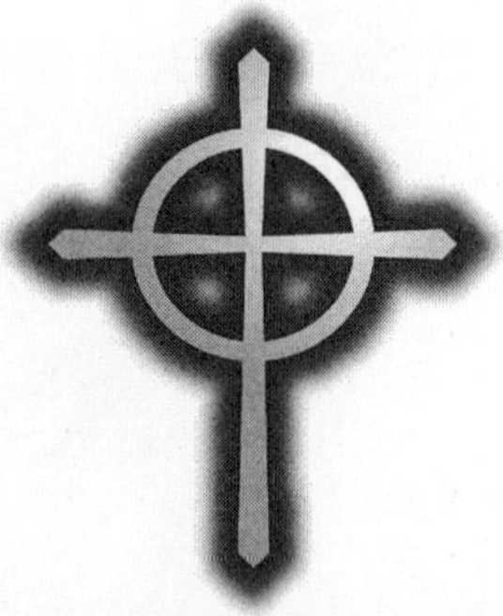

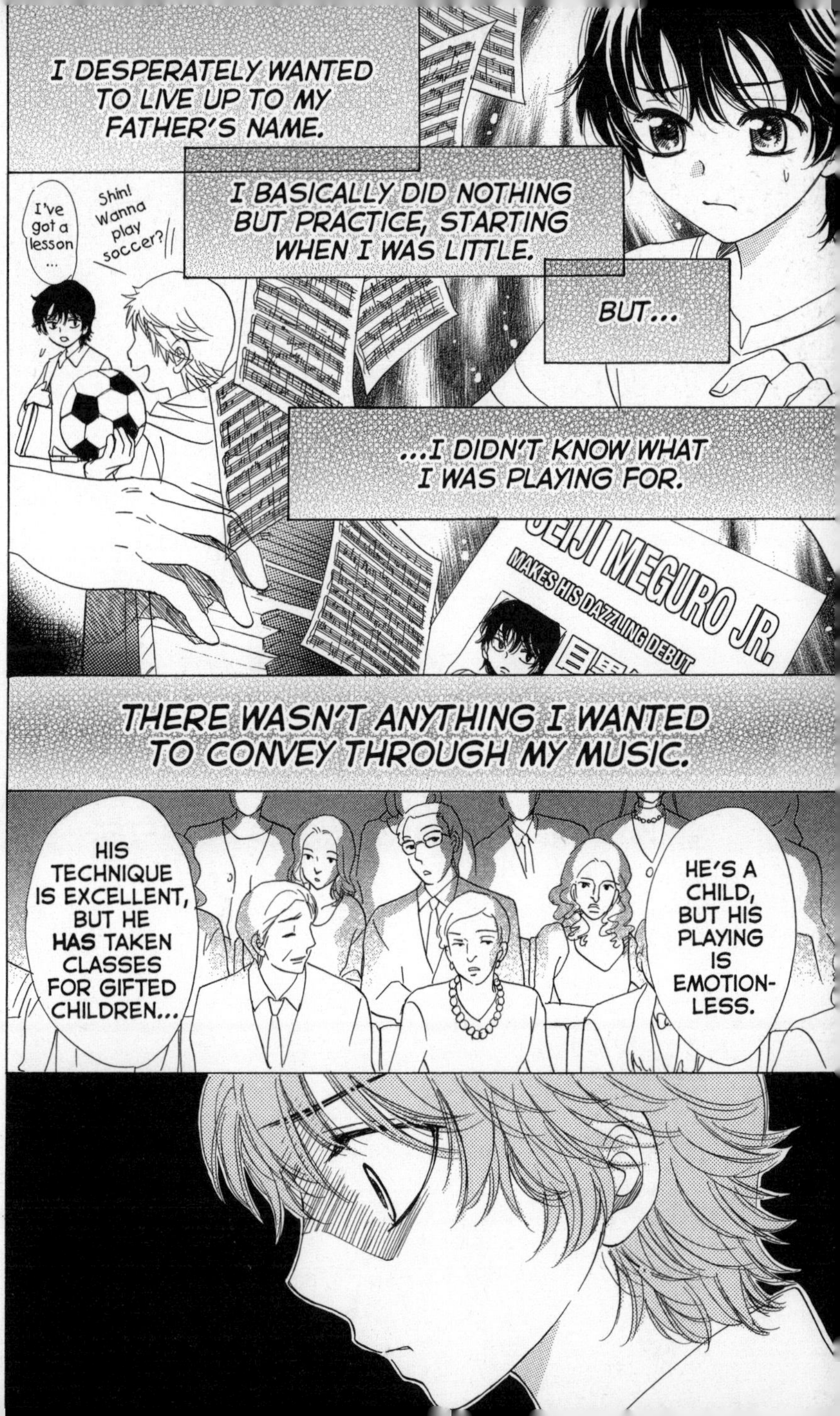
I DESPERATELY WANTED TO LIVE UP TO MY FATHER'S NAME.
I BASICALLY DID NOTHING BUT PRACTICE, STARTING WHEN I WAS LITTLE.
Shin! Wanna play soccer?
I've got a lesson...
BUT...
...I DIDN'T KNOW WHAT I WAS PLAYING FOR.
SEIJI MEGURO JR.
MAKES HIS DAZZLING DEBUT
THERE WASN'T ANYTHING I WANTED TO CONVEY THROUGH MY MUSIC.
HE'S A CHILD, BUT HIS PLAYING IS EMOTIONLESS.
HIS TECHNIQUE IS EXCELLENT, BUT HE HAS TAKEN CLASSES FOR GIFTED CHILDREN...

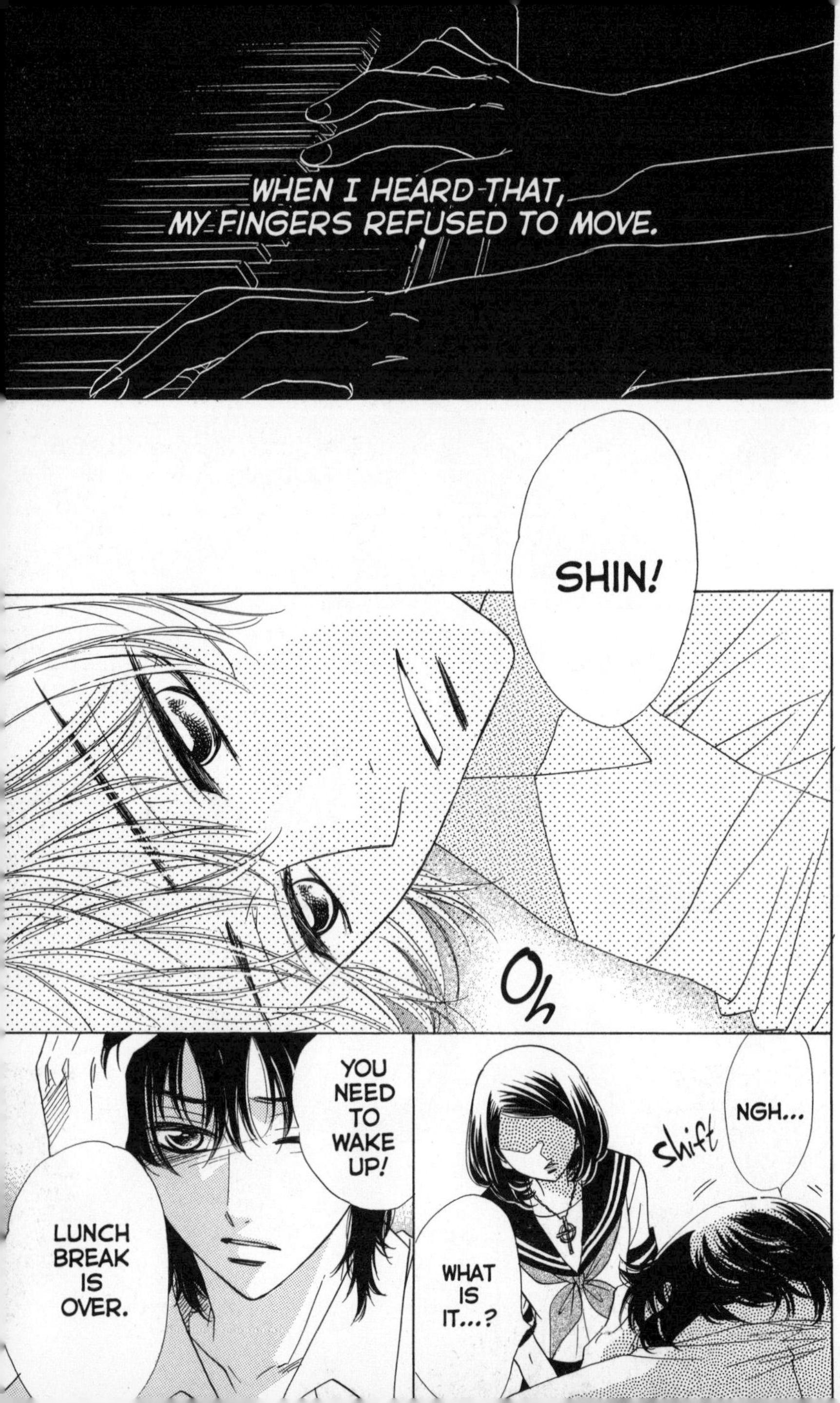
WHEN I HEARD THAT, MY FINGERS REFUSED TO MOVE.
SHIN!
Oh
NGH...
shift
WHAT IS IT...?
YOU NEED TO WAKE UP!
LUNCH BREAK IS OVER.

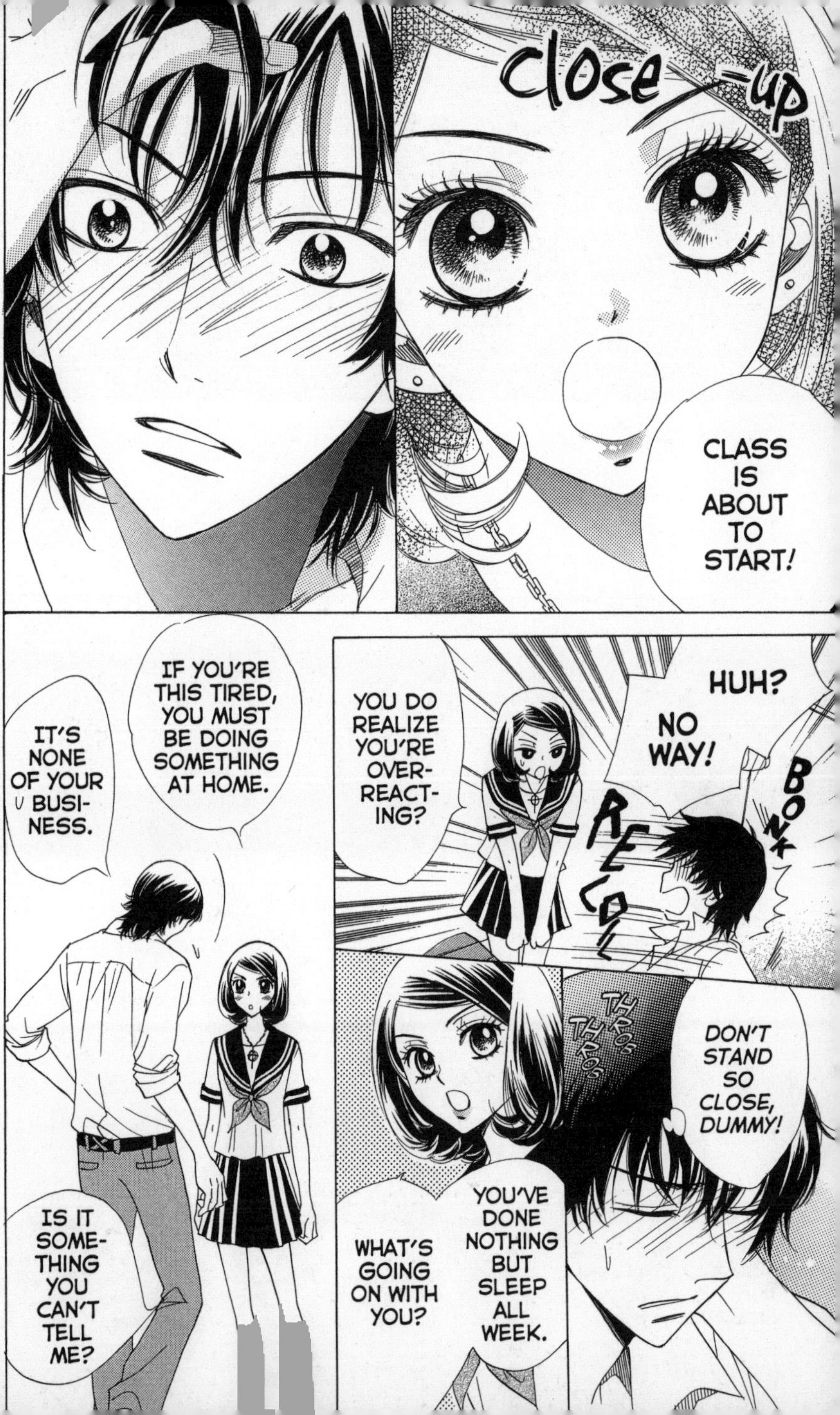
Close-up
CLASS IS ABOUT TO START!
HUH?
NO WAY!
BONK
RECOIL
YOU DO REALIZE YOU'RE OVER-REACTING?
DON'T STAND SO CLOSE, DUMMY!
THROB THROB
YOU'VE DONE NOTHING BUT SLEEP ALL WEEK.
WHAT'S GOING ON WITH YOU?
IF YOU'RE THIS TIRED, YOU MUST BE DOING SOMETHING AT HOME.
IT'S NONE OF YOUR BUSINESS.
IS IT SOMETHING YOU CAN'T TELL ME?

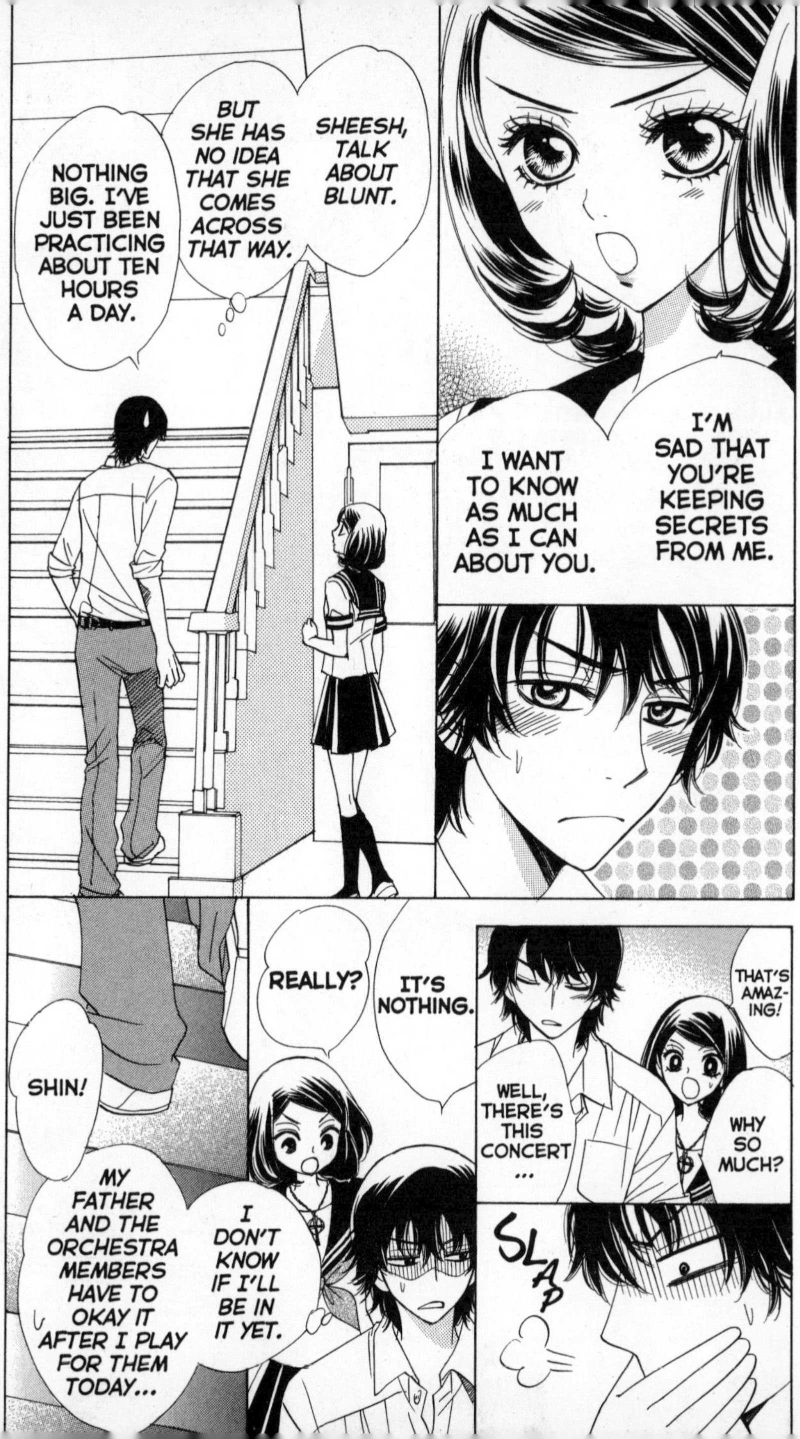
I'M SAD THAT YOU'RE KEEPING SECRETS FROM ME.
I WANT TO KNOW AS MUCH AS I CAN ABOUT YOU.
NOTHING BIG. I'VE JUST BEEN PRACTICING ABOUT TEN HOURS A DAY.
BUT SHE HAS NO IDEA THAT SHE COMES ACROSS THAT WAY.
SHEESH, TALK ABOUT BLUNT.
THAT'S AMAZ-ING!
WHY SO MUCH?
WELL, THERE'S THIS CONCERT...
SLAP
IT'S NOTHING.
REALLY?
SHIN!
MY FATHER AND THE ORCHESTRA MEMBERS HAVE TO OKAY IT AFTER I PLAY FOR THEM TODAY...
I DON'T KNOW IF I'LL BE IN IT YET.

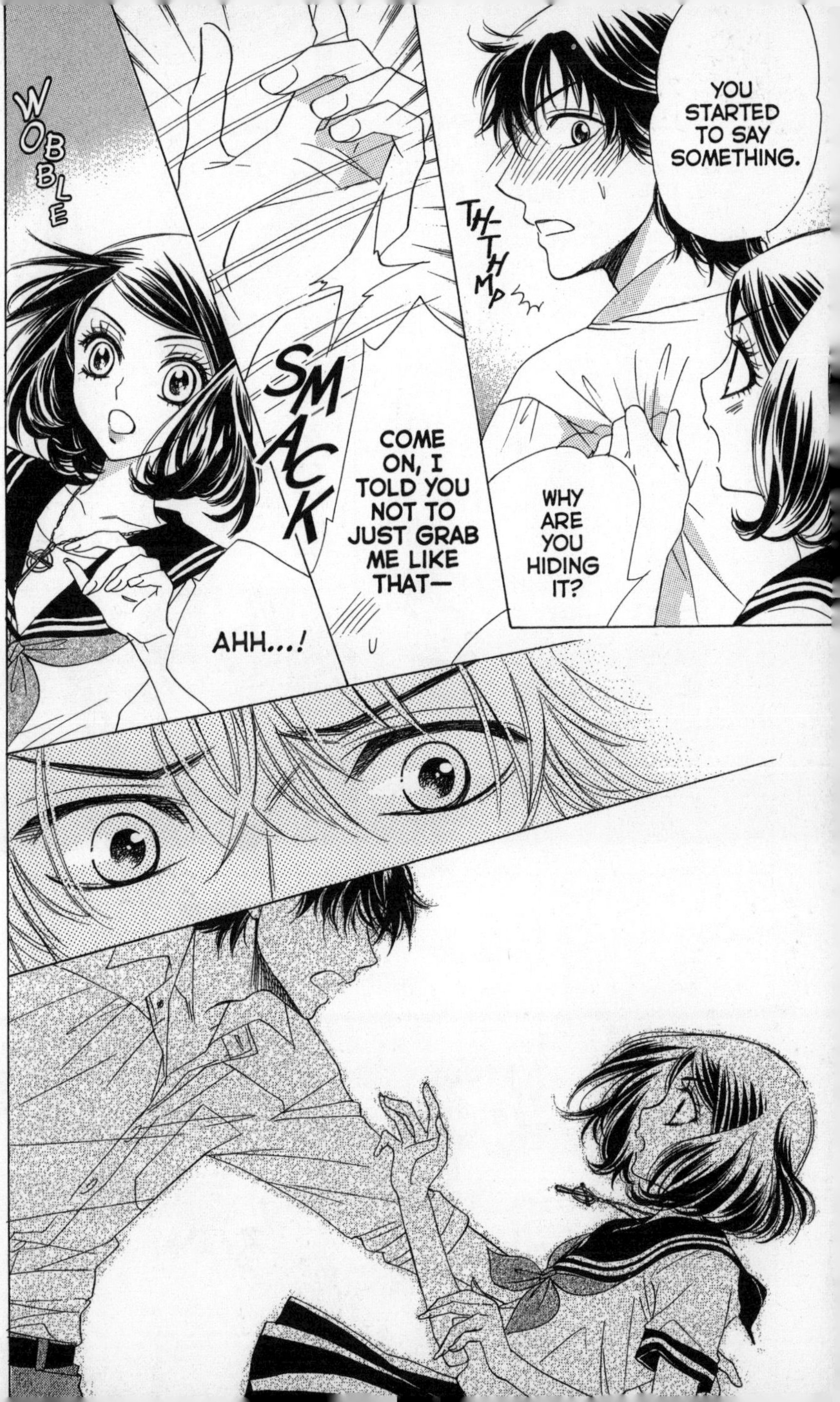
YOU STARTED TO SAY SOMETHING.
WHY ARE YOU HIDING IT?
TH-THMP
COME ON, I TOLD YOU NOT TO JUST GRAB ME LIKE THAT—
SMACK
AHH...!
WOBLE

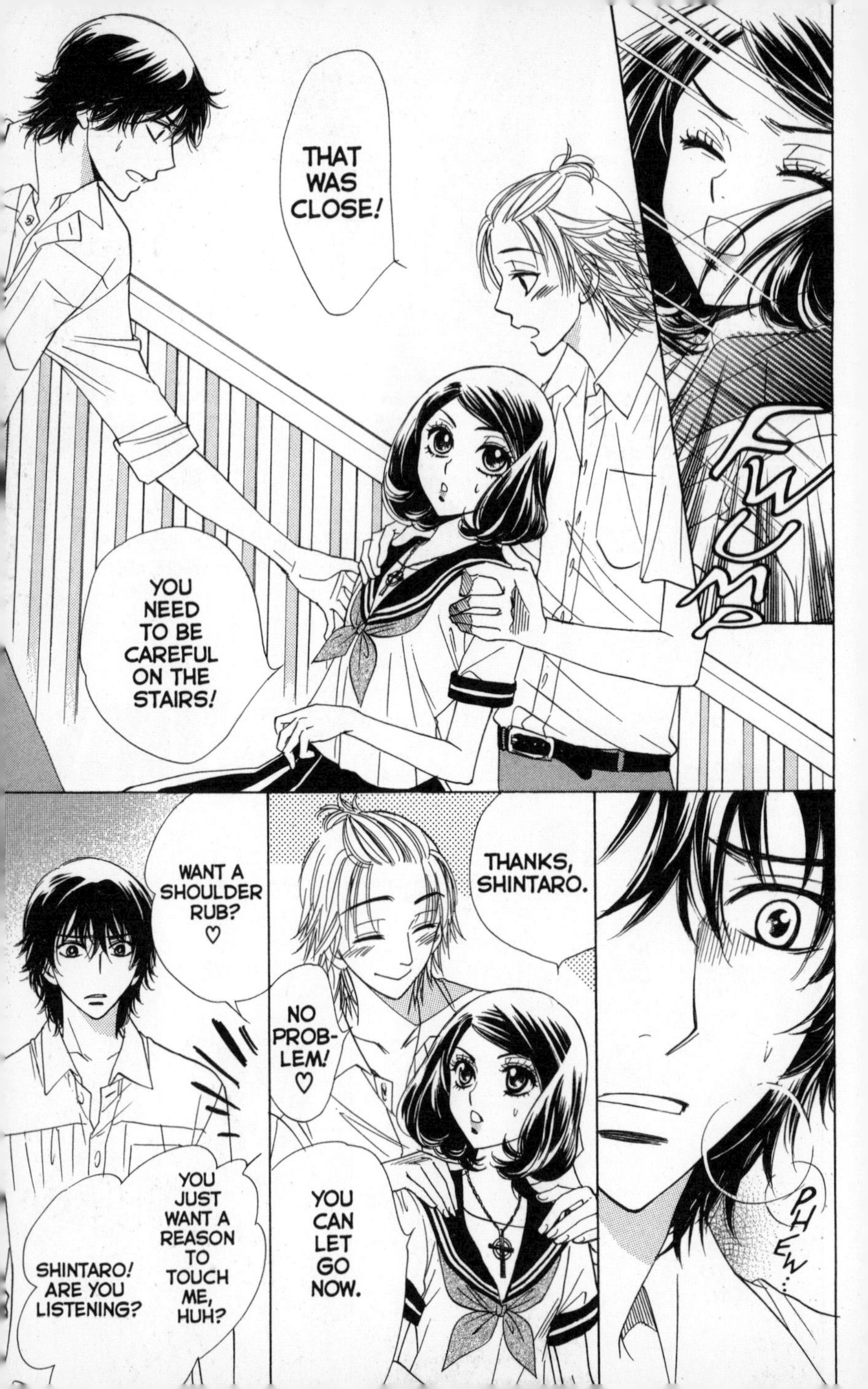
FWUMP
THAT WAS CLOSE!
YOU NEED TO BE CAREFUL ON THE STAIRS!
PHEW...
THANKS, SHINTARO.
NO PROB-LEM! ♡
YOU CAN LET GO NOW.
WANT A SHOULDER RUB? ♡
YOU JUST WANT A REASON TO TOUCH ME, HUH?
SHINTARO! ARE YOU LISTENING?

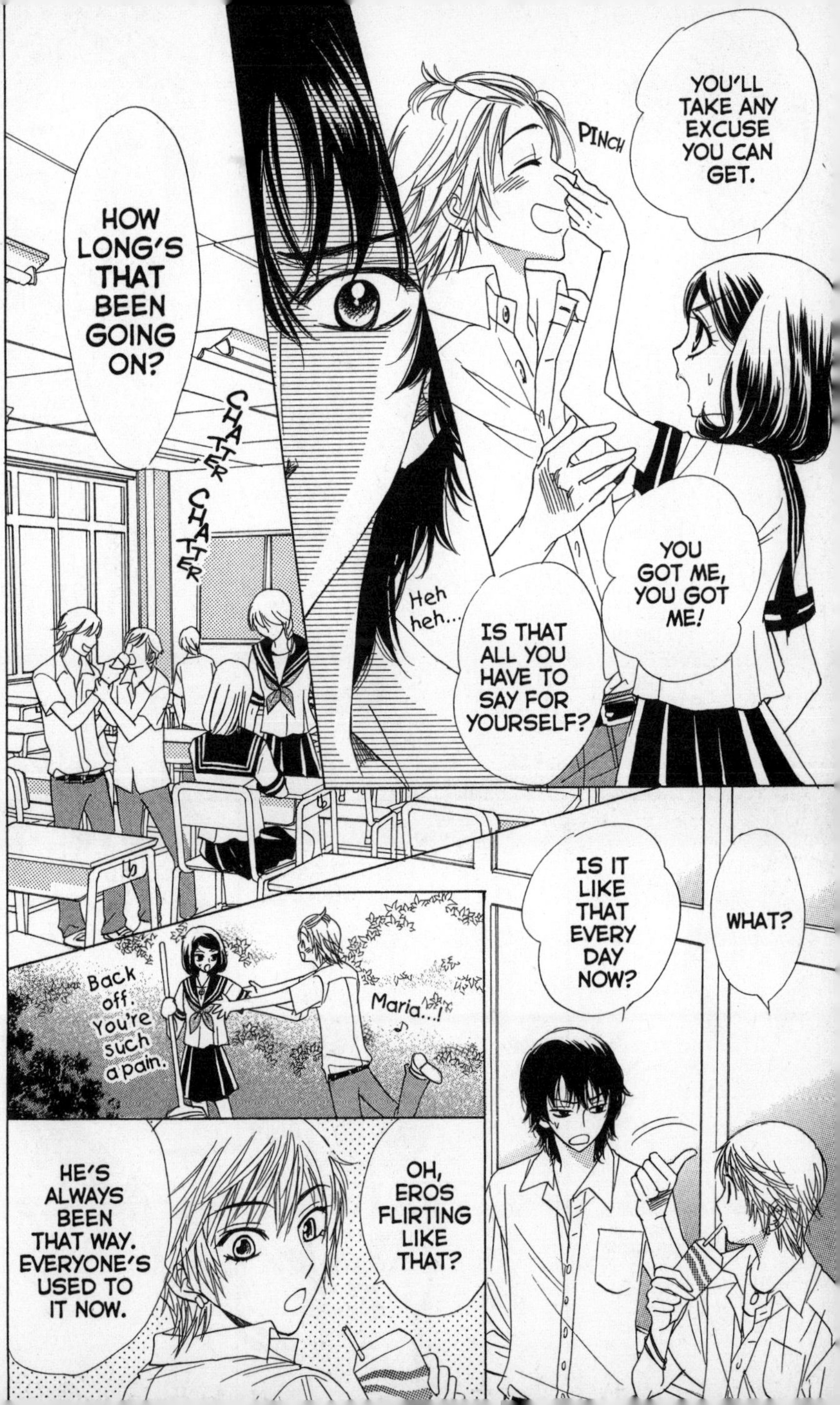
YOU'LL TAKE ANY EXCUSE YOU CAN GET.
PINCH
YOU GOT ME, YOU GOT ME!
IS THAT ALL YOU HAVE TO SAY FOR YOURSELF?
Heh heh...
HOW LONG'S THAT BEEN GOING ON?
CHATTER CHATTER
WHAT?
IS IT LIKE THAT EVERY DAY NOW?
Maria...!
Back off. You're such a pain.
OH, EROS FLIRTING LIKE THAT?
HE'S ALWAYS BEEN THAT WAY. EVERYONE'S USED TO IT NOW.

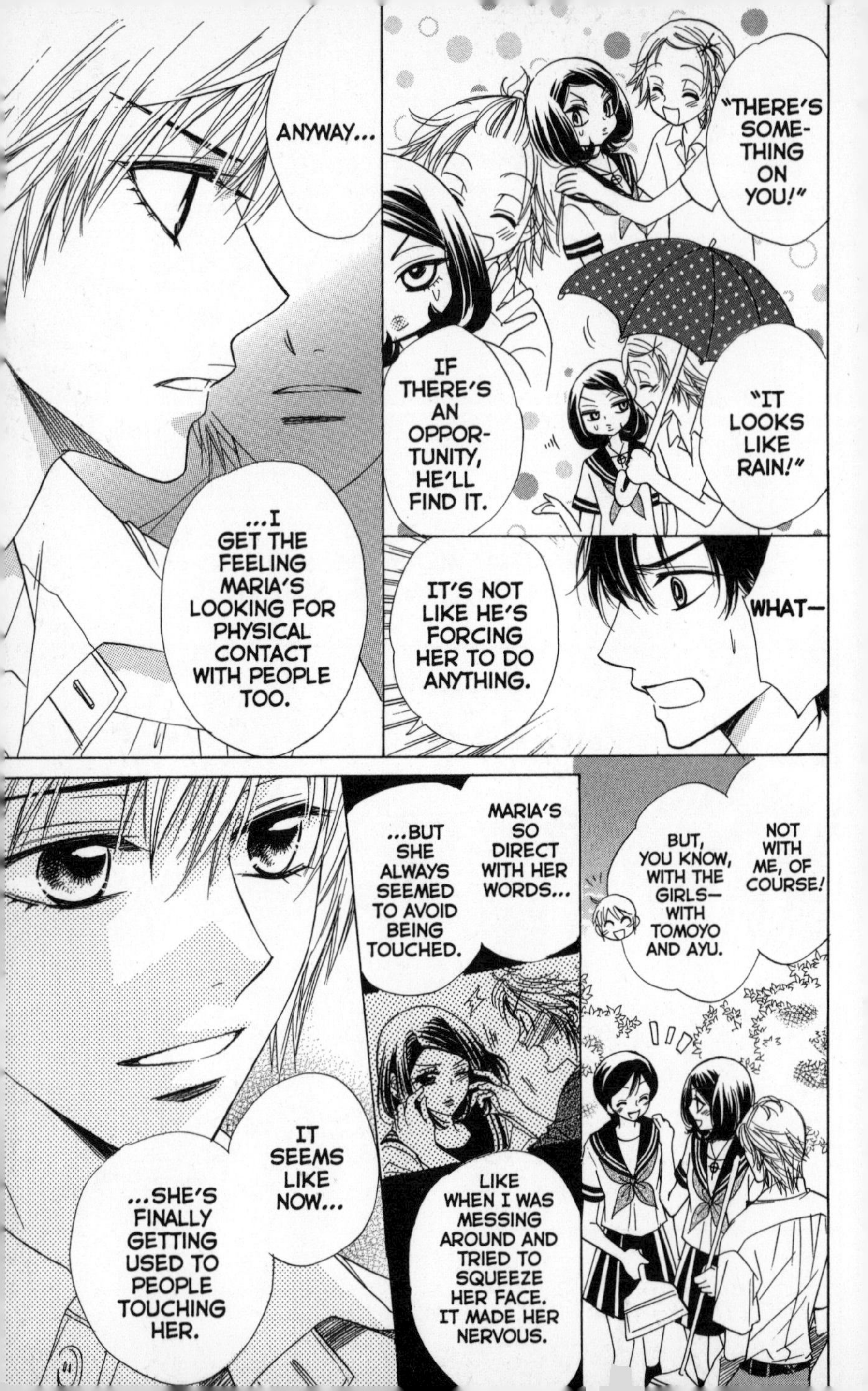
"THERE'S SOMETHING ON YOU!"
"IT LOOKS LIKE RAIN!"
IF THERE'S AN OPPORTUNITY, HE'LL FIND IT.
WHAT—
IT'S NOT LIKE HE'S FORCING HER TO DO ANYTHING.
ANYWAY...
...I GET THE FEELING MARIA'S LOOKING FOR PHYSICAL CONTACT WITH PEOPLE TOO.
NOT WITH ME, OF COURSE!
BUT, YOU KNOW, WITH THE GIRLS— WITH TOMOYO AND AYU.
MARIA'S SO DIRECT WITH HER WORDS...
...BUT SHE ALWAYS SEEMED TO AVOID BEING TOUCHED.
LIKE WHEN I WAS MESSING AROUND AND TRIED TO SQUEEZE HER FACE. IT MADE HER NERVOUS.
IT SEEMS LIKE NOW...
...SHE'S FINALLY GETTING USED TO PEOPLE TOUCHING HER.

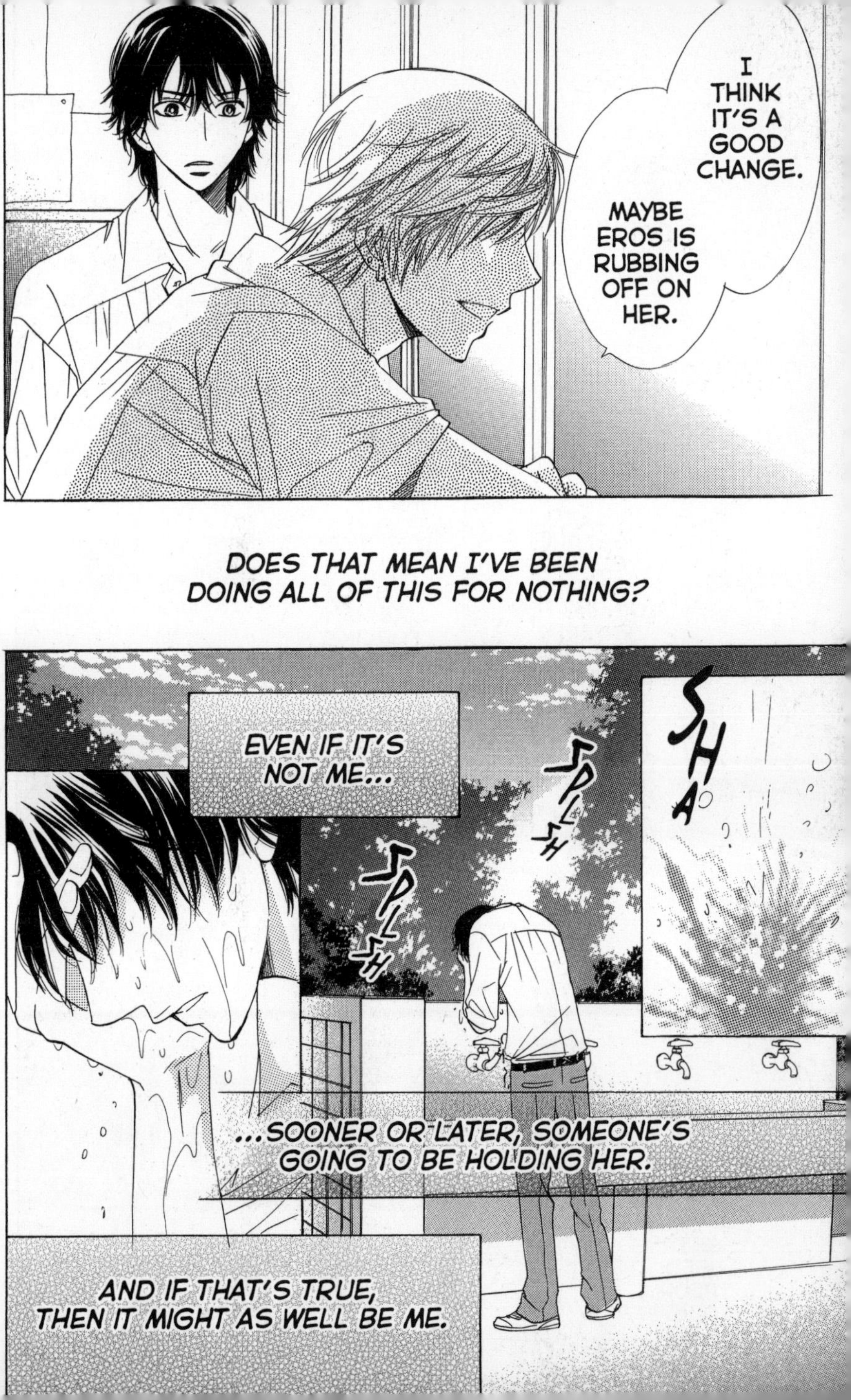
I THINK IT'S A GOOD CHANGE.
MAYBE EROS IS RUBBING OFF ON HER.
DOES THAT MEAN I'VE BEEN DOING ALL OF THIS FOR NOTHING?
SHA
SPLASH
SPLASH
EVEN IF IT'S NOT ME...
...SOONER OR LATER, SOMEONE'S GOING TO BE HOLDING HER.
AND IF THAT'S TRUE, THEN IT MIGHT AS WELL BE ME.

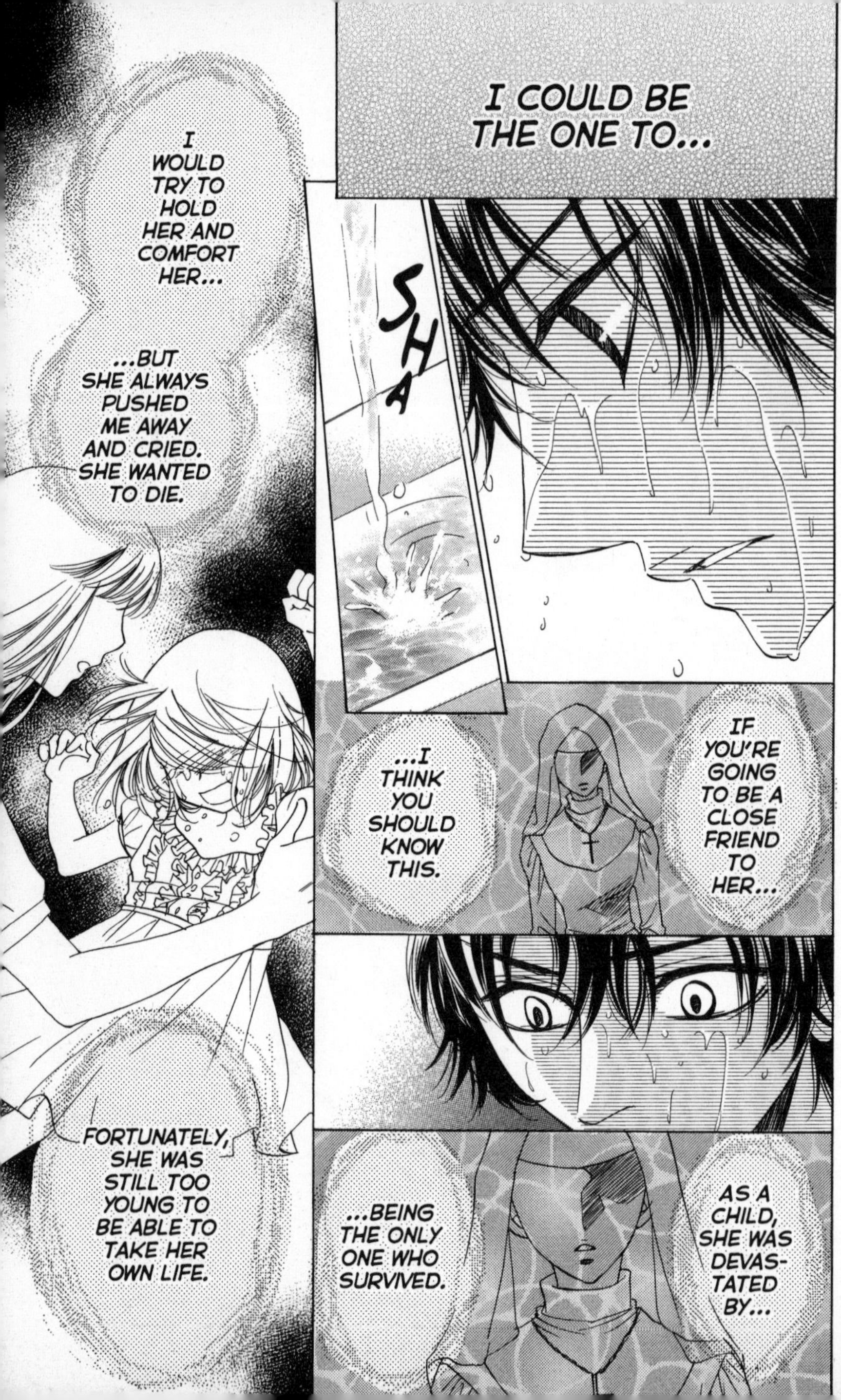
I COULD BE THE ONE TO...
SHA
IF YOU'RE GOING TO BE A CLOSE FRIEND TO HER...
...I THINK YOU SHOULD KNOW THIS.
AS A CHILD, SHE WAS DEVAS-TATED BY...
...BEING THE ONLY ONE WHO SURVIVED.
I WOULD TRY TO HOLD HER AND COMFORT HER...
...BUT SHE ALWAYS PUSHED ME AWAY AND CRIED. SHE WANTED TO DIE.
FORTUNATELY, SHE WAS STILL TOO YOUNG TO BE ABLE TO TAKE HER OWN LIFE.

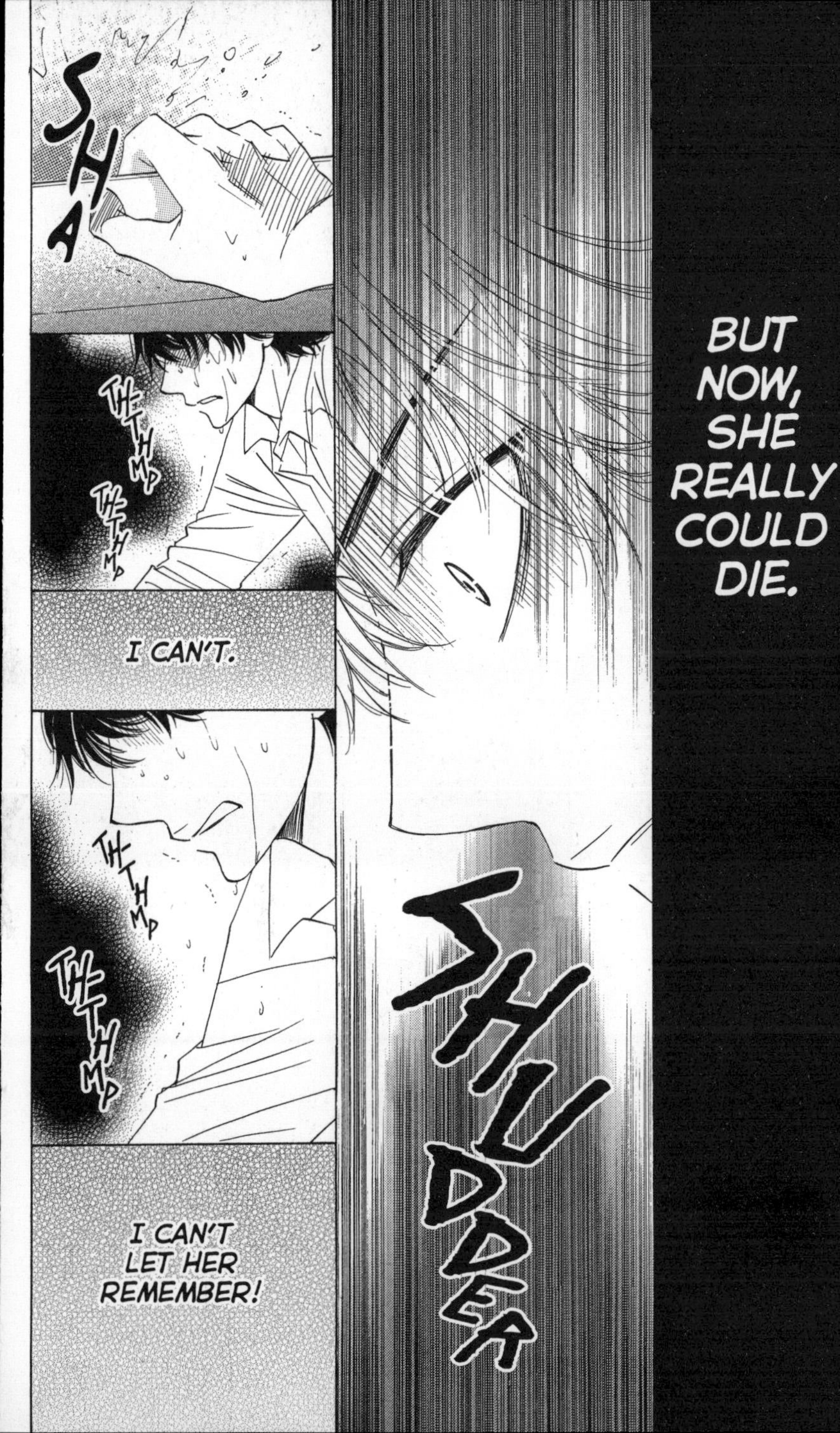
BUT NOW, SHE REALLY COULD DIE.
SHUDDER
SHA
THTHMP THTHMP
I CAN'T.
TH-THMP THTHMP
I CAN'T LET HER REMEMBER!

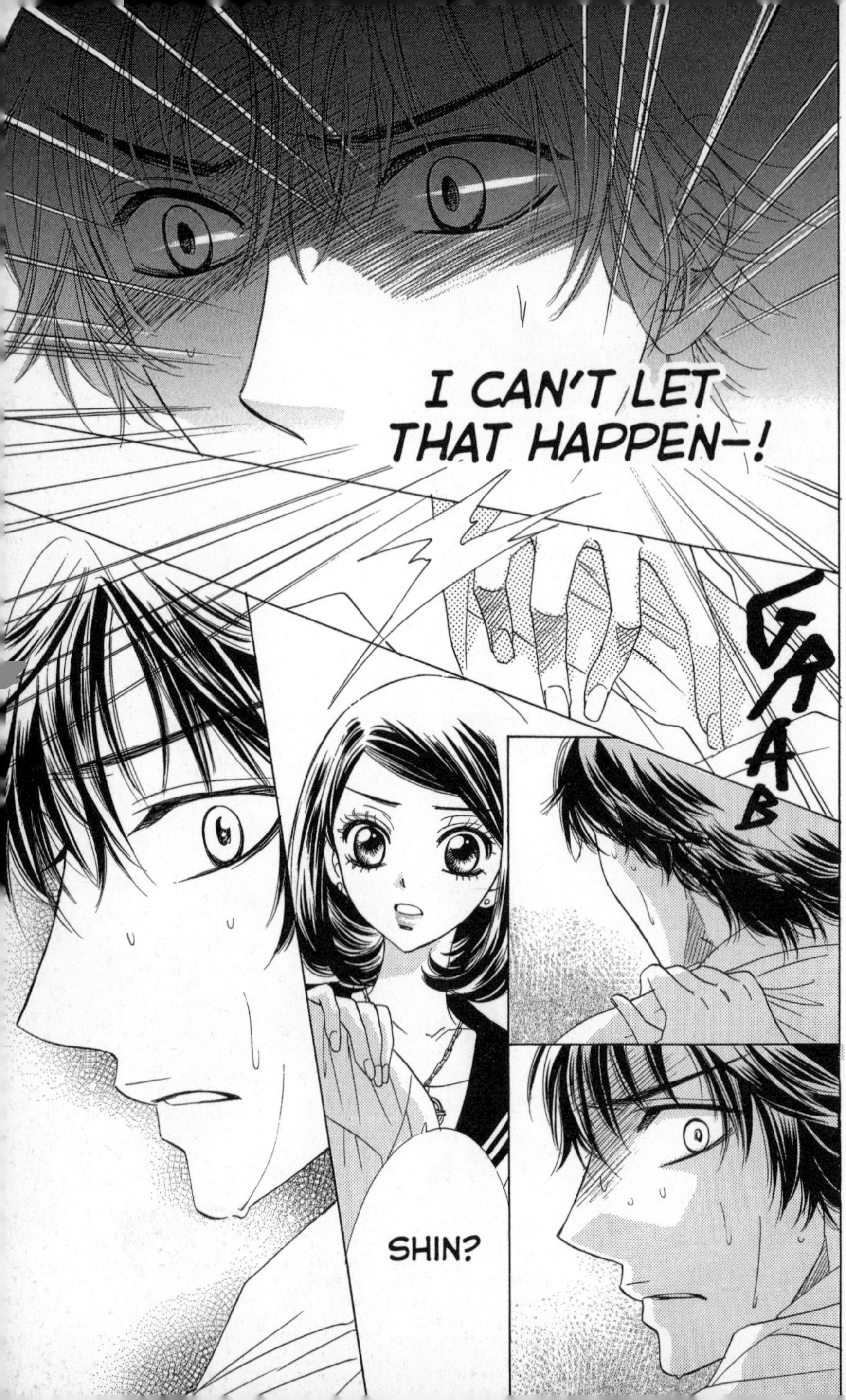
I CAN'T LET THAT HAPPEN-!
GRAB
SHIN?

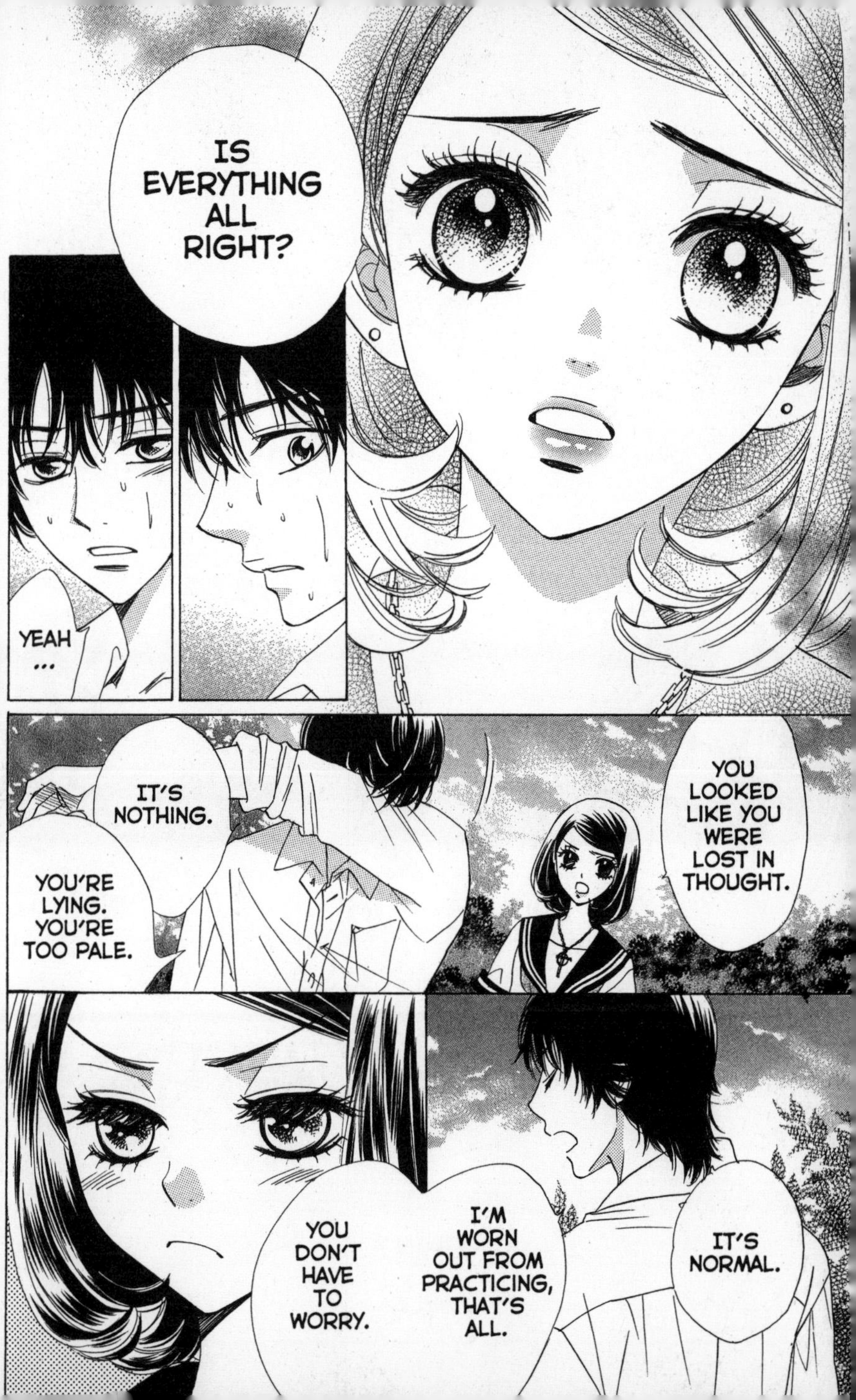
IS EVERYTHING ALL RIGHT?
YEAH ...
YOU LOOKED LIKE YOU WERE LOST IN THOUGHT.
IT'S NOTHING.
YOU'RE LYING. YOU'RE TOO PALE.
IT'S NORMAL.
I'M WORN OUT FROM PRACTICING, THAT'S ALL.
YOU DON'T HAVE TO WORRY.

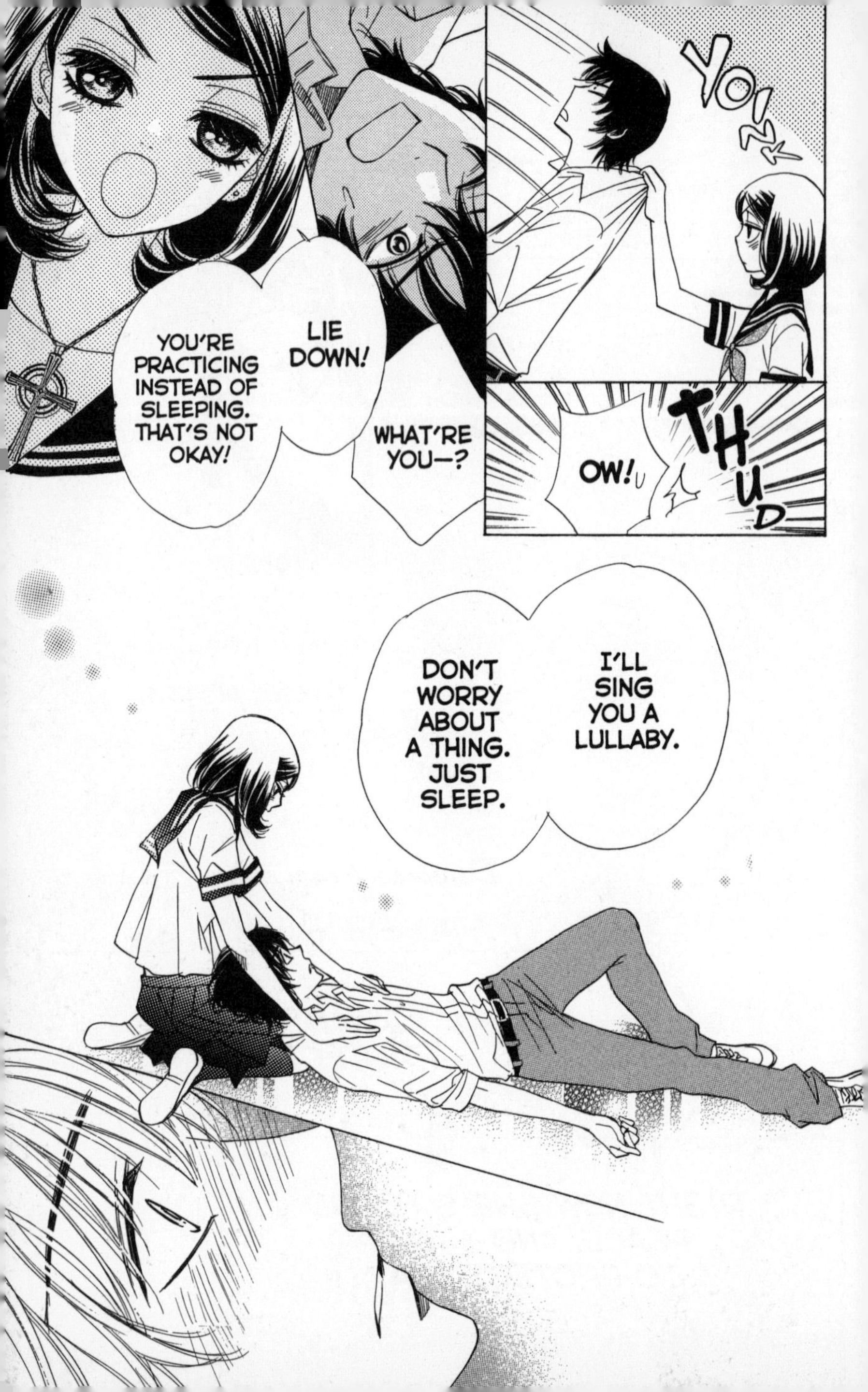
YOINK
OW!
THUD
WHAT'RE YOU—?
LIE DOWN!
YOU'RE PRACTICING INSTEAD OF SLEEPING. THAT'S NOT OKAY!
DON'T WORRY ABOUT A THING. JUST SLEEP.
I'LL SING YOU A LULLABY.

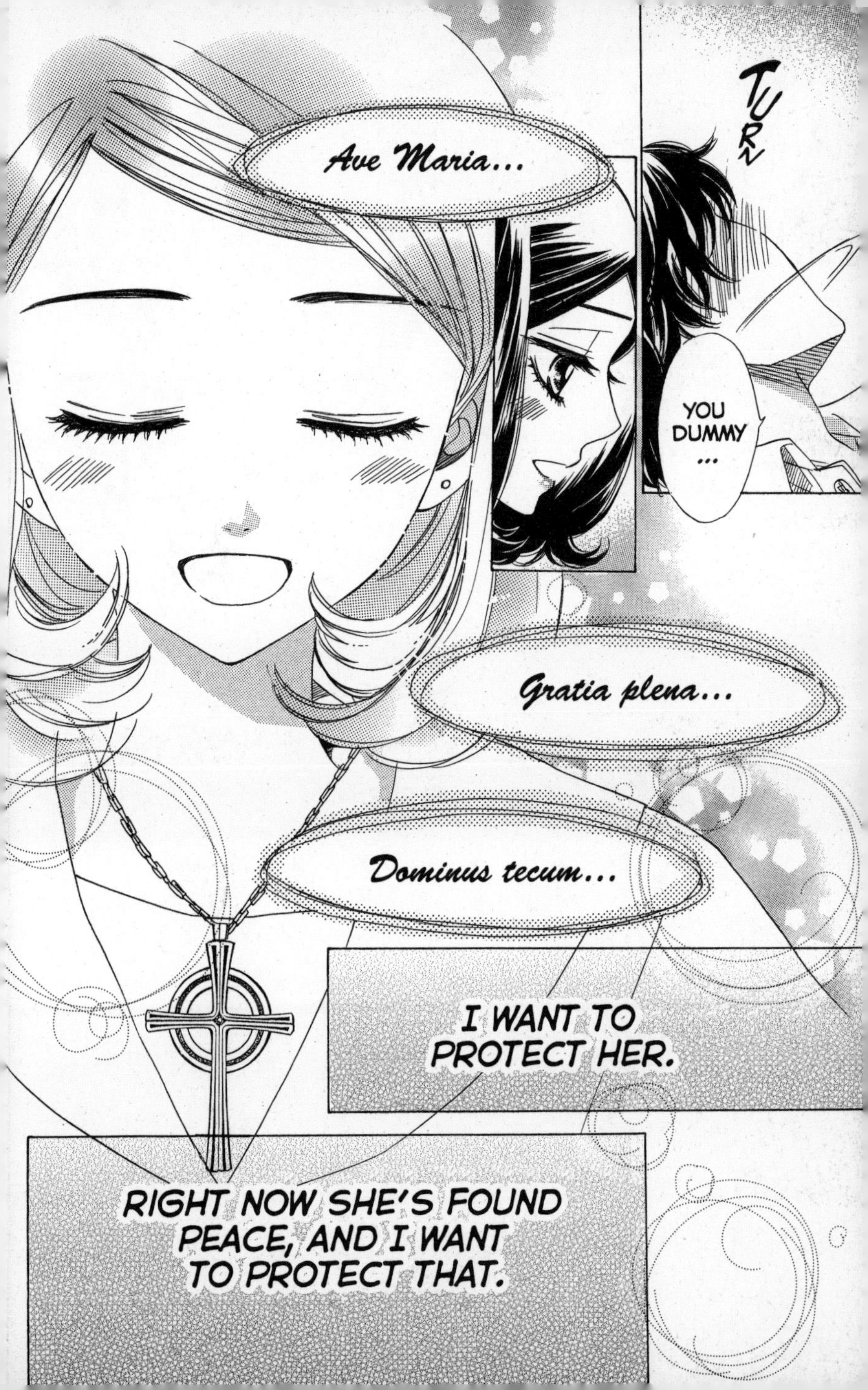
TURN
YOU DUMMY ...
Ave Maria...
Gratia plena...
Dominus tecum...
I WANT TO PROTECT HER.
RIGHT NOW SHE'S FOUND PEACE, AND I WANT TO PROTECT THAT.

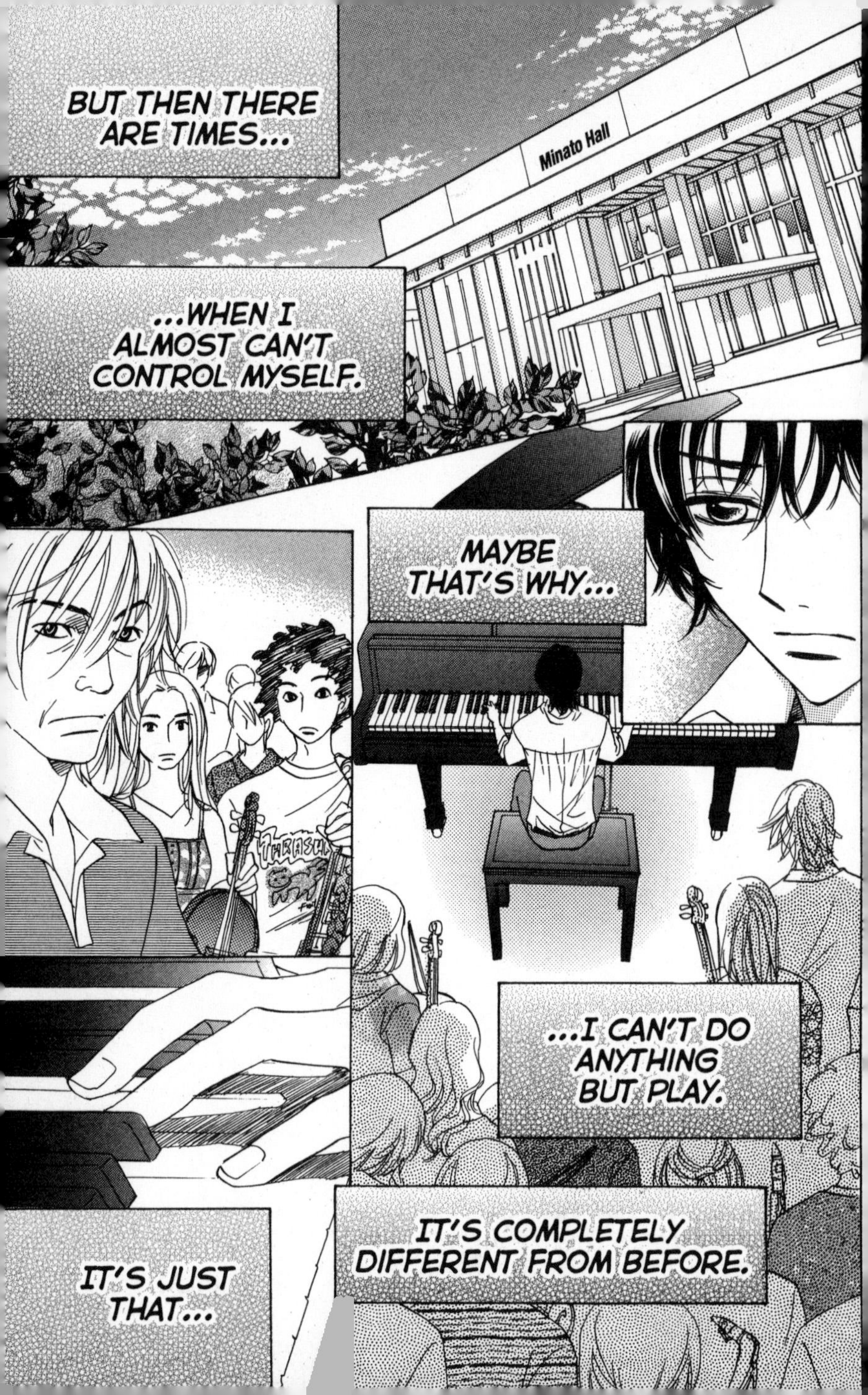
BUT THEN THERE ARE TIMES...
Minato Hall
...WHEN I ALMOST CAN'T CONTROL MYSELF.
MAYBE THAT'S WHY...
...I CAN'T DO ANYTHING BUT PLAY.
IT'S COMPLETELY DIFFERENT FROM BEFORE.
IT'S JUST THAT...

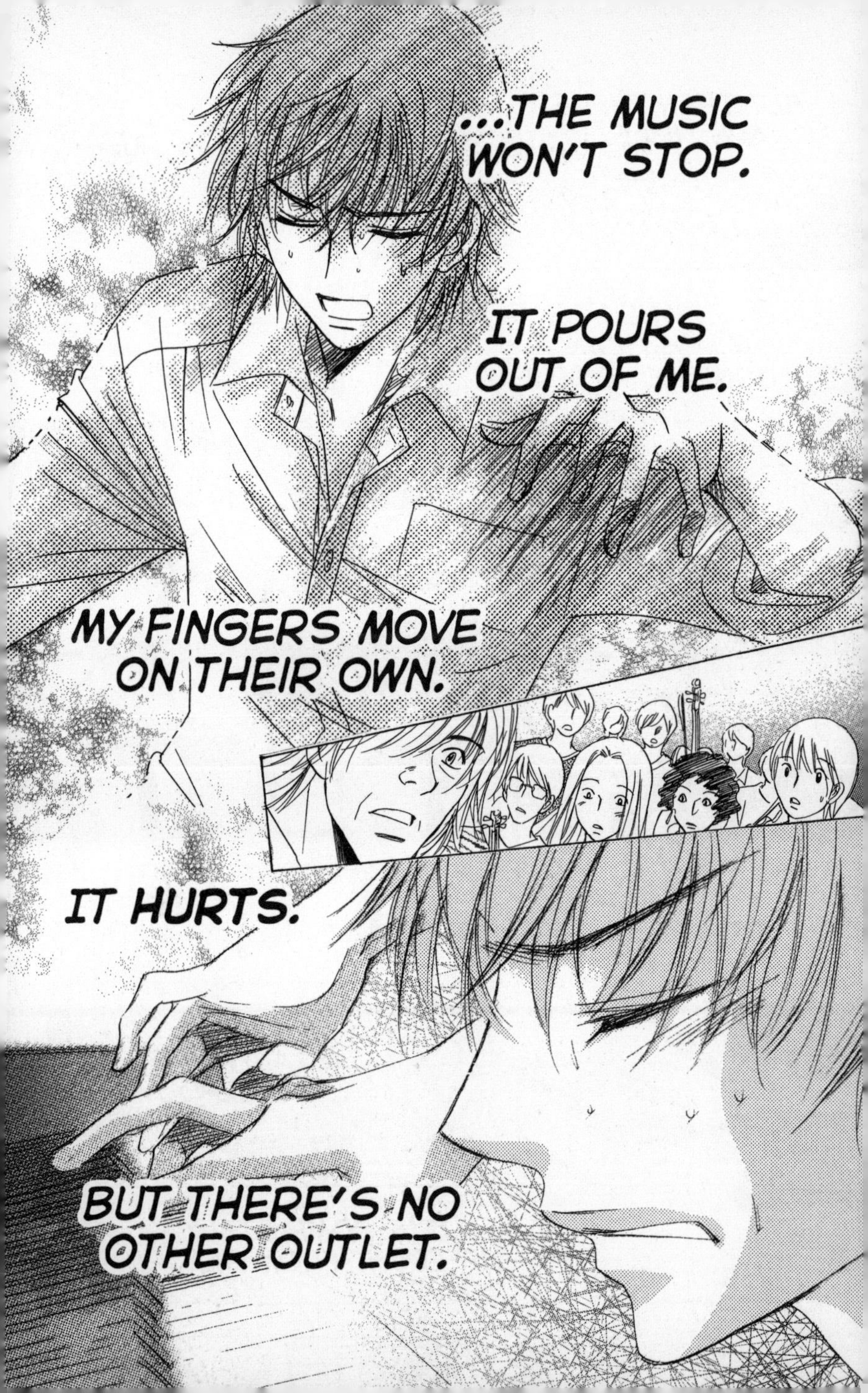
...THE MUSIC WON'T STOP.
IT POURS OUT OF ME.
MY FINGERS MOVE ON THEIR OWN.
IT HURTS.
BUT THERE'S NO OTHER OUTLET.

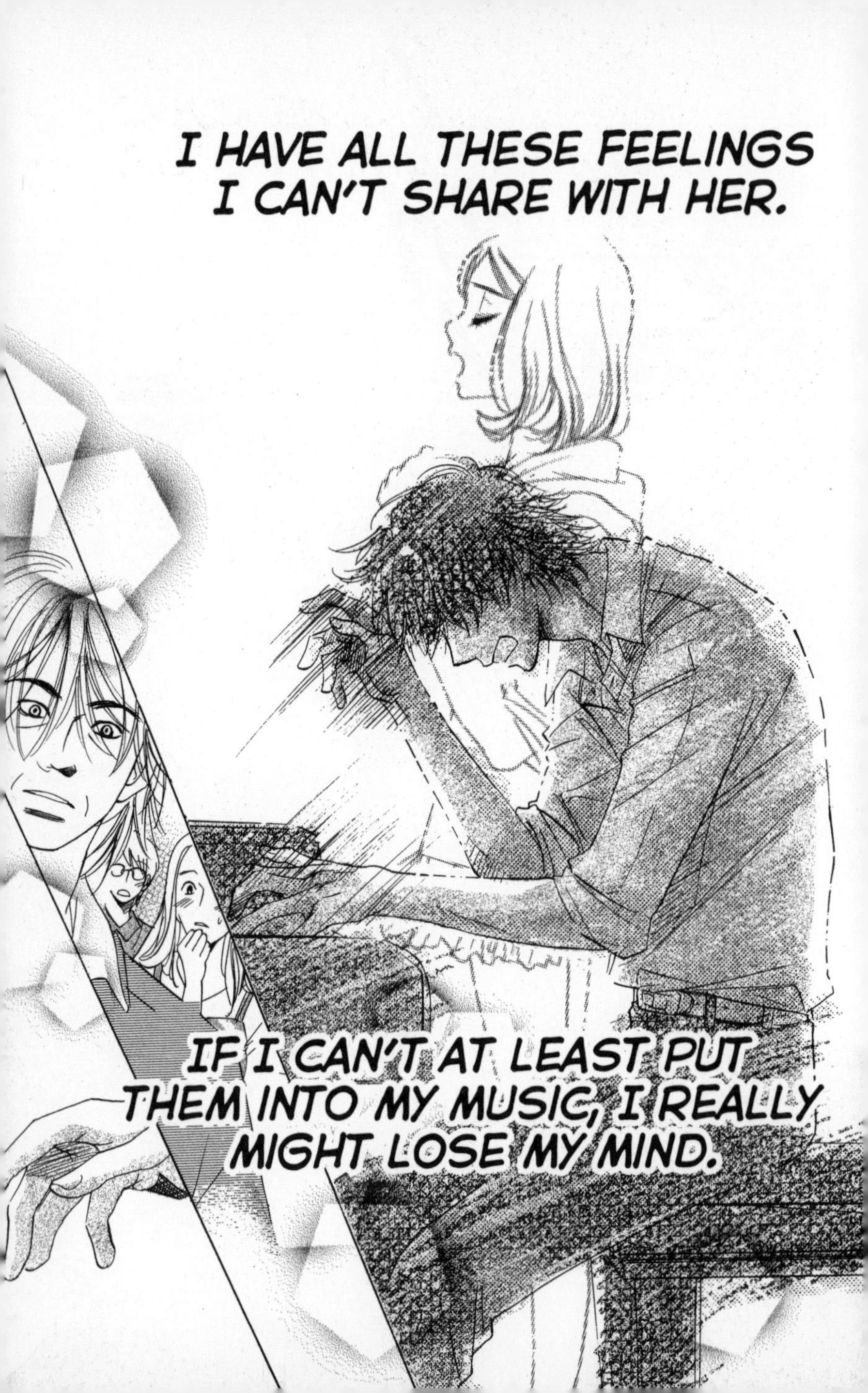
I HAVE ALL THESE FEELINGS I CAN'T SHARE WITH HER.
IF I CAN'T AT LEAST PUT THEM INTO MY MUSIC, I REALLY MIGHT LOSE MY MIND.

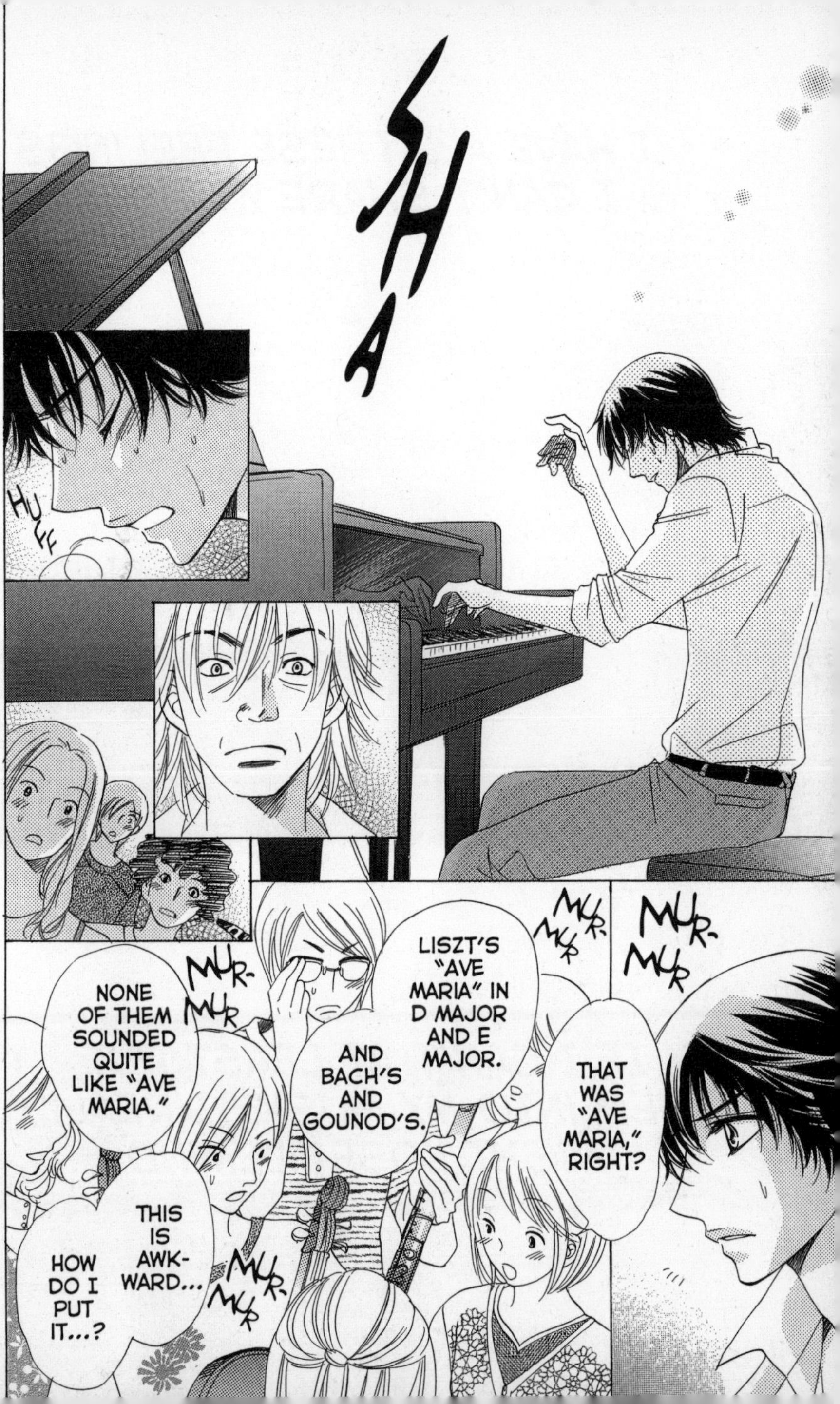
SHA
HUFF
MUR-MUR
MUR-MUR
LISZT'S "AVE MARIA" IN D MAJOR AND E MAJOR.
THAT WAS "AVE MARIA," RIGHT?
MUR-MUR
NONE OF THEM SOUNDED QUITE LIKE "AVE MARIA."
AND BACH'S AND GOUNOD'S.
MUR-MUR
THIS IS AWK-WARD...
HOW DO I PUT IT...?

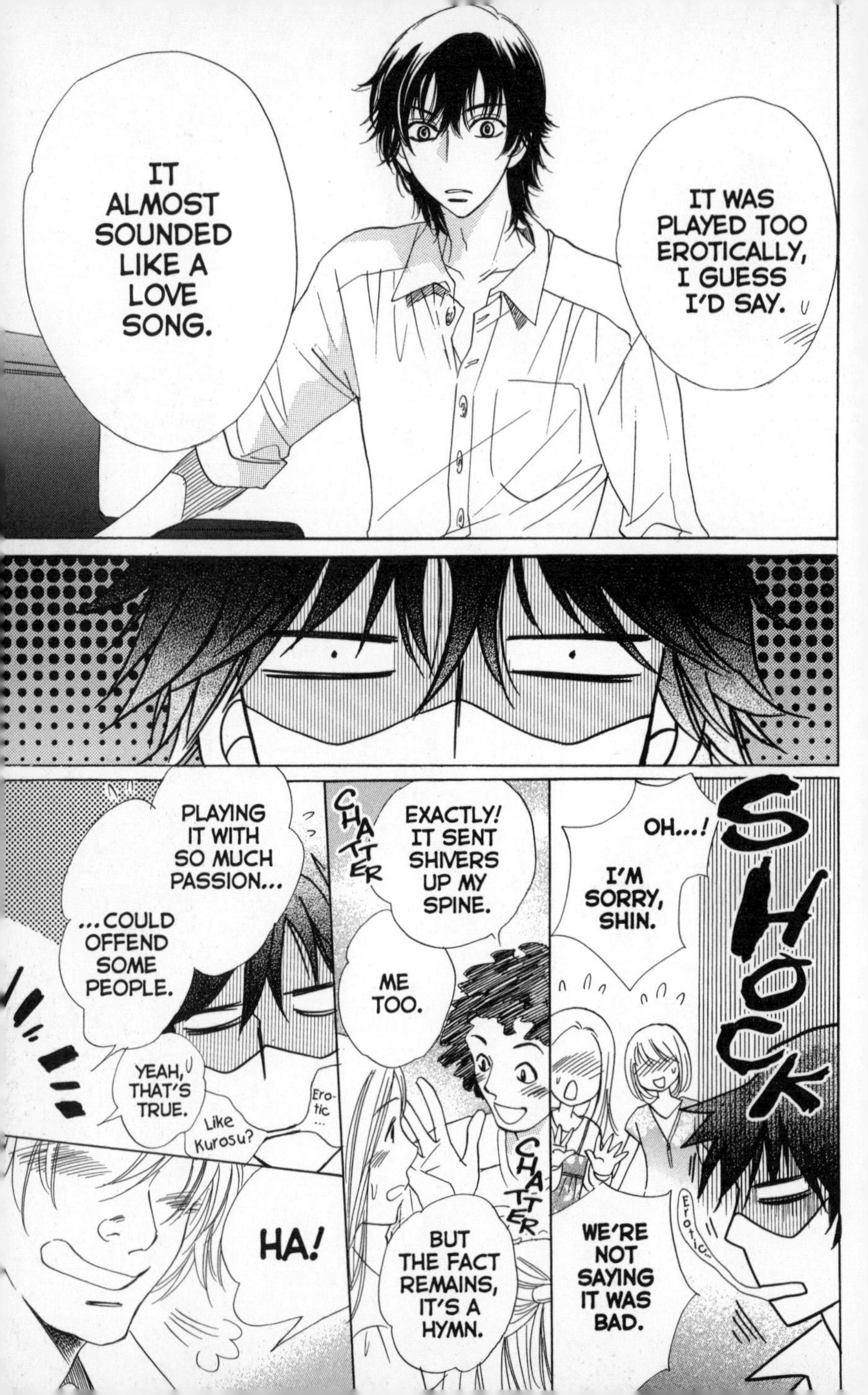
IT WAS PLAYED TOO EROTICALLY, I GUESS I'D SAY.
IT ALMOST SOUNDED LIKE A LOVE SONG.
SHOCK
OH...!
I'M SORRY, SHIN.
WE'RE NOT SAYING IT WAS BAD.
Erotic...
EXACTLY! IT SENT SHIVERS UP MY SPINE.
CHATTER
ME TOO.
CHATTER
BUT THE FACT REMAINS, IT'S A HYMN.
PLAYING IT WITH SO MUCH PASSION...
...COULD OFFEND SOME PEOPLE.
YEAH, THAT'S TRUE.
Erotic...
Like Kurosu?
HA!

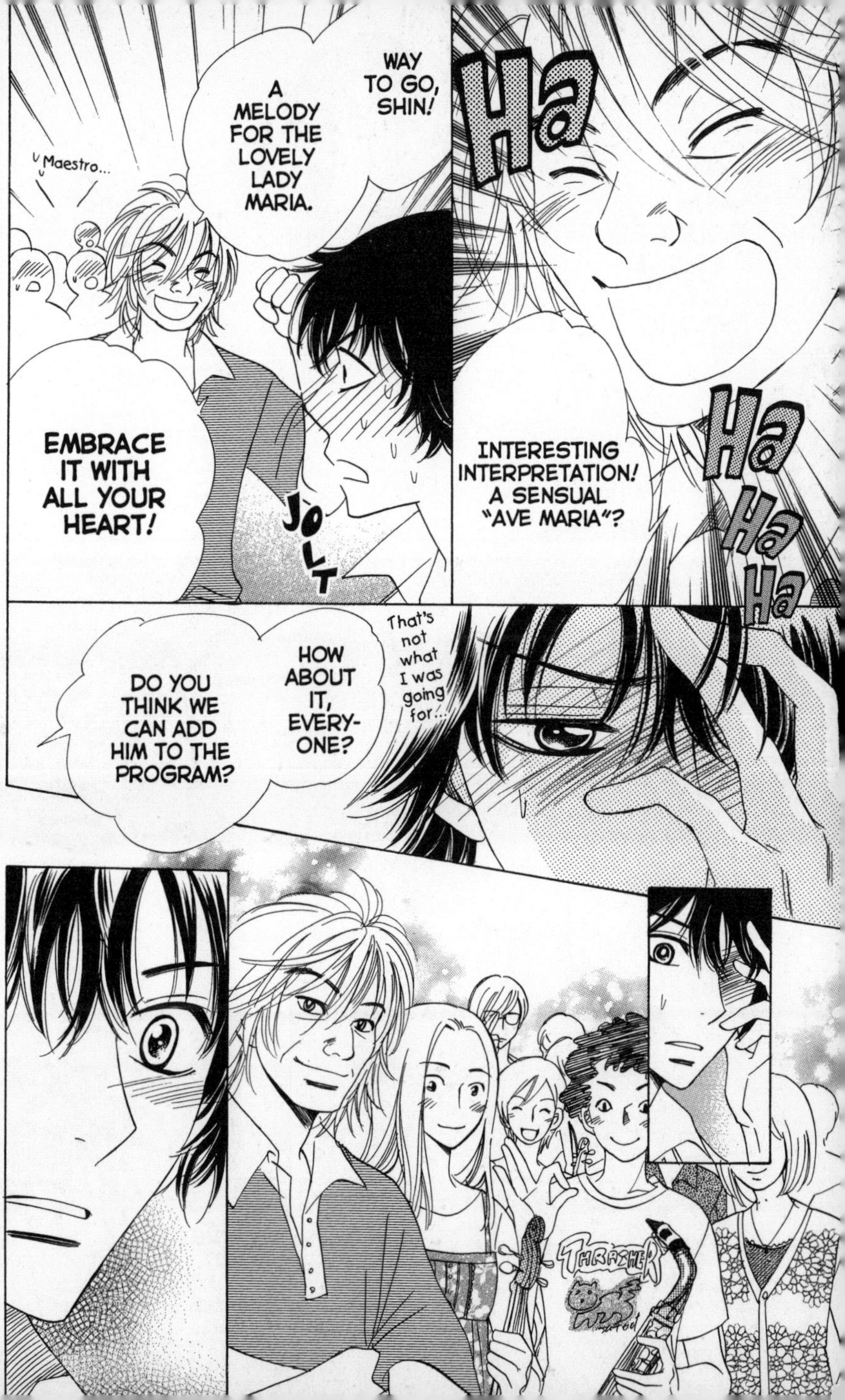
Ha
Ha Ha Ha Ha
INTERESTING INTERPRETATION! A SENSUAL "AVE MARIA"?
WAY TO GO, SHIN!
A MELODY FOR THE LOVELY LADY MARIA.
Maestro...
EMBRACE IT WITH ALL YOUR HEART!
JOLT
That's not what I was going for...
HOW ABOUT IT, EVERYONE?
DO YOU THINK WE CAN ADD HIM TO THE PROGRAM?
THRASHER

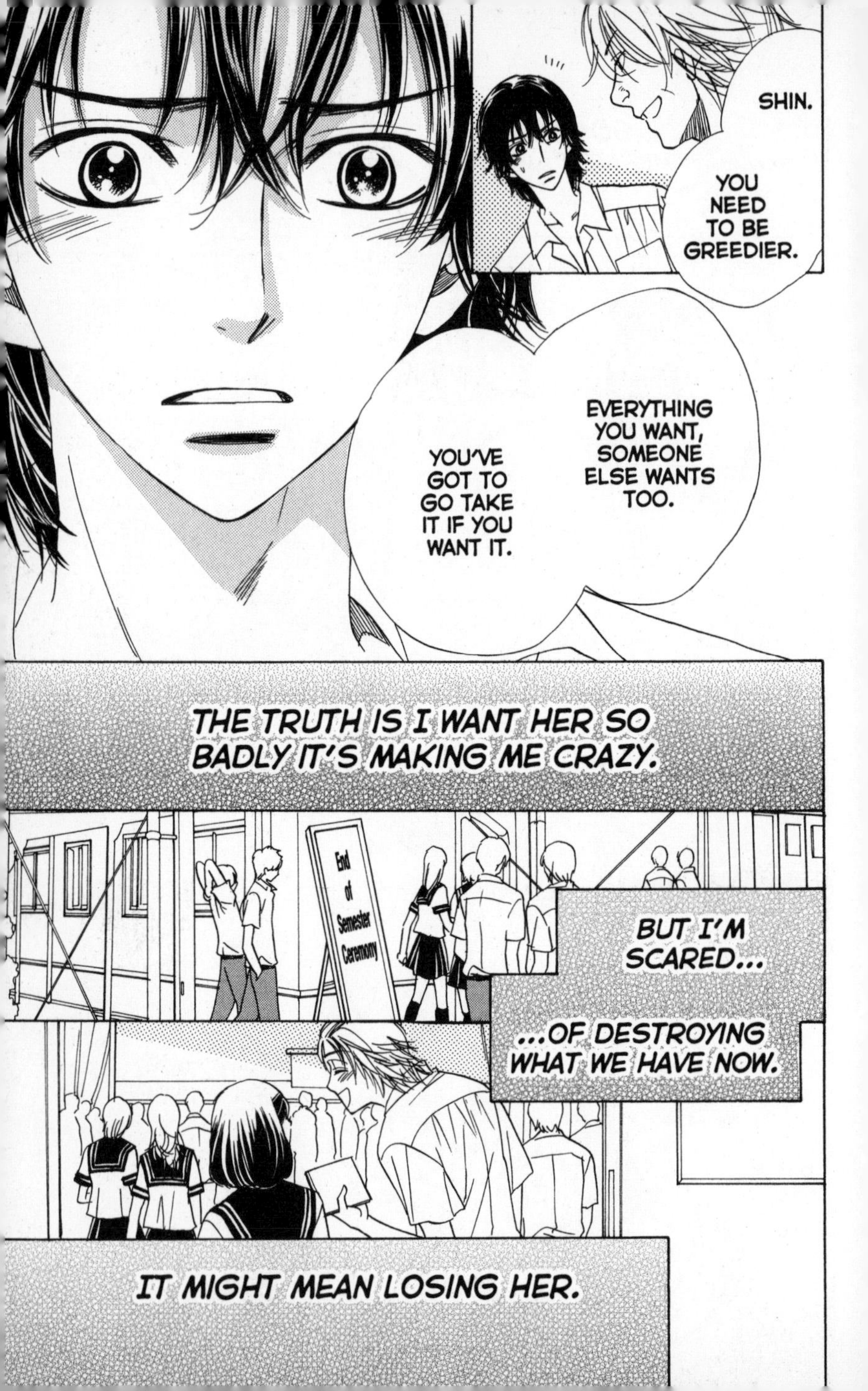
SHIN.
YOU NEED TO BE GREEDIER.
EVERYTHING YOU WANT, SOMEONE ELSE WANTS TOO.
YOU'VE GOT TO GO TAKE IT IF YOU WANT IT.
THE TRUTH IS I WANT HER SO BADLY IT'S MAKING ME CRAZY.
End of Semester Ceremony
BUT I'M SCARED...
...OF DESTROYING WHAT WE HAVE NOW.
IT MIGHT MEAN LOSING HER.

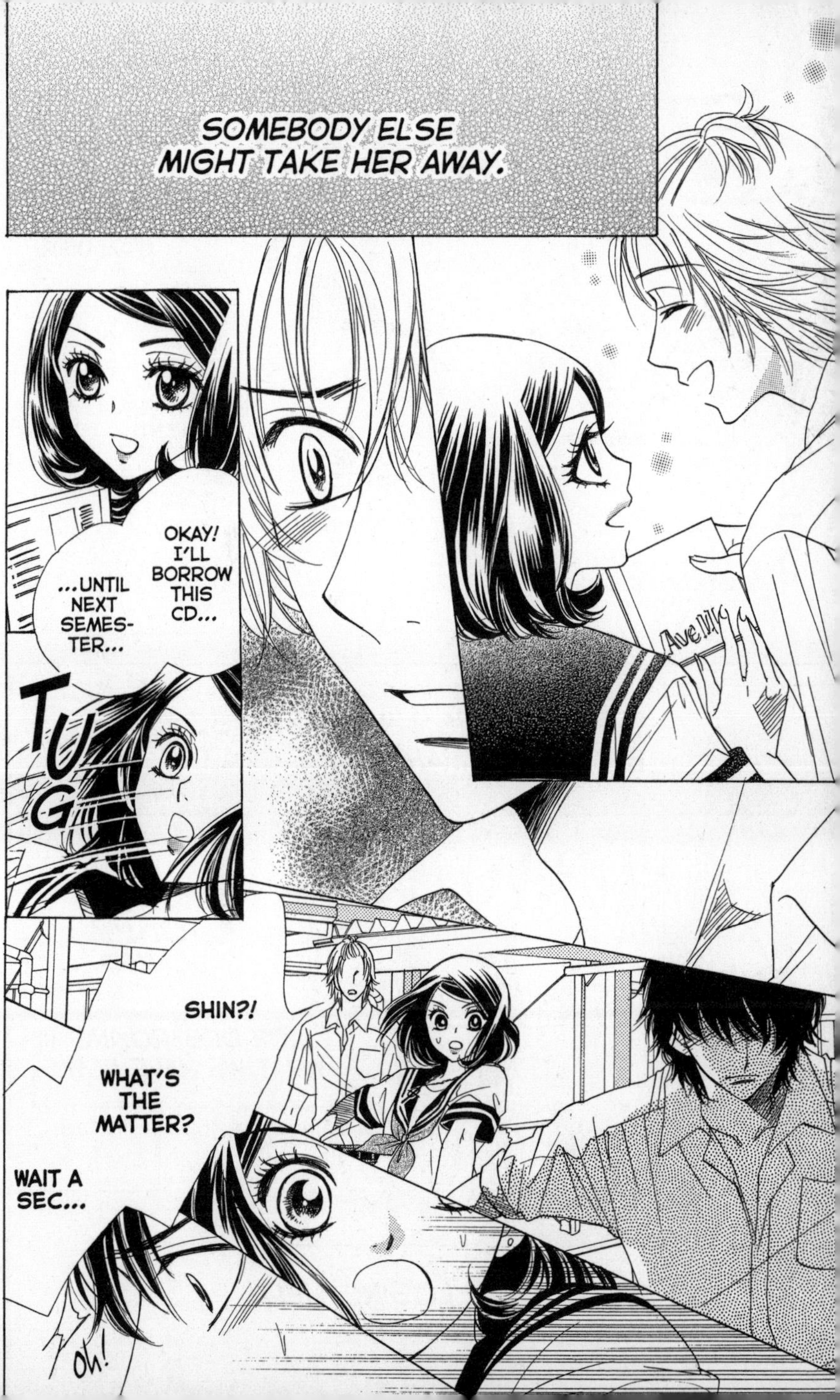
SOMEBODY ELSE MIGHT TAKE HER AWAY.
Ave Maria
OKAY! I'LL BORROW THIS CD...
...UNTIL NEXT SEMESTER...
TUG
SHIN?!
WHAT'S THE MATTER?
WAIT A SEC...
Oh!

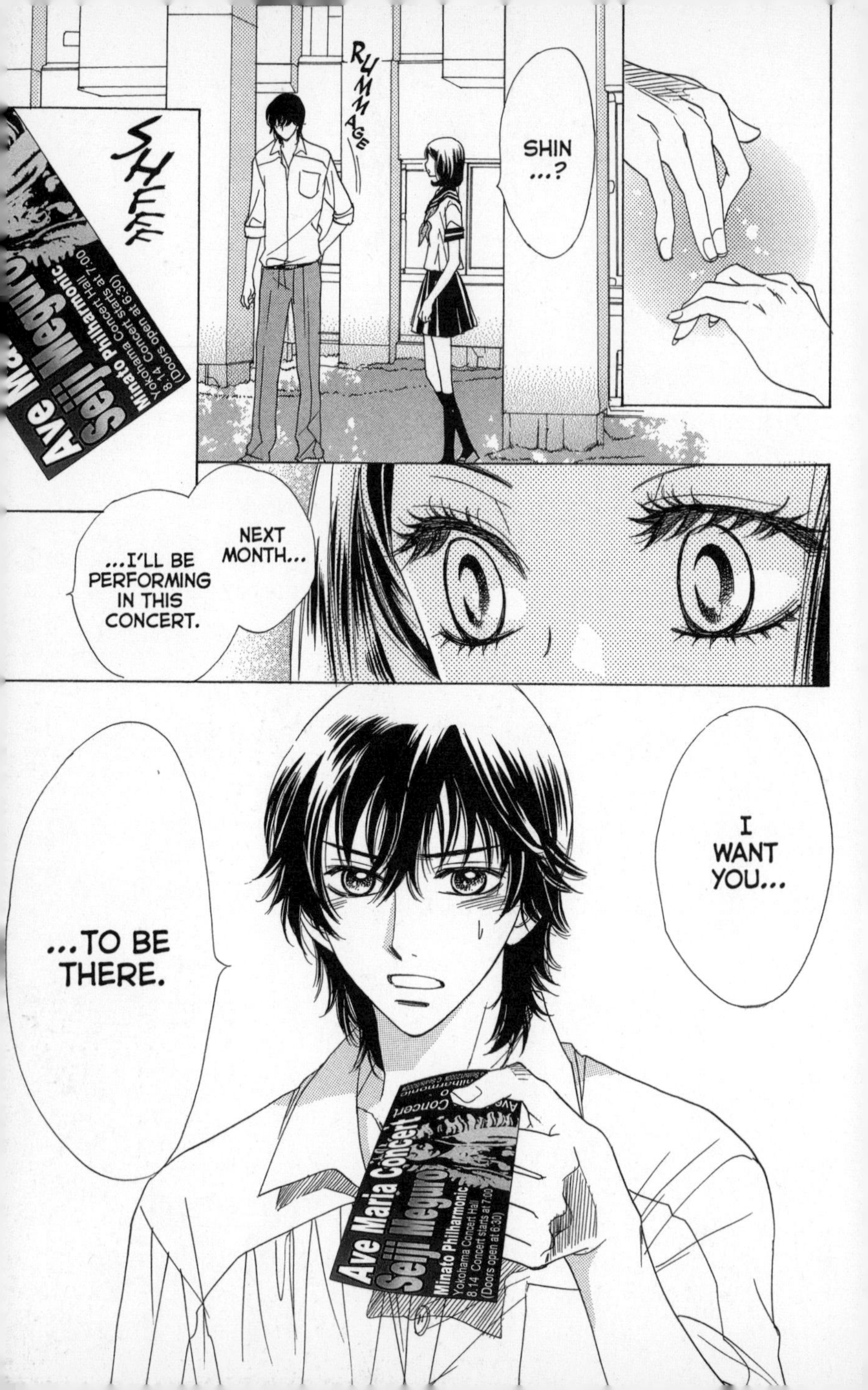
SHIN ...?
RUMMAGE
SHFFF
Ave Maria Concert
Seiji Meguro
Minato Philharmonic
Yokohama Concert Hall
8.14 Concert starts at 7:00
(Doors open at 6:30)
NEXT MONTH...
...I'LL BE PERFORMING IN THIS CONCERT.
I WANT YOU...
...TO BE THERE.

A Devil and
Her Love Song

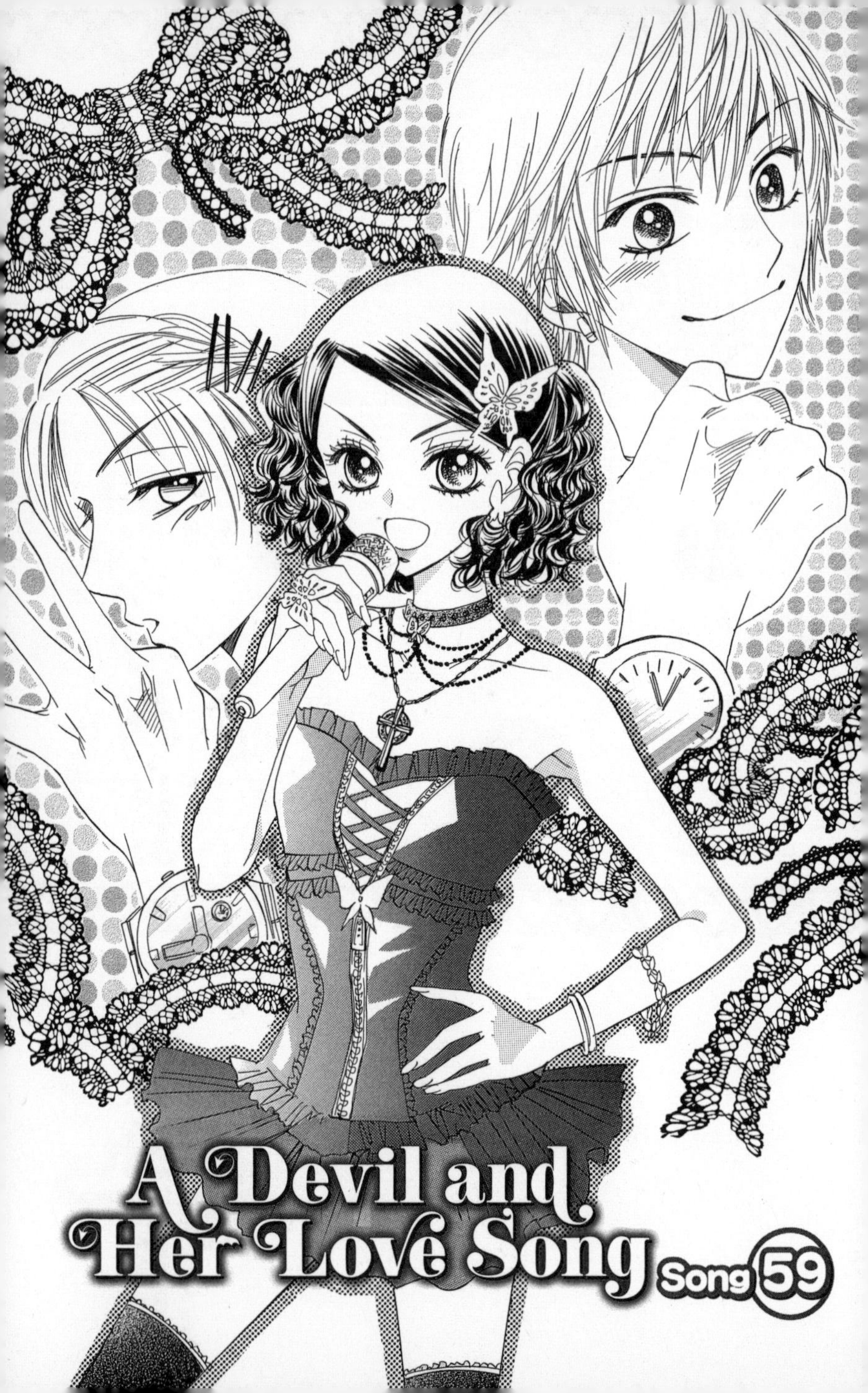
A Devil and Her Love Song
Song 59

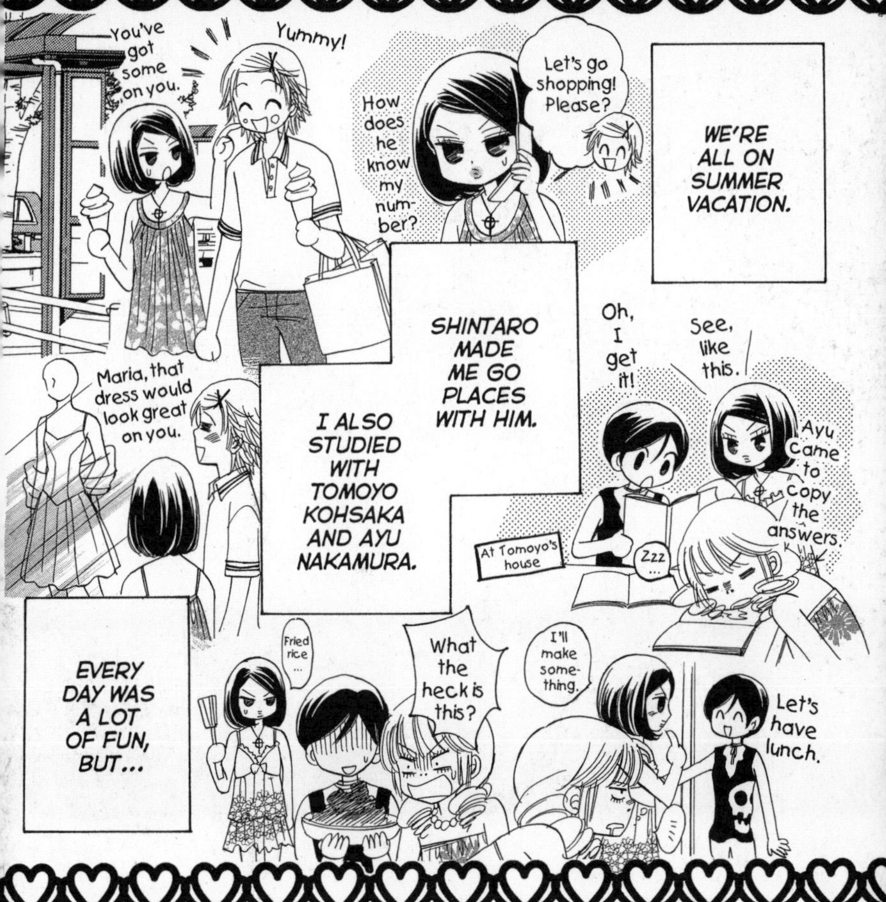
WE'RE ALL ON SUMMER VACATION.
Let's go shopping! Please?
How does he know my number?
Yummy!
You've got some on you.
SHINTARO MADE ME GO PLACES WITH HIM.
Maria, that dress would look great on you.
See, like this.
Oh, I get it!
Ayu came to copy the answers.
At Tomoyo's house
Zzz...
I ALSO STUDIED WITH TOMOYO KOHSAKA AND AYU NAKAMURA.
Let's have lunch.
I'll make something.
What the heck is this?
Fried rice...
EVERY DAY WAS A LOT OF FUN, BUT...

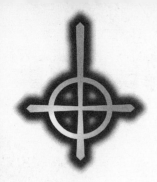

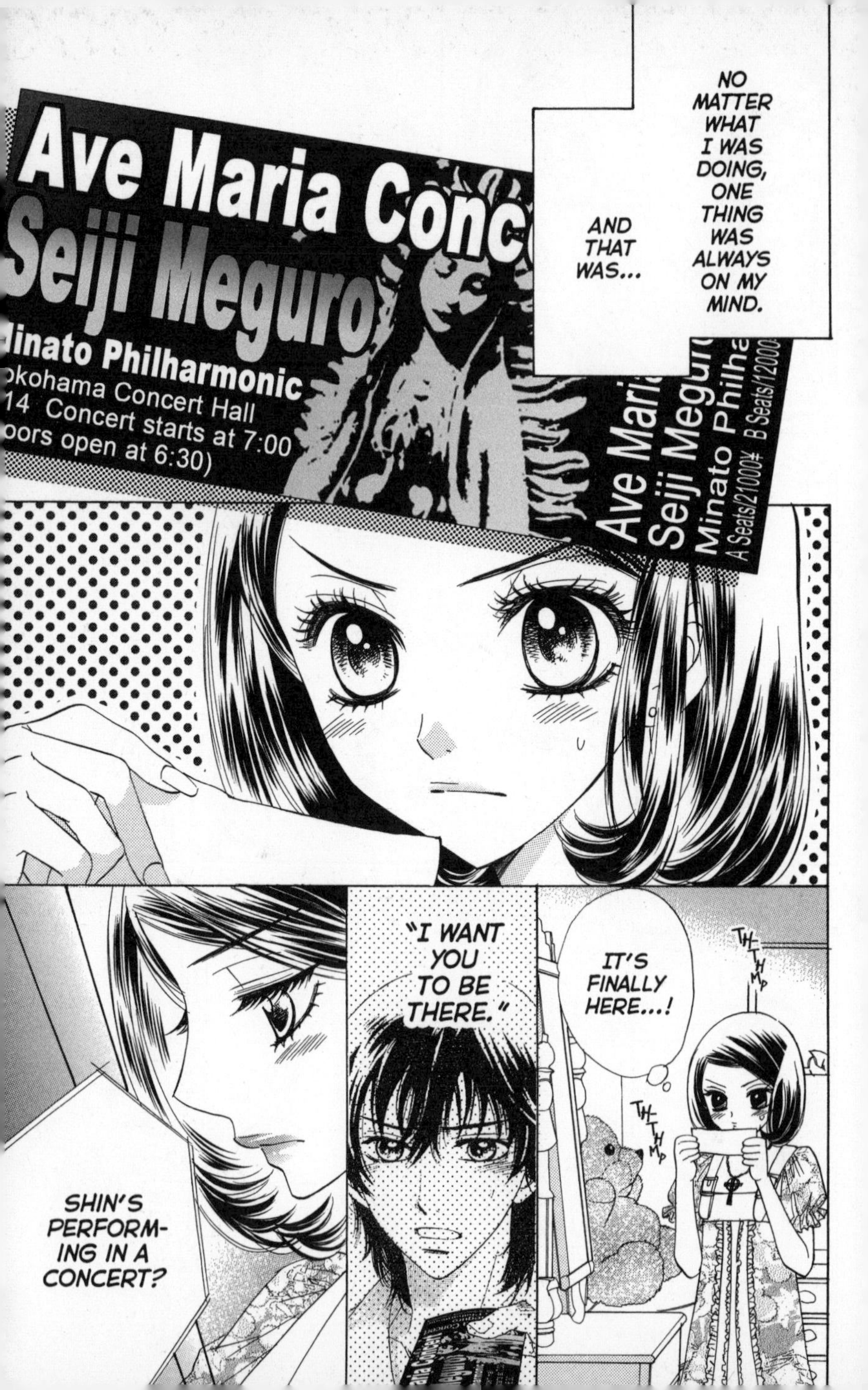
NO MATTER WHAT I WAS DOING, ONE THING WAS ALWAYS ON MY MIND.
AND THAT WAS...
Ave Maria Conc
Seiji Meguro
linato Philharmonic
okohama Concert Hall
14 Concert starts at 7:00
oors open at 6:30)
Ave Mari
Seiji Megur
Minato Philha
A Seats/21000¥ B Seats/12000
TH-THMP
IT'S FINALLY HERE...!
TH-THMP
"I WANT YOU TO BE THERE."
SHIN'S PERFORM-ING IN A CONCERT?

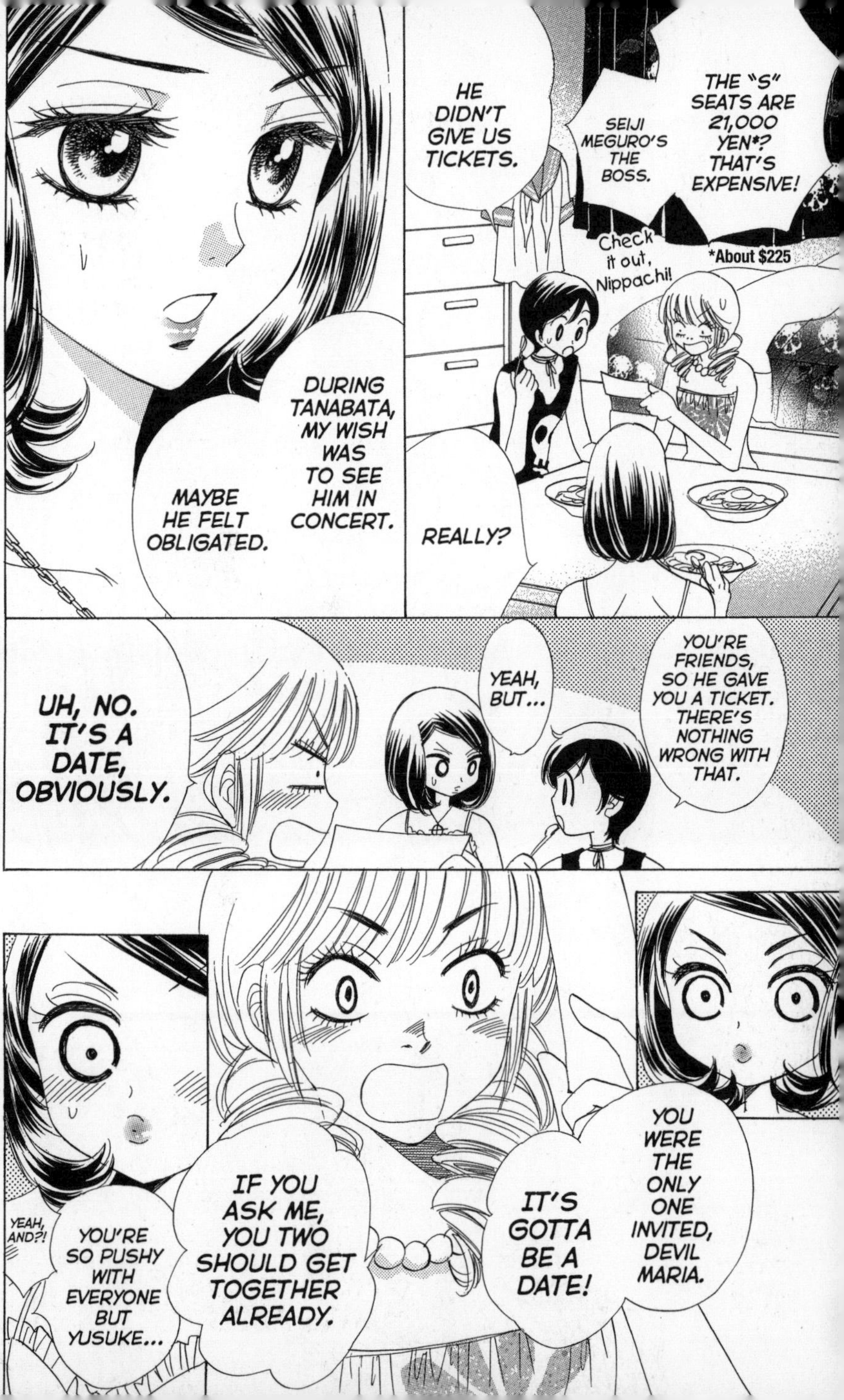
THE "S" SEATS ARE 21,000 YEN*? THAT'S EXPENSIVE!
SEIJI MEGURO'S THE BOSS.
HE DIDN'T GIVE US TICKETS.
Check it out, Nippachi!
*About $225
REALLY?
DURING TANABATA, MY WISH WAS TO SEE HIM IN CONCERT.
MAYBE HE FELT OBLIGATED.
YOU'RE FRIENDS, SO HE GAVE YOU A TICKET. THERE'S NOTHING WRONG WITH THAT.
YEAH, BUT...
UH, NO. IT'S A DATE, OBVIOUSLY.
YOU WERE THE ONLY ONE INVITED, DEVIL MARIA.
IT'S GOTTA BE A DATE!
IF YOU ASK ME, YOU TWO SHOULD GET TOGETHER ALREADY.
YOU'RE SO PUSHY WITH EVERYONE BUT YUSUKE...
YEAH, AND?!

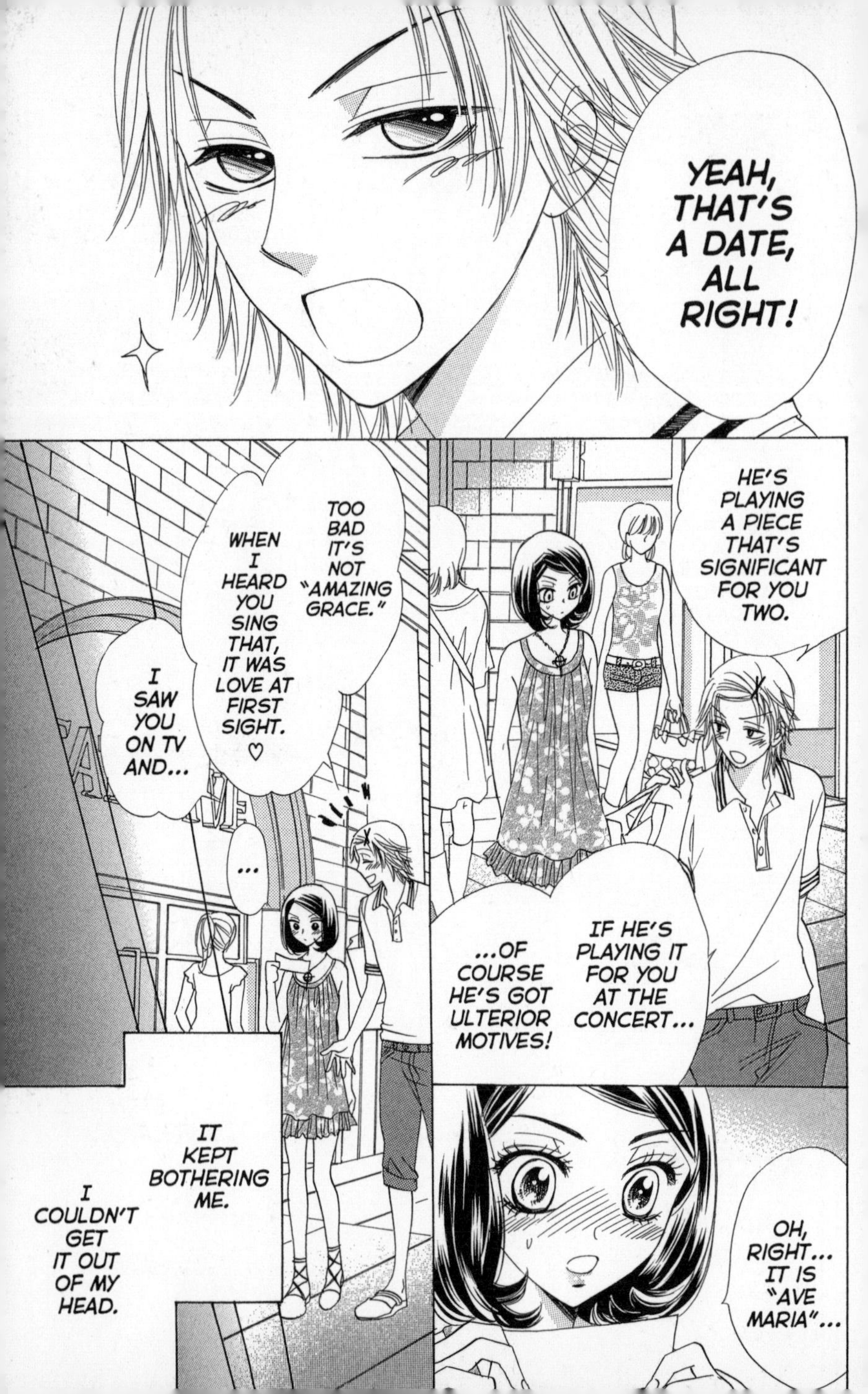
YEAH, THAT'S A DATE, ALL RIGHT!
HE'S PLAYING A PIECE THAT'S SIGNIFICANT FOR YOU TWO.
IF HE'S PLAYING IT FOR YOU AT THE CONCERT...
...OF COURSE HE'S GOT ULTERIOR MOTIVES!
OH, RIGHT... IT IS "AVE MARIA"...
TOO BAD IT'S NOT "AMAZING GRACE."
WHEN I HEARD YOU SING THAT, IT WAS LOVE AT FIRST SIGHT. ♡
I SAW YOU ON TV AND...
...
IT KEPT BOTHERING ME.
I COULDN'T GET IT OUT OF MY HEAD.

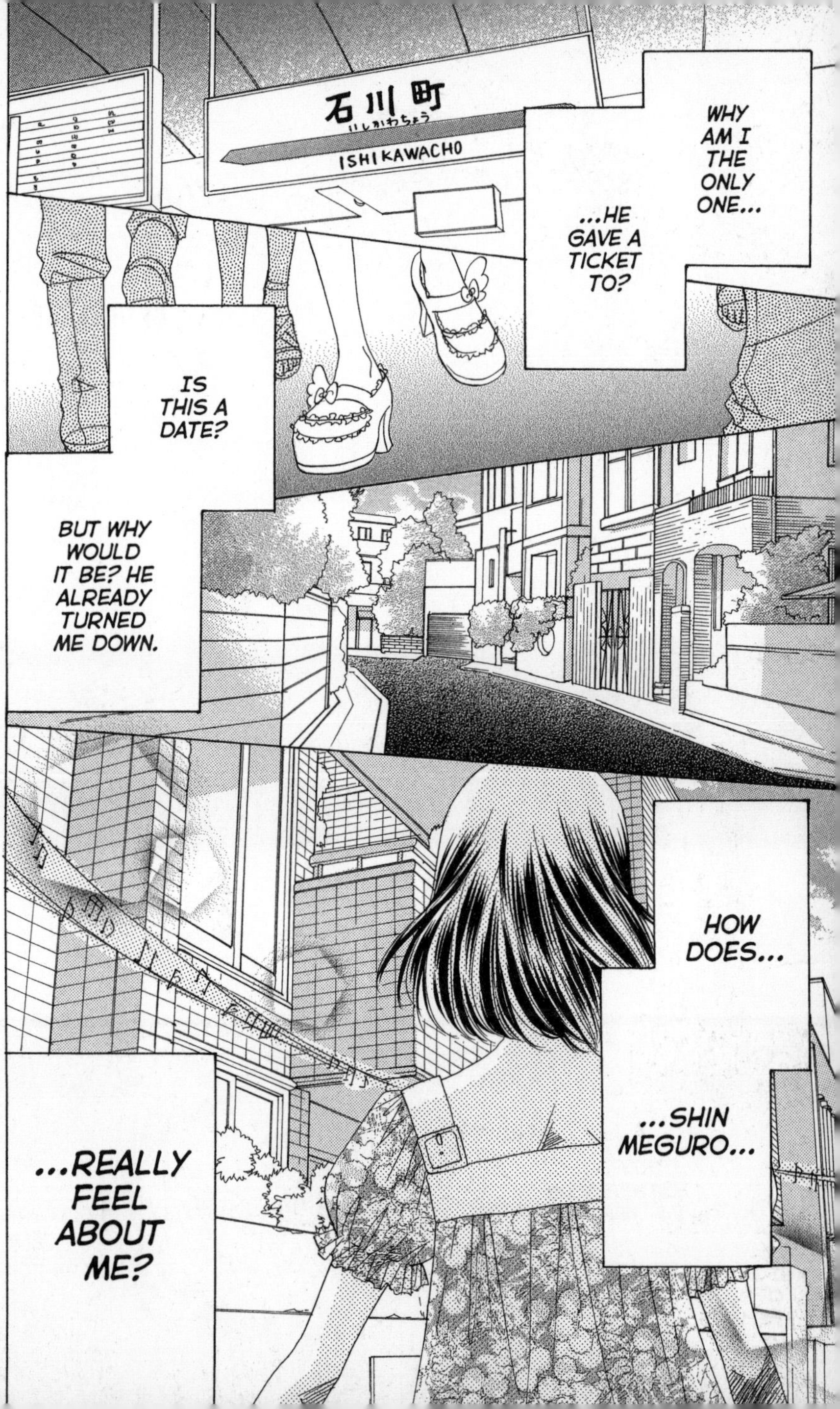
石川町
いしかわちょう
ISHIKAWACHO
WHY AM I THE ONLY ONE...
...HE GAVE A TICKET TO?
IS THIS A DATE?
BUT WHY WOULD IT BE? HE ALREADY TURNED ME DOWN.
HOW DOES...
...SHIN MEGURO...
...REALLY FEEL ABOUT ME?

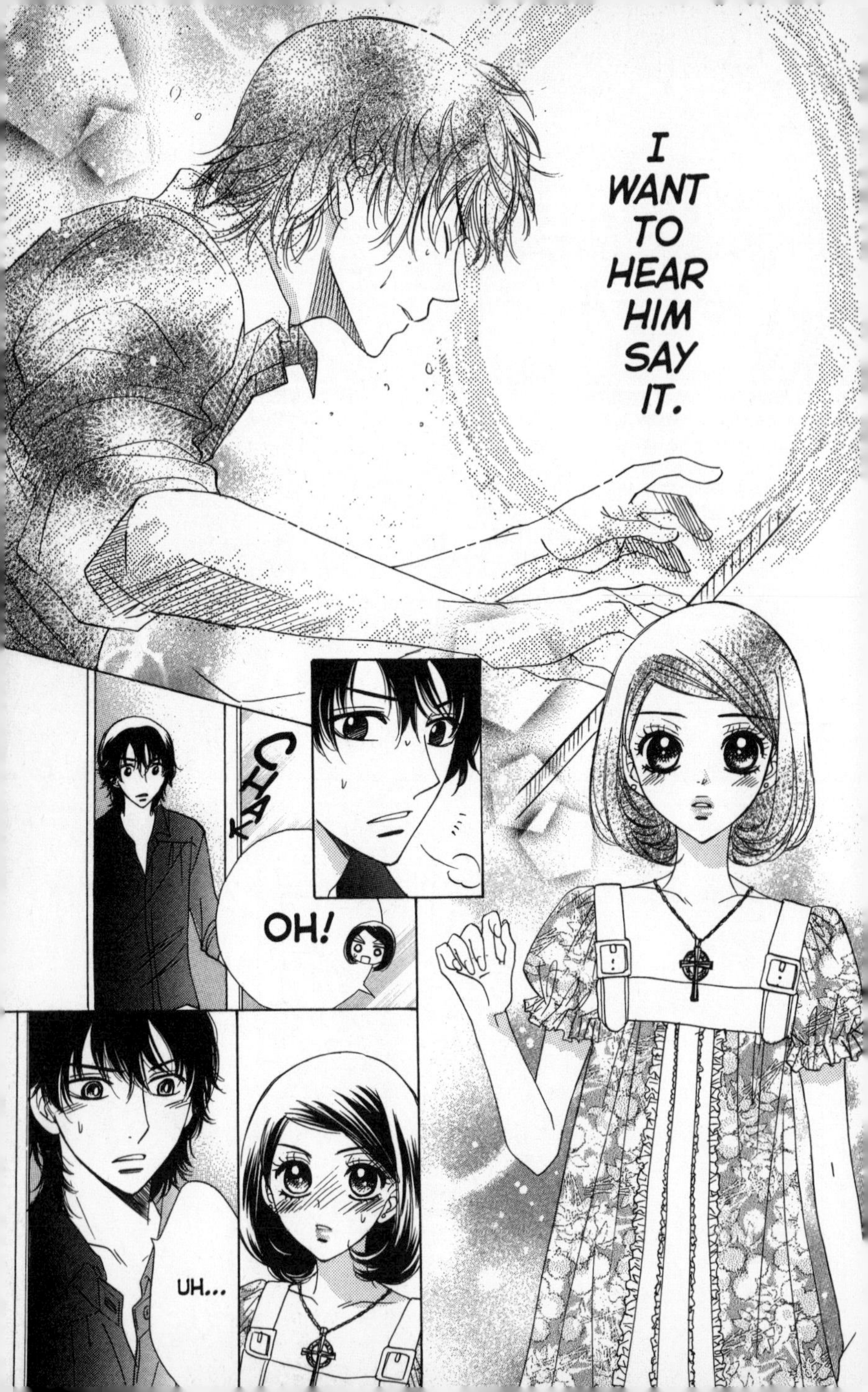
I WANT TO HEAR HIM SAY IT.
CHAT
OH!
UH...

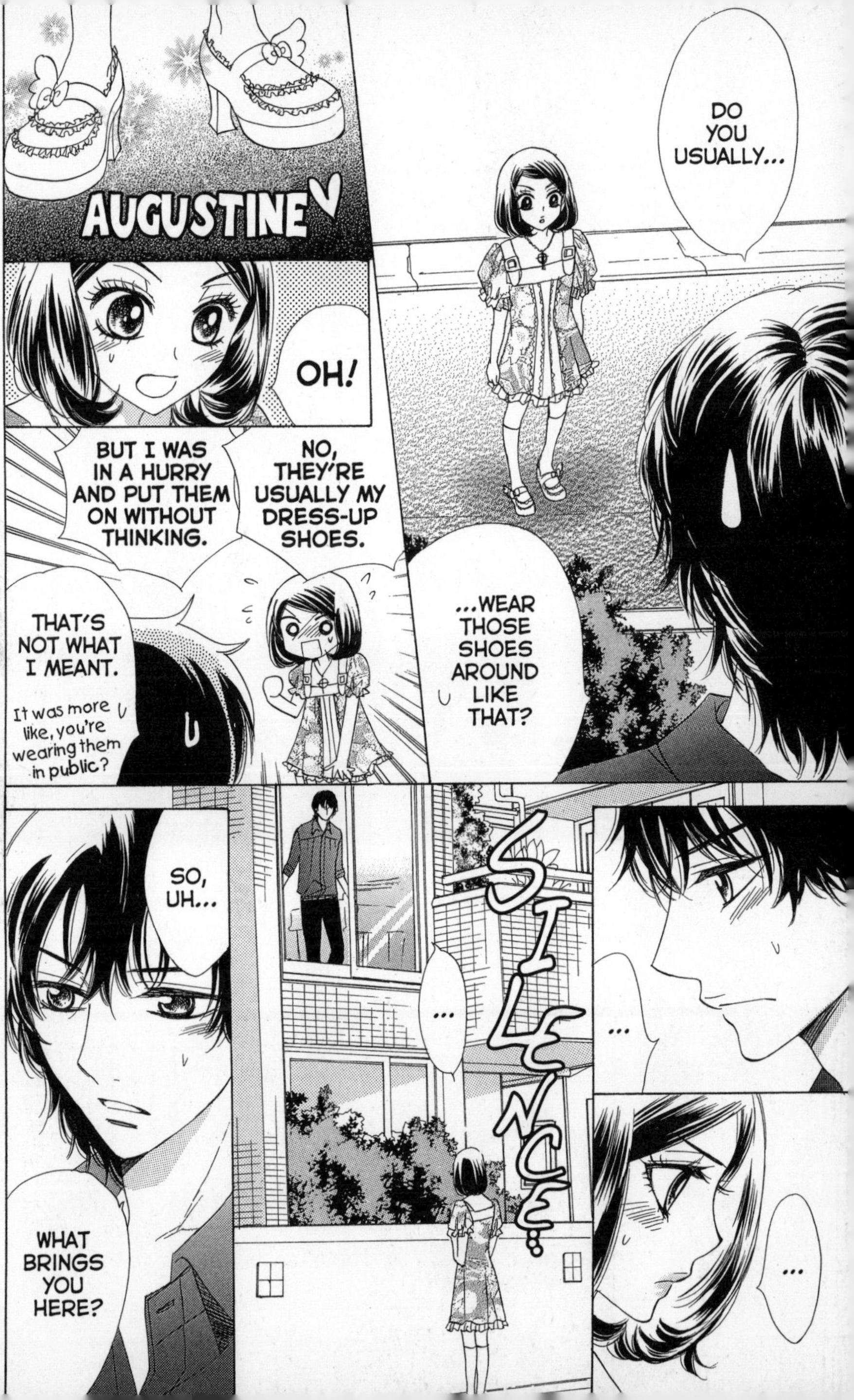
DO YOU USUALLY...
...WEAR THOSE SHOES AROUND LIKE THAT?
AUGUSTINE♥
OH!
NO, THEY'RE USUALLY MY DRESS-UP SHOES.
BUT I WAS IN A HURRY AND PUT THEM ON WITHOUT THINKING.
THAT'S NOT WHAT I MEANT.
It was more like, you're wearing them in public?
...
...
SILENCE...
...
SO, UH...
WHAT BRINGS YOU HERE?

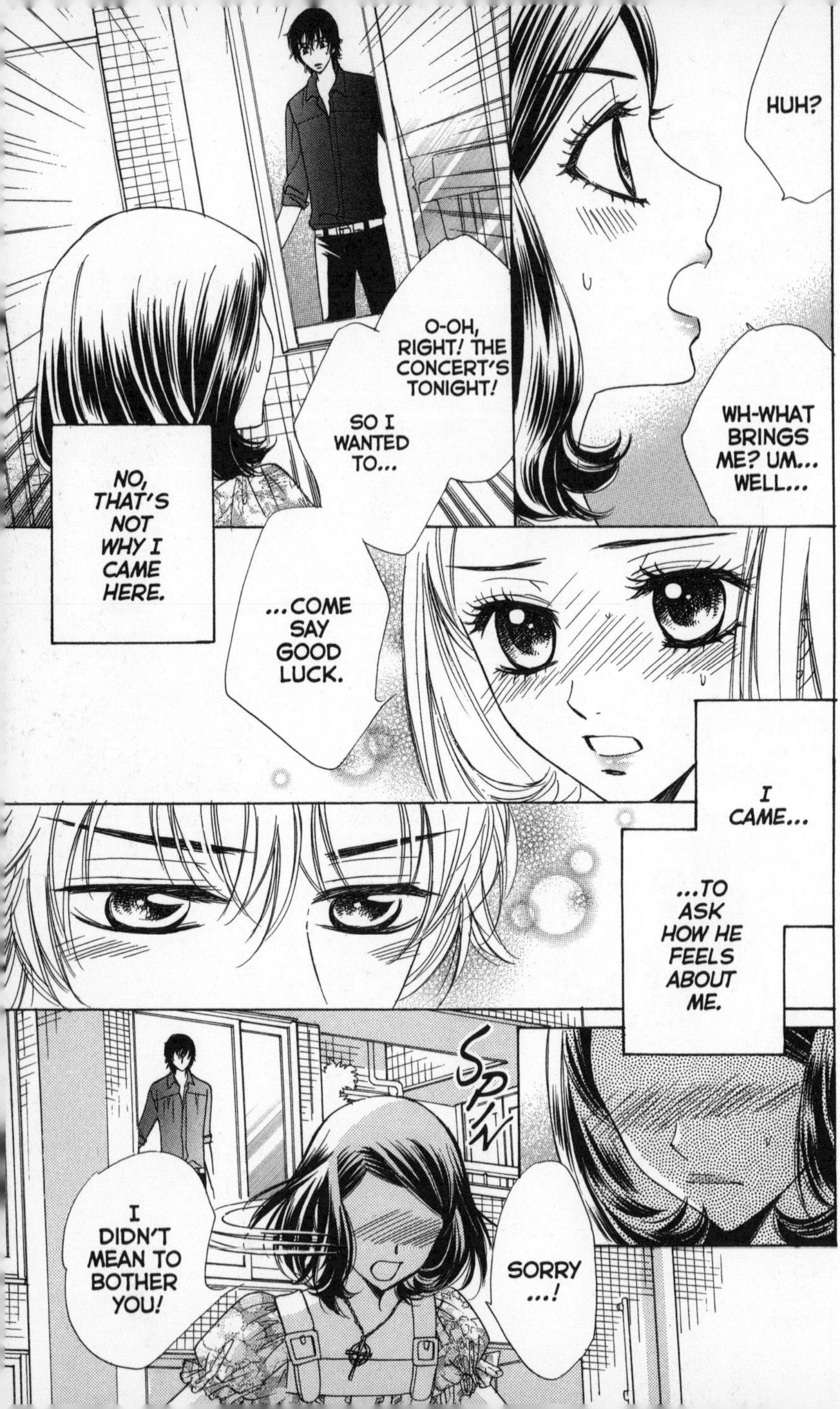
HUH?
WH-WHAT BRINGS ME? UM... WELL...
O-OH, RIGHT! THE CONCERT'S TONIGHT!
SO I WANTED TO...
NO, THAT'S NOT WHY I CAME HERE.
...COME SAY GOOD LUCK.
I CAME...
...TO ASK HOW HE FEELS ABOUT ME.
SPIN
SORRY ...!
I DIDN'T MEAN TO BOTHER YOU!

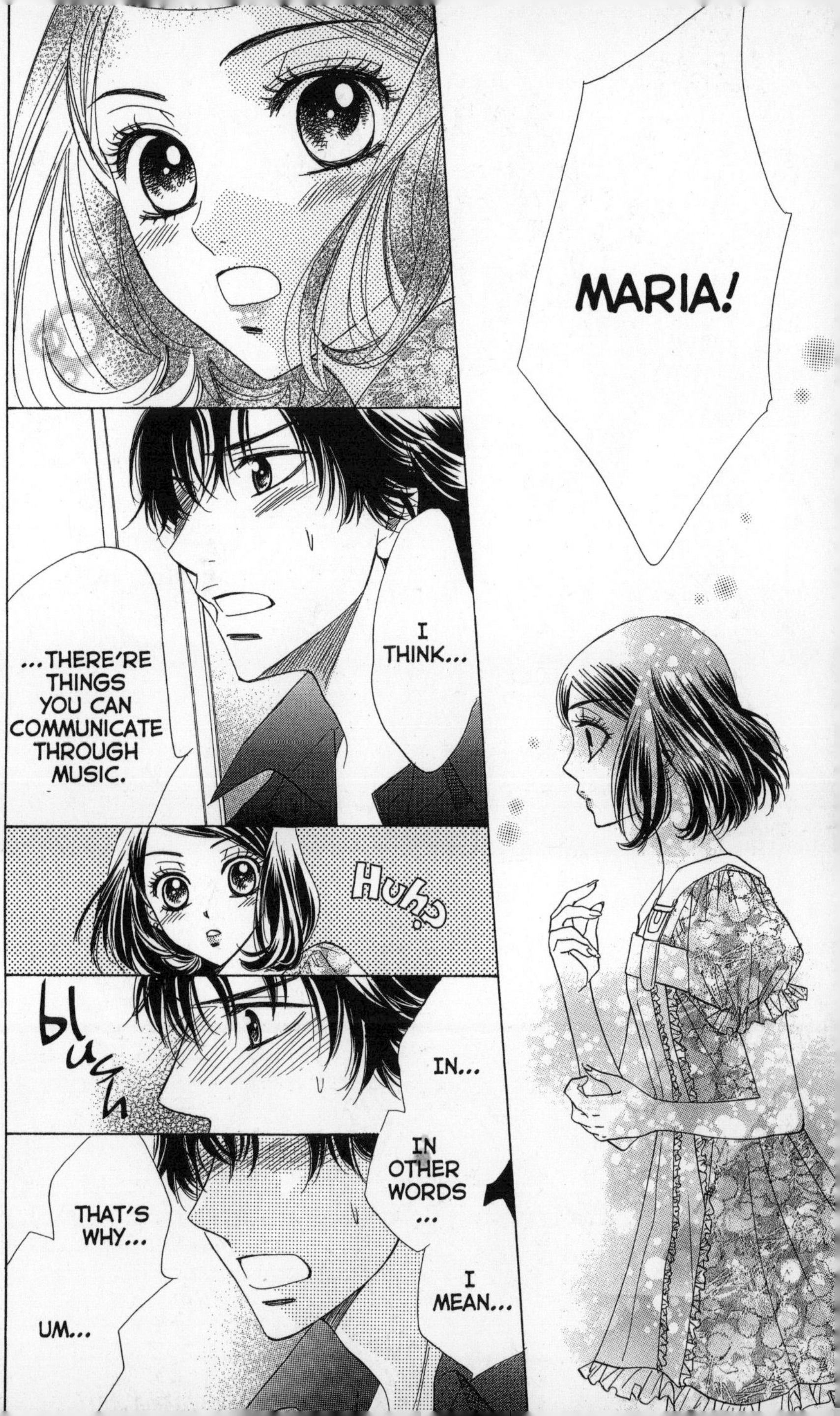
MARIA!
I THINK...
...THERE'RE THINGS YOU CAN COMMUNICATE THROUGH MUSIC.
Huh?
IN...
blush
IN OTHER WORDS...
I MEAN...
THAT'S WHY...
UM...

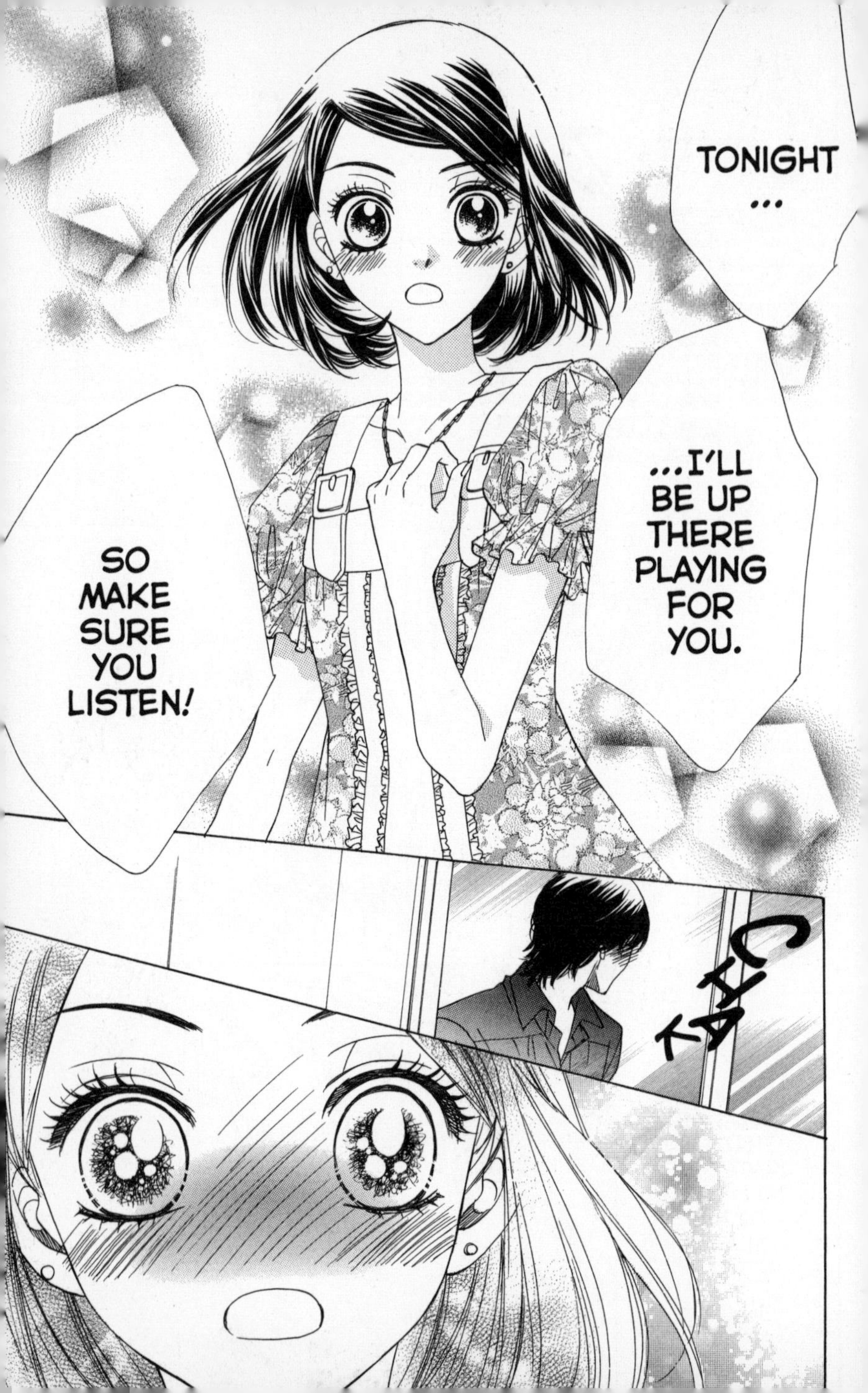
TONIGHT ...
...I'LL BE UP THERE PLAYING FOR YOU.
SO MAKE SURE YOU LISTEN!
CHA KA

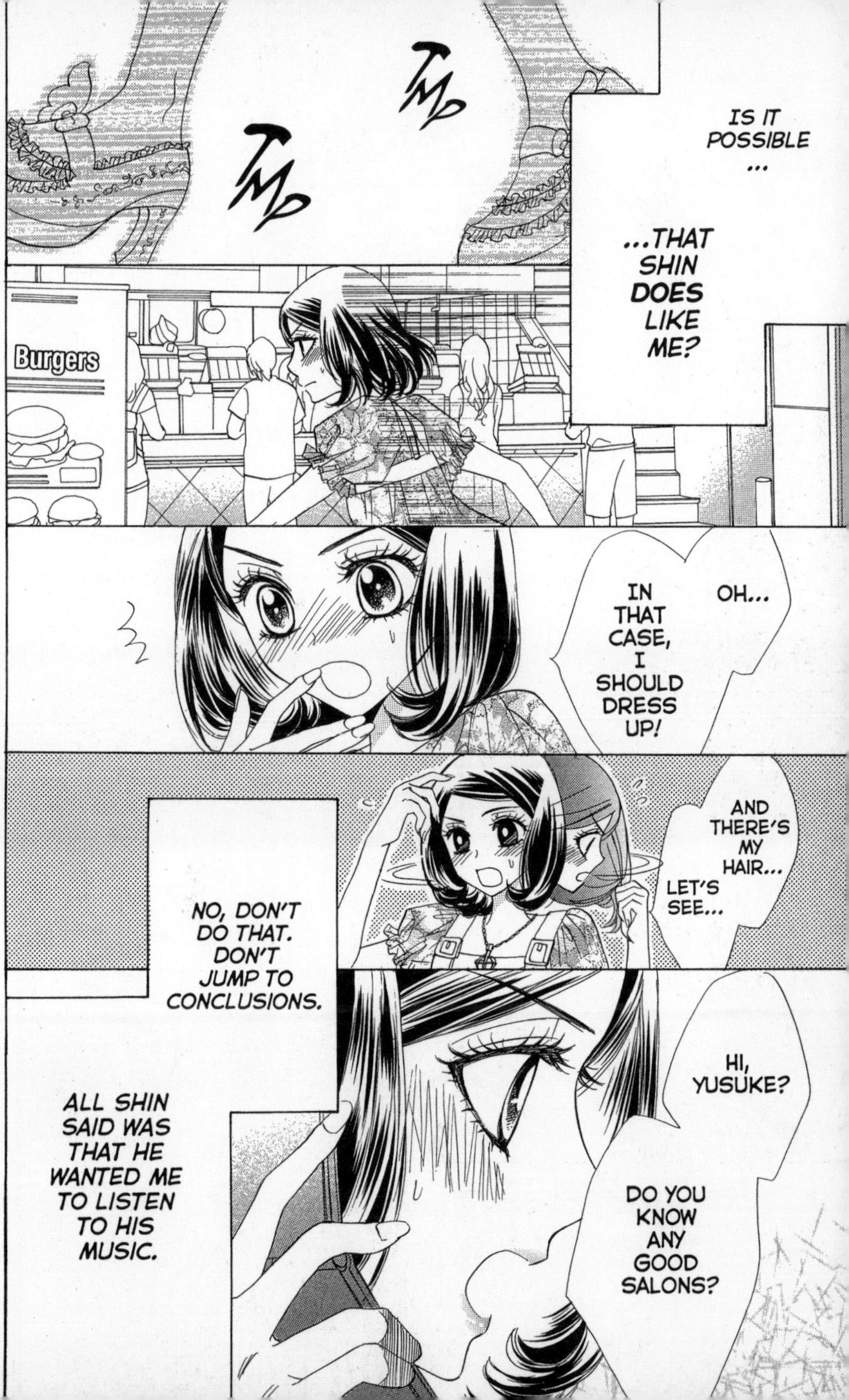
IS IT POSSIBLE ...
TMP
TMP
...THAT SHIN DOES LIKE ME?
Burgers
OH...
IN THAT CASE, I SHOULD DRESS UP!
AND THERE'S MY HAIR...
LET'S SEE...
NO, DON'T DO THAT. DON'T JUMP TO CONCLUSIONS.
HI, YUSUKE?
DO YOU KNOW ANY GOOD SALONS?
ALL SHIN SAID WAS THAT HE WANTED ME TO LISTEN TO HIS MUSIC.

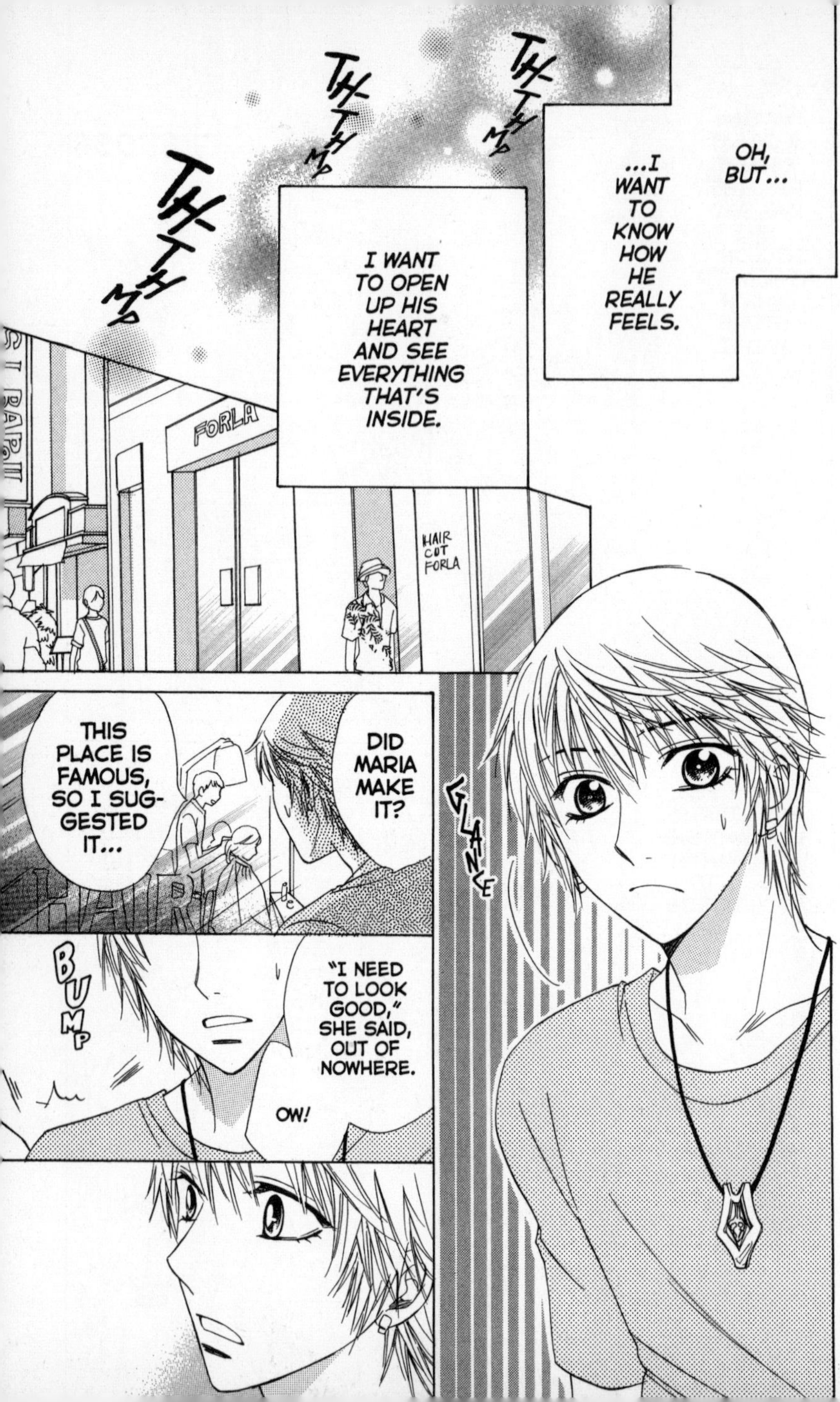
OH, BUT...
...I WANT TO KNOW HOW HE REALLY FEELS.
I WANT TO OPEN UP HIS HEART AND SEE EVERYTHING THAT'S INSIDE.
THMP
THMP
THMP
FORLA
HAIR CUT FORLA
GLANCE
DID MARIA MAKE IT?
THIS PLACE IS FAMOUS, SO I SUG-GESTED IT...
"I NEED TO LOOK GOOD," SHE SAID, OUT OF NOWHERE.
BUMP
OW!

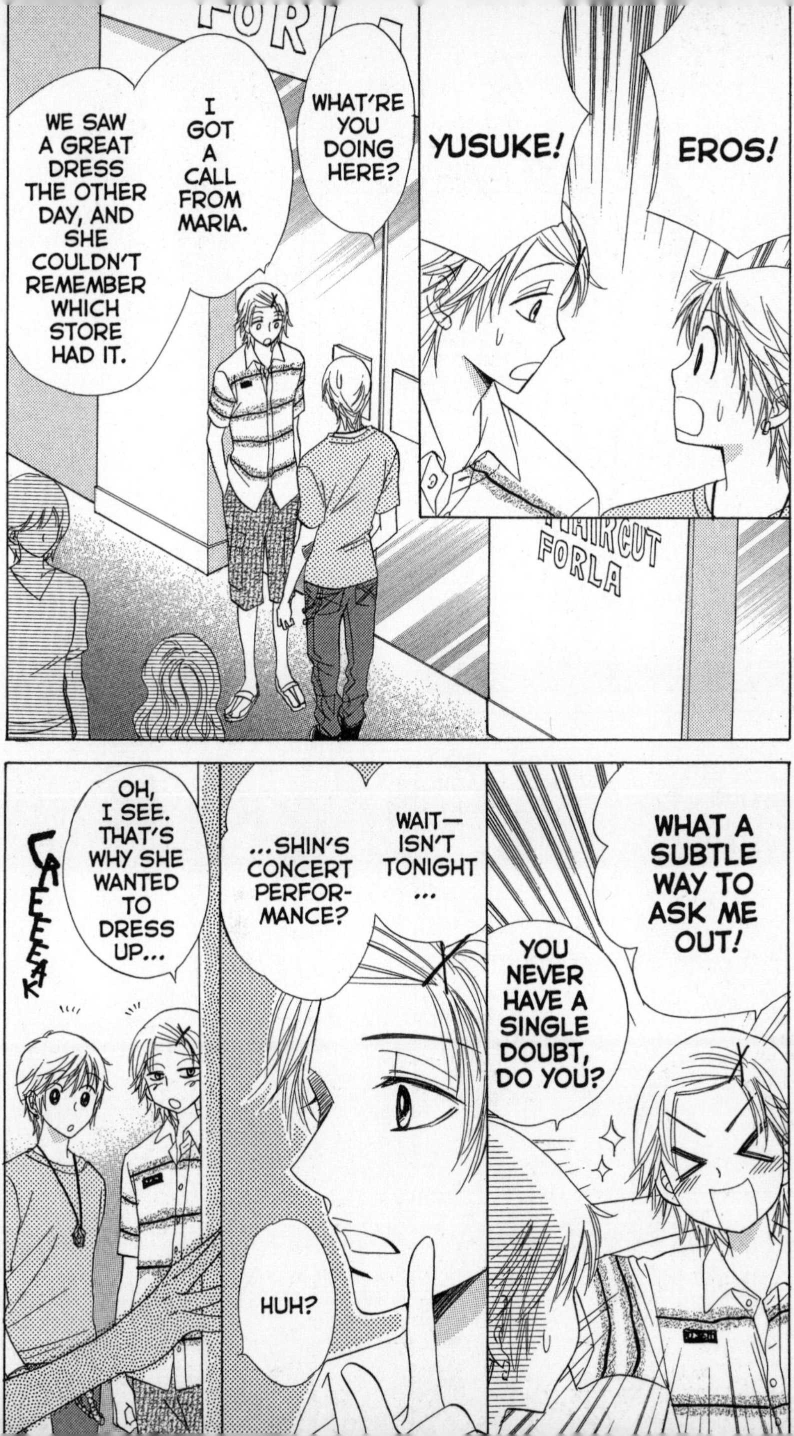
EROS!
YUSUKE!
FORLA
WHAT'RE YOU DOING HERE?
I GOT A CALL FROM MARIA.
WE SAW A GREAT DRESS THE OTHER DAY, AND SHE COULDN'T REMEMBER WHICH STORE HAD IT.
FORLA
WHAT A SUBTLE WAY TO ASK ME OUT!
YOU NEVER HAVE A SINGLE DOUBT, DO YOU?
WAIT— ISN'T TONIGHT ...
...SHIN'S CONCERT PERFOR-MANCE?
HUH?
OH, I SEE. THAT'S WHY SHE WANTED TO DRESS UP...
CREEEAK

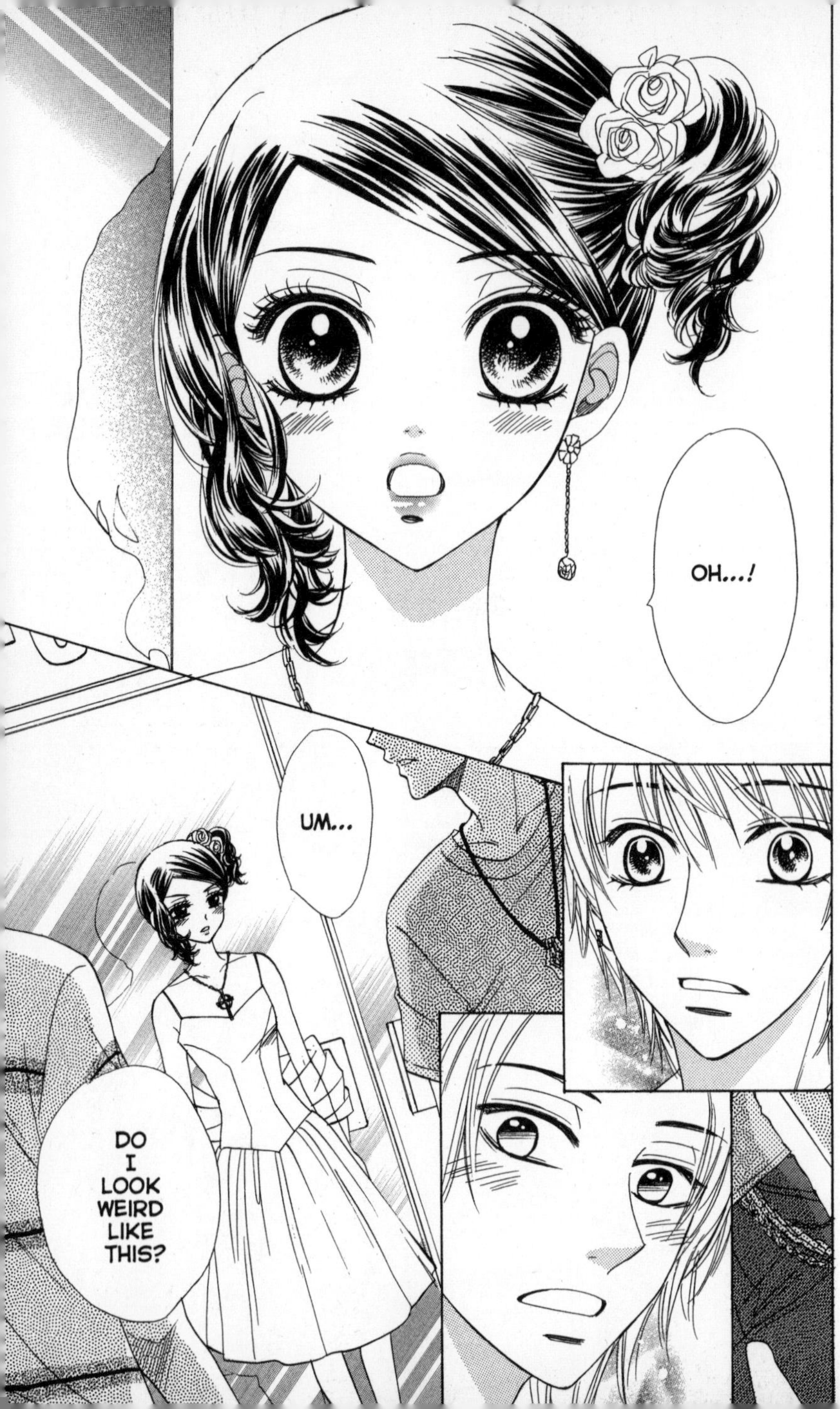
OH...!
UM...
DO I LOOK WEIRD LIKE THIS?

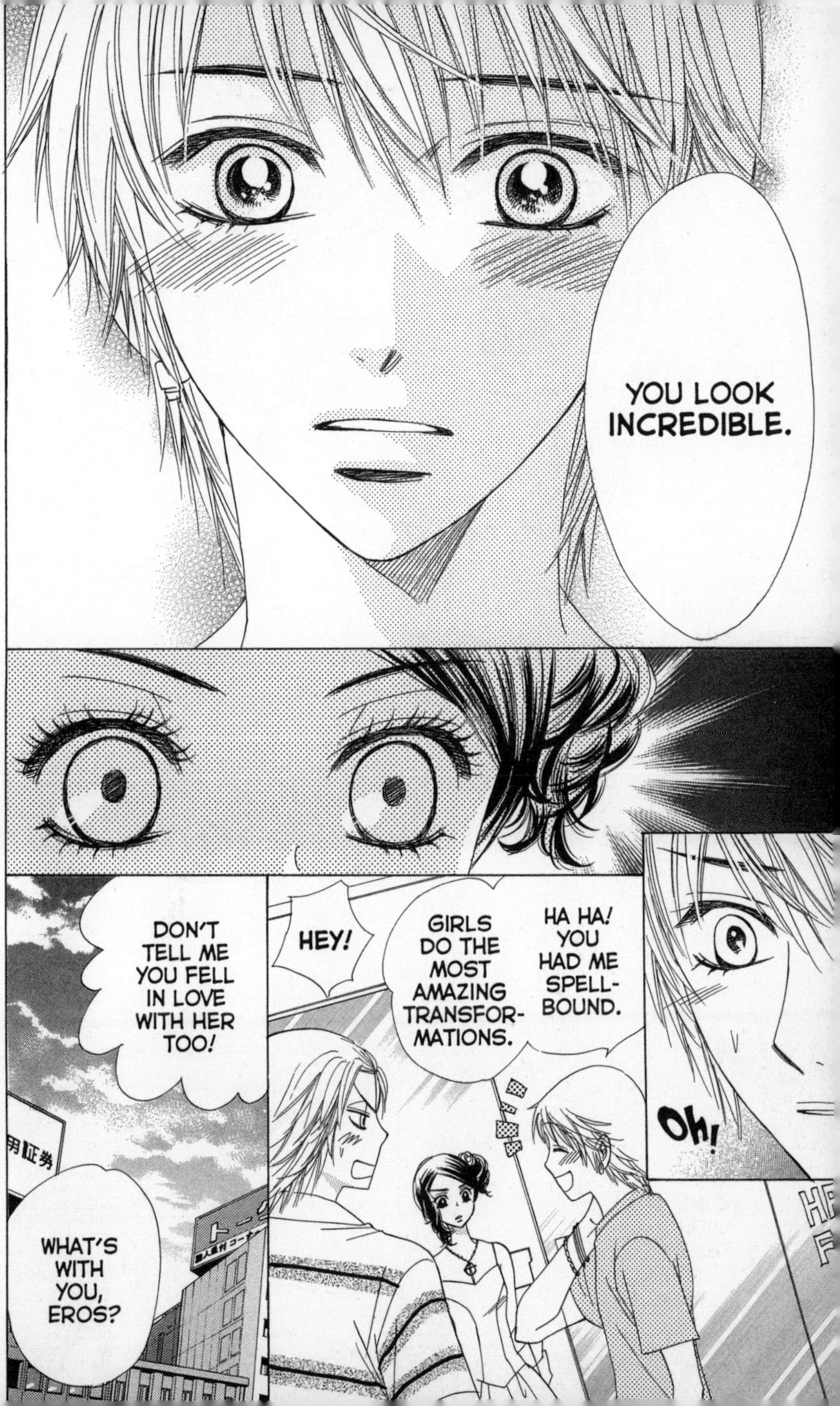
YOU LOOK INCREDIBLE.
Oh!
HA HA! YOU HAD ME SPELL-BOUND.
GIRLS DO THE MOST AMAZING TRANSFOR-MATIONS.
HEY!
DON'T TELL ME YOU FELL IN LOVE WITH HER TOO!
WHAT'S WITH YOU, EROS?

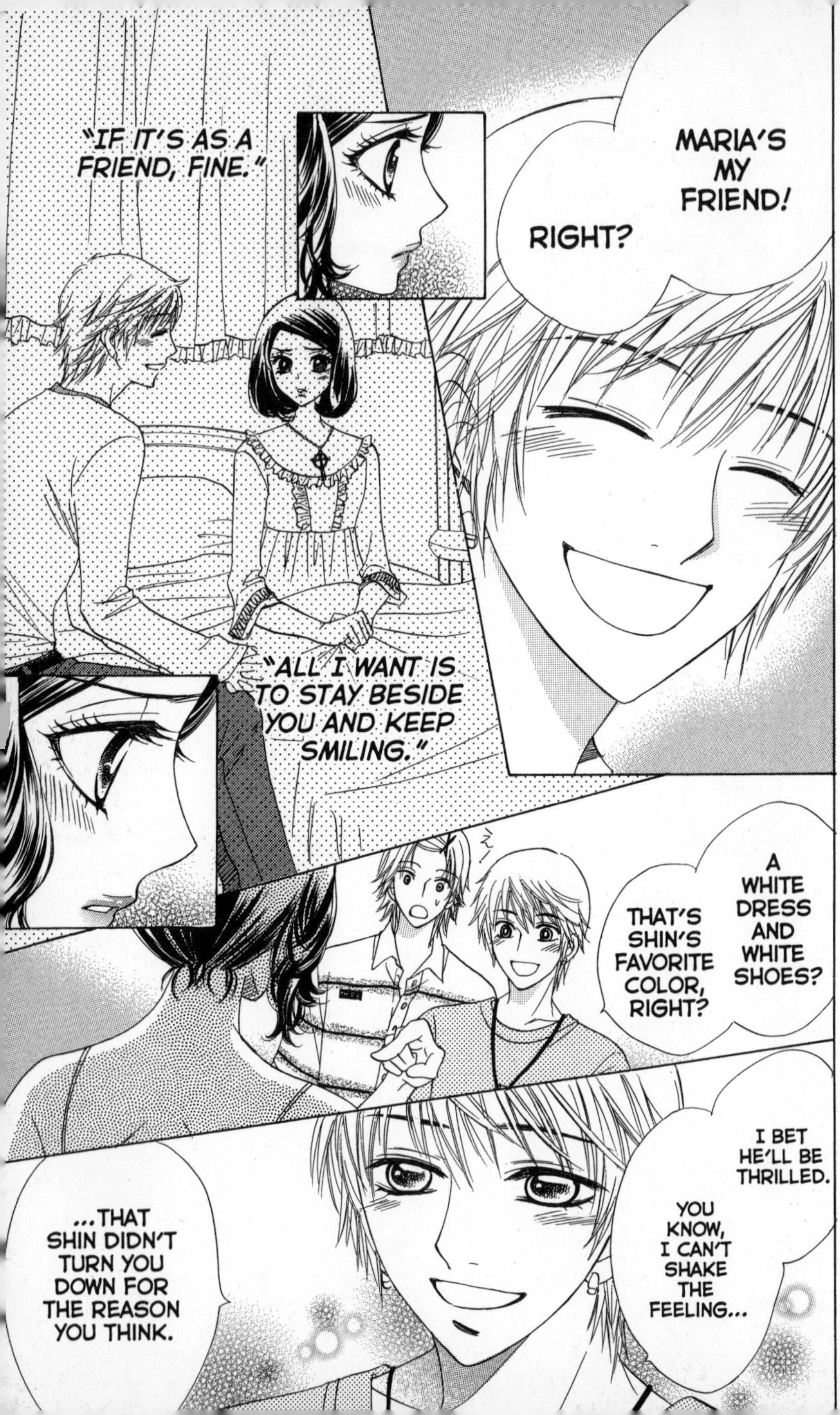
MARIA'S MY FRIEND!
RIGHT?
"IF IT'S AS A FRIEND, FINE."
"ALL I WANT IS TO STAY BESIDE YOU AND KEEP SMILING."
A WHITE DRESS AND WHITE SHOES?
THAT'S SHIN'S FAVORITE COLOR, RIGHT?
I BET HE'LL BE THRILLED.
YOU KNOW, I CAN'T SHAKE THE FEELING...
...THAT SHIN DIDN'T TURN YOU DOWN FOR THE REASON YOU THINK.

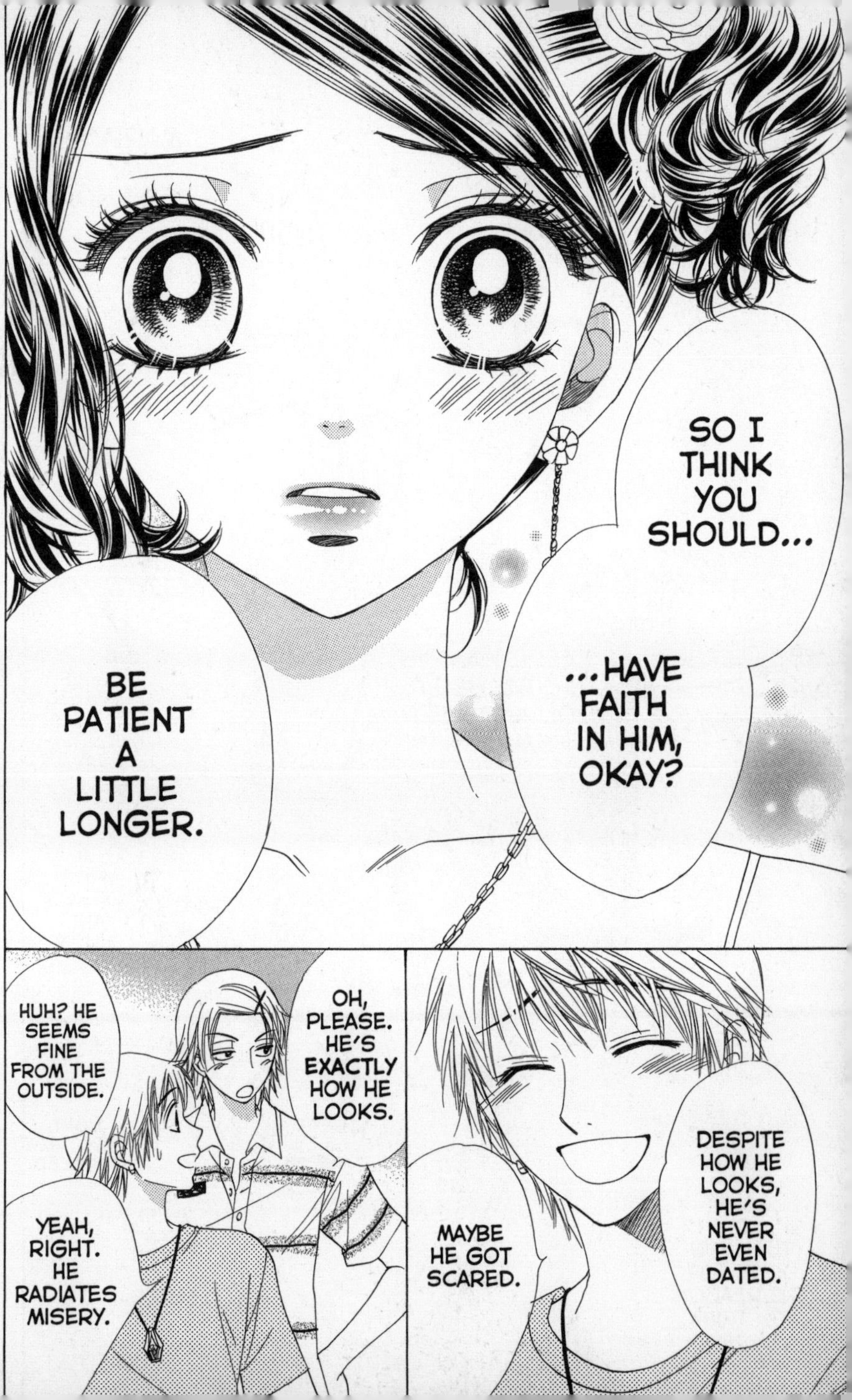
SO I THINK YOU SHOULD...
...HAVE FAITH IN HIM, OKAY?
BE PATIENT A LITTLE LONGER.
DESPITE HOW HE LOOKS, HE'S NEVER EVEN DATED.
MAYBE HE GOT SCARED.
OH, PLEASE. HE'S EXACTLY HOW HE LOOKS.
HUH? HE SEEMS FINE FROM THE OUTSIDE.
YEAH, RIGHT. HE RADIATES MISERY.

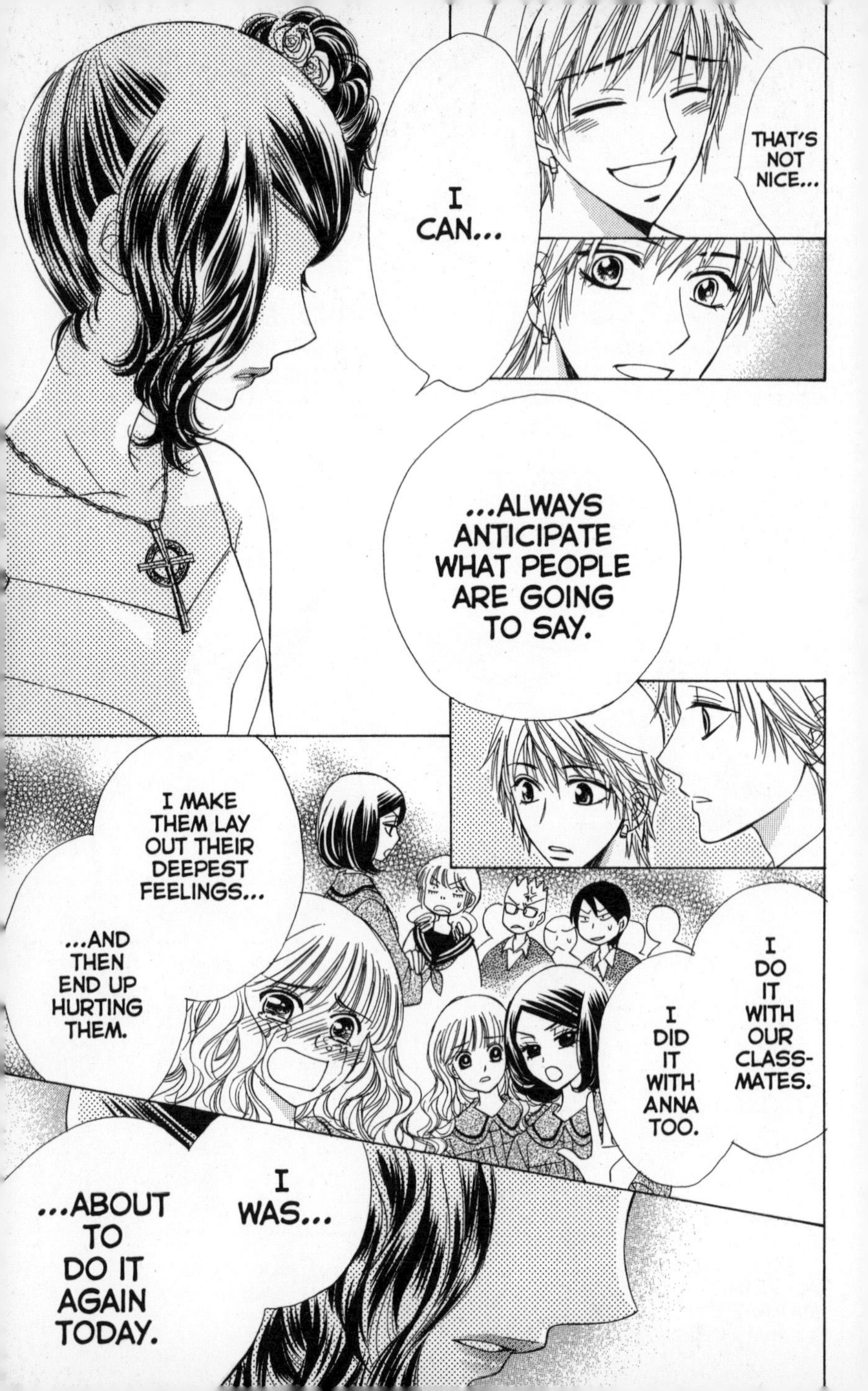
THAT'S NOT NICE...
I CAN...
...ALWAYS ANTICIPATE WHAT PEOPLE ARE GOING TO SAY.
I DO IT WITH OUR CLASS-MATES.
I DID IT WITH ANNA TOO.
I MAKE THEM LAY OUT THEIR DEEPEST FEELINGS...
...AND THEN END UP HURTING THEM.
I WAS...
...ABOUT TO DO IT AGAIN TODAY.

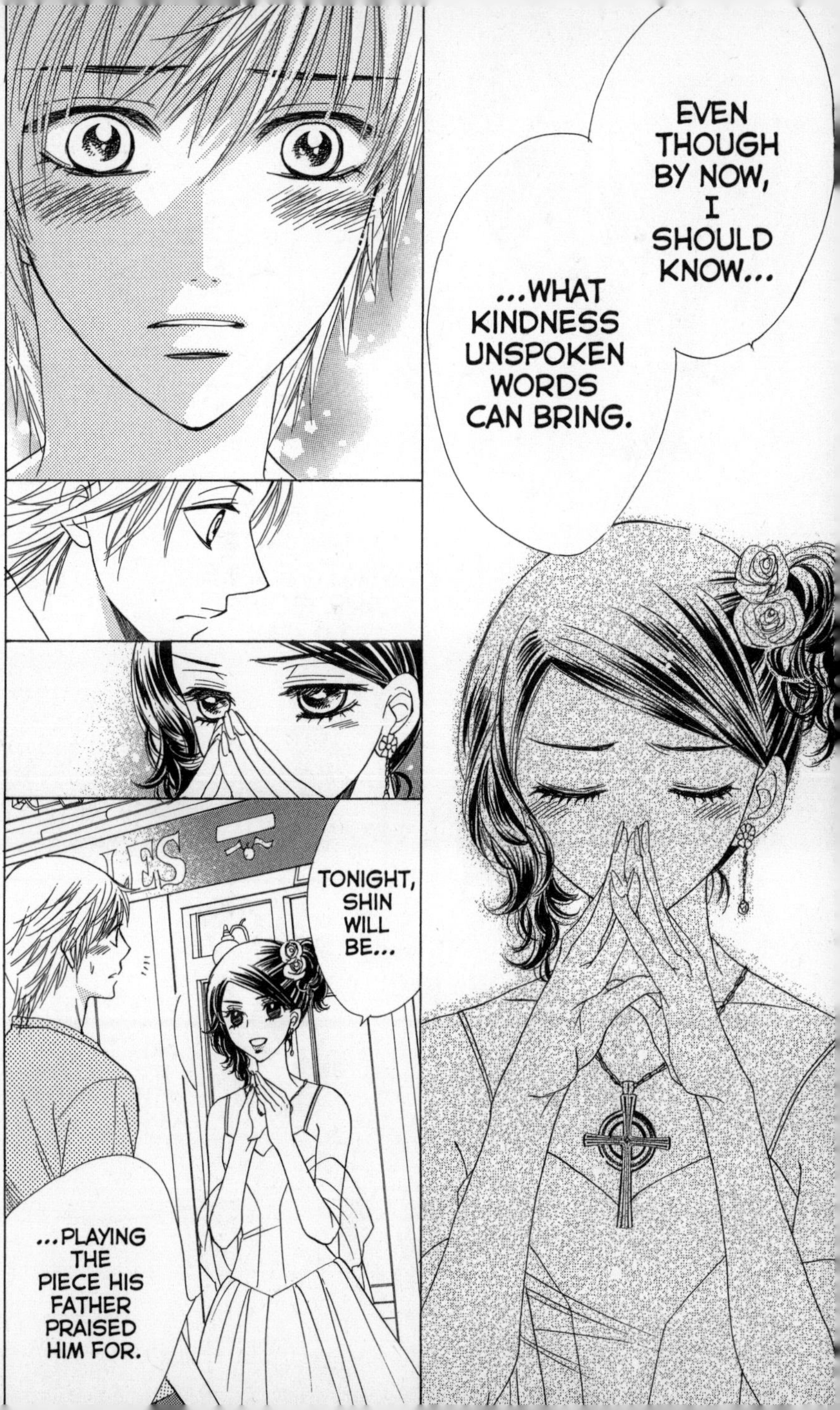
EVEN THOUGH BY NOW, I SHOULD KNOW...
...WHAT KINDNESS UNSPOKEN WORDS CAN BRING.
TONIGHT, SHIN WILL BE...
...PLAYING THE PIECE HIS FATHER PRAISED HIM FOR.

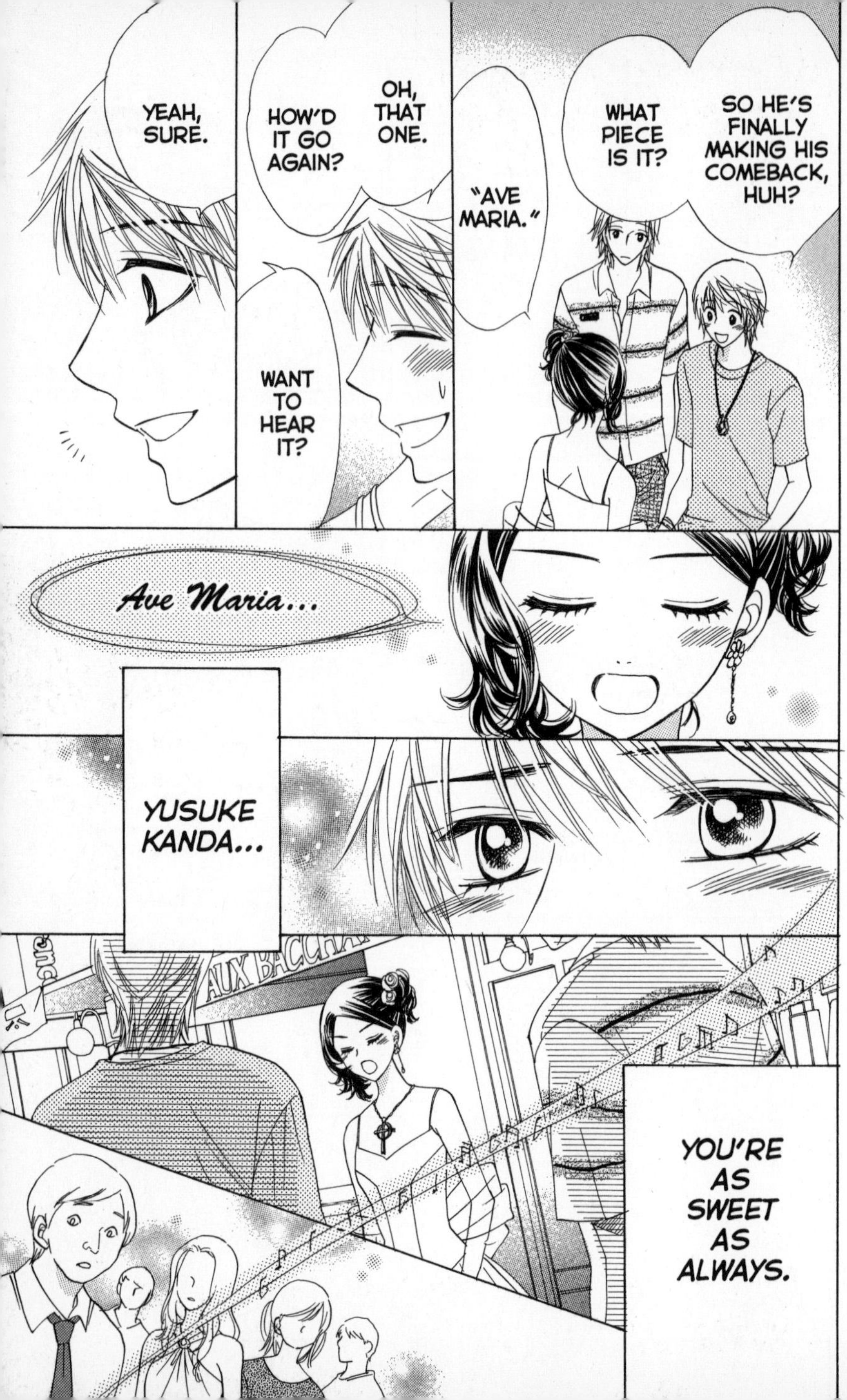
SO HE'S FINALLY MAKING HIS COMEBACK, HUH?
WHAT PIECE IS IT?
"AVE MARIA."
OH, THAT ONE.
HOW'D IT GO AGAIN?
WANT TO HEAR IT?
YEAH, SURE.
Ave Maria...
YUSUKE KANDA...
YOU'RE AS SWEET AS ALWAYS.
AUX BACCHA

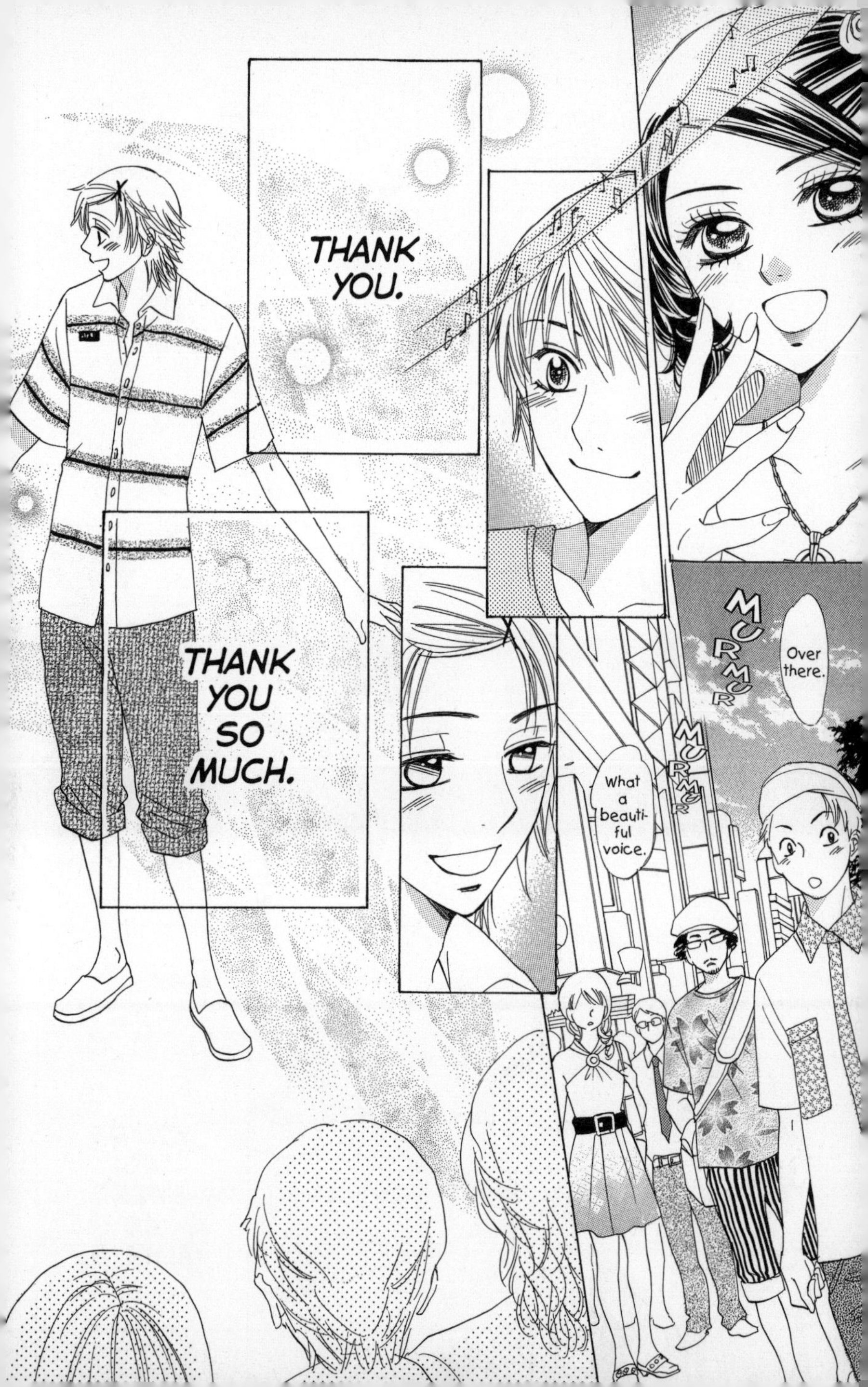
THANK YOU.
Over there.
MURMUR
MURMUR
What a beautiful voice.
THANK YOU SO MUCH.

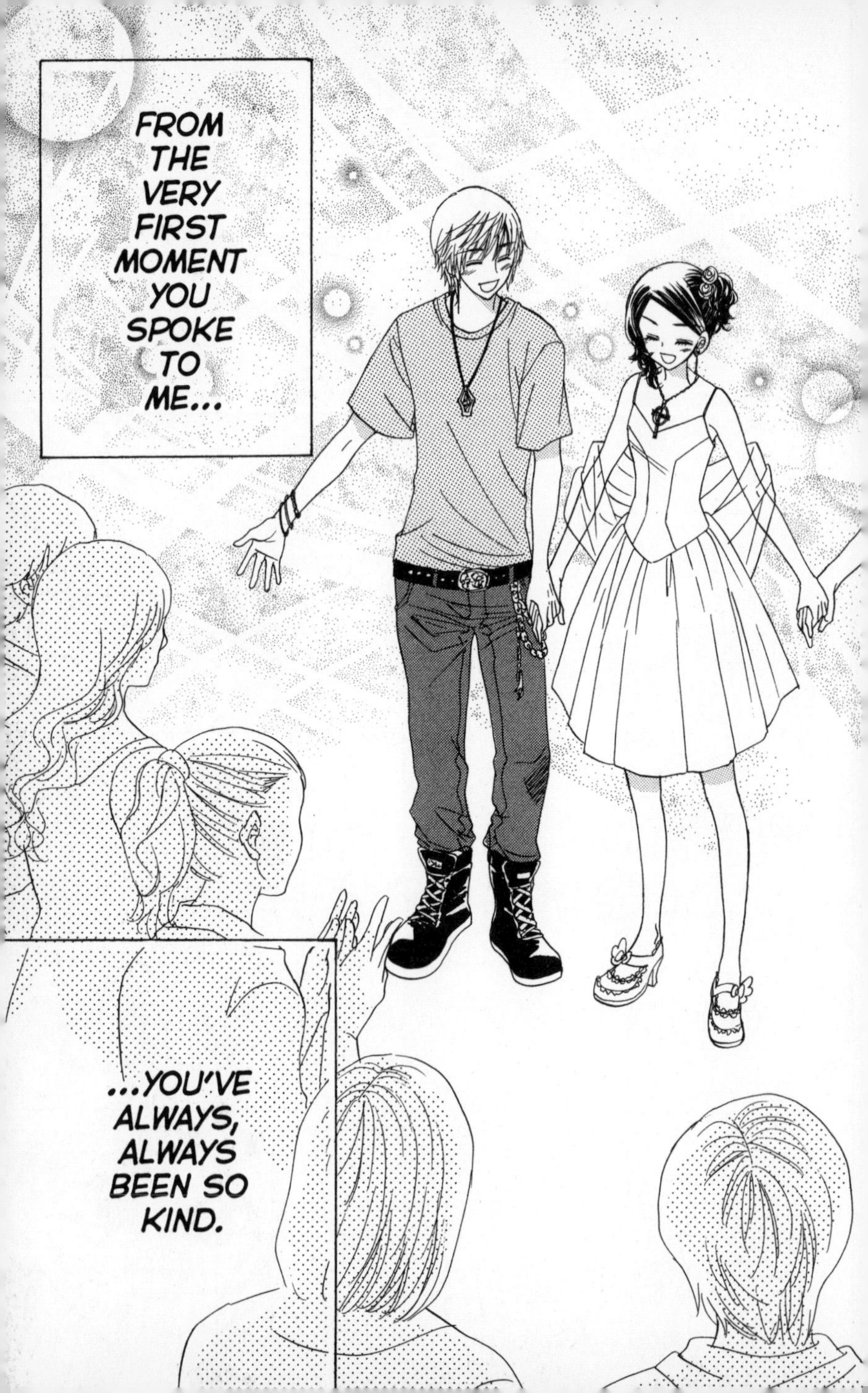
FROM THE VERY FIRST MOMENT YOU SPOKE TO ME...
...YOU'VE ALWAYS, ALWAYS BEEN SO KIND.

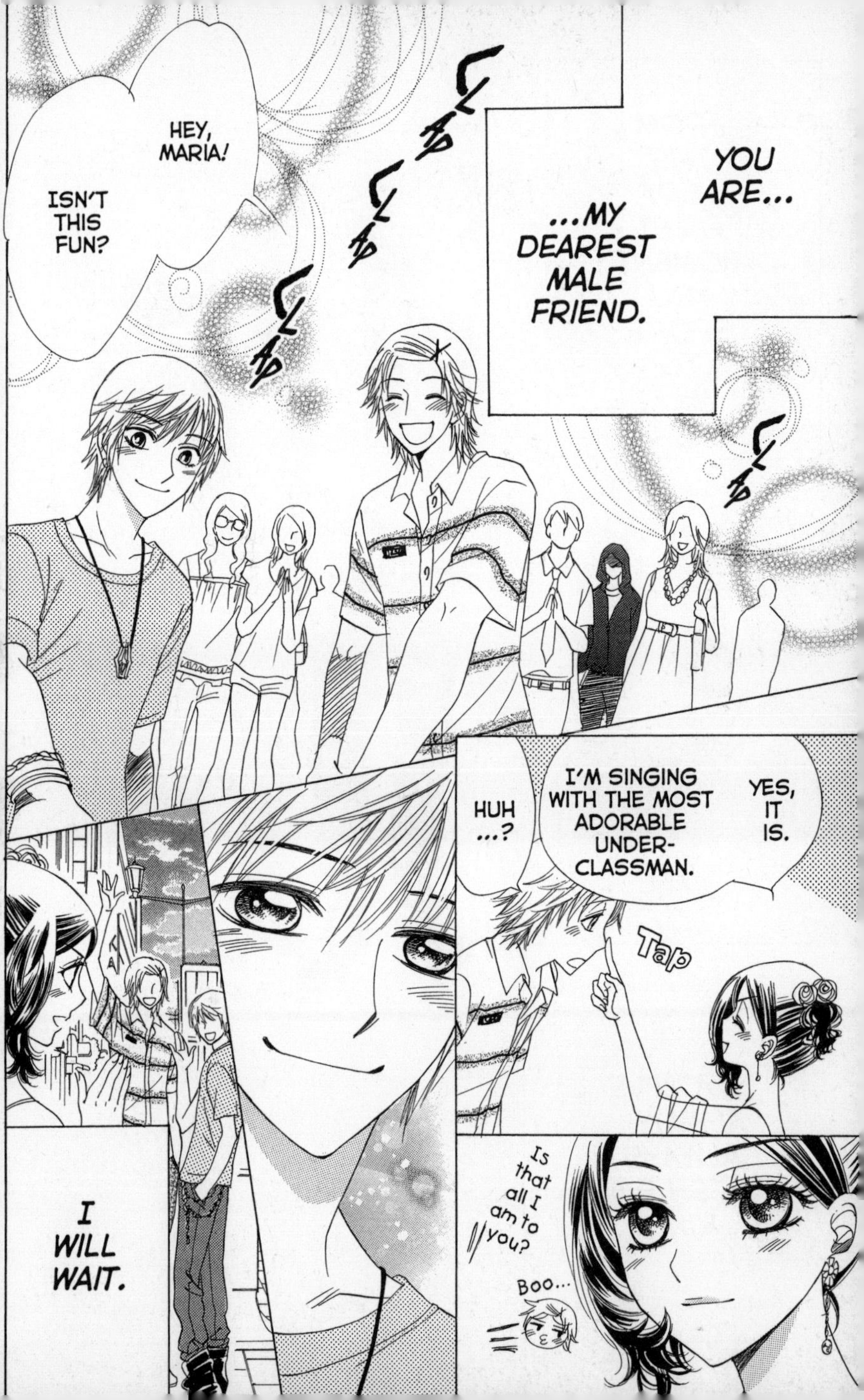
YOU ARE...
...MY DEAREST MALE FRIEND.
CLAP CLAP CLAP CLAP
HEY, MARIA!
ISN'T THIS FUN?
YES, IT IS.
I'M SINGING WITH THE MOST ADORABLE UNDER-CLASSMAN.
HUH ...?
Tap
Is that all I am to you?
Boo...
I WILL WAIT.

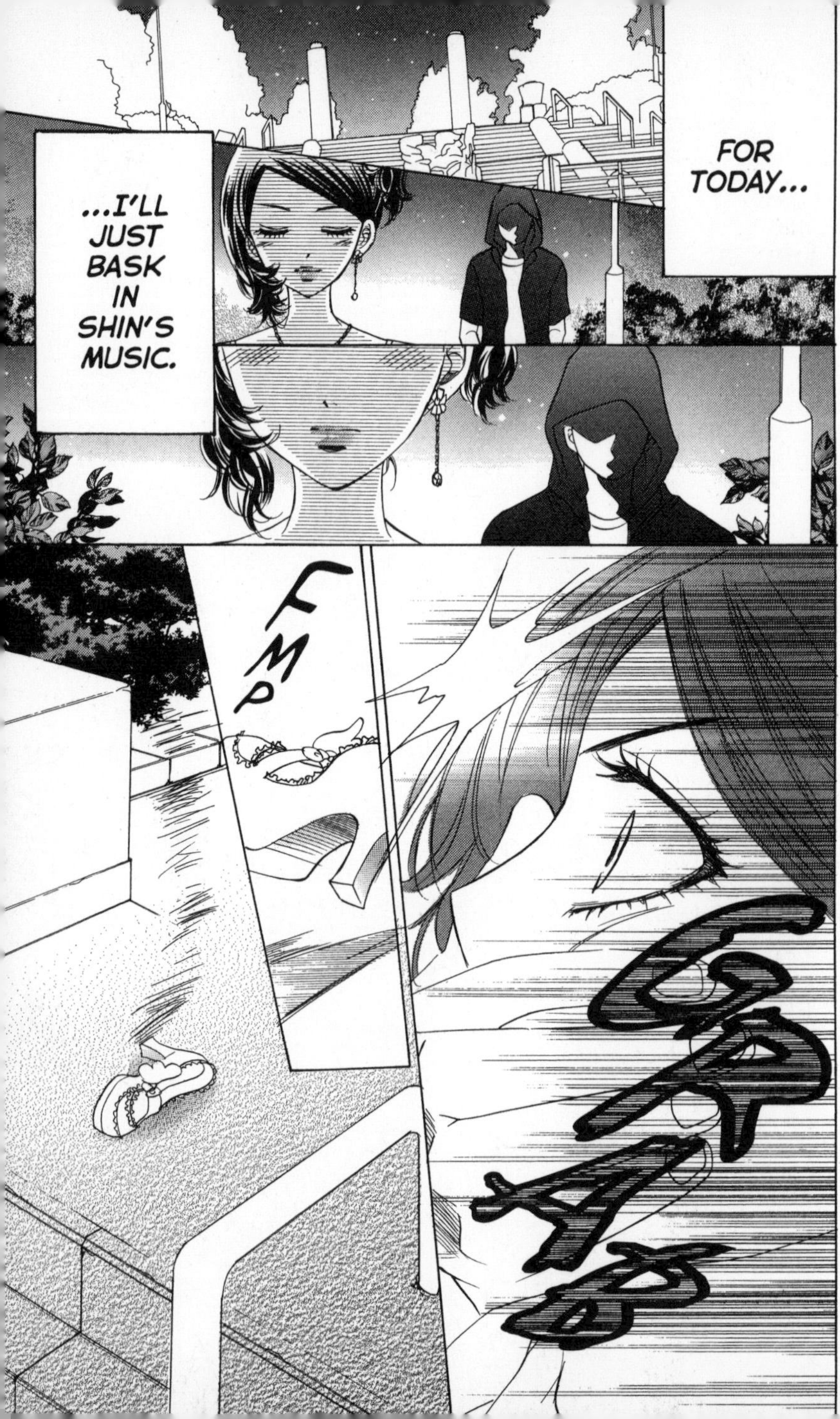
FOR TODAY...
...I'LL JUST BASK IN SHIN'S MUSIC.
FMP
GRAB

A Devil and
Her Love Song

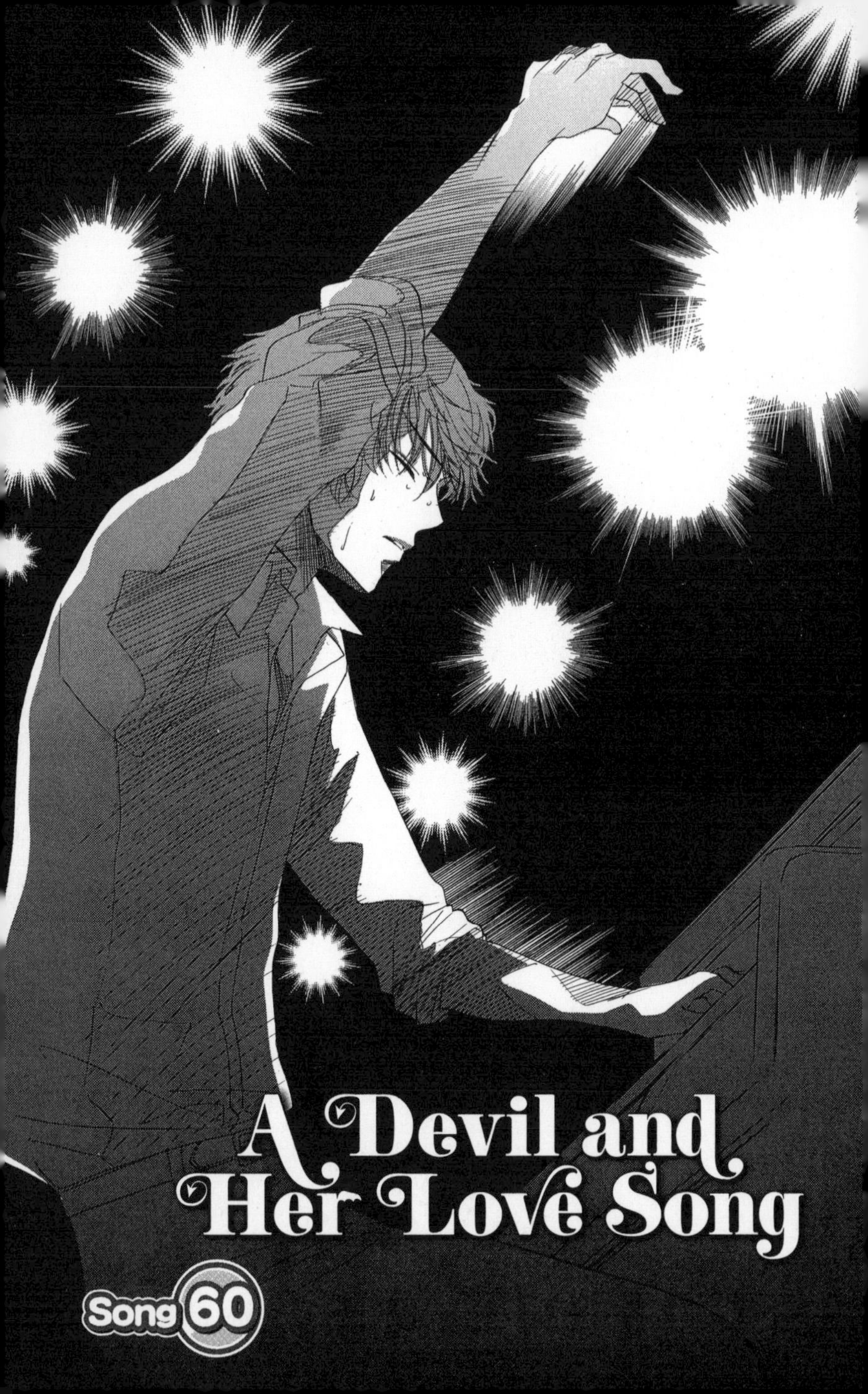
A Devil and Her Love Song
Song 60

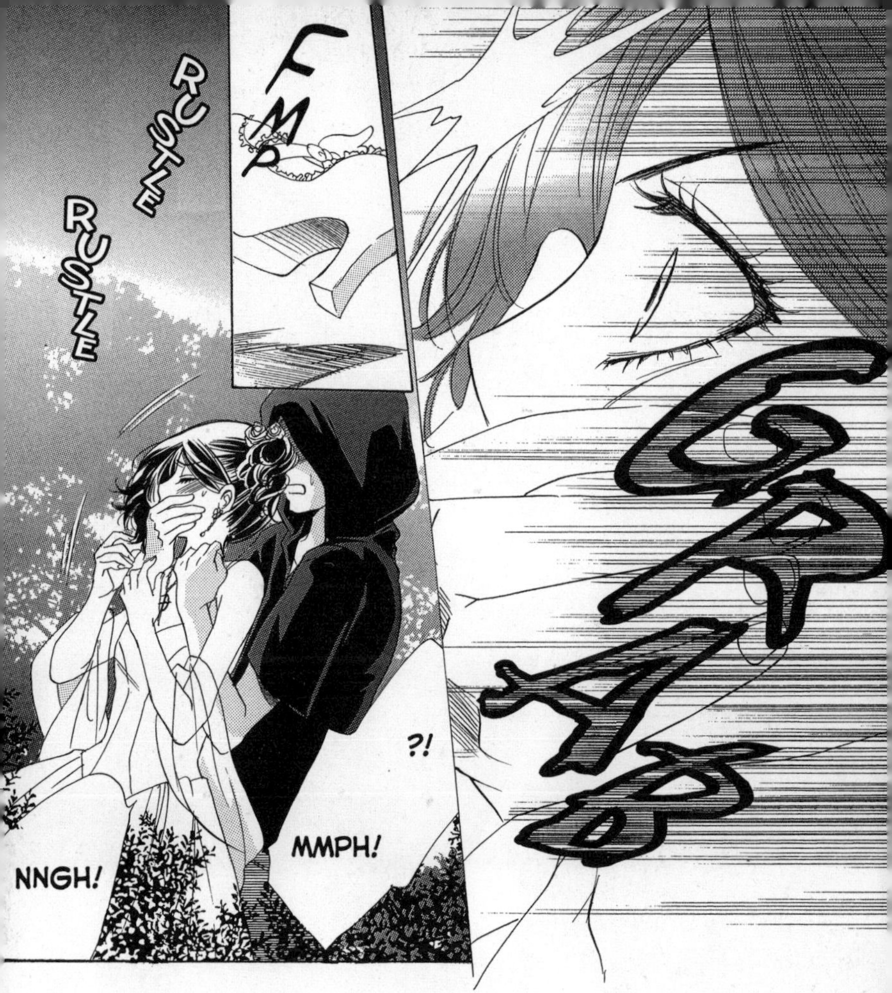
FMP
?!
MMPH!
NNGH!
RUSTLE
RUSTLE

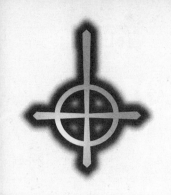

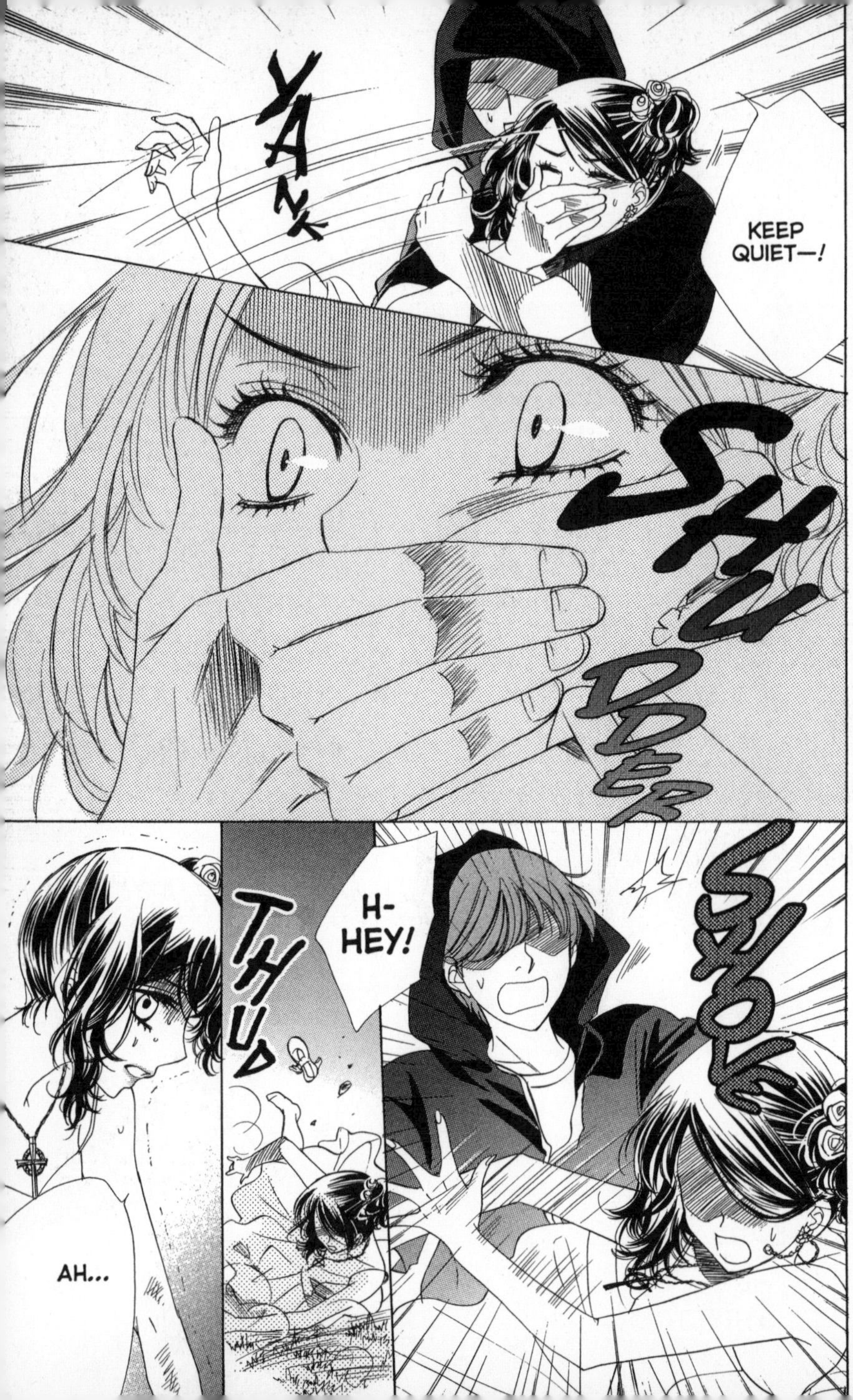
KEEP QUIET—!
YANK
SHUDDER
SHOVE
H- HEY!
THUD
AH...

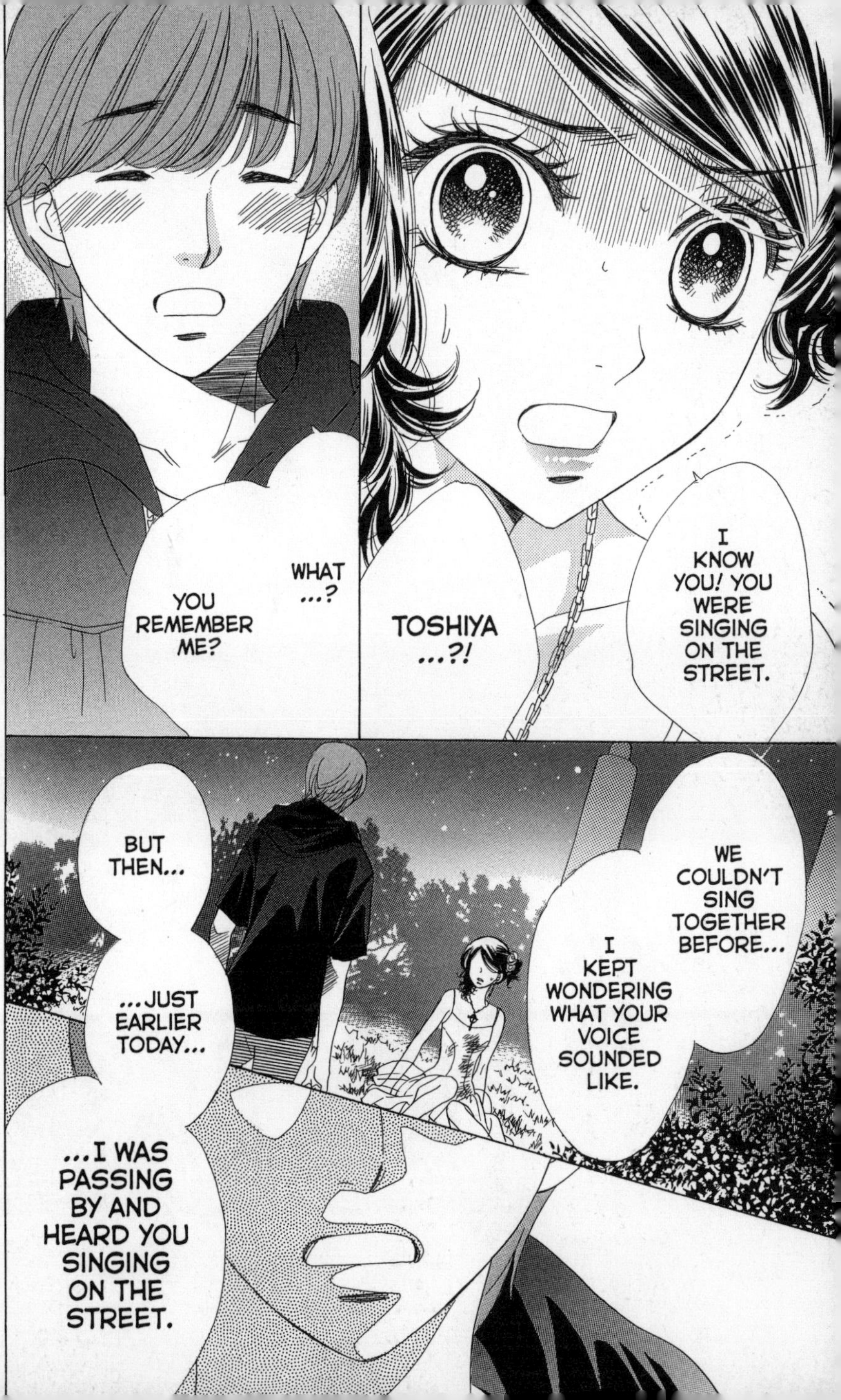
TOSHIYA ...?!
I KNOW YOU! YOU WERE SINGING ON THE STREET.
WHAT ...?
YOU REMEMBER ME?
WE COULDN'T SING TOGETHER BEFORE...
I KEPT WONDERING WHAT YOUR VOICE SOUNDED LIKE.
BUT THEN...
...JUST EARLIER TODAY...
...I WAS PASSING BY AND HEARD YOU SINGING ON THE STREET.

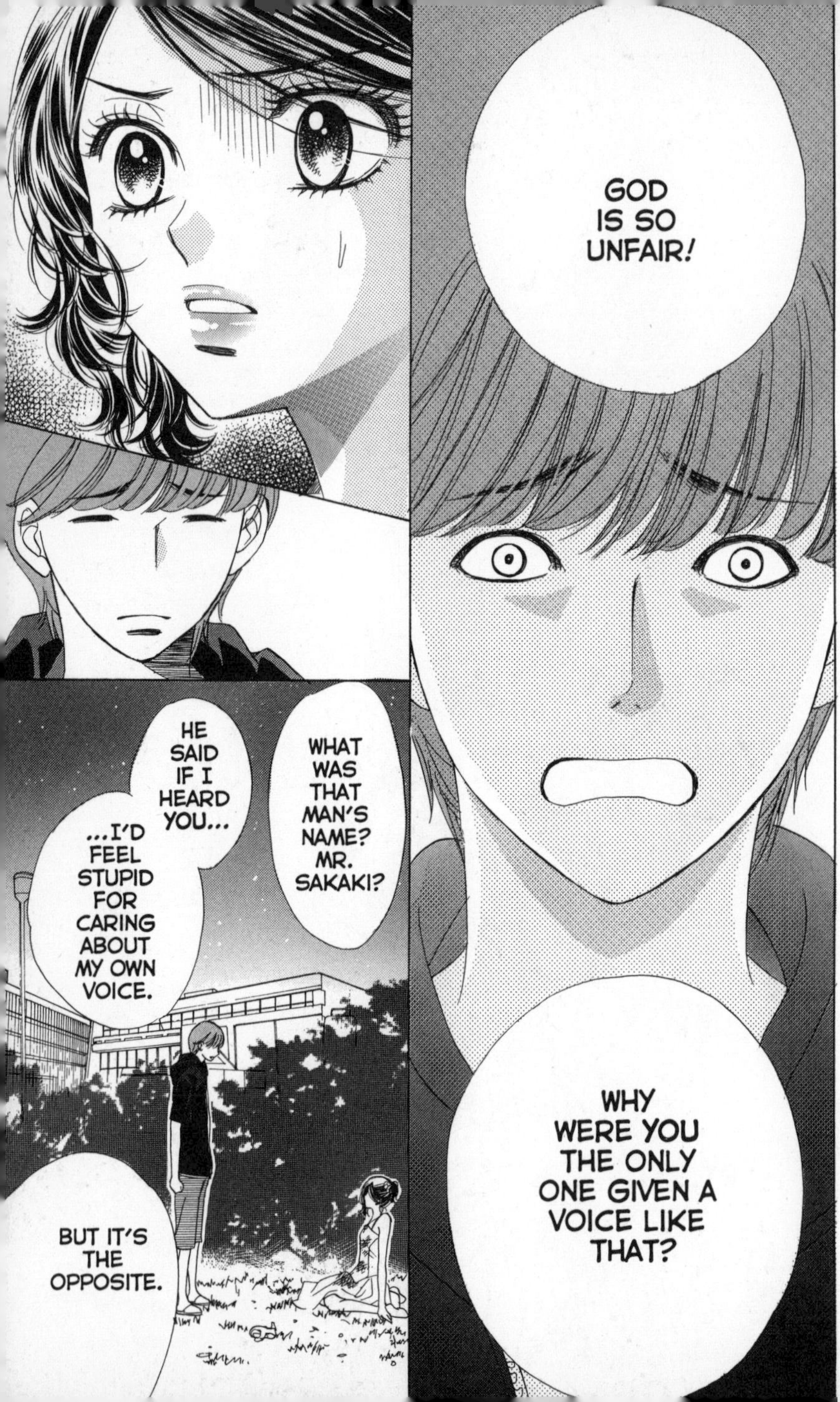
GOD IS SO UNFAIR!
WHY WERE YOU THE ONLY ONE GIVEN A VOICE LIKE THAT?
WHAT WAS THAT MAN'S NAME? MR. SAKAKI?
HE SAID IF I HEARD YOU...
...I'D FEEL STUPID FOR CARING ABOUT MY OWN VOICE.
BUT IT'S THE OPPOSITE.

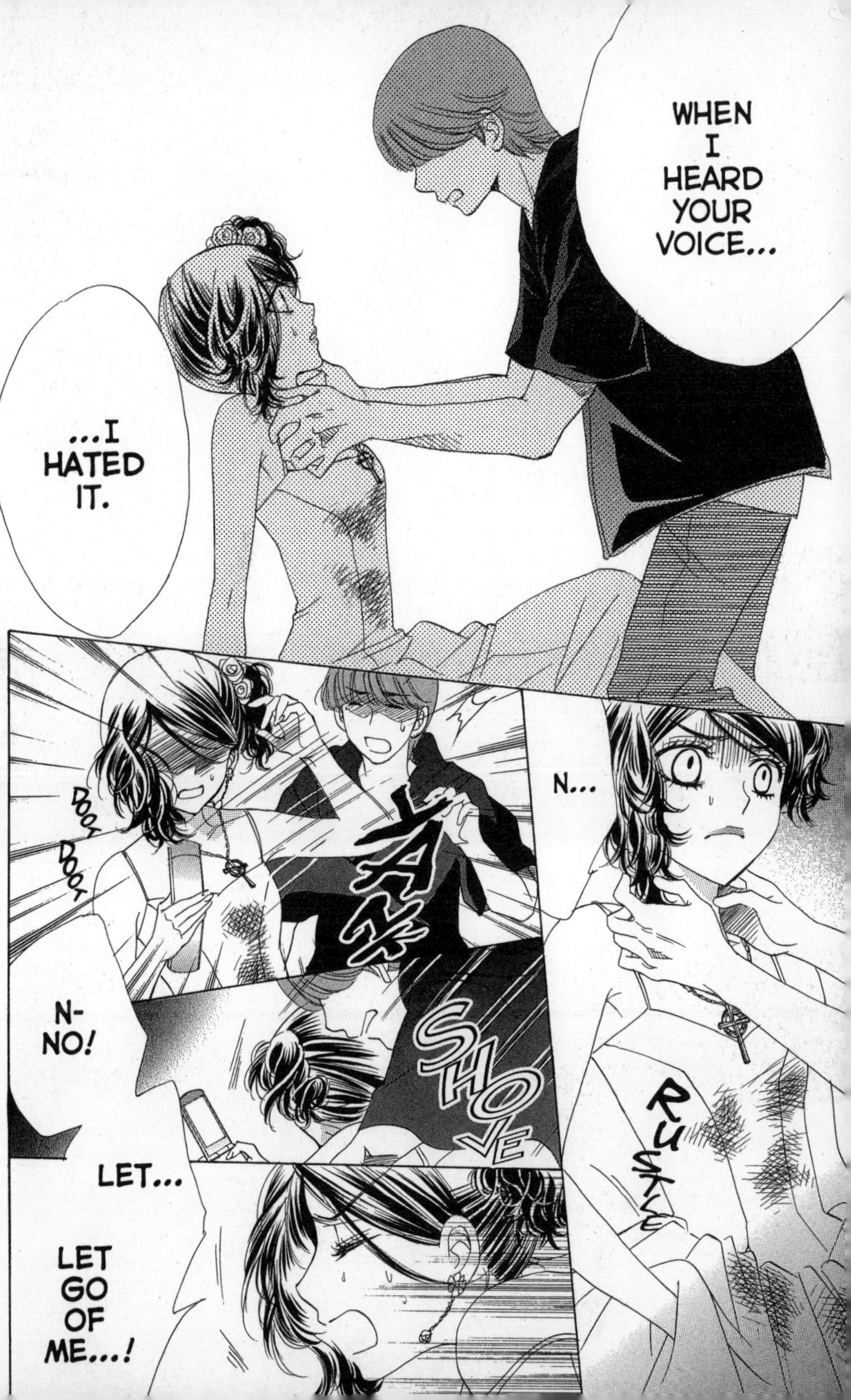
WHEN I HEARD YOUR VOICE...
...I HATED IT.
N...
RUSTLE
DOOT DOOT
YANK
N-NO!
SHOVE
LET...
LET GO OF ME...!

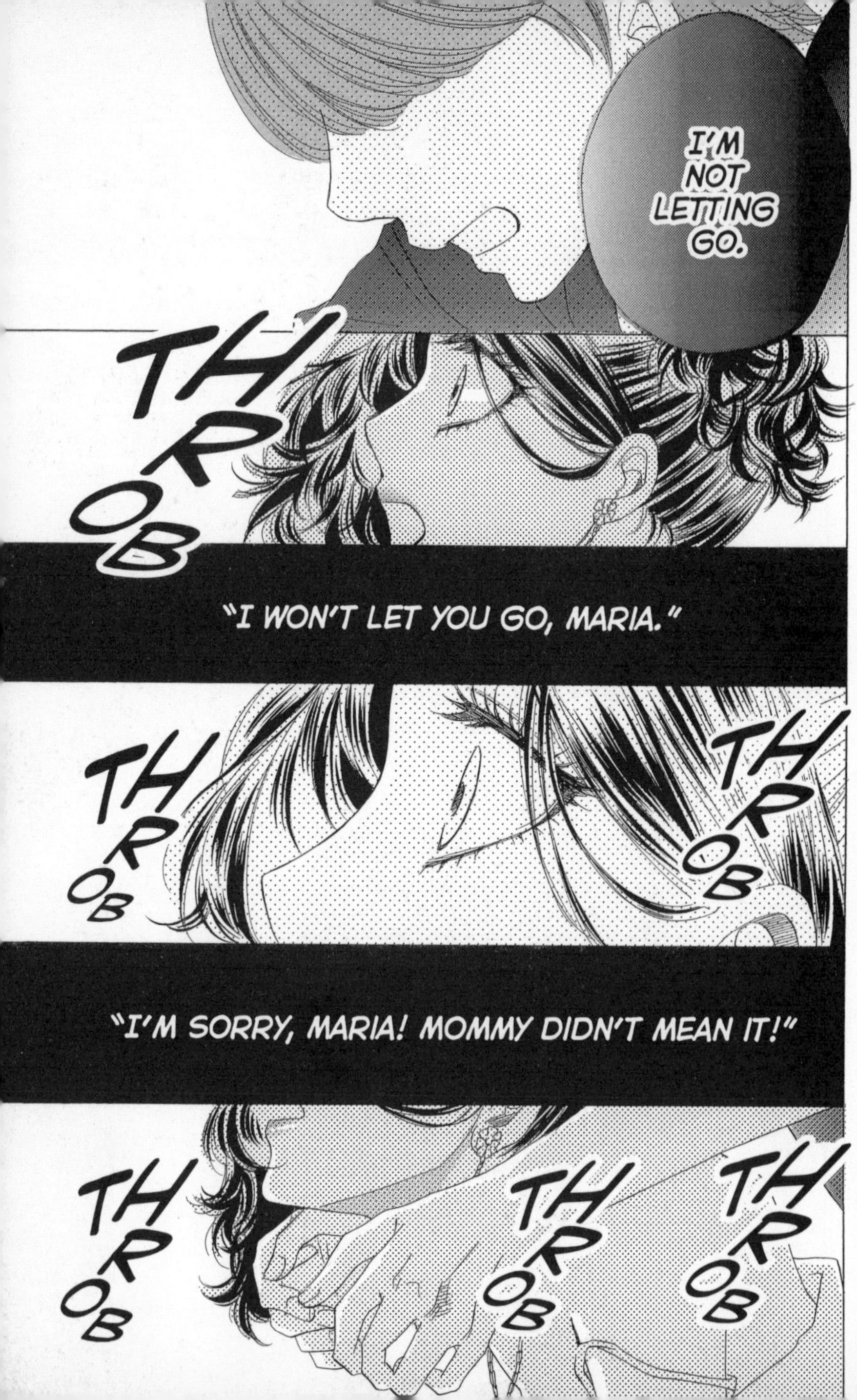
I'M NOT LETTING GO.
THROB
"I WON'T LET YOU GO, MARIA."
THROB
THROB
"I'M SORRY, MARIA! MOMMY DIDN'T MEAN IT!"
THROB
THROB
THROB

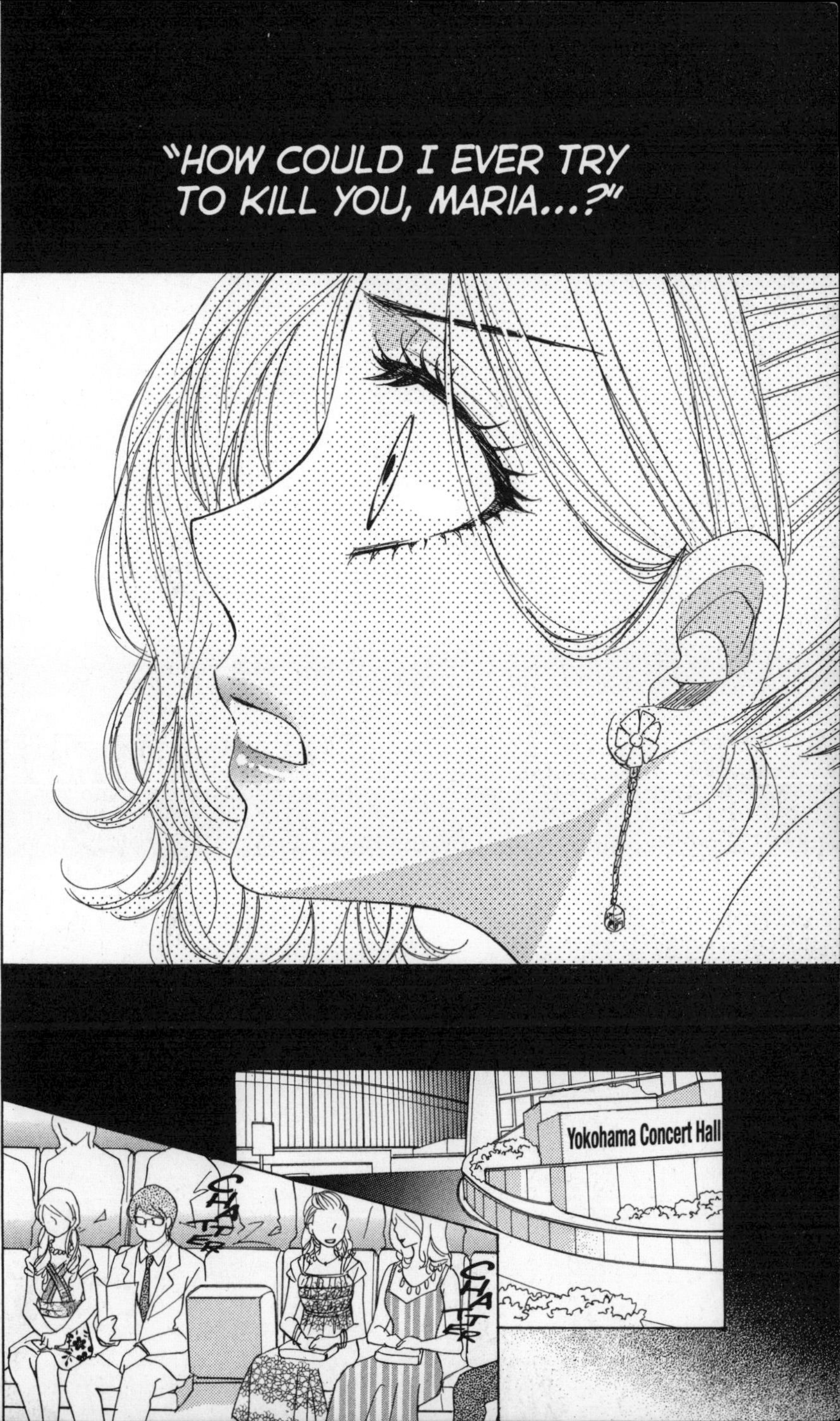
"HOW COULD I EVER TRY TO KILL YOU, MARIA...?"
Yokohama Concert Hall
CHATTER
CHATTER

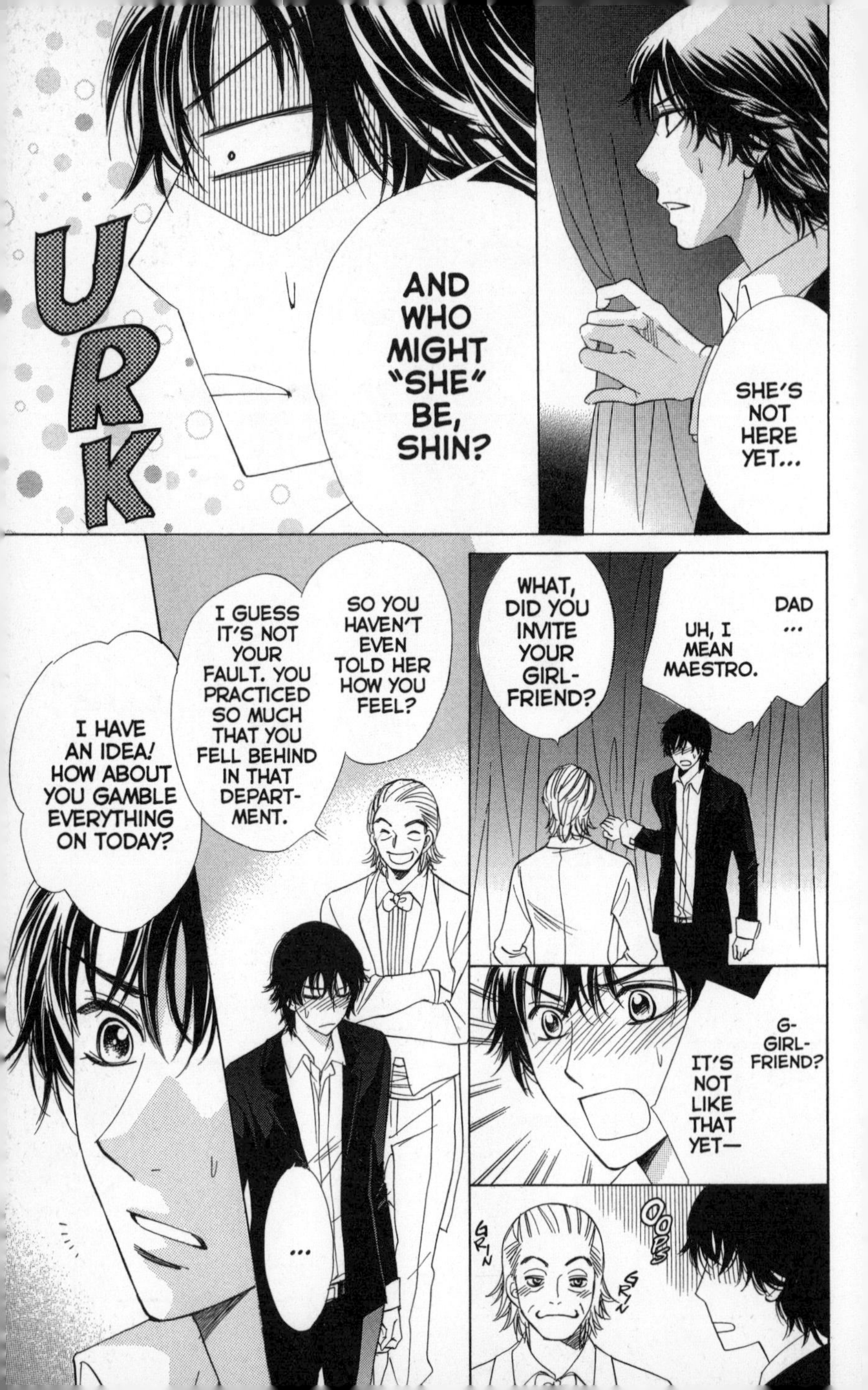
SHE'S NOT HERE YET...
AND WHO MIGHT "SHE" BE, SHIN?
URK
DAD ... UH, I MEAN MAESTRO.
WHAT, DID YOU INVITE YOUR GIRL-FRIEND?
G-GIRL-FRIEND?
IT'S NOT LIKE THAT YET—
OOPS
GRIN
GRIN
SO YOU HAVEN'T EVEN TOLD HER HOW YOU FEEL?
I GUESS IT'S NOT YOUR FAULT. YOU PRACTICED SO MUCH THAT YOU FELL BEHIND IN THAT DEPART-MENT.
I HAVE AN IDEA! HOW ABOUT YOU GAMBLE EVERYTHING ON TODAY?
...

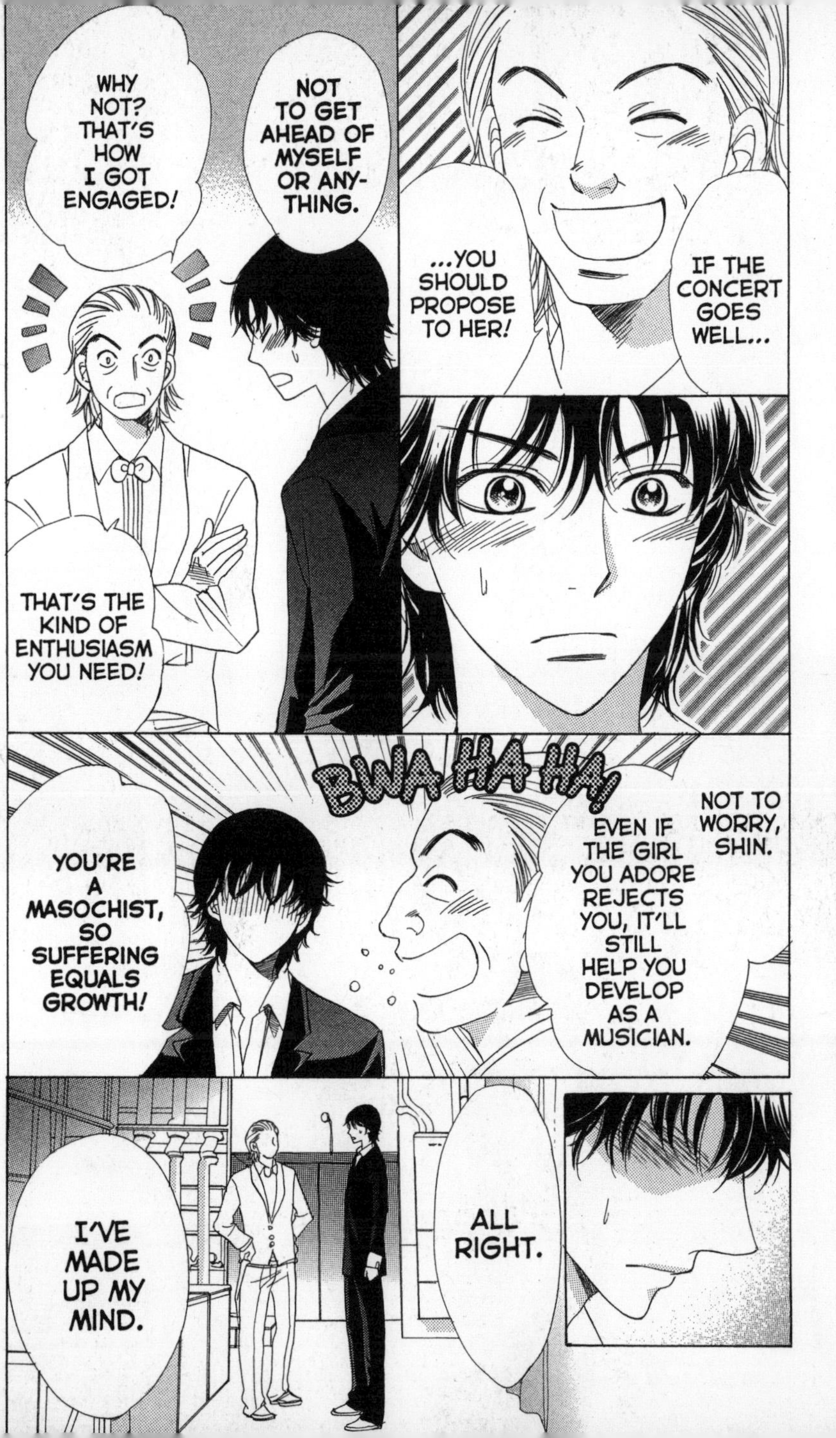
IF THE CONCERT GOES WELL...
...YOU SHOULD PROPOSE TO HER!
NOT TO GET AHEAD OF MYSELF OR ANY-THING.
WHY NOT? THAT'S HOW I GOT ENGAGED!
THAT'S THE KIND OF ENTHUSIASM YOU NEED!
NOT TO WORRY, SHIN.
EVEN IF THE GIRL YOU ADORE REJECTS YOU, IT'LL STILL HELP YOU DEVELOP AS A MUSICIAN.
BWA HA HA!
YOU'RE A MASOCHIST, SO SUFFERING EQUALS GROWTH!
ALL RIGHT.
I'VE MADE UP MY MIND.

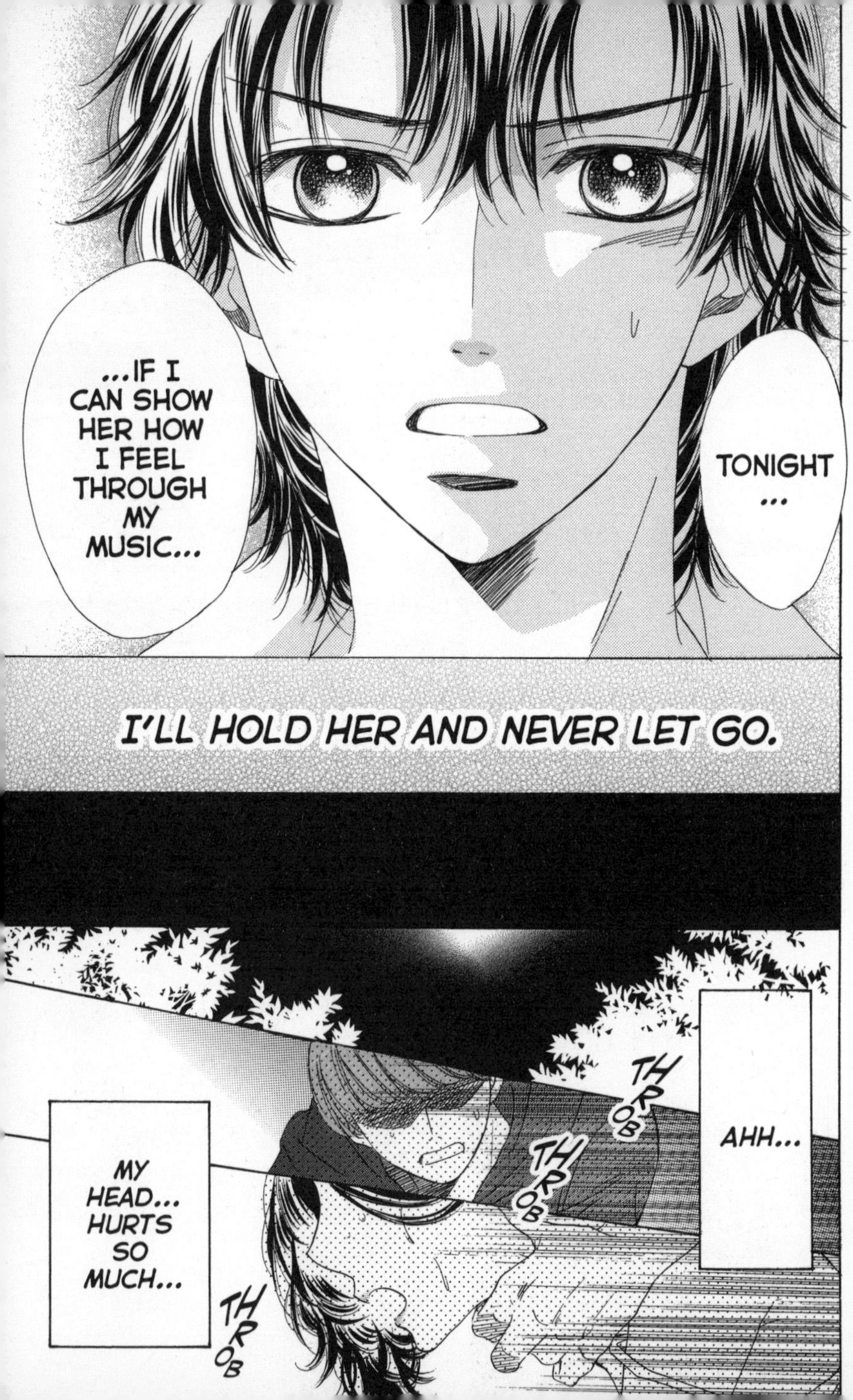
TONIGHT...
...IF I CAN SHOW HER HOW I FEEL THROUGH MY MUSIC...
I'LL HOLD HER AND NEVER LET GO.
AHH...
THROB
THROB
MY HEAD... HURTS SO MUCH...
THROB

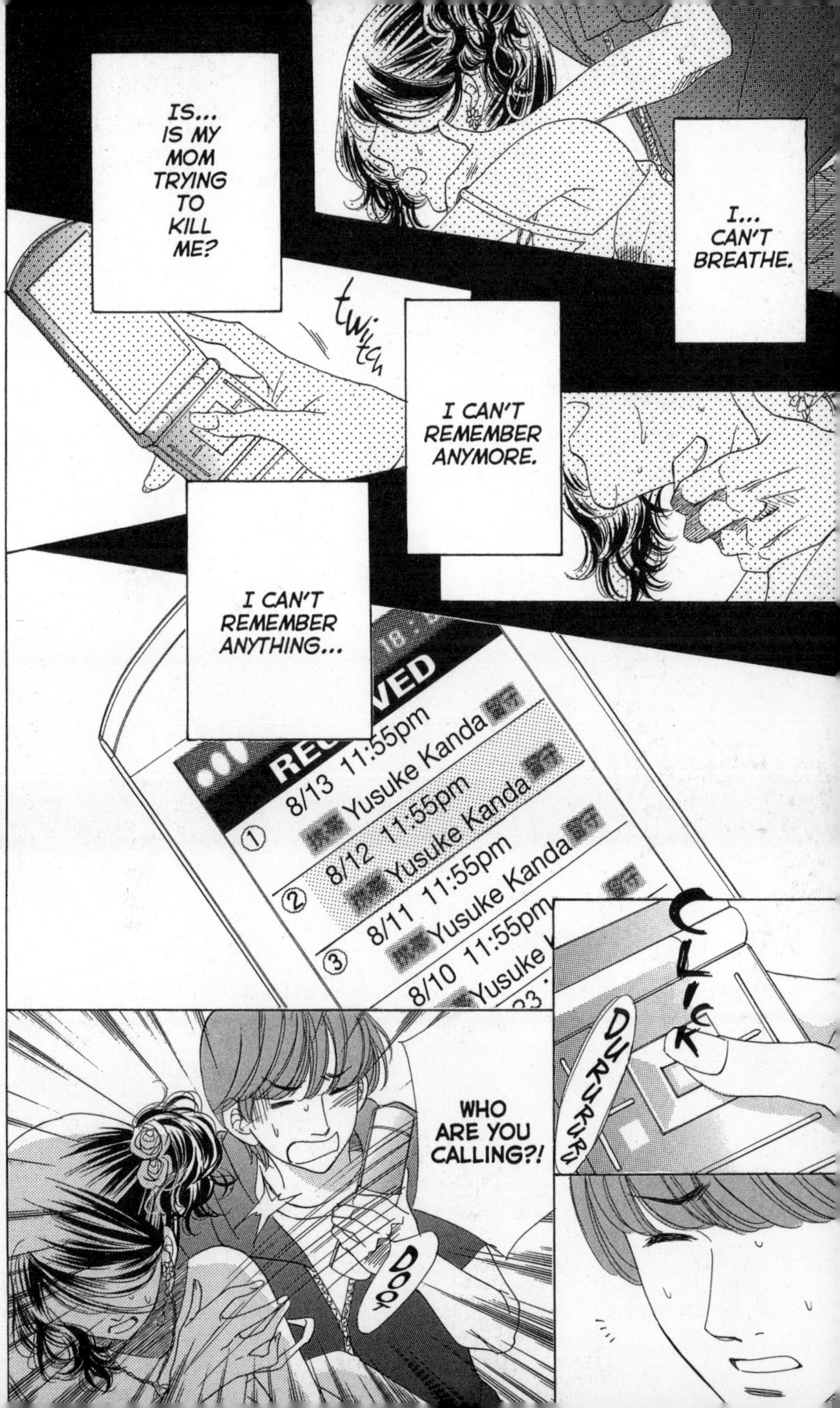
I... CAN'T BREATHE.
IS... IS MY MOM TRYING TO KILL ME?
twitch
I CAN'T REMEMBER ANYMORE.
I CAN'T REMEMBER ANYTHING...
RE
VED
8/13 11:55pm
Yusuke Kanda
8/12 11:55pm
Yusuke Kanda
8/11 11:55pm
Yusuke Kanda
8/10 11:55pm
Yusuke
CLICK
DURURURU
WHO ARE YOU CALLING?!
DOOF

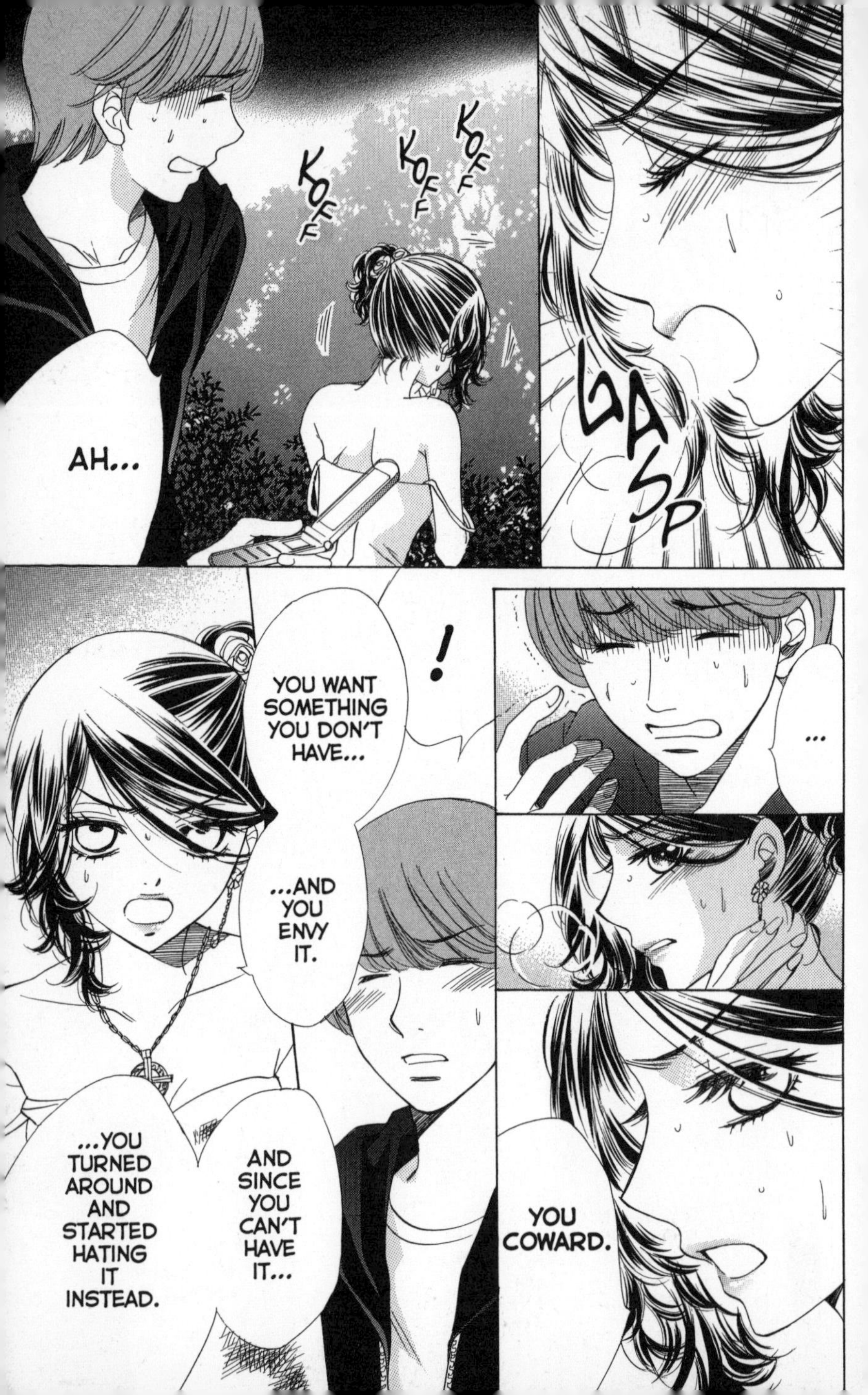
GASP
KOFF KOFF KOFF
AH...
...
YOU COWARD.
!
YOU WANT SOMETHING YOU DON'T HAVE...
...AND YOU ENVY IT.
AND SINCE YOU CAN'T HAVE IT...
...YOU TURNED AROUND AND STARTED HATING IT INSTEAD.

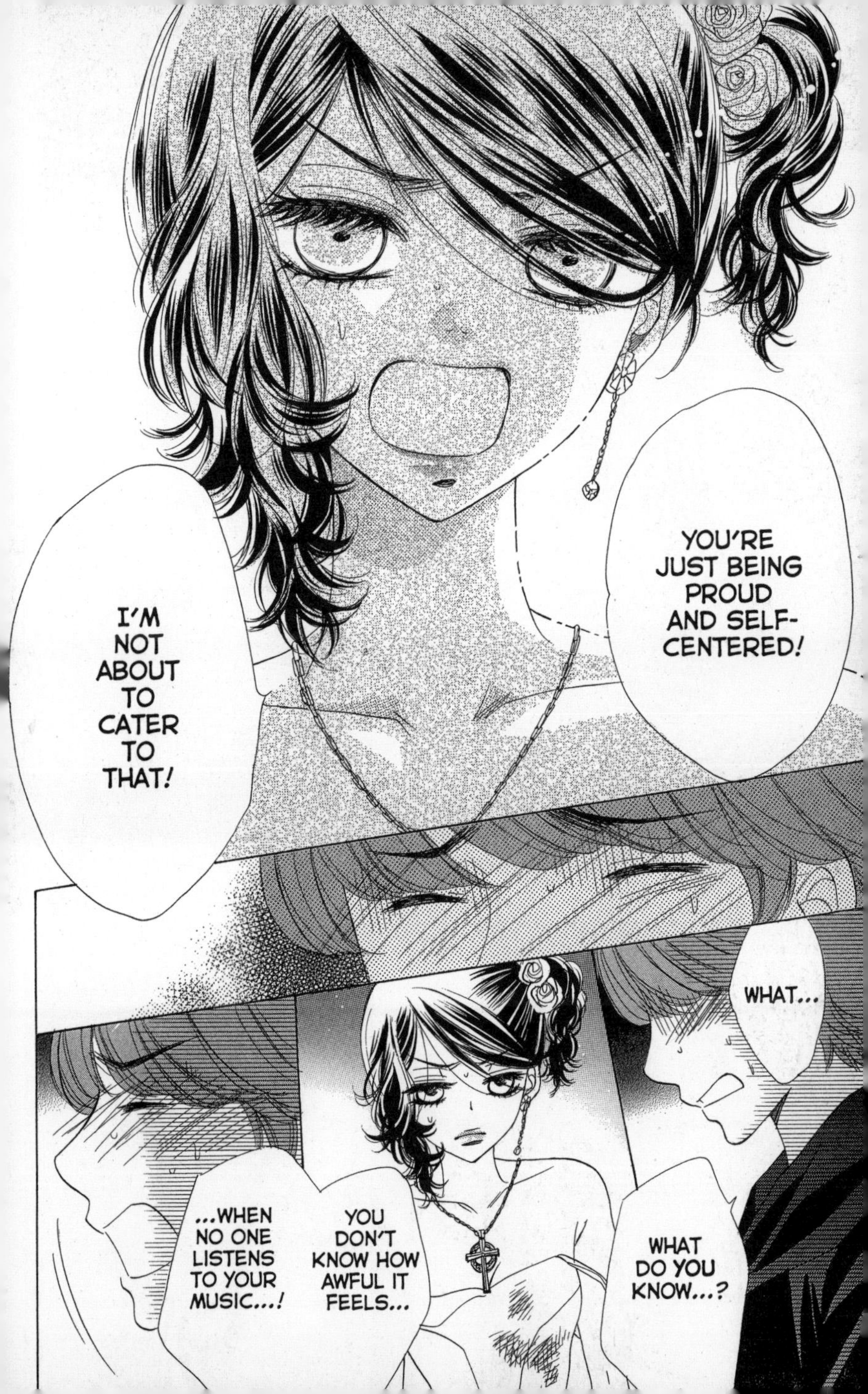
YOU'RE JUST BEING PROUD AND SELF-CENTERED!
I'M NOT ABOUT TO CATER TO THAT!
WHAT...
WHAT DO YOU KNOW...?
YOU DON'T KNOW HOW AWFUL IT FEELS...
...WHEN NO ONE LISTENS TO YOUR MUSIC...!

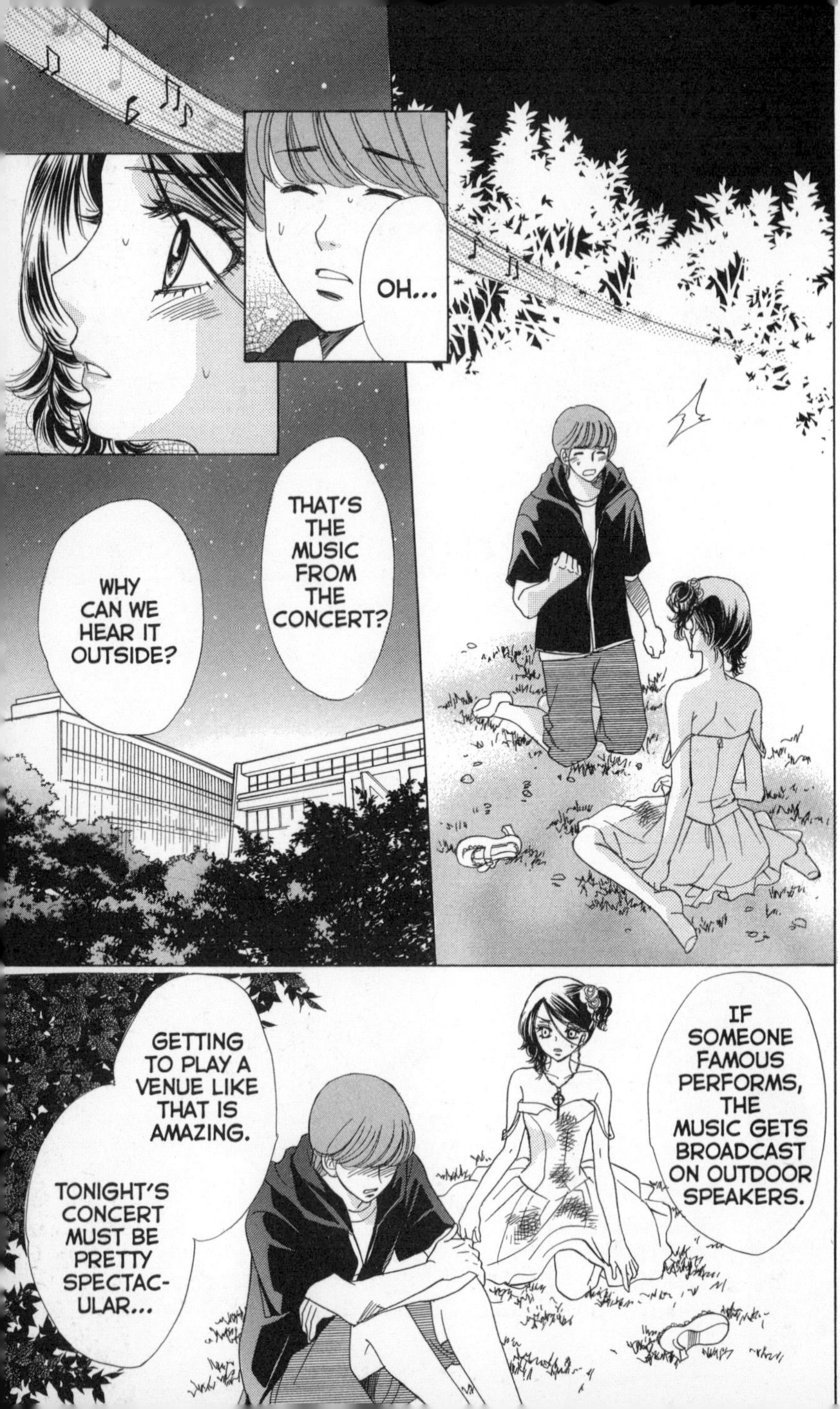
OH...
THAT'S THE MUSIC FROM THE CONCERT?
WHY CAN WE HEAR IT OUTSIDE?
IF SOMEONE FAMOUS PERFORMS, THE MUSIC GETS BROADCAST ON OUTDOOR SPEAKERS.
GETTING TO PLAY A VENUE LIKE THAT IS AMAZING.
TONIGHT'S CONCERT MUST BE PRETTY SPECTAC-ULAR...

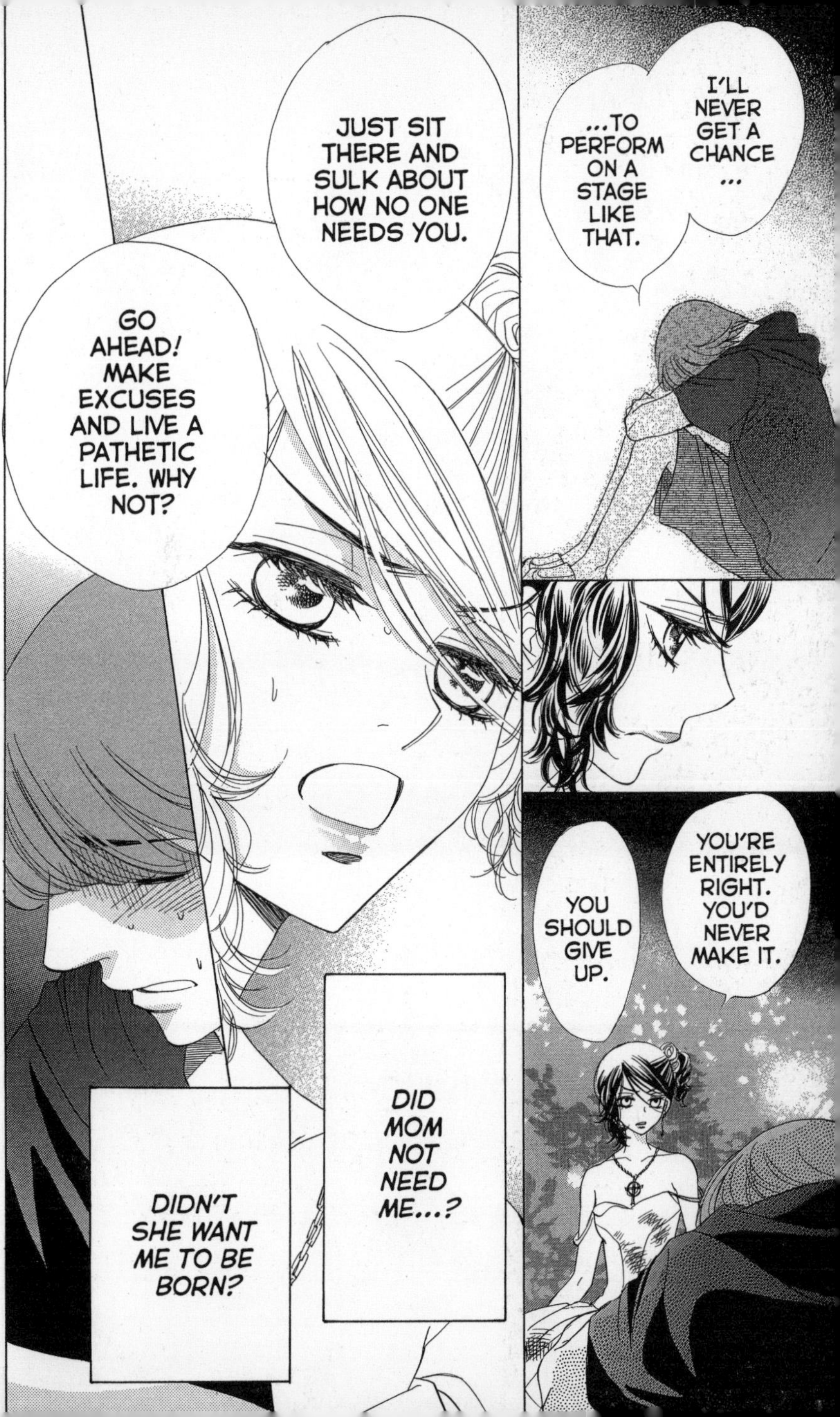
I'LL NEVER GET A CHANCE ...
...TO PERFORM ON A STAGE LIKE THAT.
YOU'RE ENTIRELY RIGHT. YOU'D NEVER MAKE IT.
YOU SHOULD GIVE UP.
JUST SIT THERE AND SULK ABOUT HOW NO ONE NEEDS YOU.
GO AHEAD! MAKE EXCUSES AND LIVE A PATHETIC LIFE. WHY NOT?
DID MOM NOT NEED ME...?
DIDN'T SHE WANT ME TO BE BORN?

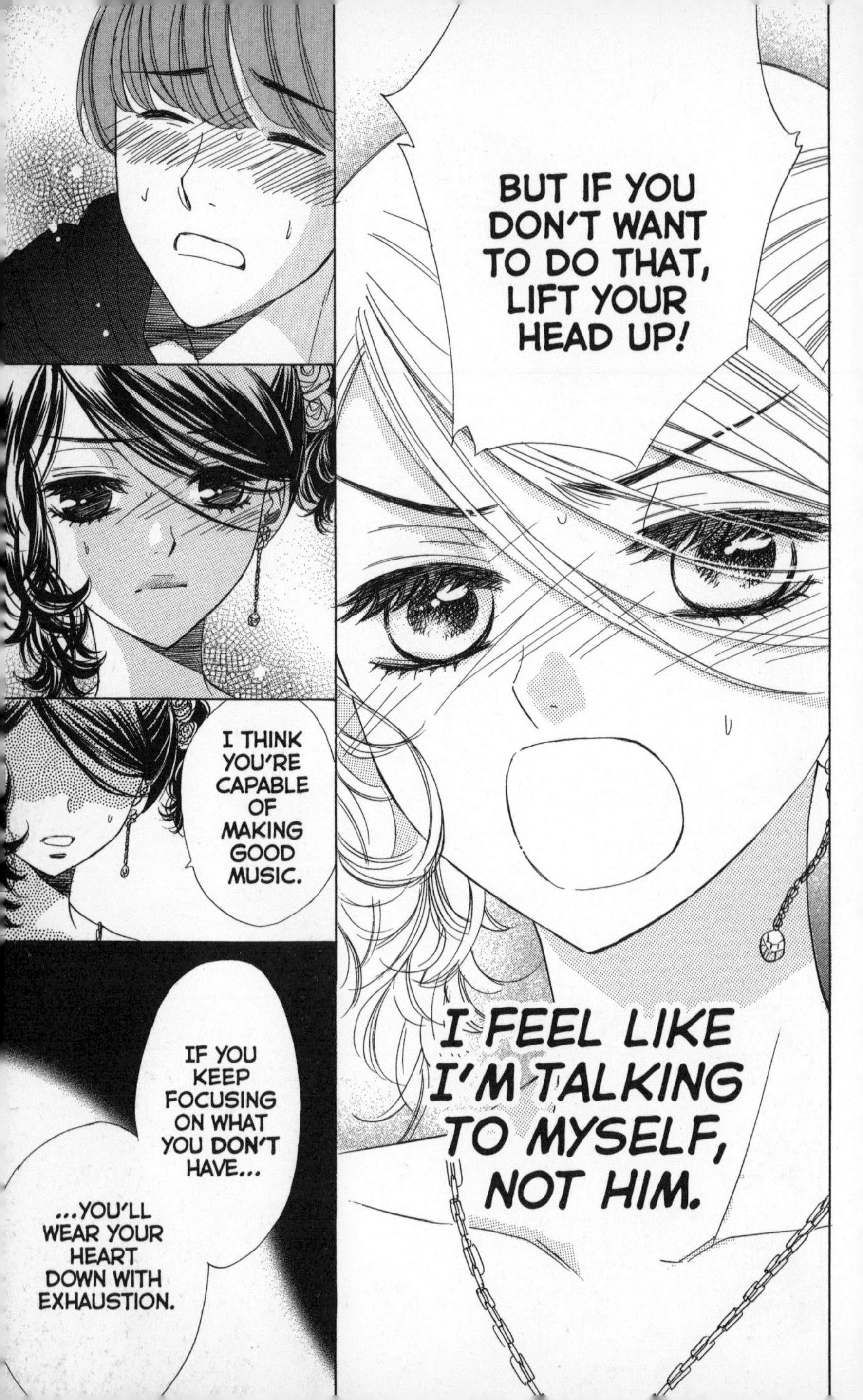
BUT IF YOU DON'T WANT TO DO THAT, LIFT YOUR HEAD UP!
I FEEL LIKE I'M TALKING TO MYSELF, NOT HIM.
I THINK YOU'RE CAPABLE OF MAKING GOOD MUSIC.
IF YOU KEEP FOCUSING ON WHAT YOU DON'T HAVE...
...YOU'LL WEAR YOUR HEART DOWN WITH EXHAUSTION.

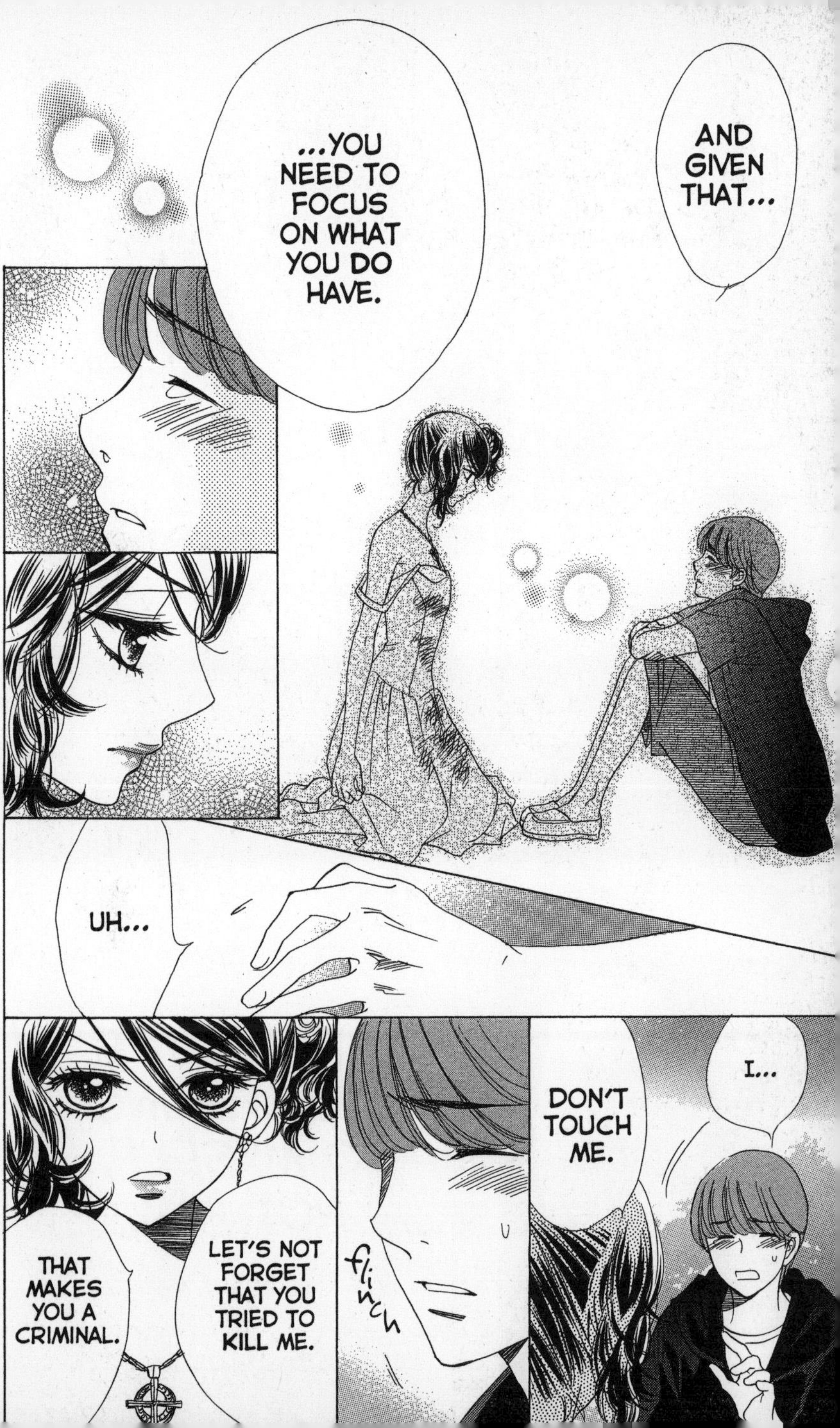
AND GIVEN THAT...
...YOU NEED TO FOCUS ON WHAT YOU DO HAVE.
UH...
I...
DON'T TOUCH ME.
flinch
LET'S NOT FORGET THAT YOU TRIED TO KILL ME.
THAT MAKES YOU A CRIMINAL.

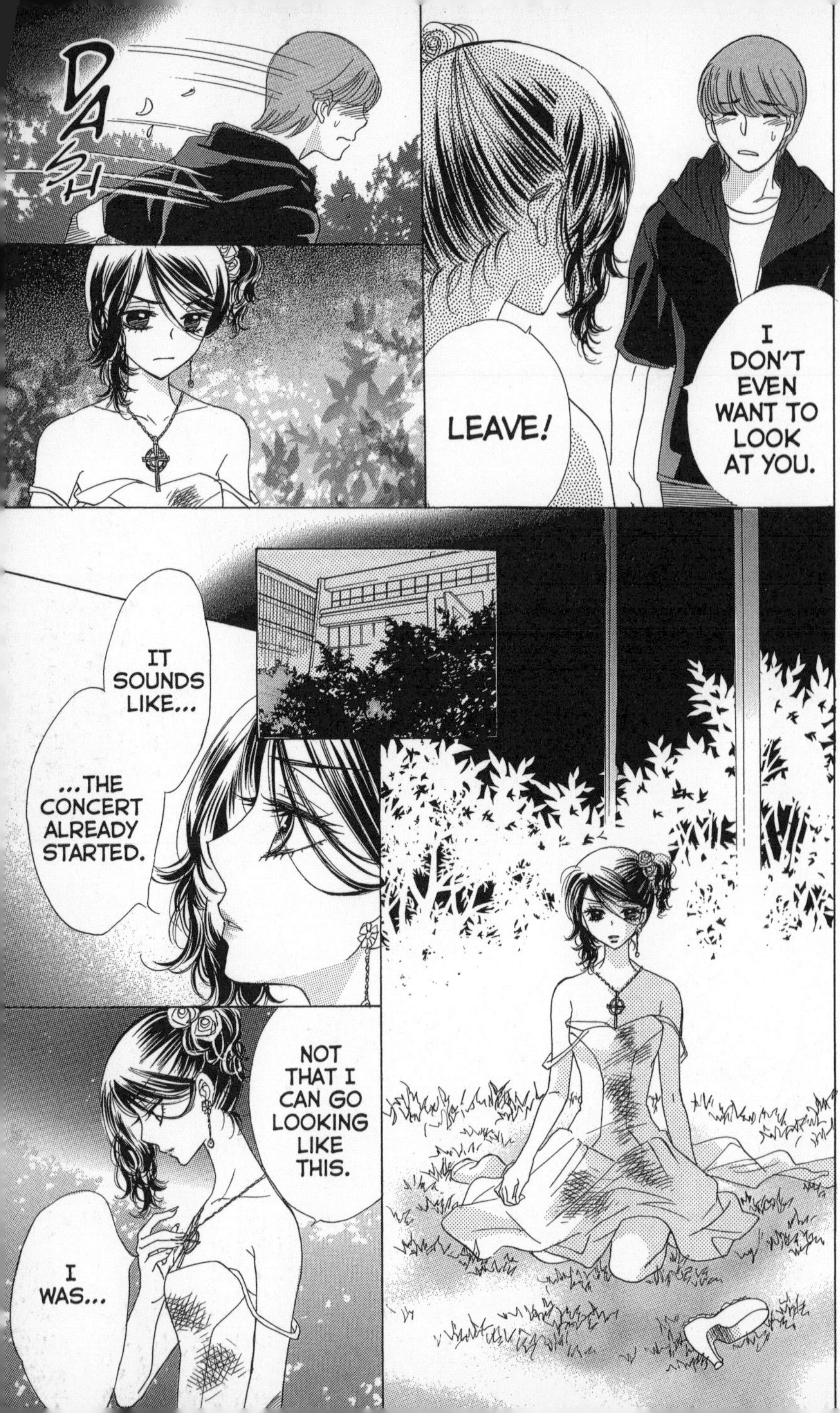
I DON'T EVEN WANT TO LOOK AT YOU.
LEAVE!
DASH
IT SOUNDS LIKE...
...THE CONCERT ALREADY STARTED.
NOT THAT I CAN GO LOOKING LIKE THIS.
I WAS...

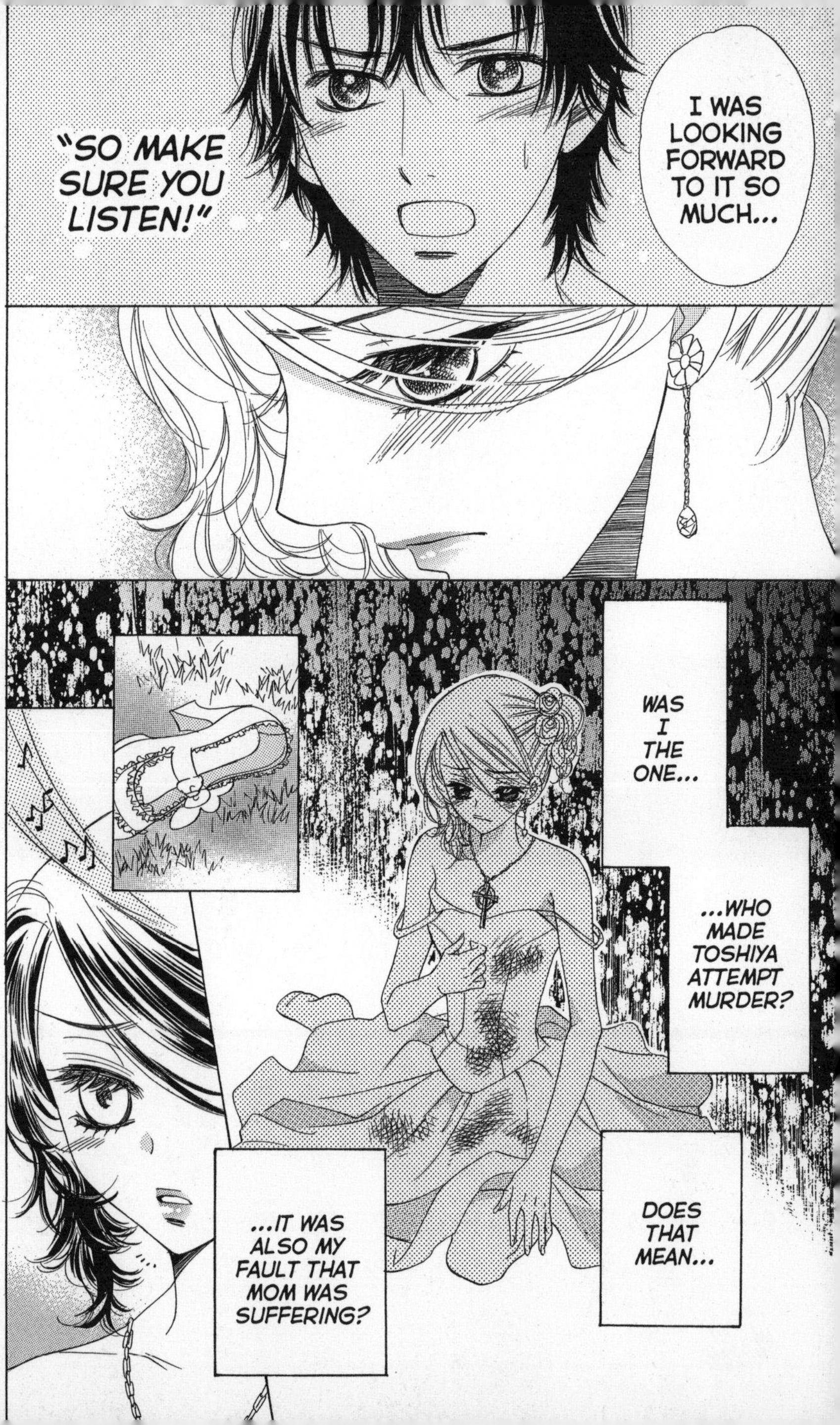
I WAS LOOKING FORWARD TO IT SO MUCH...
"SO MAKE SURE YOU LISTEN!"
WAS I THE ONE...
...WHO MADE TOSHIYA ATTEMPT MURDER?
DOES THAT MEAN...
...IT WAS ALSO MY FAULT THAT MOM WAS SUFFERING?

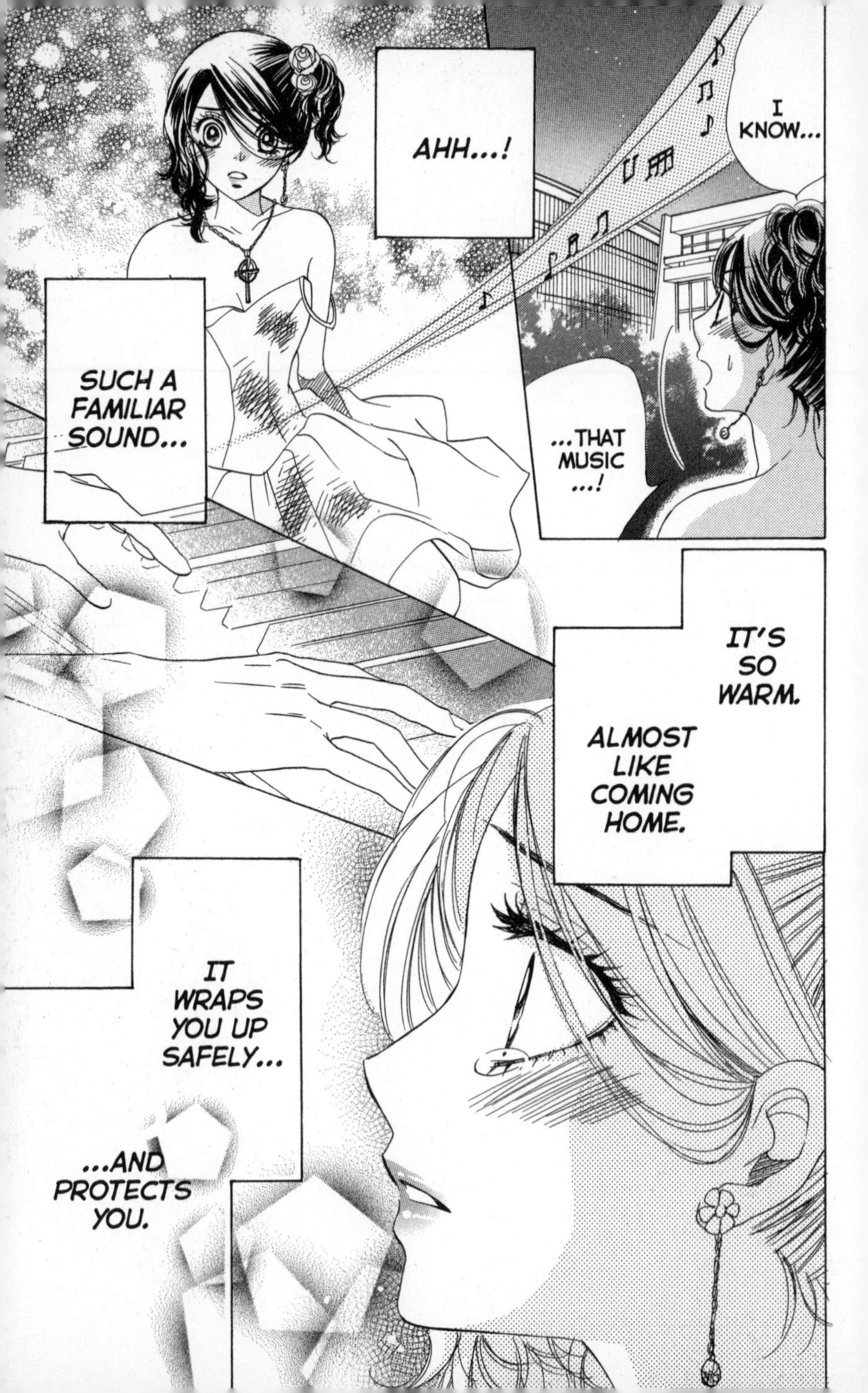
I KNOW...
...THAT MUSIC ...!
AHH...!
SUCH A FAMILIAR SOUND...
IT'S SO WARM.
ALMOST LIKE COMING HOME.
IT WRAPS YOU UP SAFELY...
...AND PROTECTS YOU.

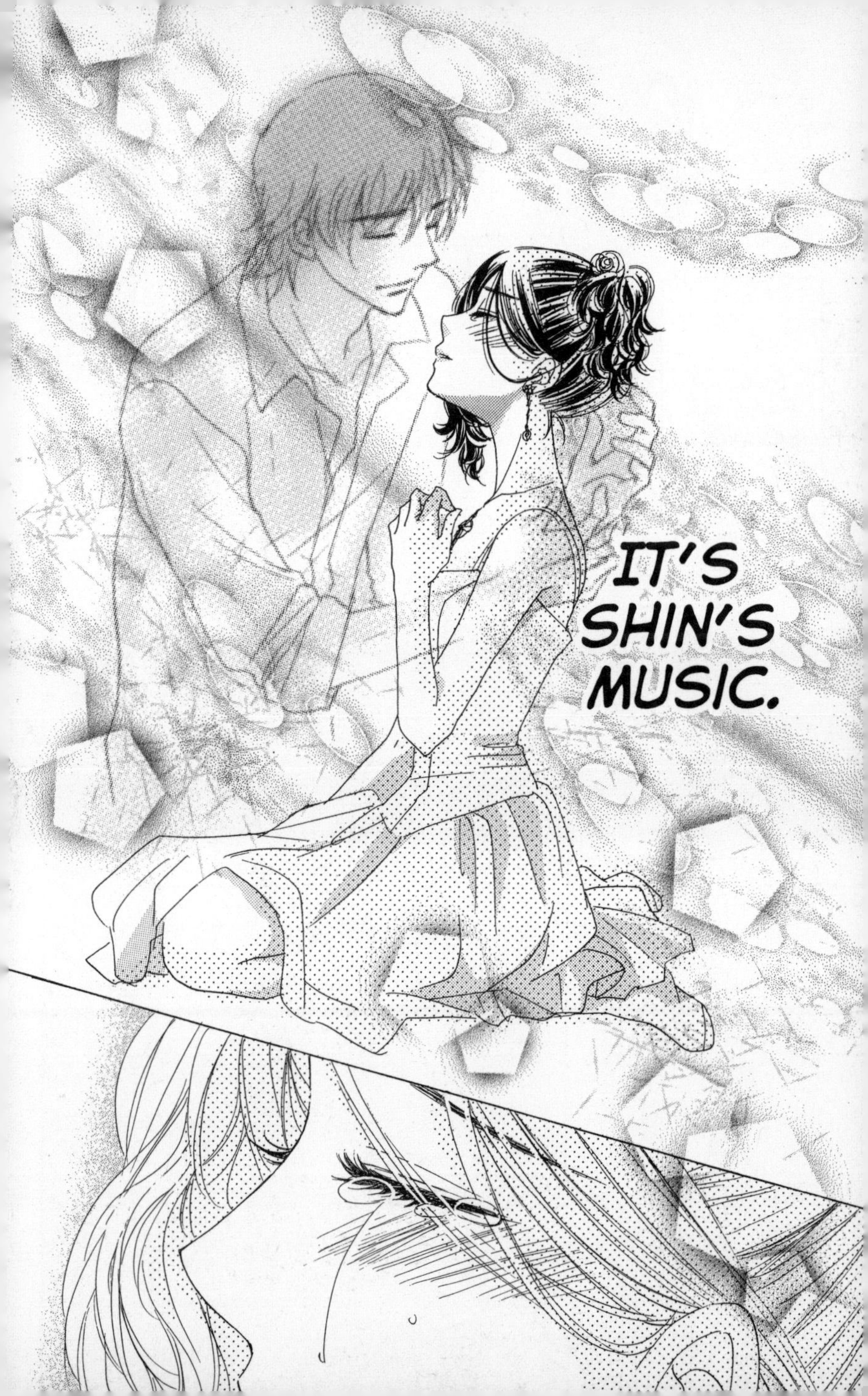
IT'S SHIN'S MUSIC.

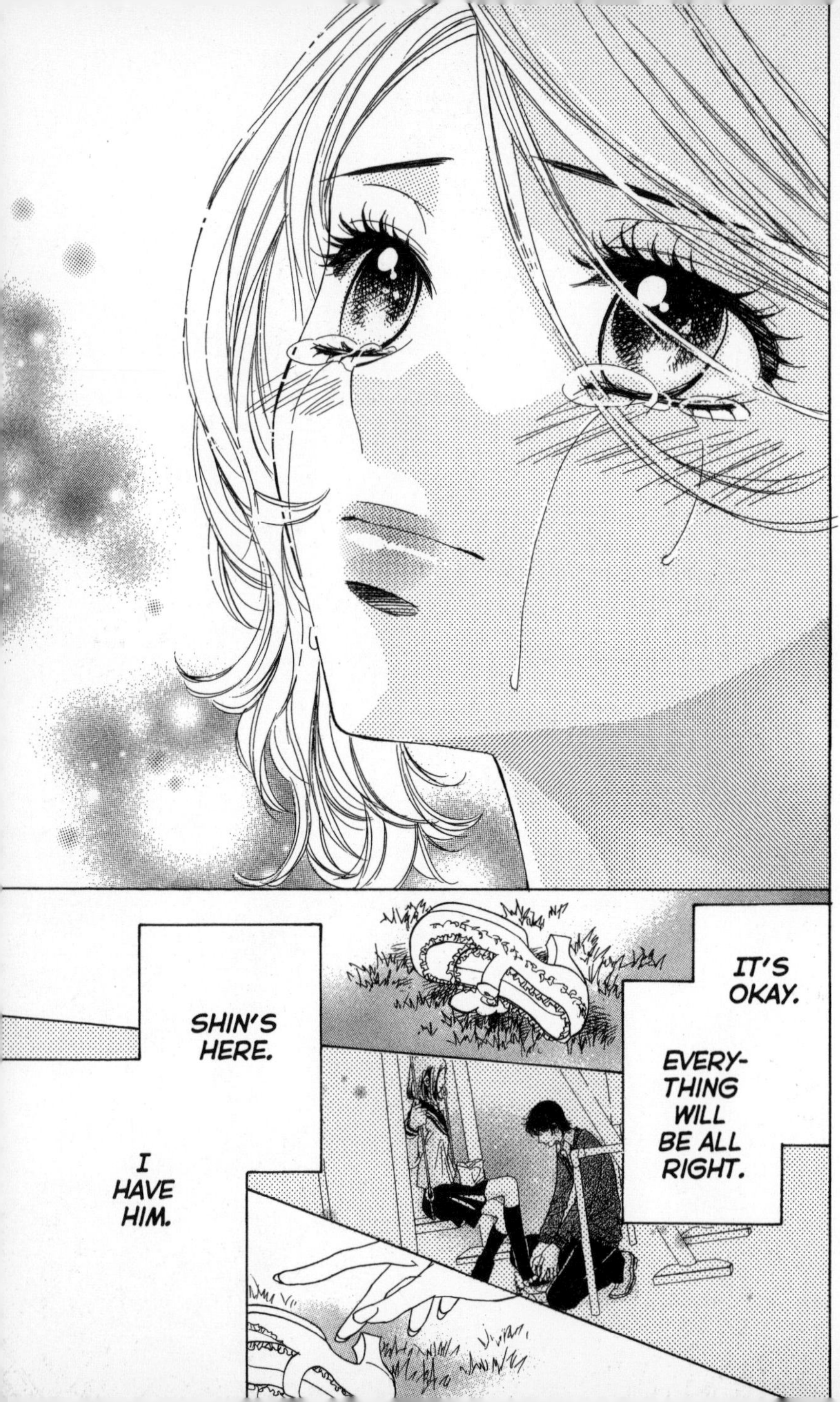
IT'S OKAY.
EVERY-THING WILL BE ALL RIGHT.
SHIN'S HERE.
I HAVE HIM.

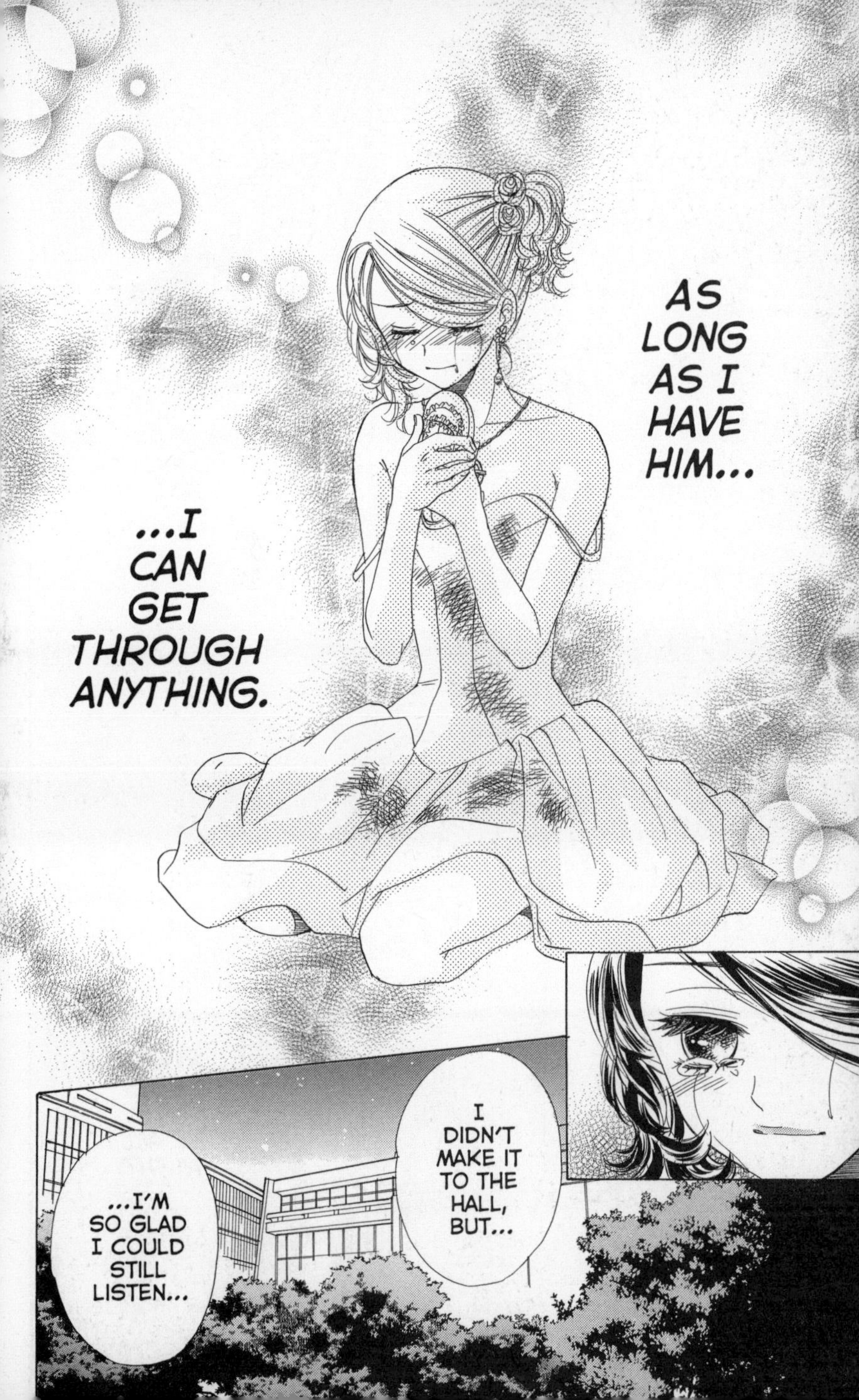
AS LONG AS I HAVE HIM...
...I CAN GET THROUGH ANYTHING.
I DIDN'T MAKE IT TO THE HALL, BUT...
...I'M SO GLAD I COULD STILL LISTEN...

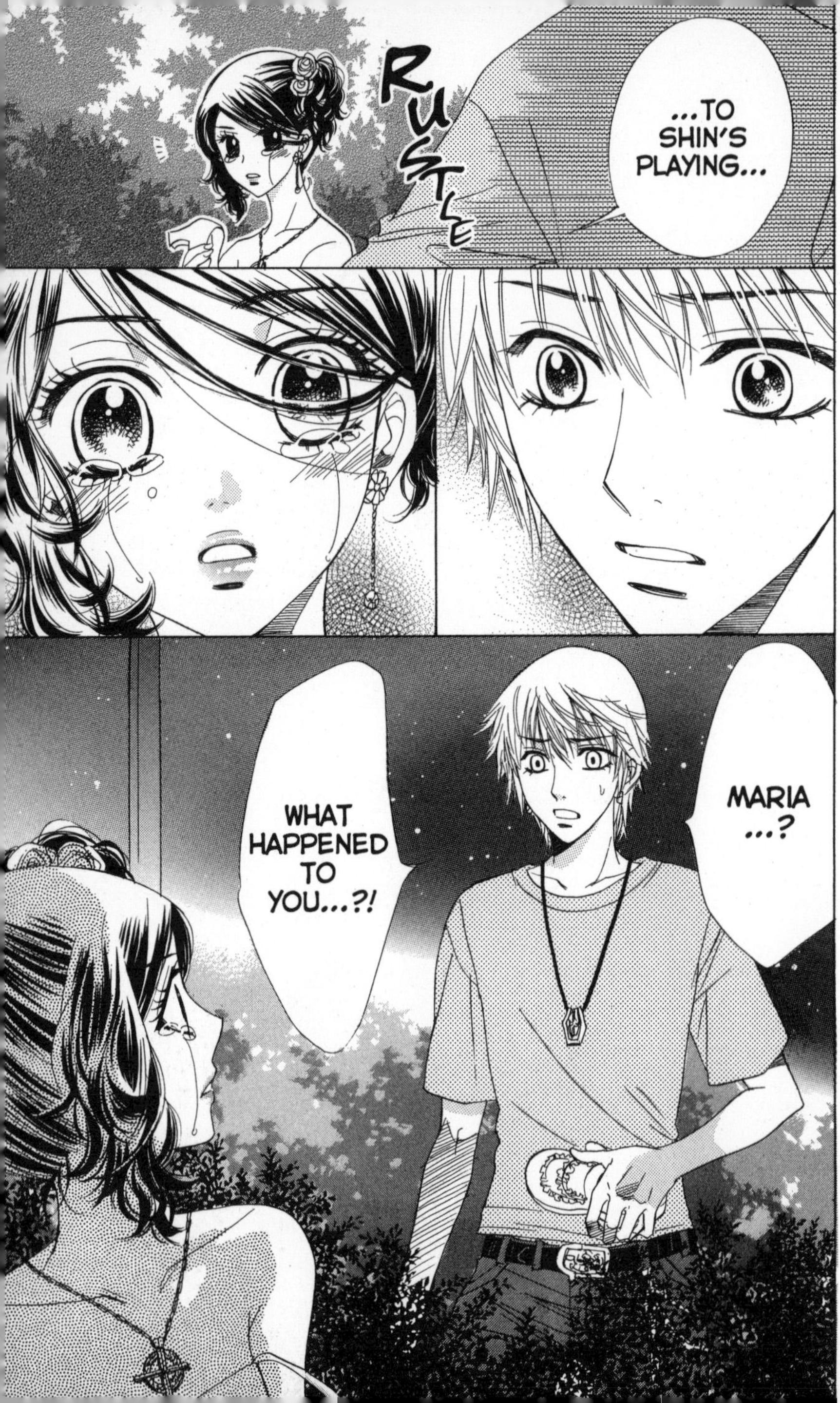
...TO SHIN'S PLAYING...
RUSTLE
MARIA ...?
WHAT HAPPENED TO YOU...?!

A Devil and
Her Love Song

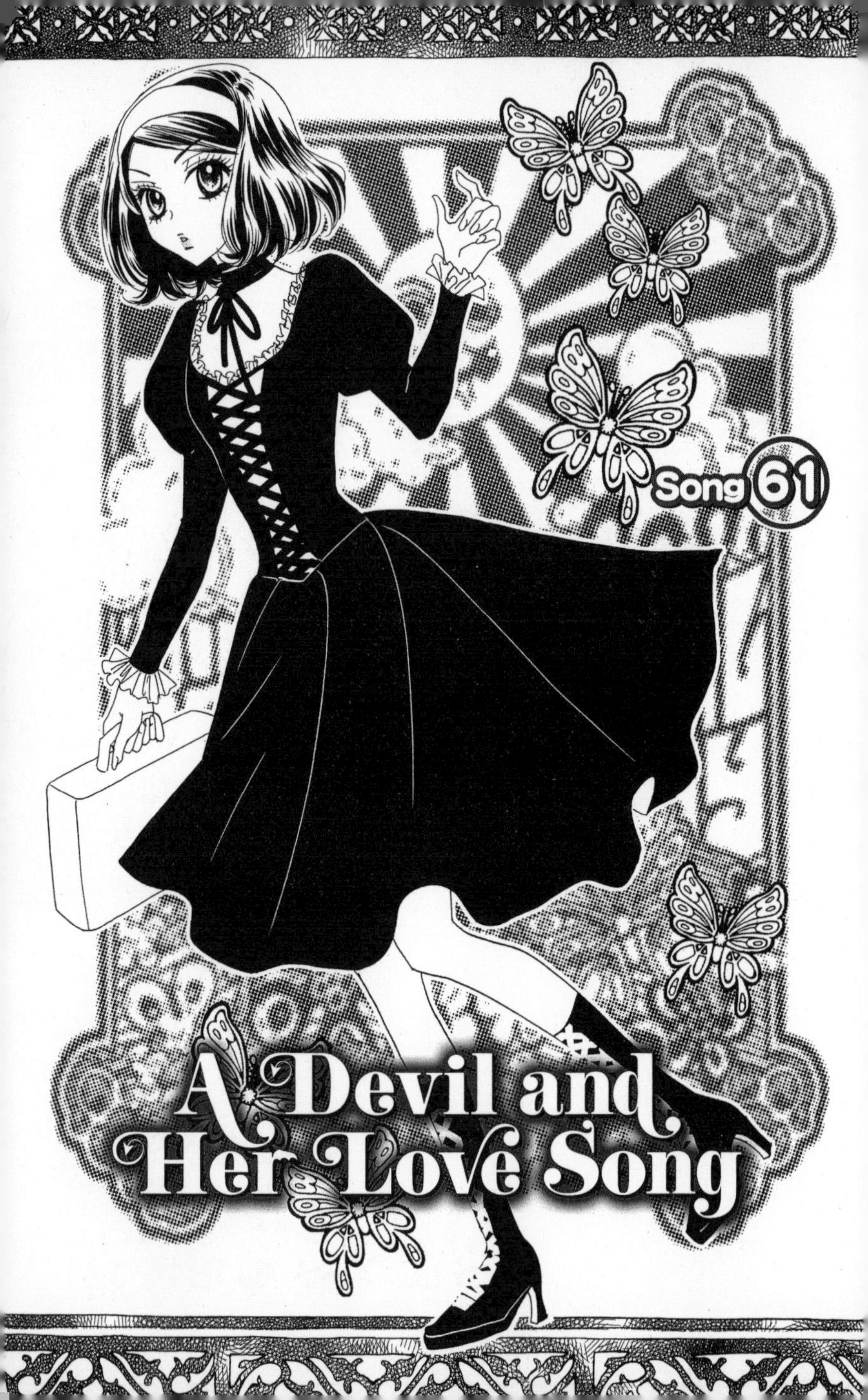
Song 61
A Devil and Her Love Song

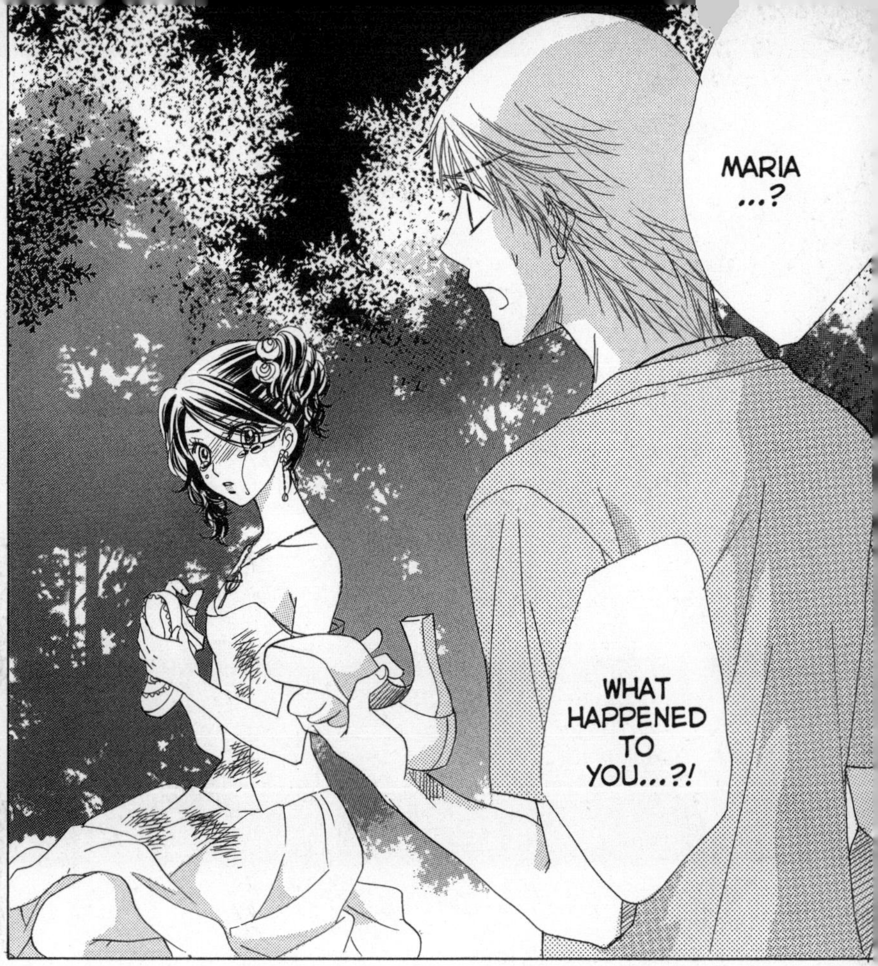
MARIA ...?
WHAT HAPPENED TO YOU...?!

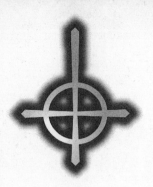

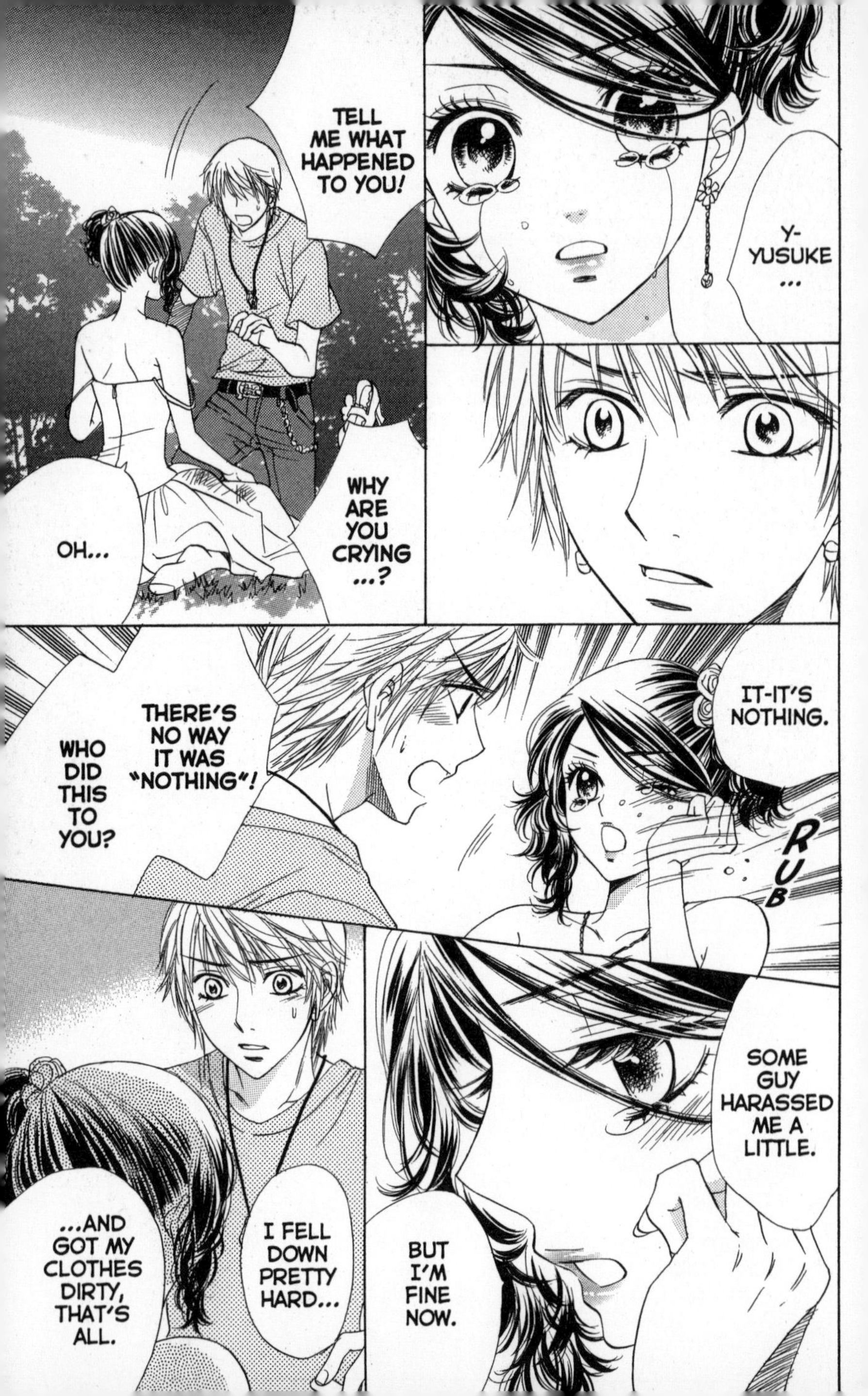
Y-YUSUKE...
TELL ME WHAT HAPPENED TO YOU!
WHY ARE YOU CRYING...?
OH...
IT-IT'S NOTHING.
RUB
THERE'S NO WAY IT WAS "NOTHING"!
WHO DID THIS TO YOU?
SOME GUY HARASSED ME A LITTLE.
BUT I'M FINE NOW.
I FELL DOWN PRETTY HARD...
...AND GOT MY CLOTHES DIRTY, THAT'S ALL.

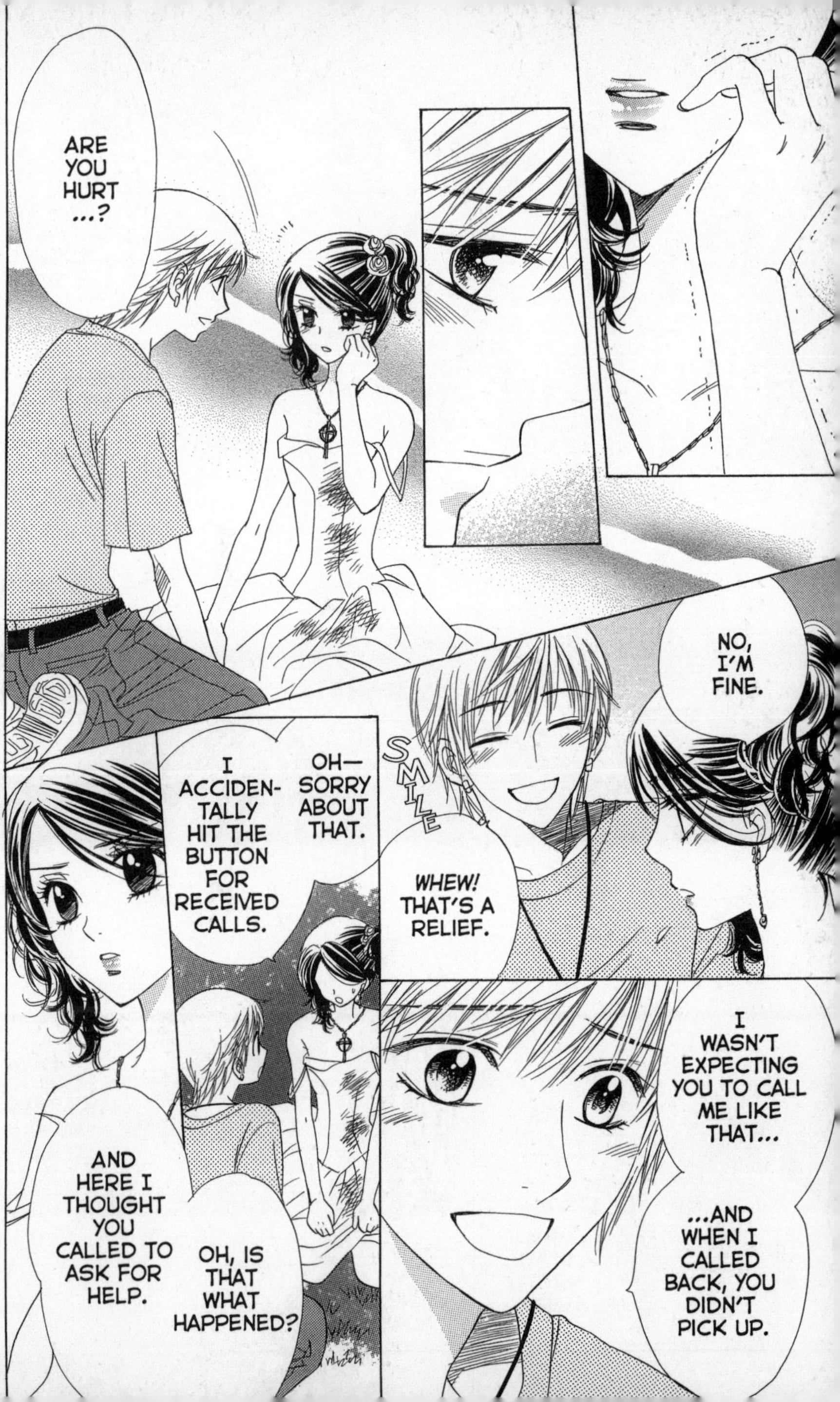
ARE YOU HURT ...?
NO, I'M FINE.
SMILE
WHEW! THAT'S A RELIEF.
OH— SORRY ABOUT THAT.
I ACCIDENTALLY HIT THE BUTTON FOR RECEIVED CALLS.
I WASN'T EXPECTING YOU TO CALL ME LIKE THAT...
...AND WHEN I CALLED BACK, YOU DIDN'T PICK UP.
OH, IS THAT WHAT HAPPENED?
AND HERE I THOUGHT YOU CALLED TO ASK FOR HELP.

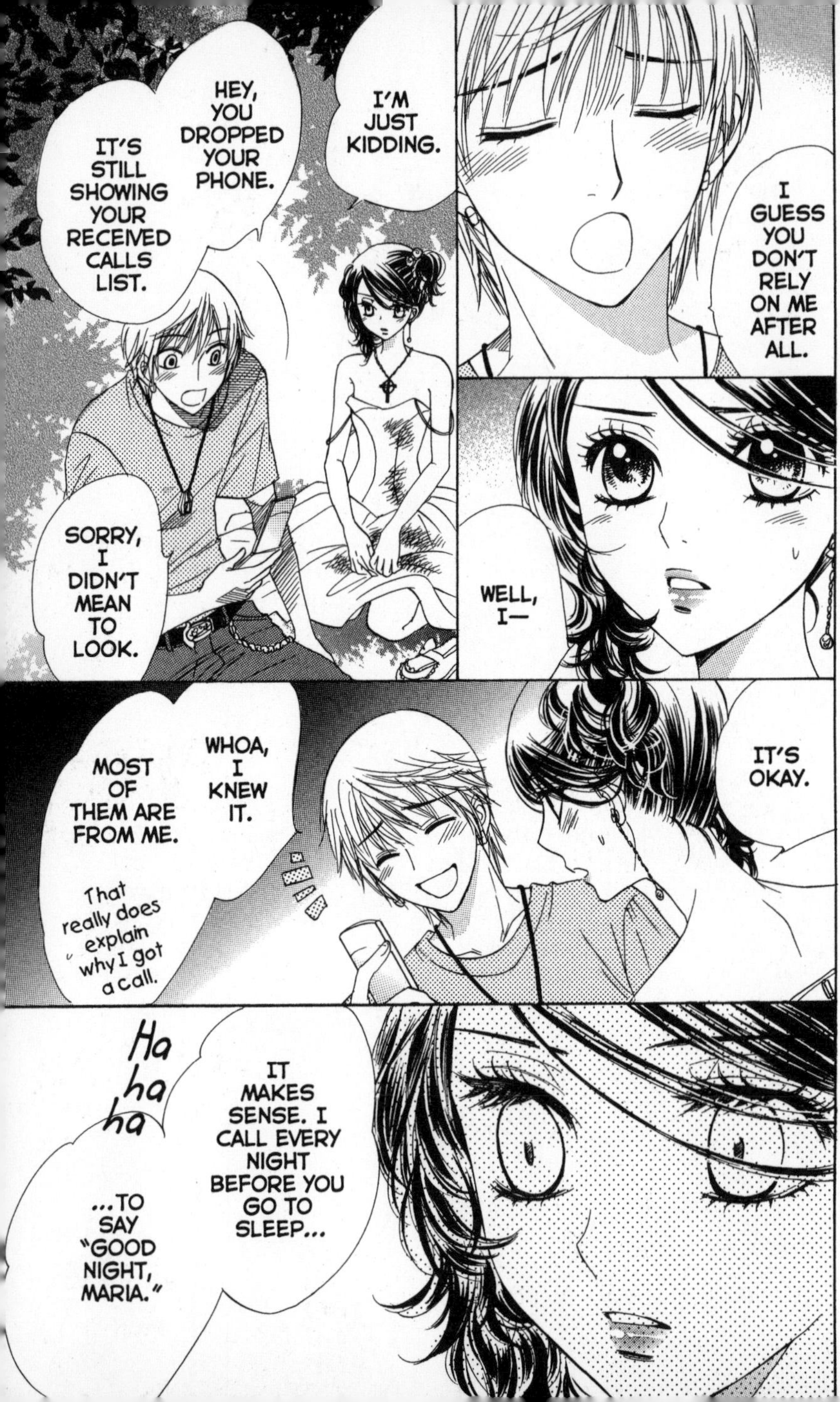
I GUESS YOU DON'T RELY ON ME AFTER ALL.
WELL, I—
I'M JUST KIDDING.
HEY, YOU DROPPED YOUR PHONE.
IT'S STILL SHOWING YOUR RECEIVED CALLS LIST.
SORRY, I DIDN'T MEAN TO LOOK.
IT'S OKAY.
WHOA, I KNEW IT.
MOST OF THEM ARE FROM ME.
That really does explain why I got a call.
IT MAKES SENSE. I CALL EVERY NIGHT BEFORE YOU GO TO SLEEP...
Ha ha ha
...TO SAY "GOOD NIGHT, MARIA."

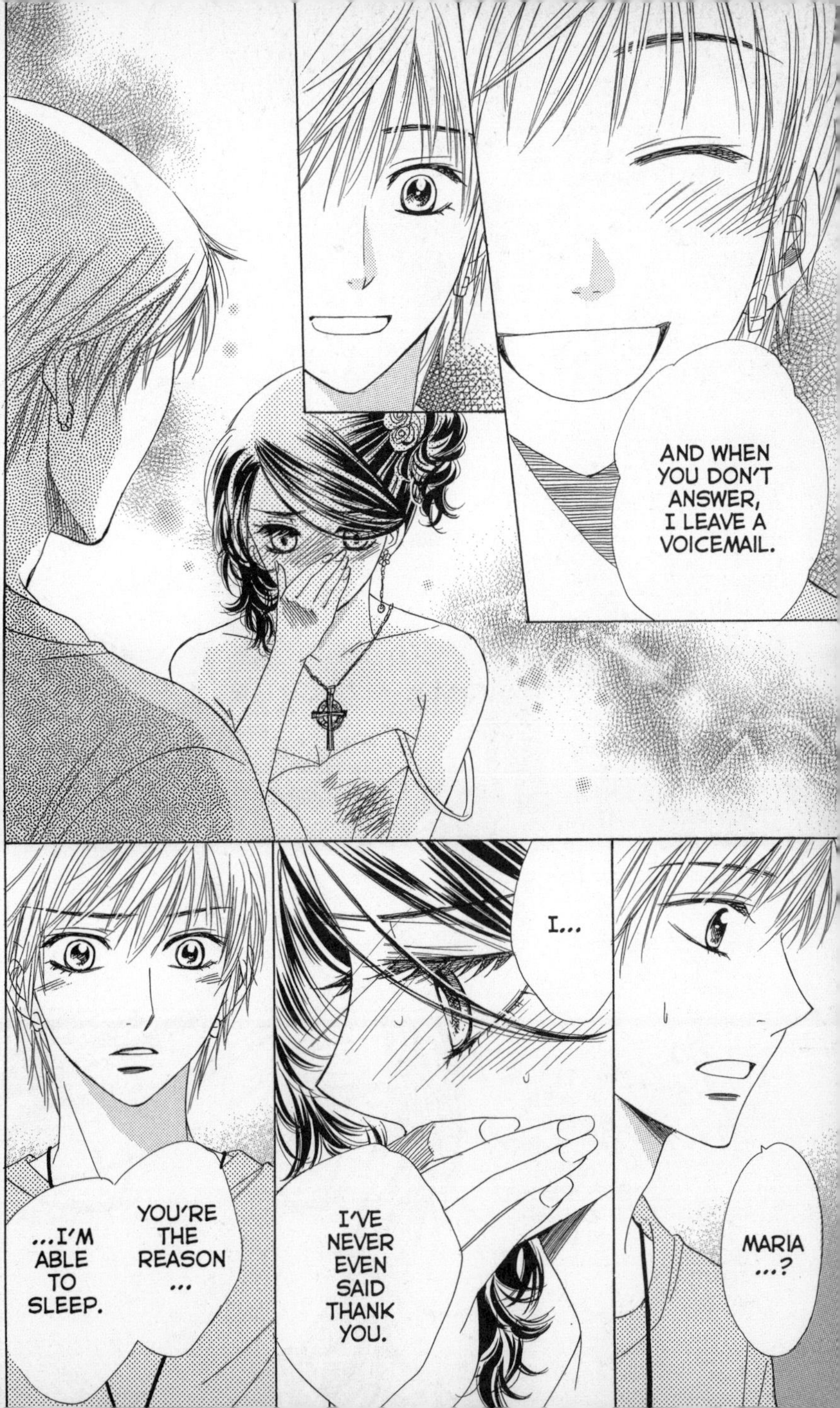
AND WHEN YOU DON'T ANSWER, I LEAVE A VOICEMAIL.
MARIA ...?
I...
I'VE NEVER EVEN SAID THANK YOU.
YOU'RE THE REASON ...
...I'M ABLE TO SLEEP.

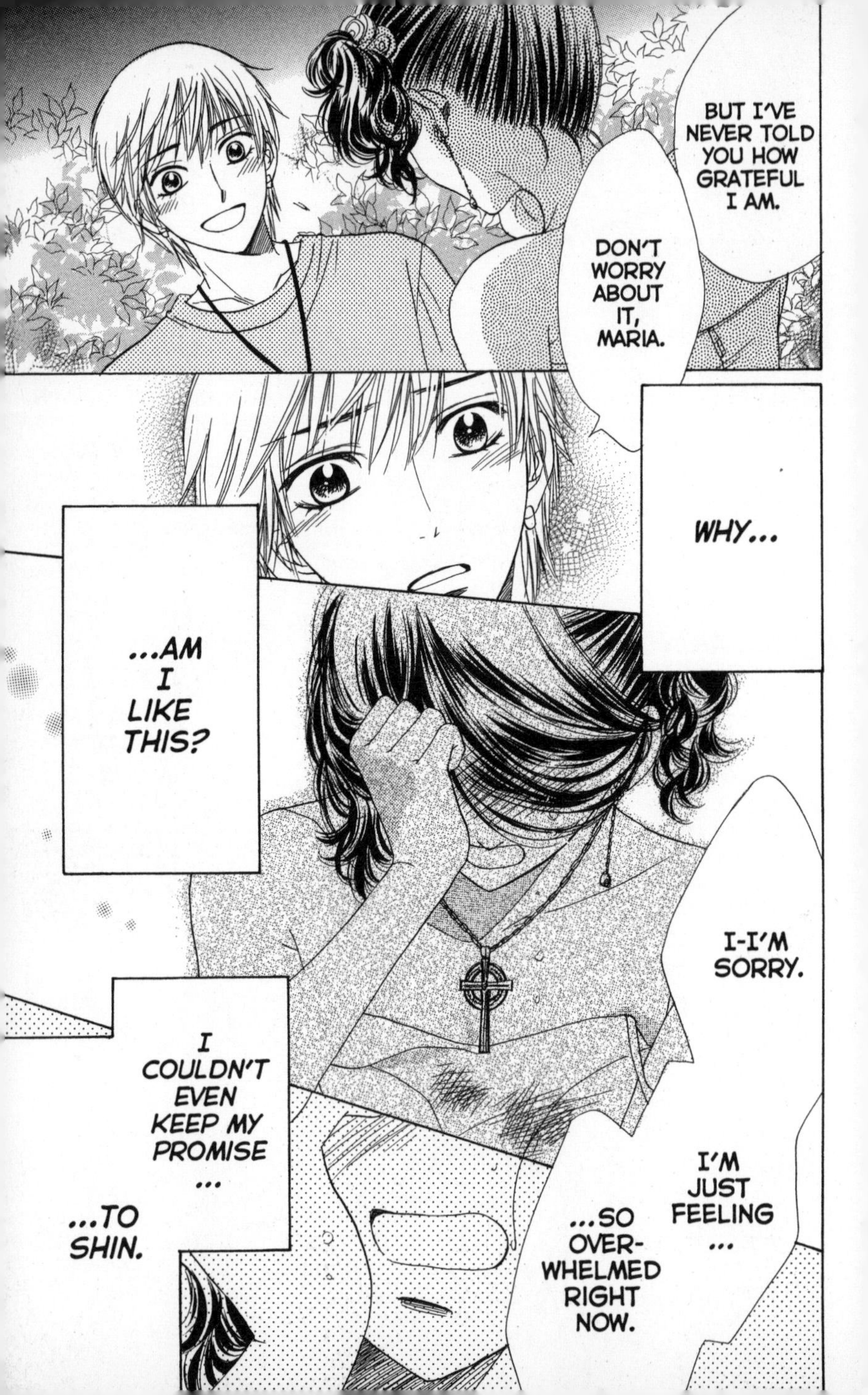
BUT I'VE NEVER TOLD YOU HOW GRATEFUL I AM.
DON'T WORRY ABOUT IT, MARIA.
WHY...
...AM I LIKE THIS?
I-I'M SORRY.
I'M JUST FEELING ...
...SO OVER-WHELMED RIGHT NOW.
I COULDN'T EVEN KEEP MY PROMISE ...
...TO SHIN.

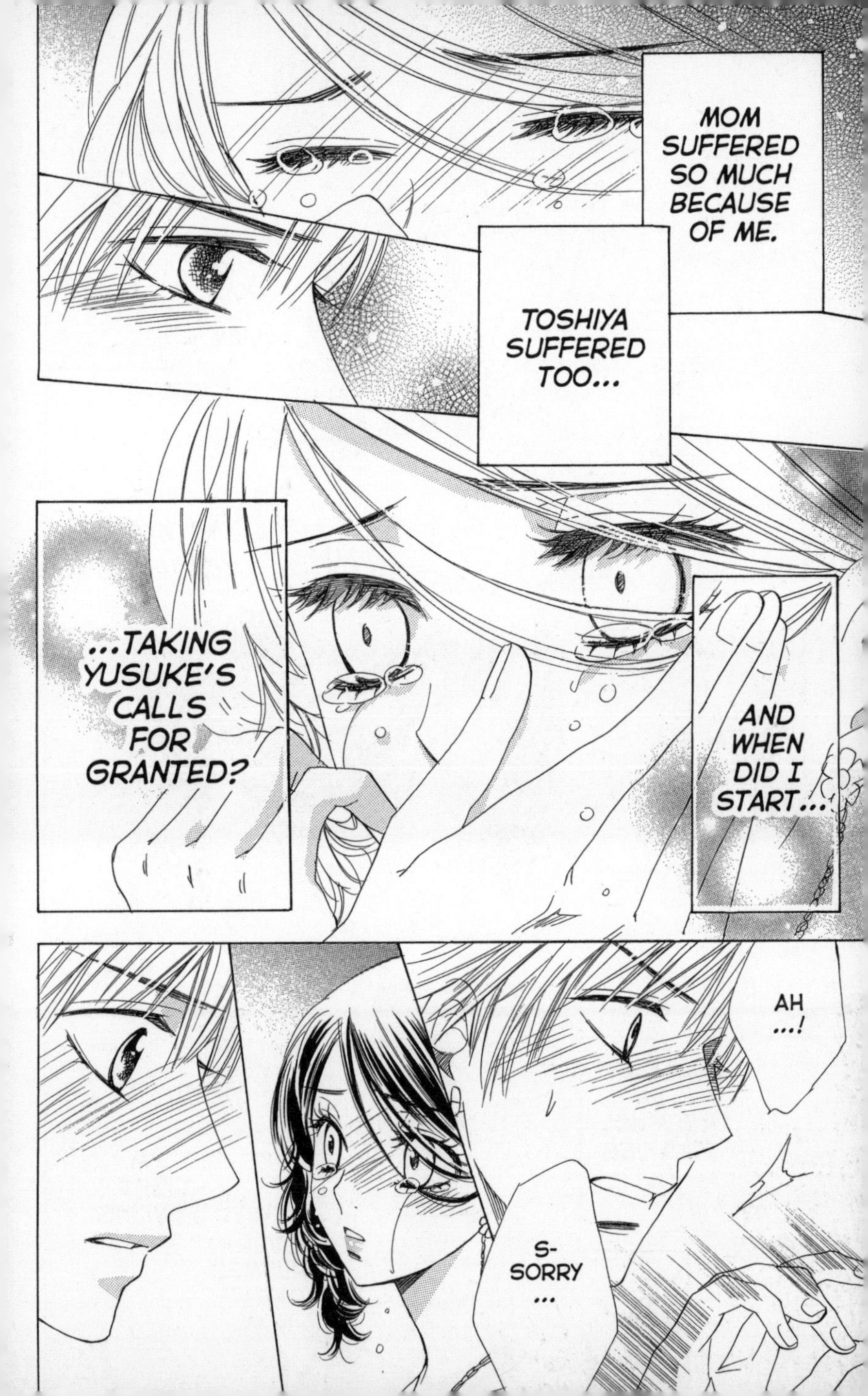
MOM SUFFERED SO MUCH BECAUSE OF ME.
TOSHIYA SUFFERED TOO...
AND WHEN DID I START...
...TAKING YUSUKE'S CALLS FOR GRANTED?
AH ...!
S- SORRY ...

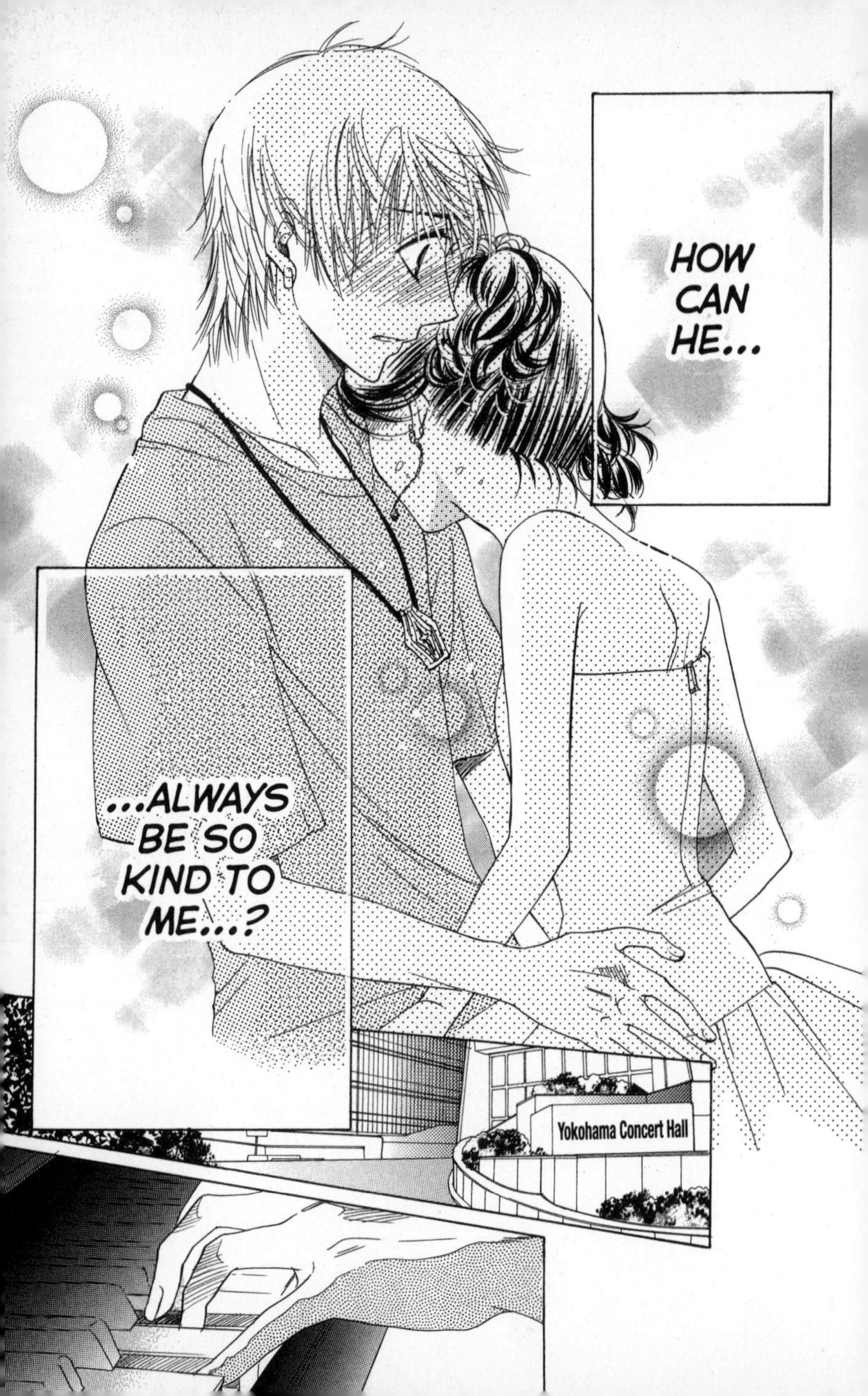
HOW CAN HE...
...ALWAYS BE SO KIND TO ME...?
Yokohama Concert Hall

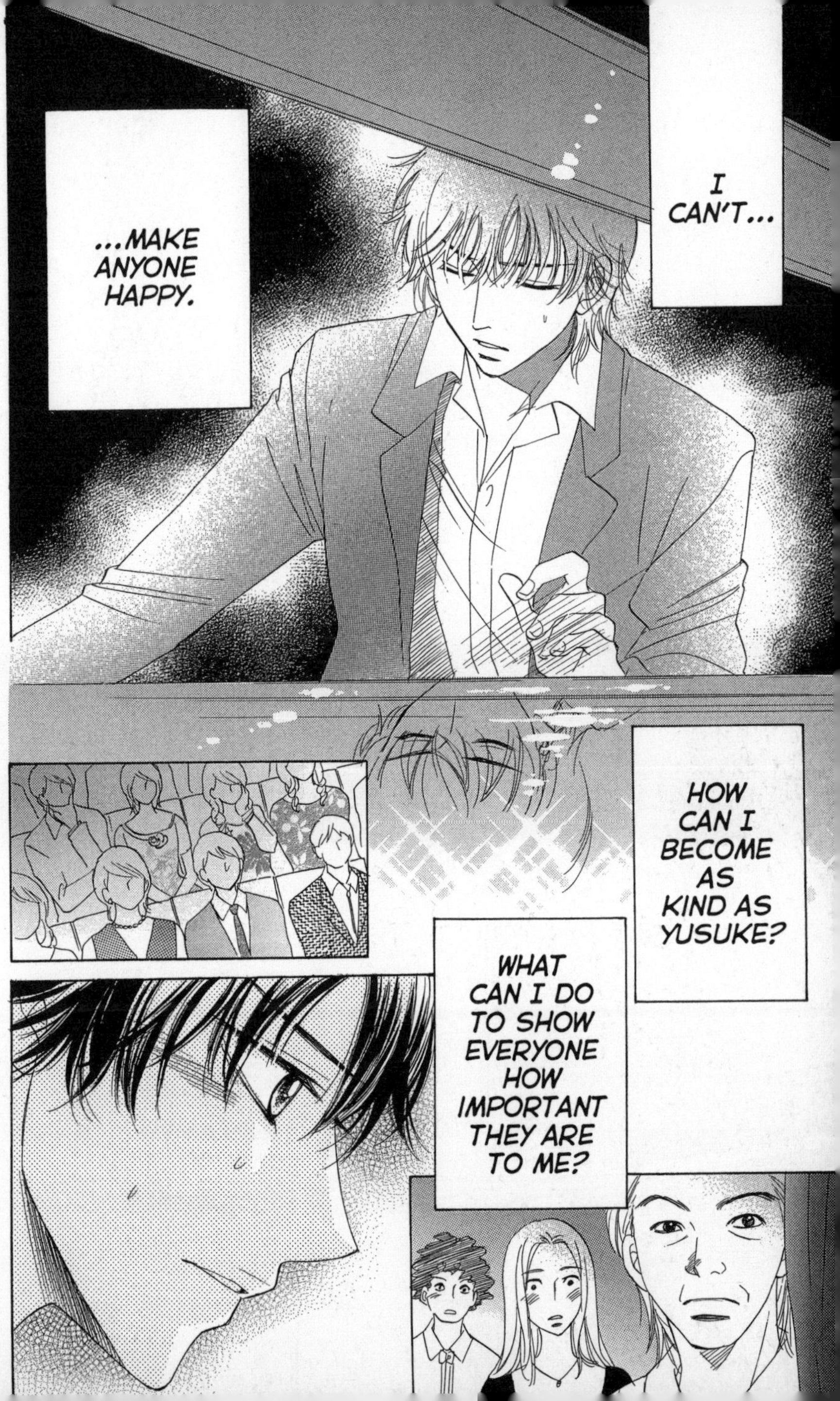
I CAN'T...
...MAKE ANYONE HAPPY.
HOW CAN I BECOME AS KIND AS YUSUKE?
WHAT CAN I DO TO SHOW EVERYONE HOW IMPORTANT THEY ARE TO ME?

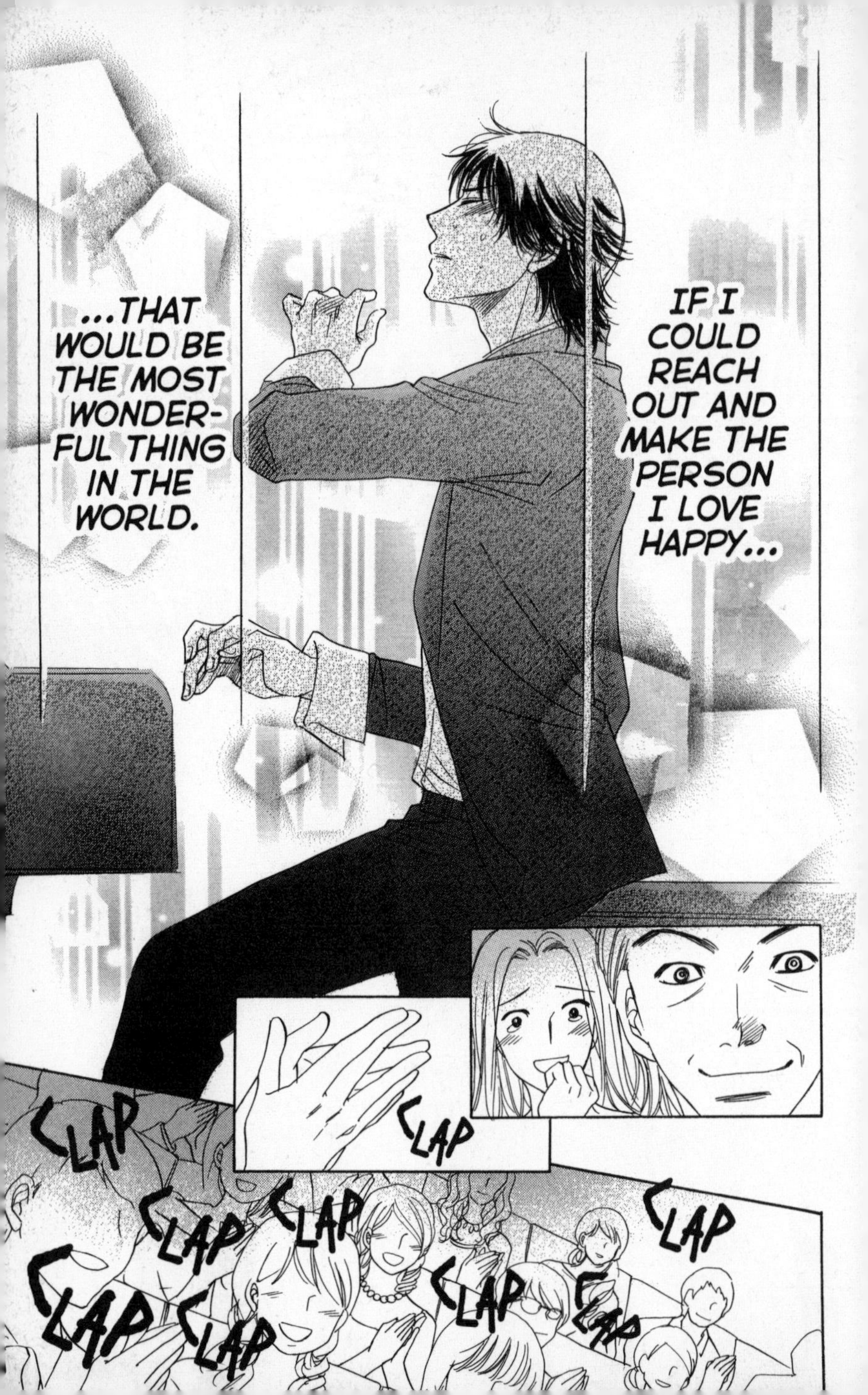
IF I COULD REACH OUT AND MAKE THE PERSON I LOVE HAPPY...
...THAT WOULD BE THE MOST WONDER-FUL THING IN THE WORLD.
CLAP
CLAP
CLAP
CLAP
CLAP
CLAP
CLAP
CLAP
CLAP
CLAP

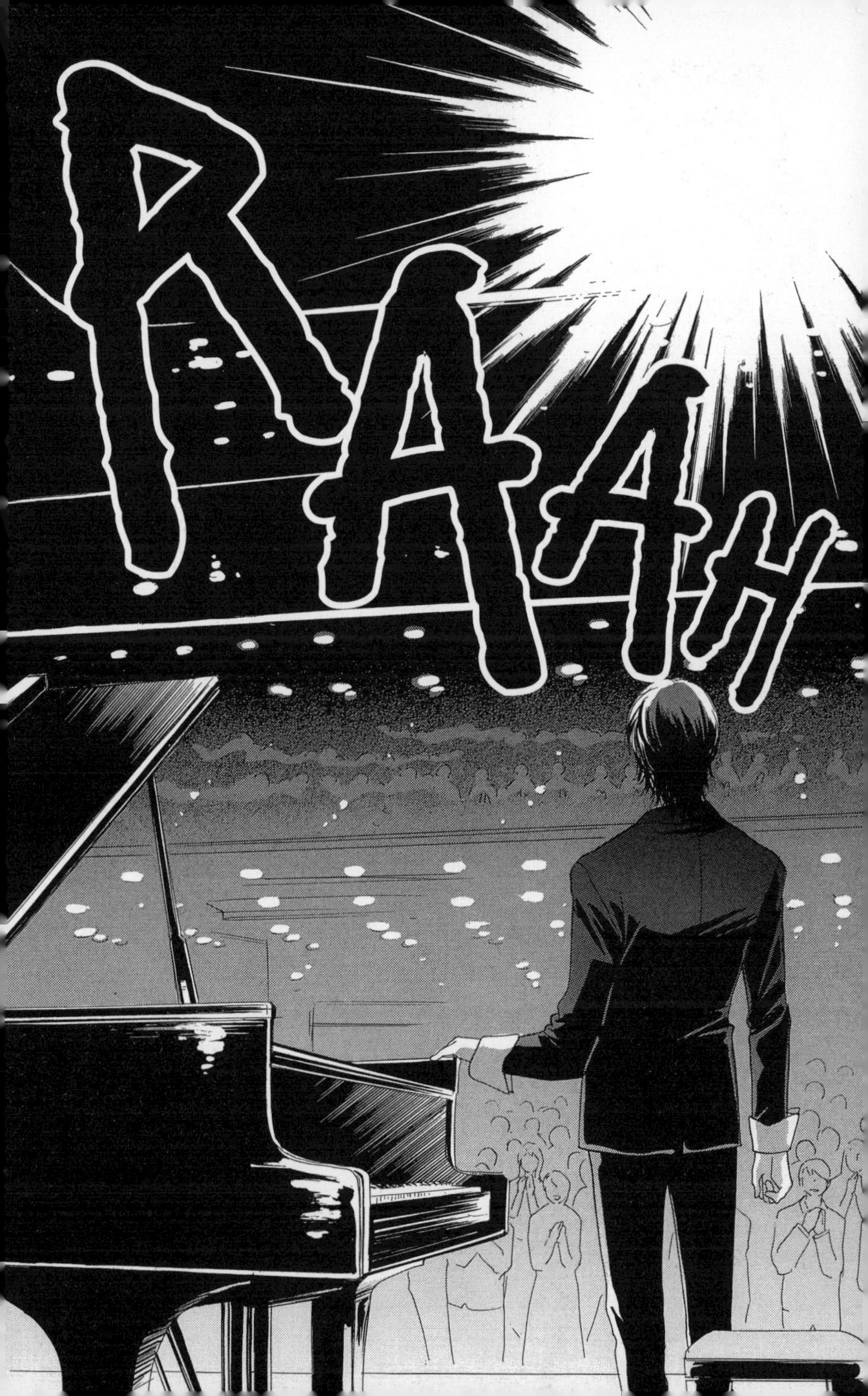
RAAH

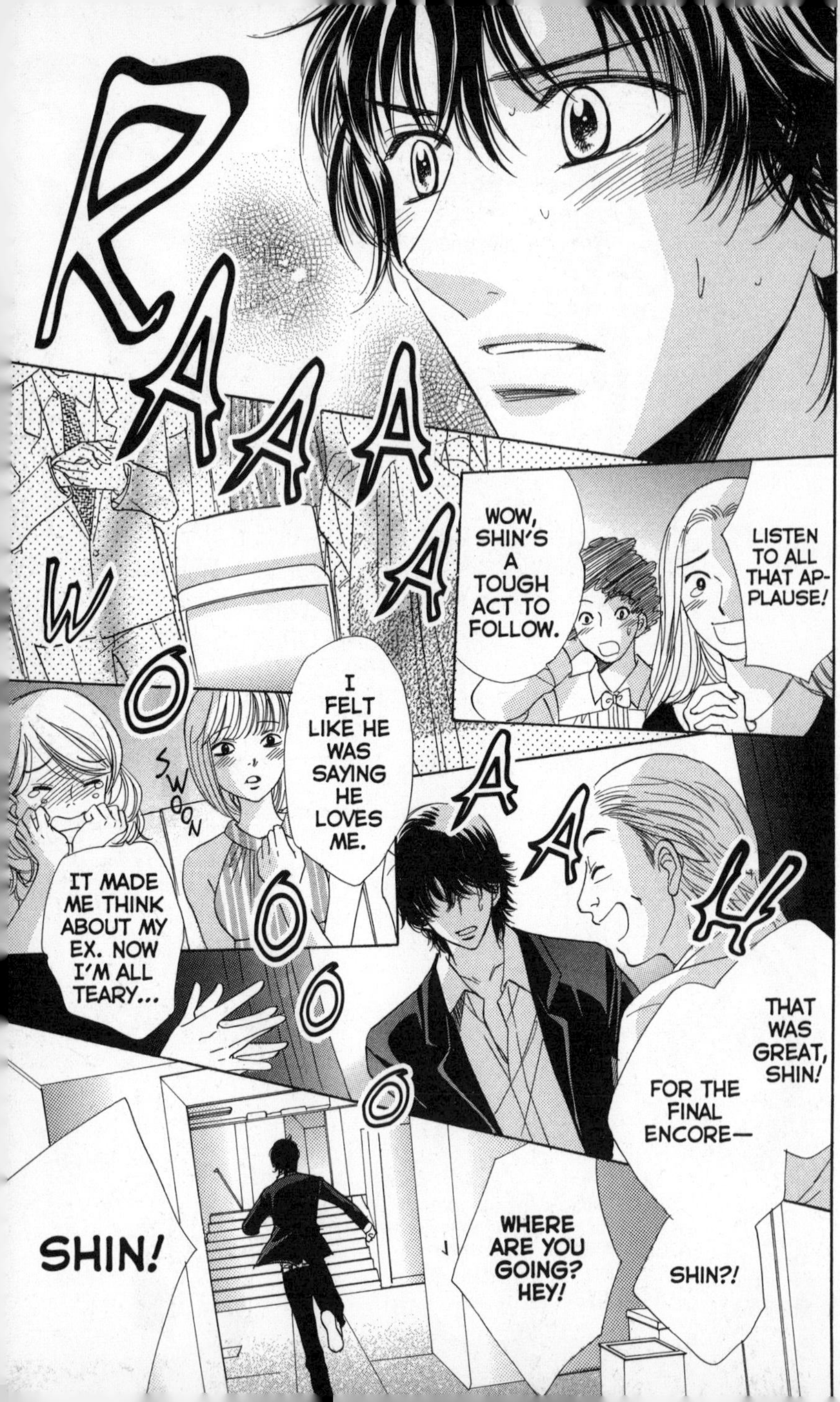
RAAAAAAAH
WOOOOOOO
LISTEN TO ALL THAT AP-PLAUSE!
WOW, SHIN'S A TOUGH ACT TO FOLLOW.
I FELT LIKE HE WAS SAYING HE LOVES ME.
SWOON
IT MADE ME THINK ABOUT MY EX. NOW I'M ALL TEARY...
THAT WAS GREAT, SHIN!
FOR THE FINAL ENCORE—
SHIN?!
WHERE ARE YOU GOING? HEY!
SHIN!

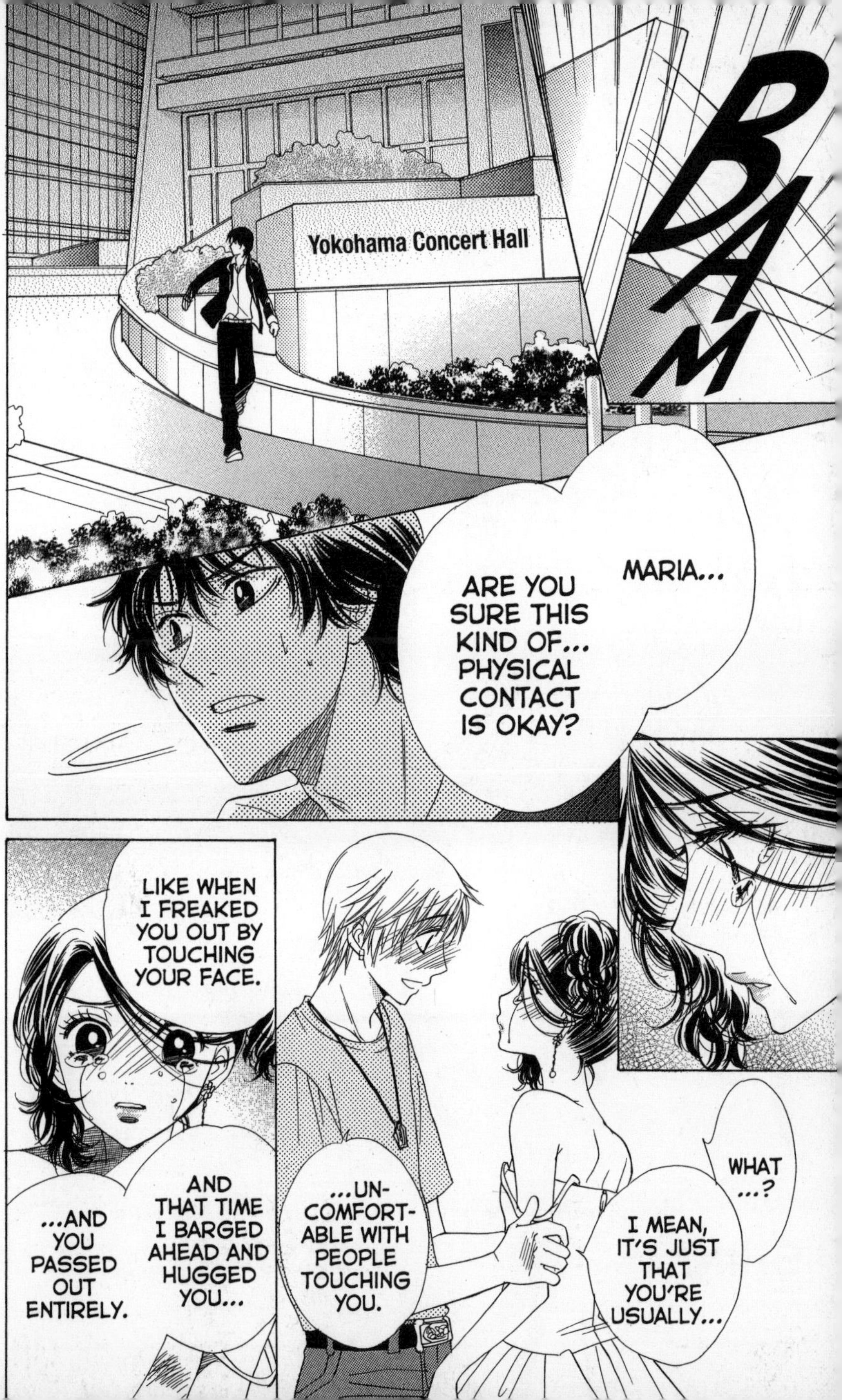
BAM
Yokohama Concert Hall
MARIA...
ARE YOU SURE THIS KIND OF... PHYSICAL CONTACT IS OKAY?
WHAT ...?
I MEAN, IT'S JUST THAT YOU'RE USUALLY...
...UN-COMFORT-ABLE WITH PEOPLE TOUCHING YOU.
LIKE WHEN I FREAKED YOU OUT BY TOUCHING YOUR FACE.
AND THAT TIME I BARGED AHEAD AND HUGGED YOU...
...AND YOU PASSED OUT ENTIRELY.

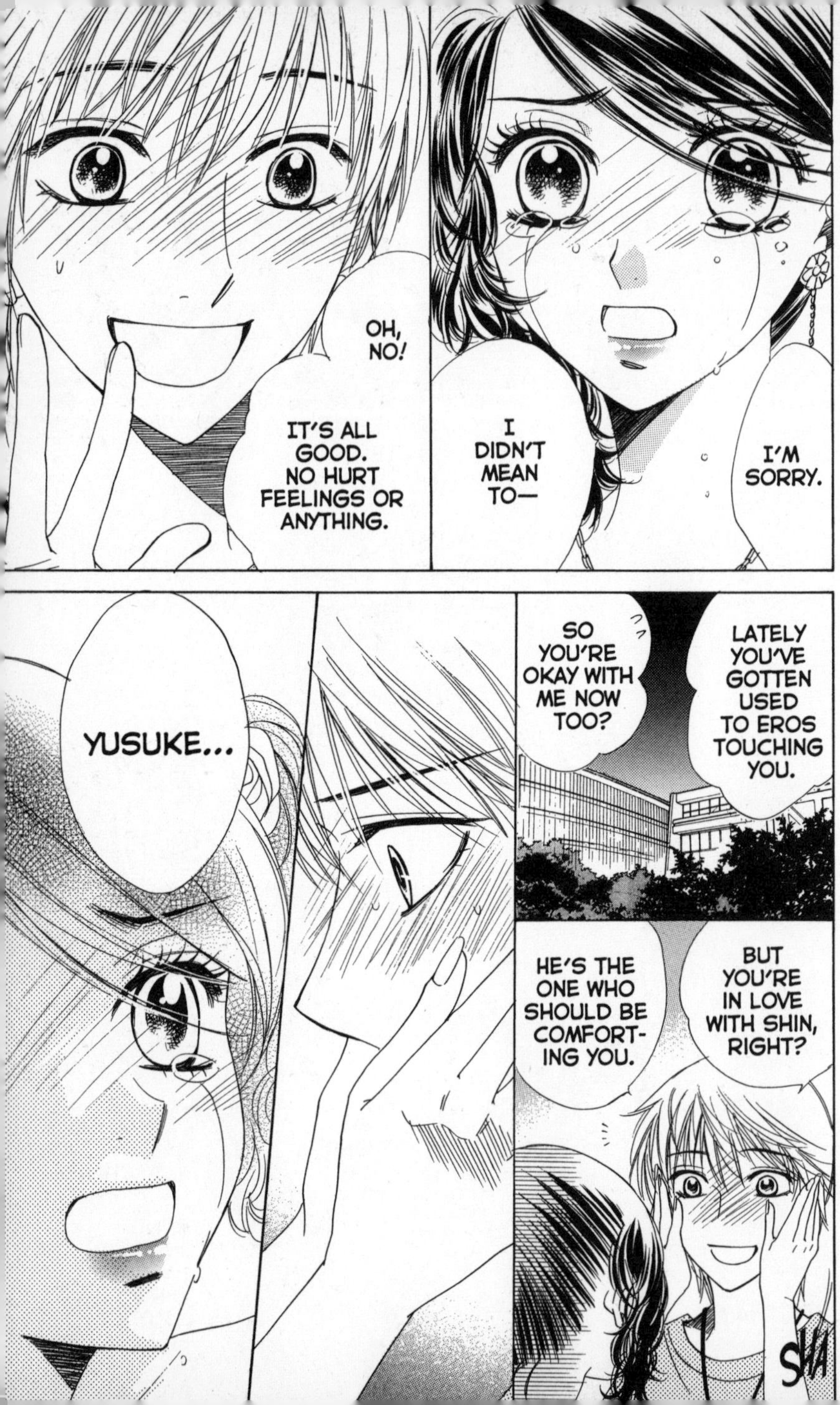
I'M SORRY.
I DIDN'T MEAN TO—
OH, NO!
IT'S ALL GOOD. NO HURT FEELINGS OR ANYTHING.
LATELY YOU'VE GOTTEN USED TO EROS TOUCHING YOU.
SO YOU'RE OKAY WITH ME NOW TOO?
BUT YOU'RE IN LOVE WITH SHIN, RIGHT?
HE'S THE ONE WHO SHOULD BE COMFORT-ING YOU.
SHA
YUSUKE...

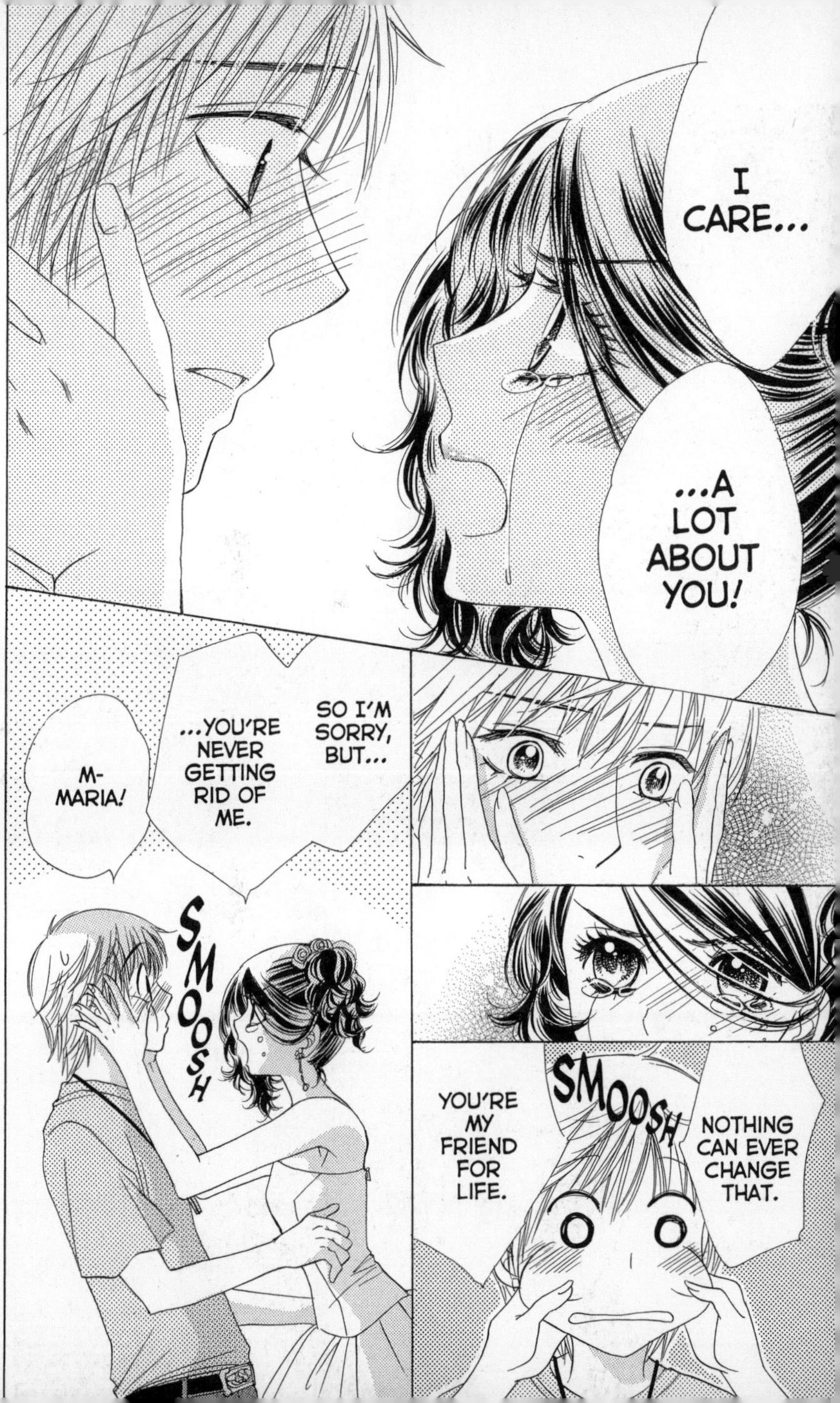

I CARE...
...A LOT ABOUT YOU!
NOTHING CAN EVER CHANGE THAT.
SMOOSH
YOU'RE MY FRIEND FOR LIFE.
SO I'M SORRY, BUT...
...YOU'RE NEVER GETTING RID OF ME.
M-MARIA!
SMOOSH

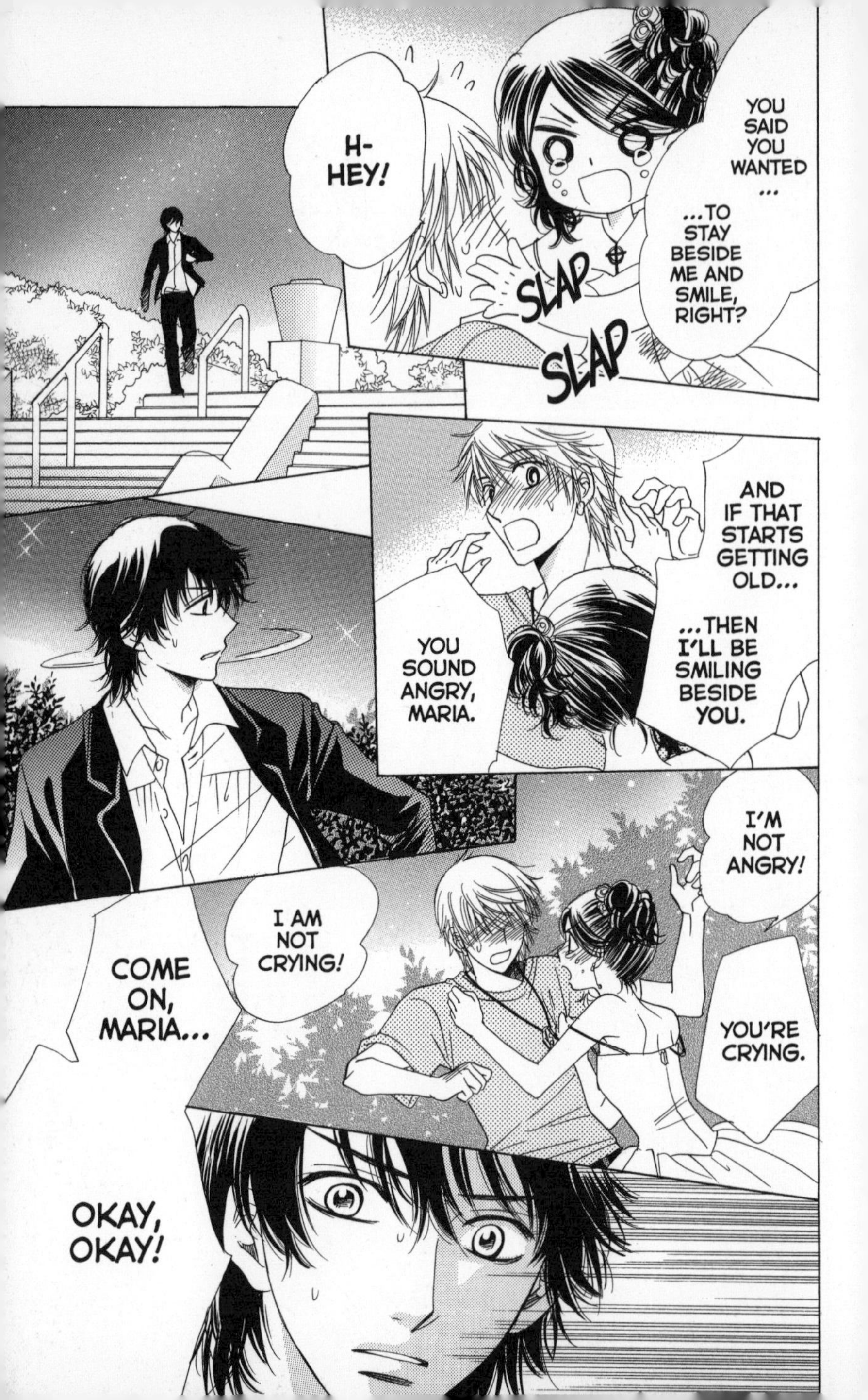
YOU SAID YOU WANTED ...
...TO STAY BESIDE ME AND SMILE, RIGHT?
SLAP
SLAP
H- HEY!
AND IF THAT STARTS GETTING OLD...
...THEN I'LL BE SMILING BESIDE YOU.
YOU SOUND ANGRY, MARIA.
I'M NOT ANGRY!
YOU'RE CRYING.
I AM NOT CRYING!
COME ON, MARIA...
OKAY, OKAY!

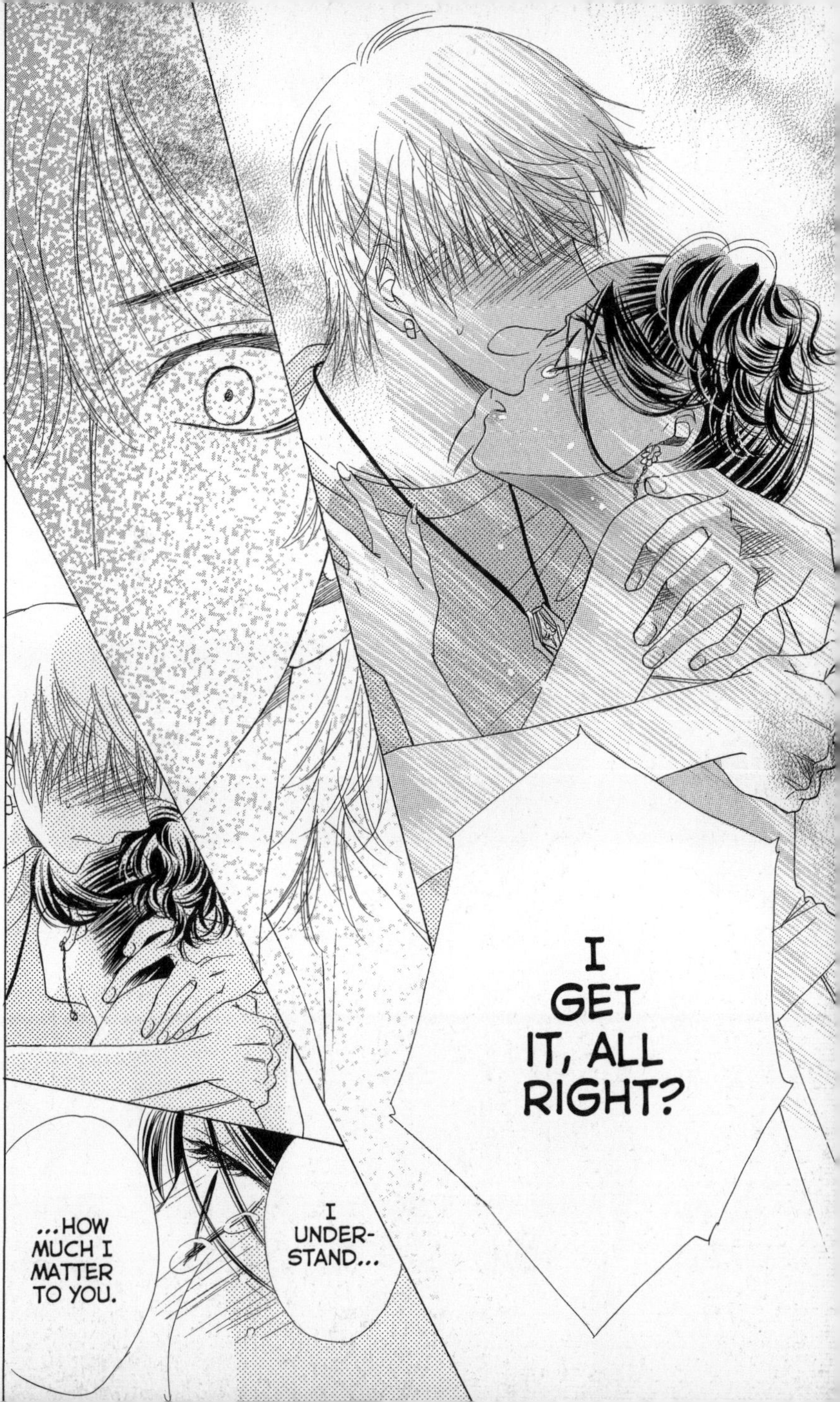
I GET IT, ALL RIGHT?
I UNDER-STAND...
...HOW MUCH I MATTER TO YOU.

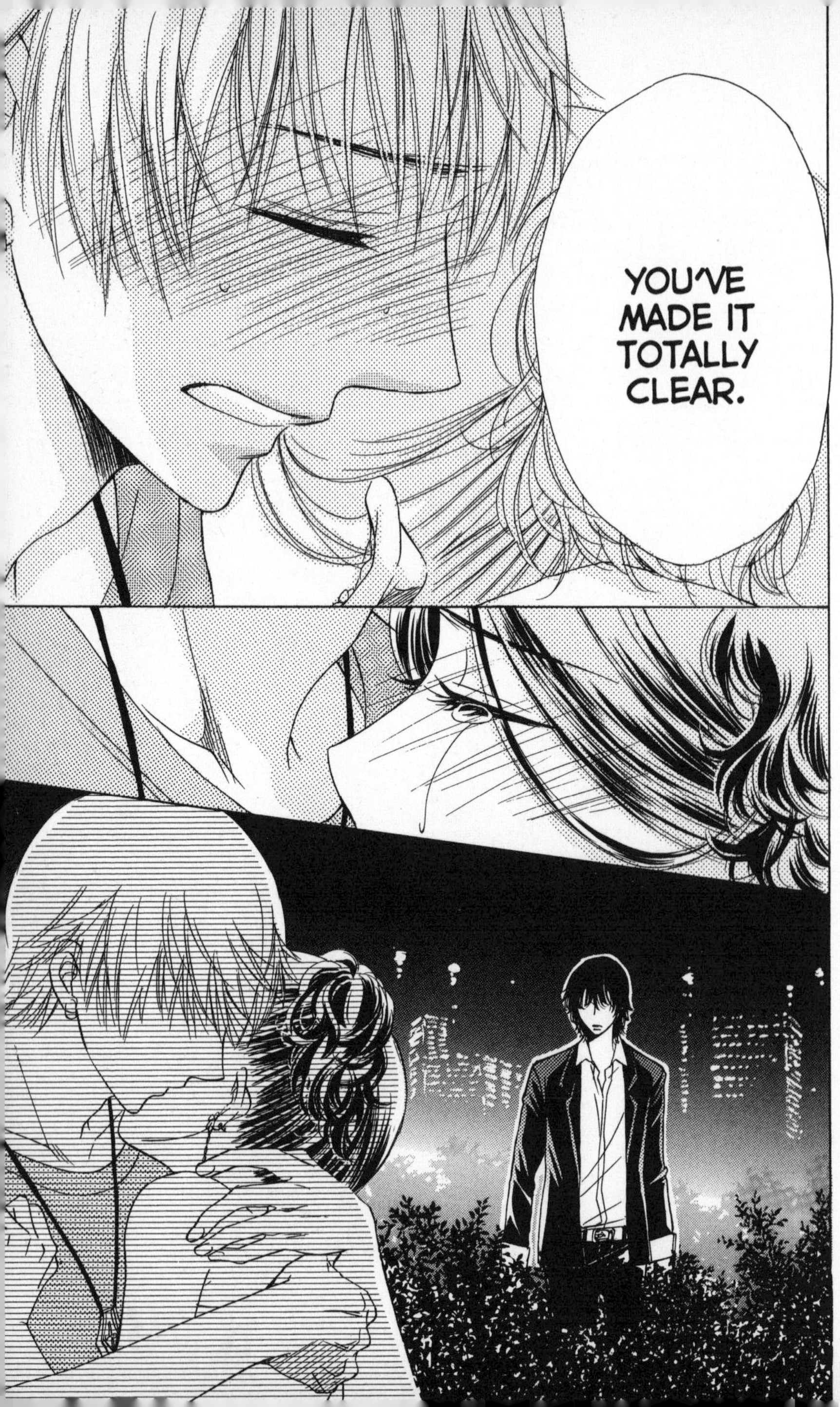
YOU'VE MADE IT TOTALLY CLEAR.

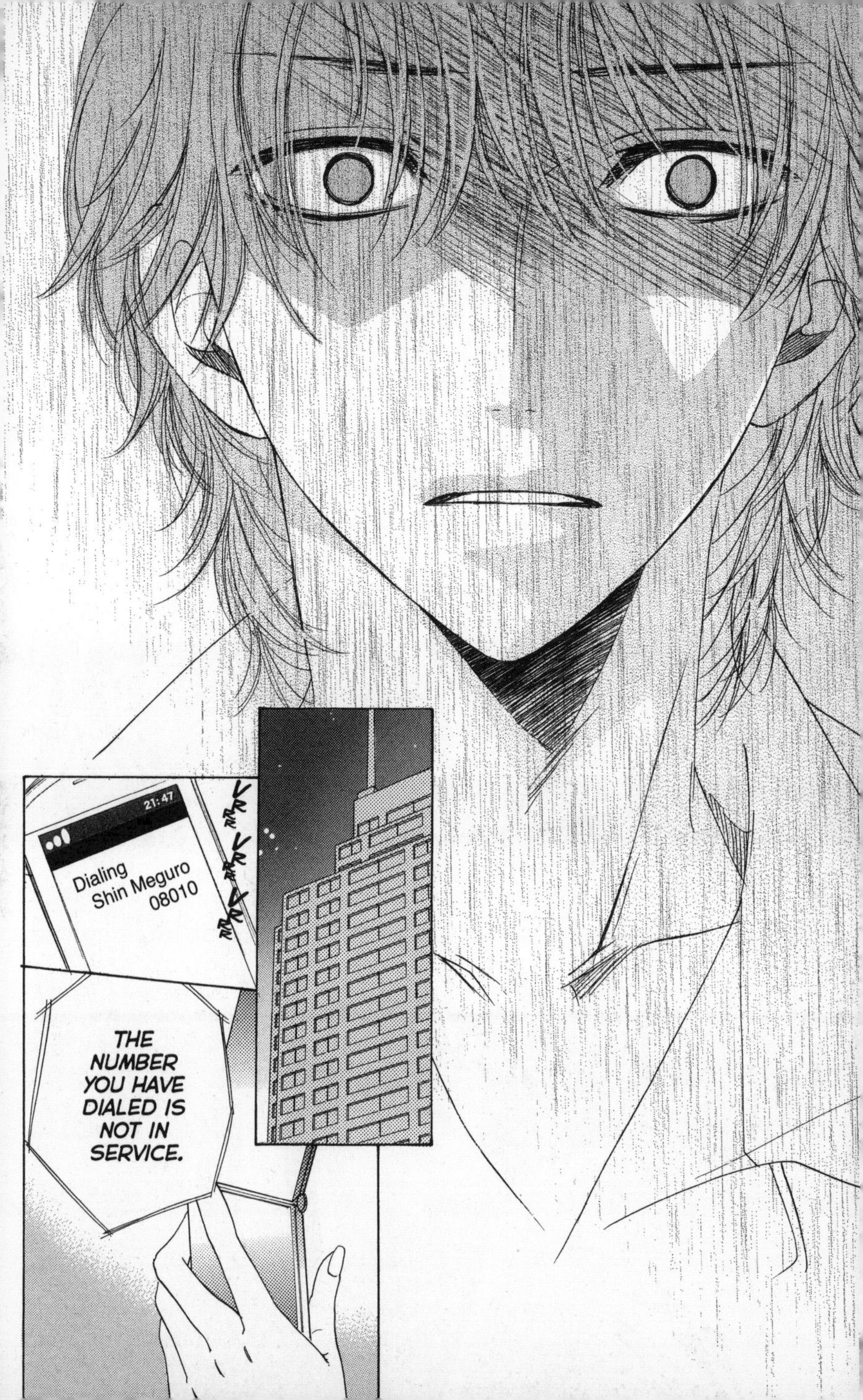
21:47
Dialing
Shin Meguro
08010
VRR VRR VRR
THE NUMBER YOU HAVE DIALED IS NOT IN SERVICE.

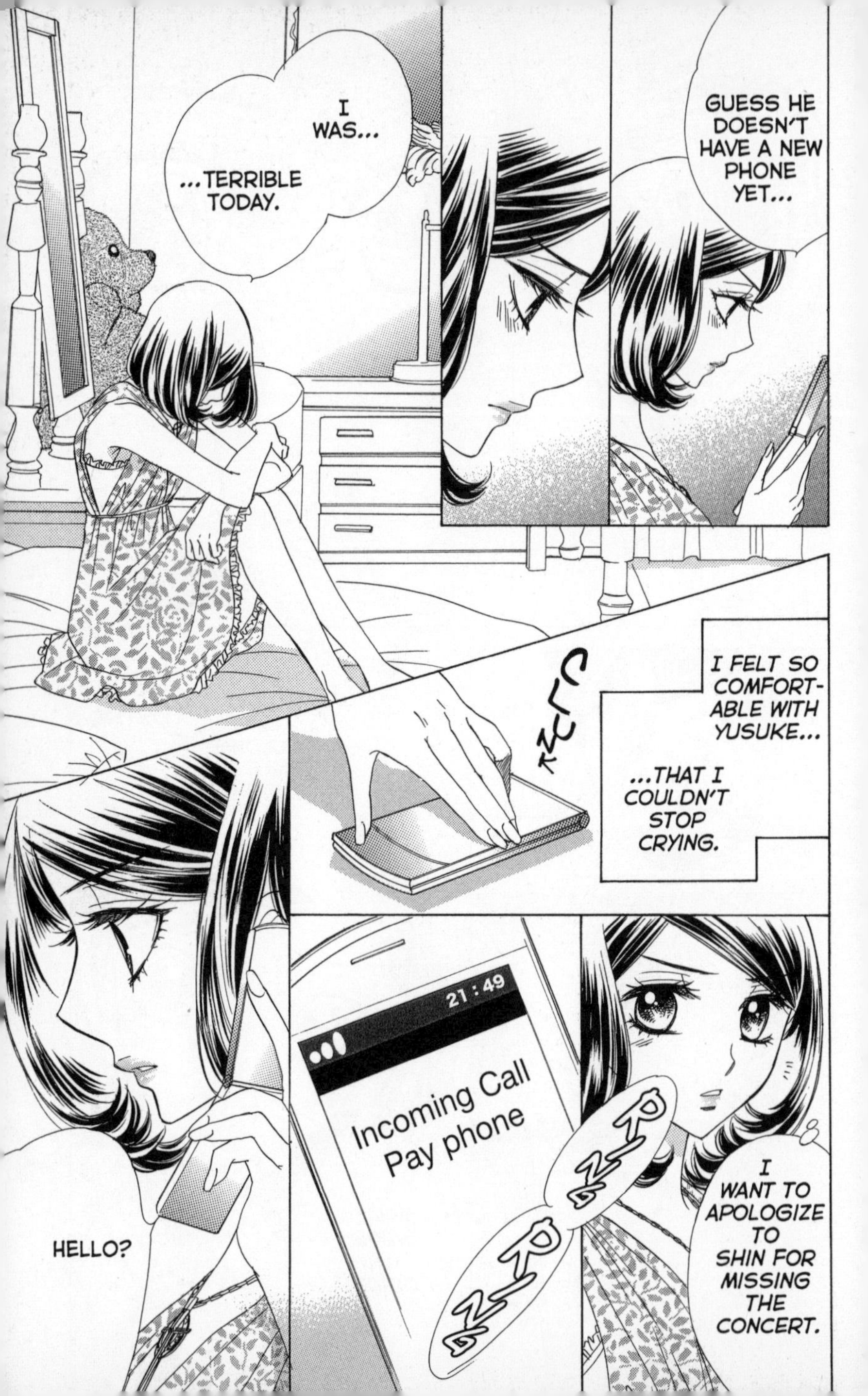
GUESS HE DOESN'T HAVE A NEW PHONE YET...
I WAS...
...TERRIBLE TODAY.
I FELT SO COMFORT-ABLE WITH YUSUKE...
...THAT I COULDN'T STOP CRYING.
CLUNK
I WANT TO APOLOGIZE TO SHIN FOR MISSING THE CONCERT.
RING RING
21 : 49
Incoming Call
Pay phone
HELLO?

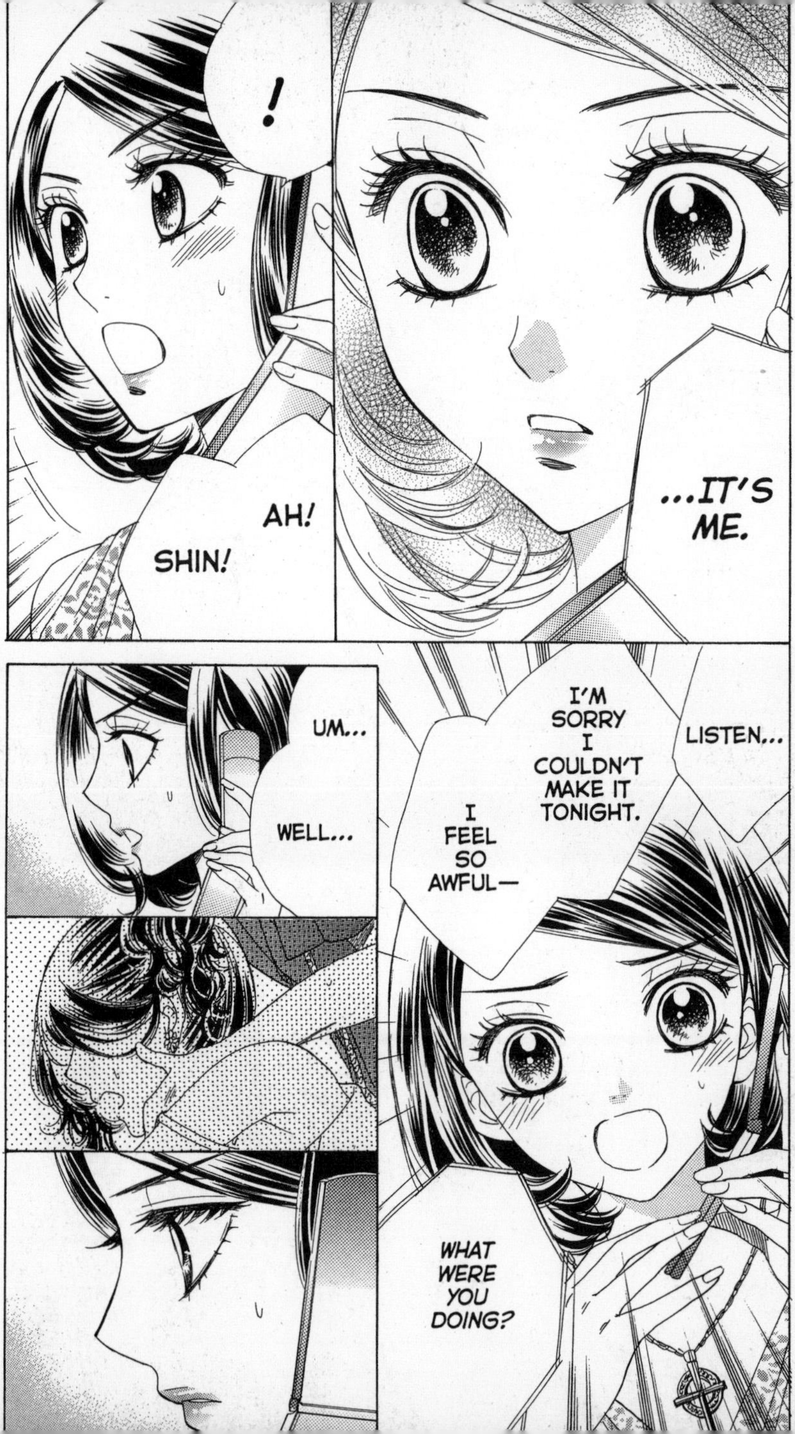
...IT'S ME.
!
AH!
SHIN!
LISTEN...
I'M SORRY I COULDN'T MAKE IT TONIGHT.
I FEEL SO AWFUL—
WHAT WERE YOU DOING?
UM...
WELL...

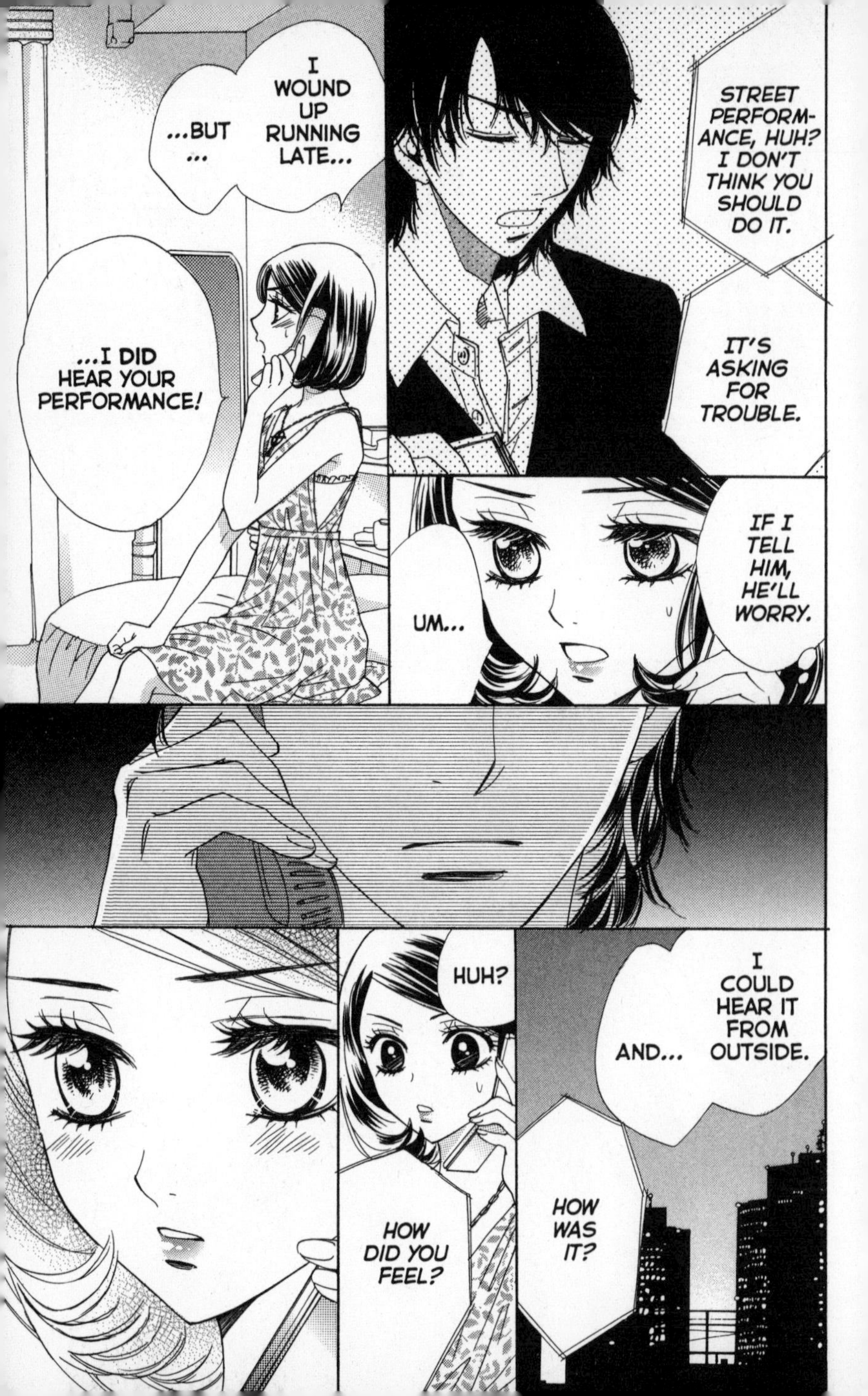
STREET PERFORMANCE, HUH? I DON'T THINK YOU SHOULD DO IT.
IT'S ASKING FOR TROUBLE.
I WOUND UP RUNNING LATE...
...BUT ...
...I DID HEAR YOUR PERFORMANCE!
IF I TELL HIM, HE'LL WORRY.
UM...
I COULD HEAR IT FROM OUTSIDE.
AND...
HOW WAS IT?
HUH?
HOW DID YOU FEEL?

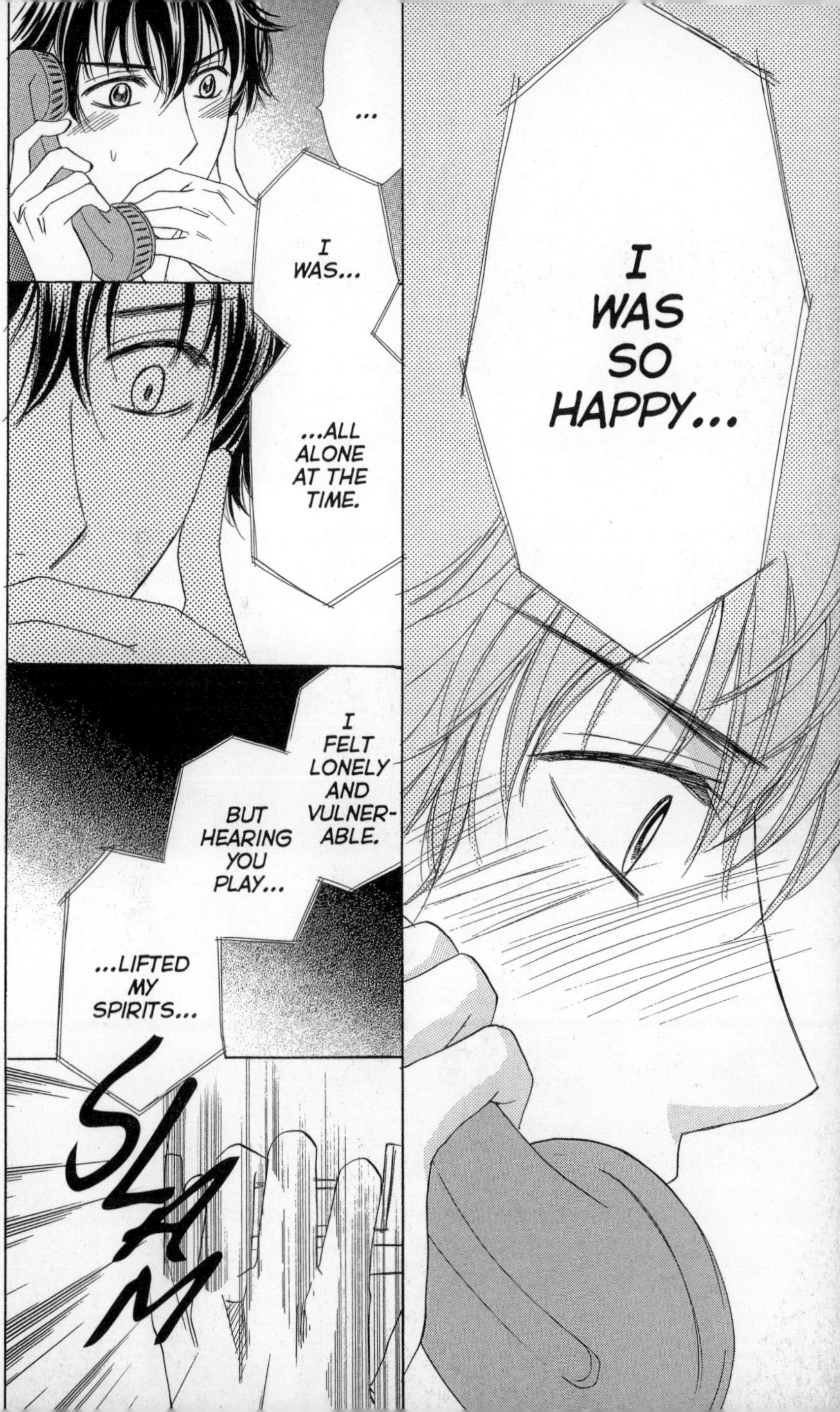
I WAS SO HAPPY...
...
I WAS...
...ALL ALONE AT THE TIME.
I FELT LONELY AND VULNER-ABLE.
BUT HEARING YOU PLAY...
...LIFTED MY SPIRITS...
SLAM

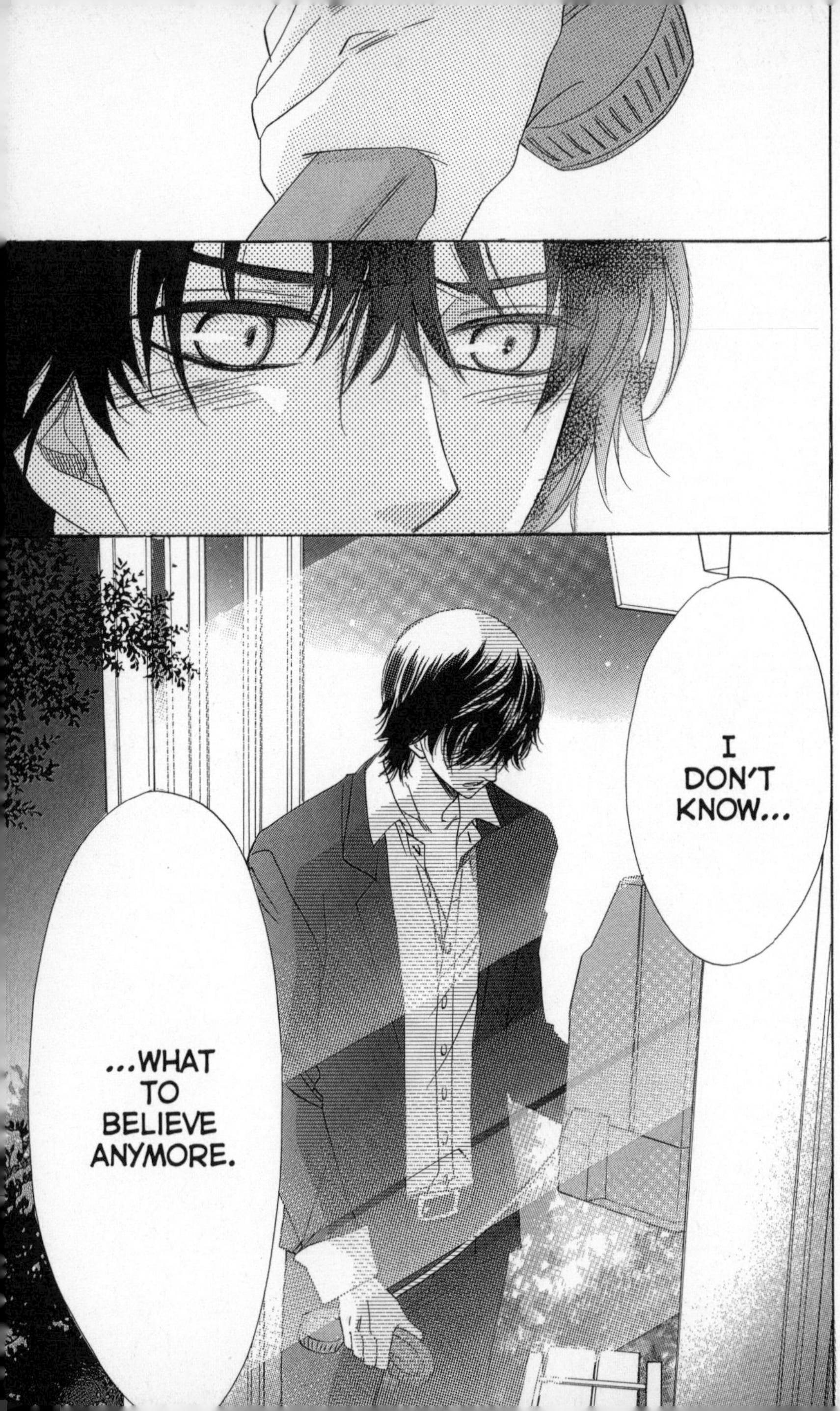
I DON'T KNOW...
...WHAT TO BELIEVE ANYMORE.

Continued in volume 10

# A Devil and Her Love Song Bonus

## A Story About Eros
Turn the page for a little something extra!

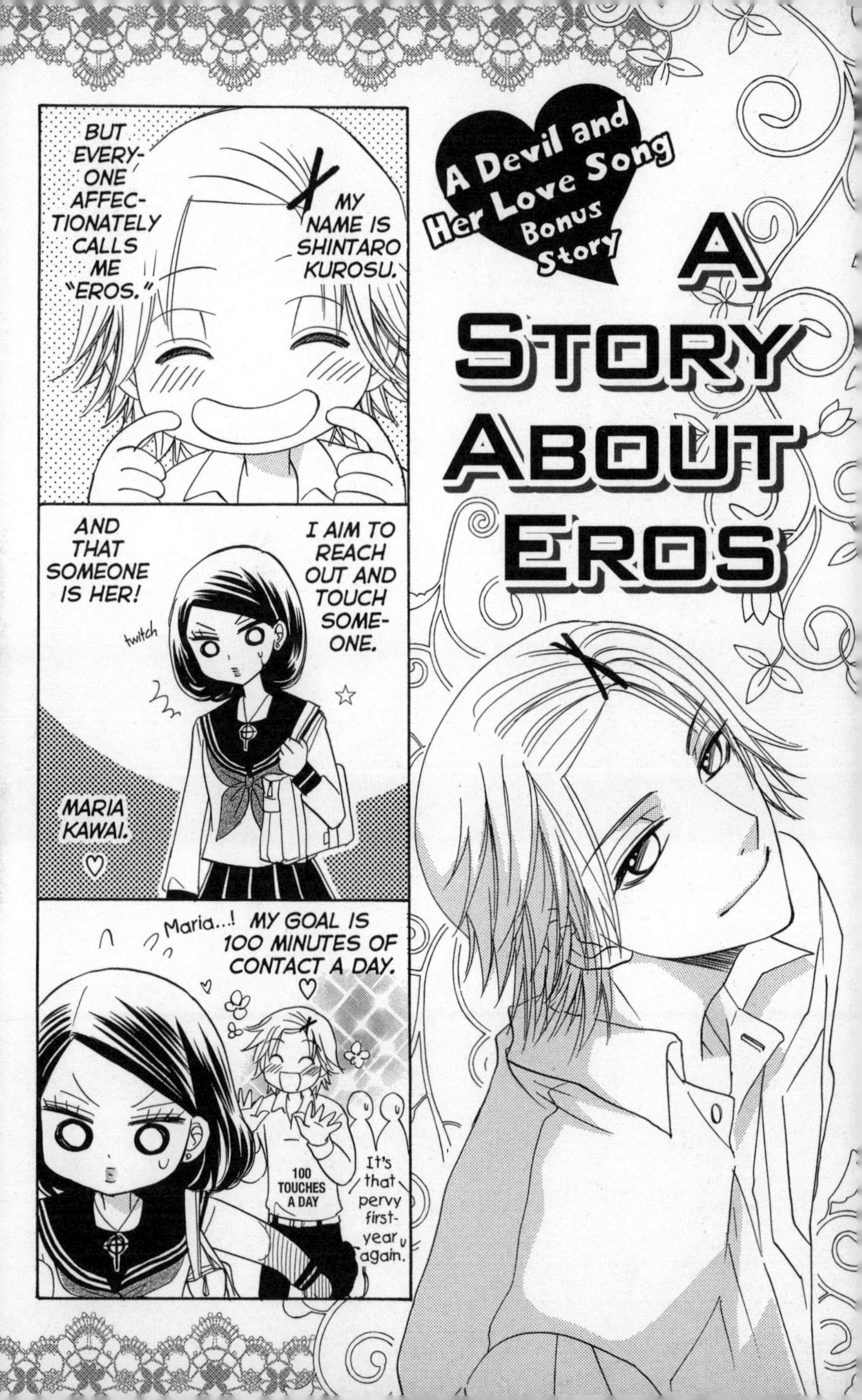
A Devil and Her Love Song Bonus Story
A STORY ABOUT EROS
MY NAME IS SHINTARO KUROSU.
BUT EVERYONE AFFECTIONATELY CALLS ME "EROS."
I AIM TO REACH OUT AND TOUCH SOMEONE.
AND THAT SOMEONE IS HER!
twitch
MARIA KAWAI.
MY GOAL IS 100 MINUTES OF CONTACT A DAY.
Maria...!
100 TOUCHES A DAY
It's that pervy first-year again.

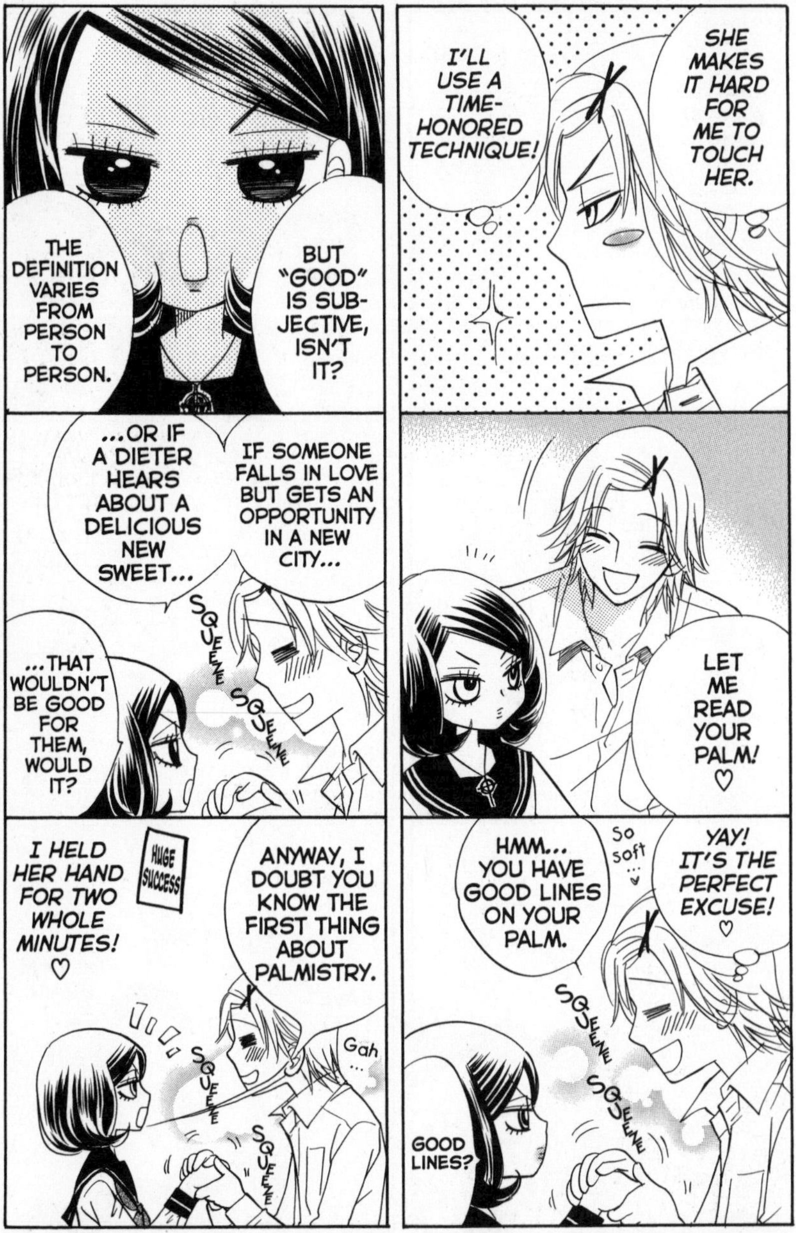
SHE MAKES IT HARD FOR ME TO TOUCH HER.
I'LL USE A TIME-HONORED TECHNIQUE!
LET ME READ YOUR PALM! ♡
YAY! IT'S THE PERFECT EXCUSE! ♡
So soft... ♥
HMM... YOU HAVE GOOD LINES ON YOUR PALM.
SQUEEZE
SQUEEZE
GOOD LINES?
BUT "GOOD" IS SUB-JECTIVE, ISN'T IT?
THE DEFINITION VARIES FROM PERSON TO PERSON.
IF SOMEONE FALLS IN LOVE BUT GETS AN OPPORTUNITY IN A NEW CITY...
...OR IF A DIETER HEARS ABOUT A DELICIOUS NEW SWEET...
SQUEEZE
SQUEEZE
...THAT WOULDN'T BE GOOD FOR THEM, WOULD IT?
ANYWAY, I DOUBT YOU KNOW THE FIRST THING ABOUT PALMISTRY.
HUGE SUCCESS
I HELD HER HAND FOR TWO WHOLE MINUTES! ♡
Gah...
SQUEEZE
SQUEEZE

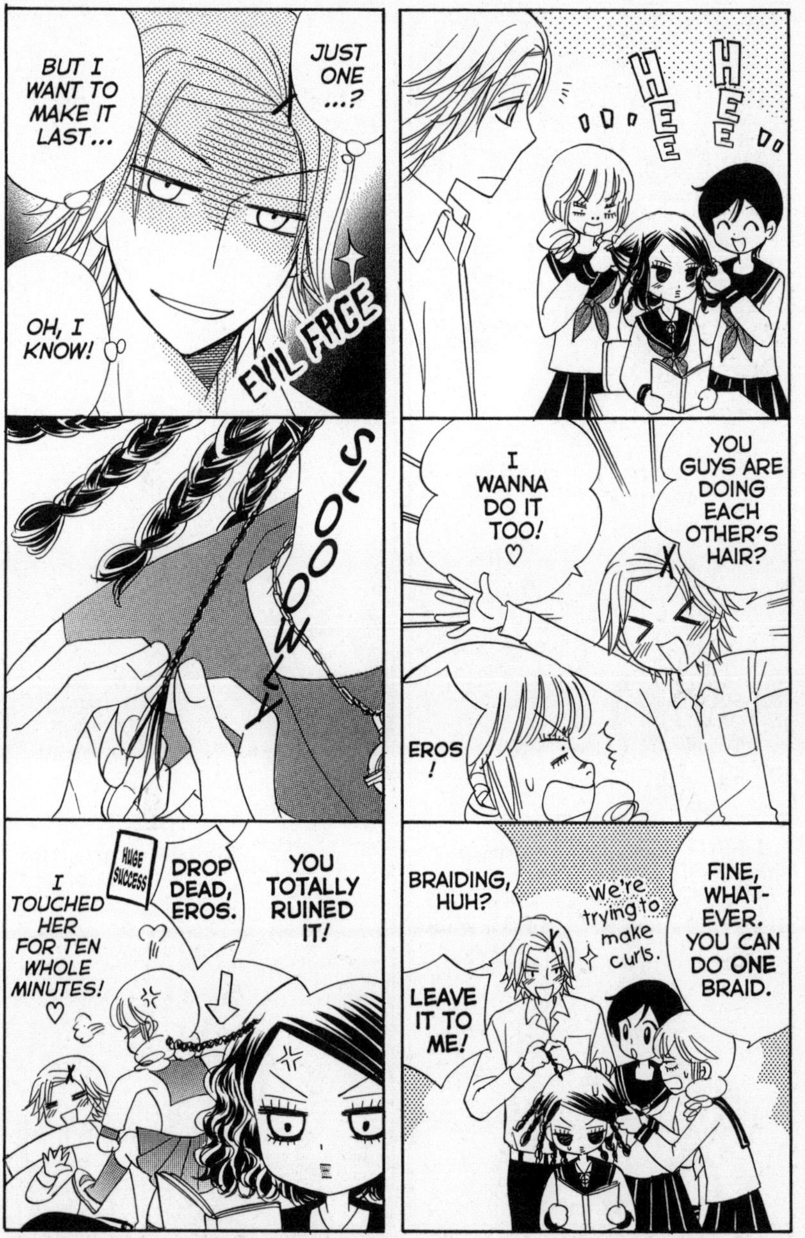
HEE HEE
YOU GUYS ARE DOING EACH OTHER'S HAIR?
I WANNA DO IT TOO! ♡
EROS!
FINE, WHAT-EVER. YOU CAN DO ONE BRAID.
We're trying to make curls.
BRAIDING, HUH?
LEAVE IT TO ME!
BUT I WANT TO MAKE IT LAST...
JUST ONE ...?
OH, I KNOW!
EVIL FACE
SLOOOOWLY
YOU TOTALLY RUINED IT!
DROP DEAD, EROS.
HUGE SUCCESS
I TOUCHED HER FOR TEN WHOLE MINUTES! ♡

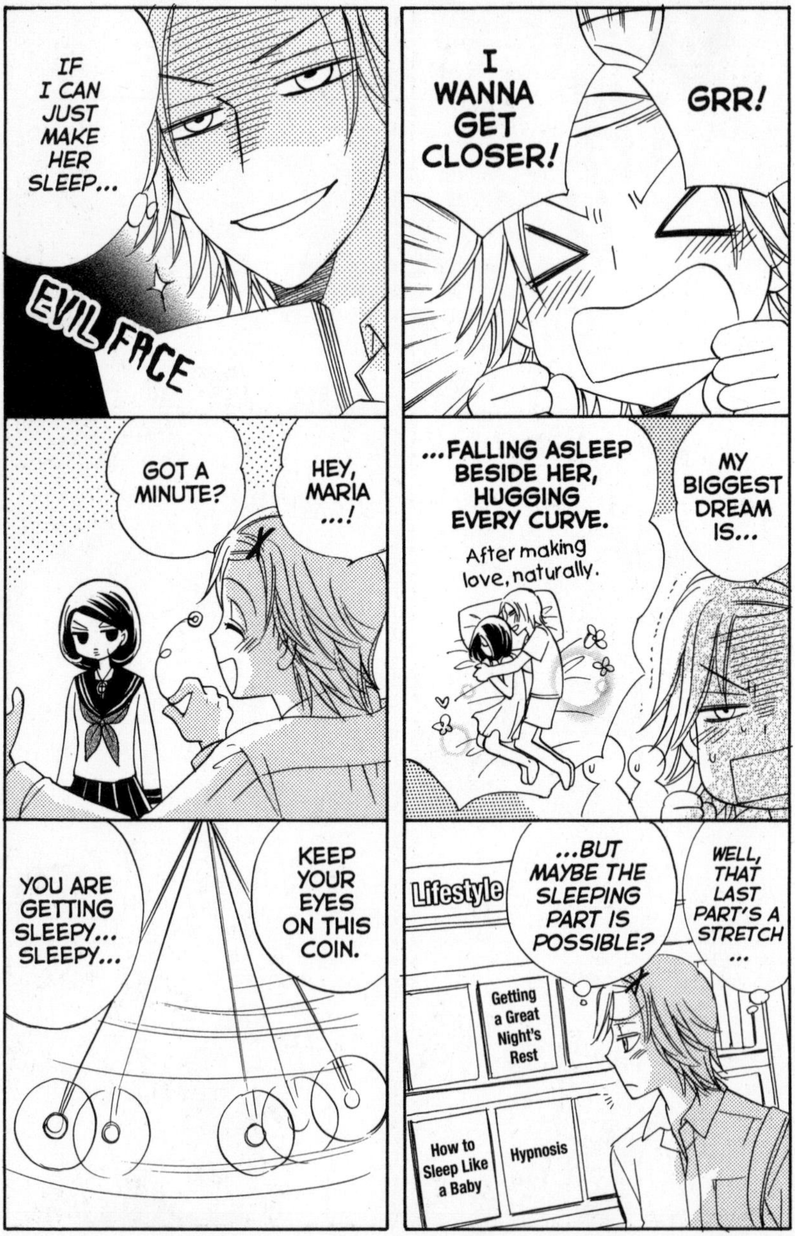
I WANNA GET CLOSER!
GRR!
MY BIGGEST DREAM IS...
...FALLING ASLEEP BESIDE HER, HUGGING EVERY CURVE.
After making love, naturally.
WELL, THAT LAST PART'S A STRETCH...
...BUT MAYBE THE SLEEPING PART IS POSSIBLE?
Lifestyle
Getting a Great Night's Rest
Hypnosis
How to Sleep Like a Baby
IF I CAN JUST MAKE HER SLEEP...
EVIL FACE
HEY, MARIA...!
GOT A MINUTE?
KEEP YOUR EYES ON THIS COIN.
YOU ARE GETTING SLEEPY... SLEEPY...

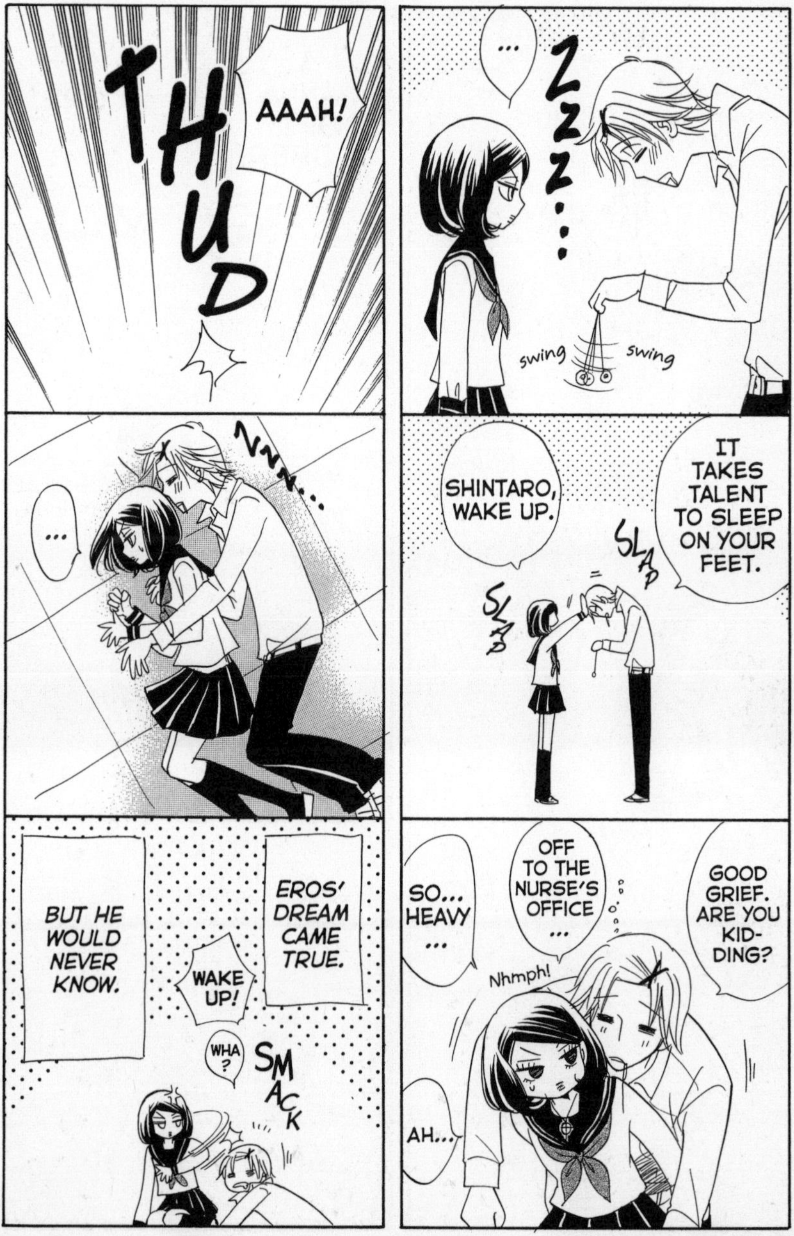
...
ZZZ...
swing swing
IT TAKES TALENT TO SLEEP ON YOUR FEET.
SHINTARO, WAKE UP.
SLAP
SLAP
GOOD GRIEF. ARE YOU KID-DING?
OFF TO THE NURSE'S OFFICE ...
SO... HEAVY ...
Nhmph!
AH...
AAAH!
THUD
NNN...
...
EROS' DREAM CAME TRUE.
BUT HE WOULD NEVER KNOW.
WAKE UP!
WHA?
SMACK

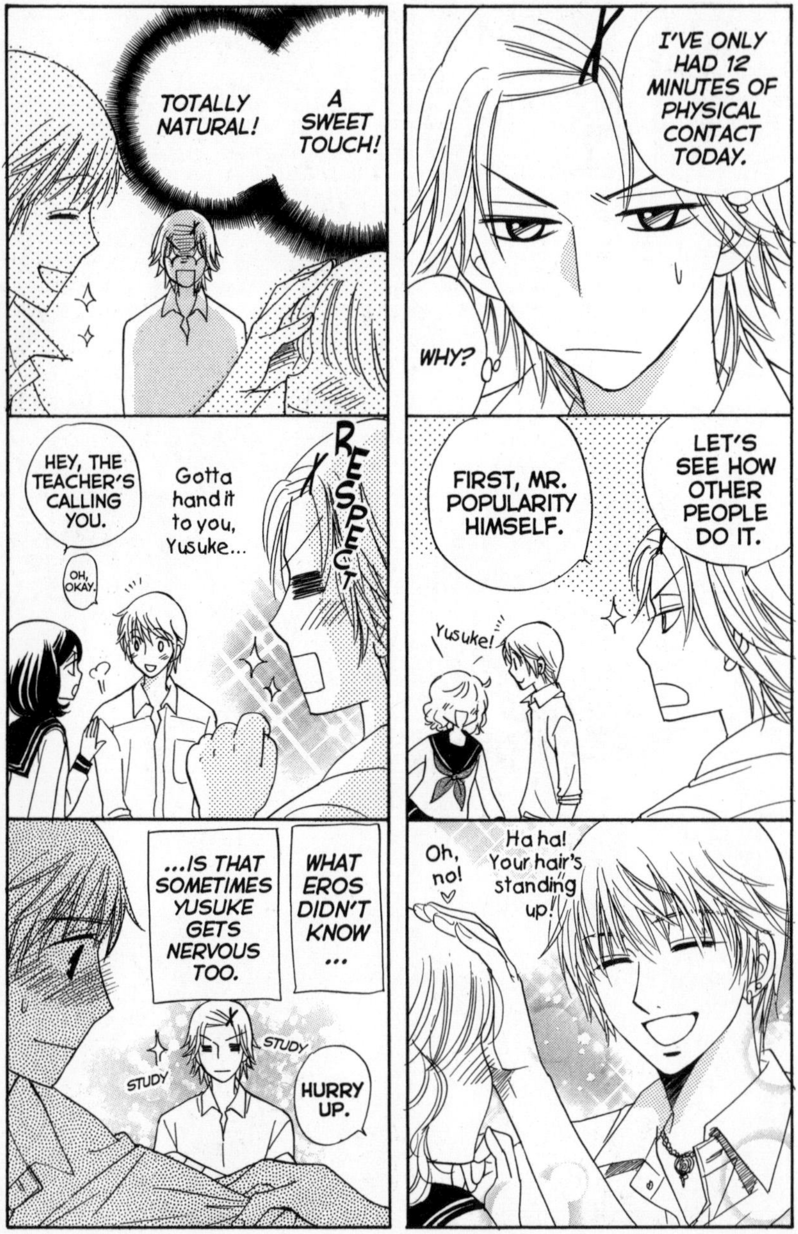
I'VE ONLY HAD 12 MINUTES OF PHYSICAL CONTACT TODAY.
WHY?
A SWEET TOUCH!
TOTALLY NATURAL!
LET'S SEE HOW OTHER PEOPLE DO IT.
FIRST, MR. POPULARITY HIMSELF.
Yusuke!
RESPECT
Gotta hand it to you, Yusuke...
HEY, THE TEACHER'S CALLING YOU.
OH, OKAY.
Ha ha! Your hair's standing up!
Oh, no!
WHAT EROS DIDN'T KNOW ...
...IS THAT SOMETIMES YUSUKE GETS NERVOUS TOO.
STUDY
STUDY
HURRY UP.

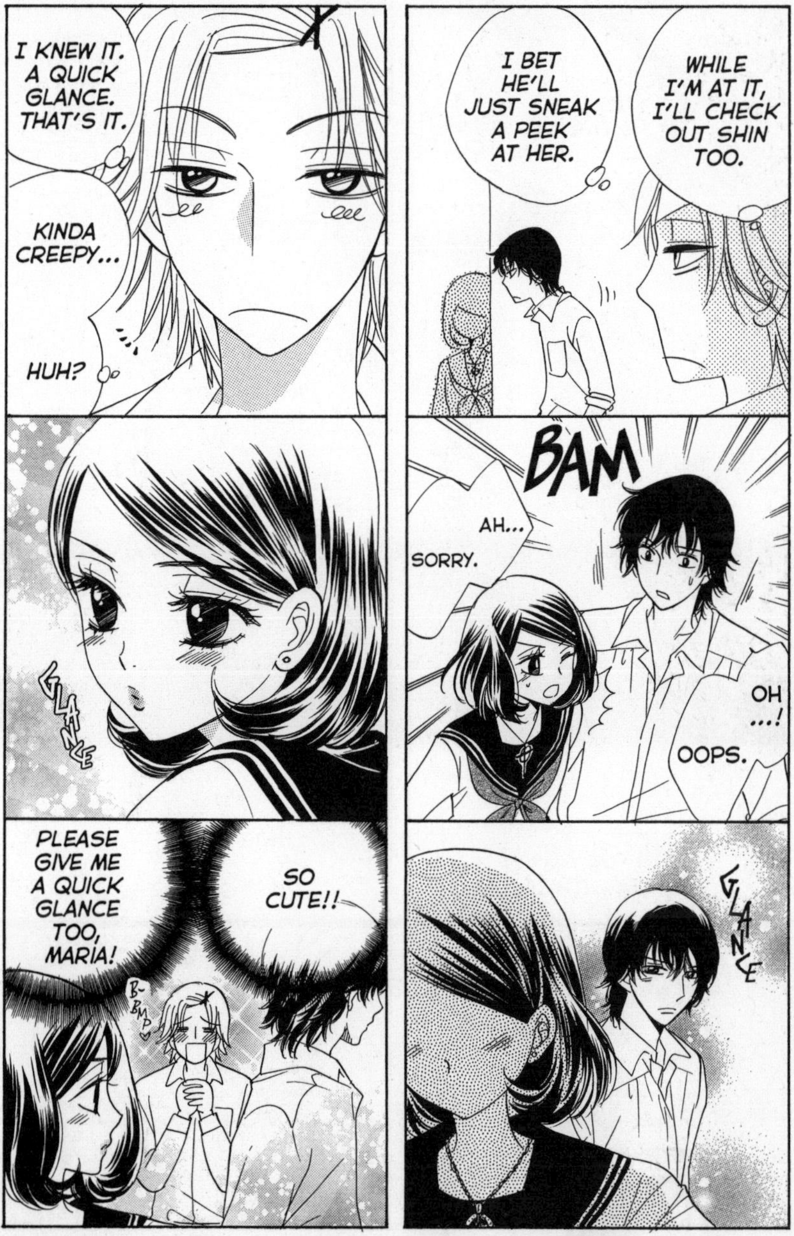
WHILE I'M AT IT, I'LL CHECK OUT SHIN TOO.
I BET HE'LL JUST SNEAK A PEEK AT HER.
I KNEW IT. A QUICK GLANCE. THAT'S IT.
KINDA CREEPY...
HUH?
BAM
AH...
SORRY.
OH ...!
OOPS.
GLANCE
GLANCE
SO CUTE!!
PLEASE GIVE ME A QUICK GLANCE TOO, MARIA!
B-BMP

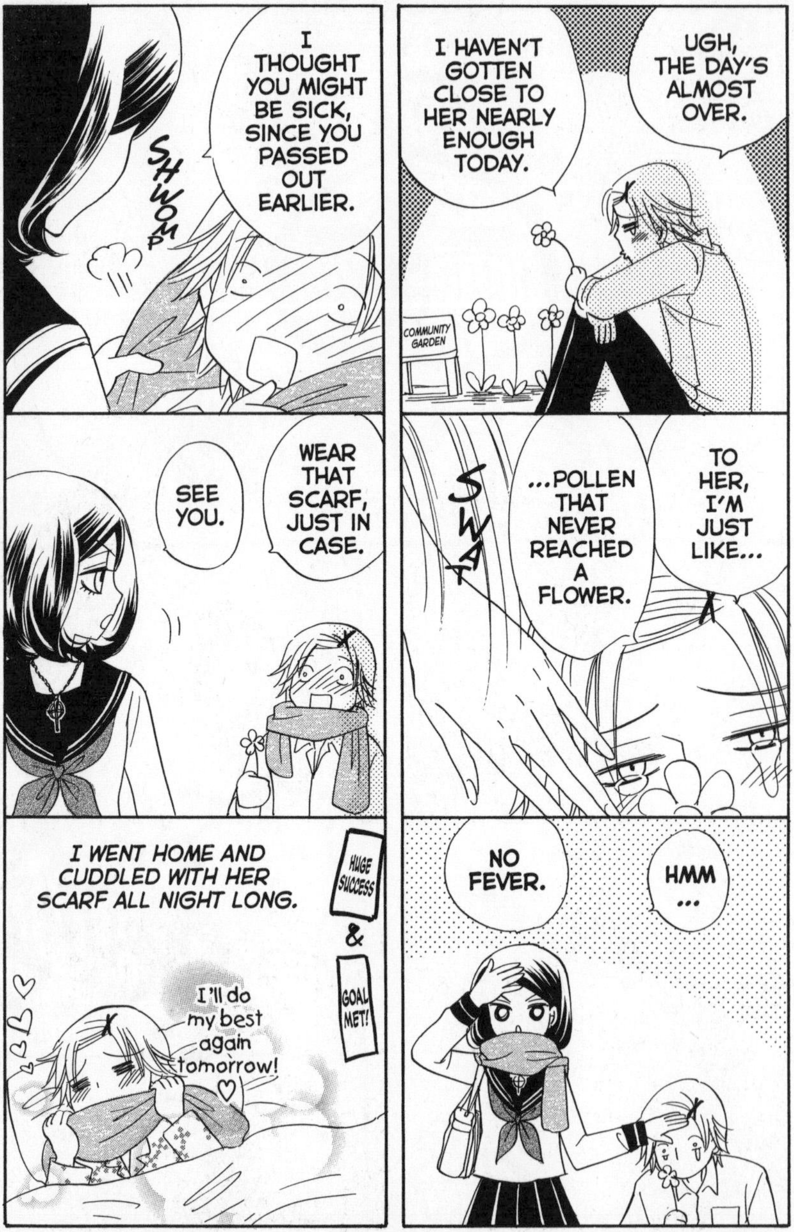
UGH, THE DAY'S ALMOST OVER.
I HAVEN'T GOTTEN CLOSE TO HER NEARLY ENOUGH TODAY.
COMMUNITY GARDEN
I THOUGHT YOU MIGHT BE SICK, SINCE YOU PASSED OUT EARLIER.
SHWOMP
TO HER, I'M JUST LIKE...
...POLLEN THAT NEVER REACHED A FLOWER.
SWAT
WEAR THAT SCARF, JUST IN CASE.
SEE YOU.
HMM ...
NO FEVER.
HUGE SUCCESS
&
GOAL MET!
I WENT HOME AND CUDDLED WITH HER SCARF ALL NIGHT LONG.
I'll do my best again tomorrow!

THE END

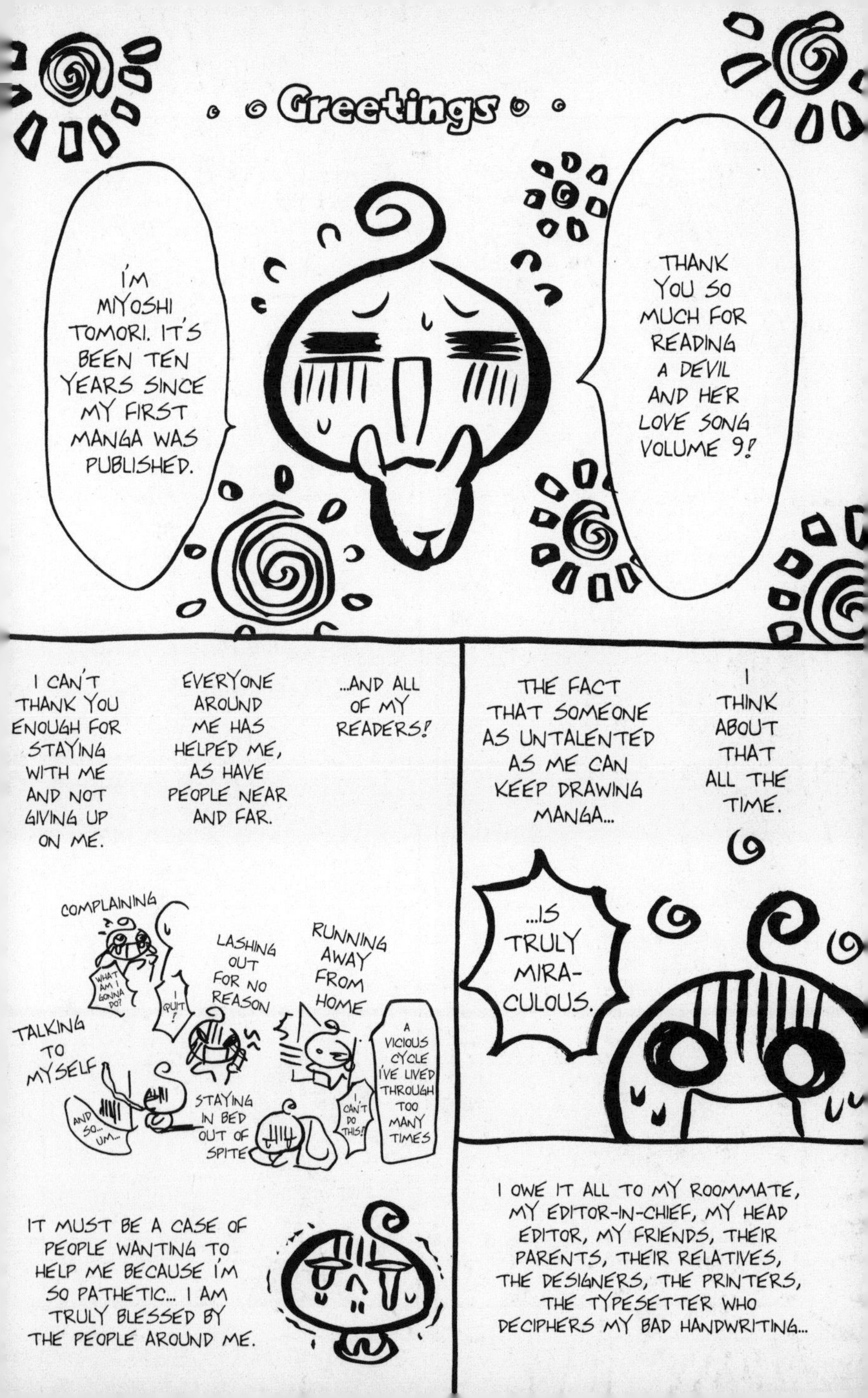
Greetings
THANK YOU SO MUCH FOR READING A DEVIL AND HER LOVE SONG VOLUME 9!
I'M MIYOSHI TOMORI. IT'S BEEN TEN YEARS SINCE MY FIRST MANGA WAS PUBLISHED.
I THINK ABOUT THAT ALL THE TIME.
THE FACT THAT SOMEONE AS UNTALENTED AS ME CAN KEEP DRAWING MANGA...
...IS TRULY MIRA-CULOUS.
I CAN'T THANK YOU ENOUGH FOR STAYING WITH ME AND NOT GIVING UP ON ME.
EVERYONE AROUND ME HAS HELPED ME, AS HAVE PEOPLE NEAR AND FAR.
...AND ALL OF MY READERS!
RUNNING AWAY FROM HOME
A VICIOUS CYCLE I'VE LIVED THROUGH TOO MANY TIMES
I CAN'T DO THIS!
LASHING OUT FOR NO REASON
I QUIT!
COMPLAINING
WHAT AM I GONNA DO?
STAYING IN BED OUT OF SPITE
TALKING TO MYSELF
AND SO... UM...
I OWE IT ALL TO MY ROOMMATE, MY EDITOR-IN-CHIEF, MY HEAD EDITOR, MY FRIENDS, THEIR PARENTS, THEIR RELATIVES, THE DESIGNERS, THE PRINTERS, THE TYPESETTER WHO DECIPHERS MY BAD HANDWRITING...
IT MUST BE A CASE OF PEOPLE WANTING TO HELP ME BECAUSE I'M SO PATHETIC... I AM TRULY BLESSED BY THE PEOPLE AROUND ME.